Wizards of Arcadia I

Wizards of Arcadia 1

Copyright © 2022 Daniel Xavier Luna

This book is a work of fiction. Names, characters, businesses, organizations, places, events and incidents either are the product of the author's imagination or are used fictitiously. Any resemblance to actual persons, living or dead, events, or locales is entirely coincidental.

Cover design by Bordin Marsinkul (hyperbooster)

ISBN (eBook): 979-8-9865274-0-6

ISBN (paperback): 979-8-9865274-1-3

ISBN (hardcover): 979-8-9865274-2-0

Second Edition: October 2022

10 9 8 7 6 5 4 3 2

Wizards of Arcadia I

Daniel Xavier Luna

Table of Contents

Dedicated to all the dreamers out there that
didn't let the realists or paralyzing fear
discourage them from achieving the unattainable.

Prologue

ount Levier. *I can't believe this is the same place we vacationed at when we were kids.* No matter where you stood, you could always hear the waves of the ocean slamming against the cliffs. The grass was the greenest hue I had ever seen, the flowers made up of the most magnificently bright colors. All of the cottages were the same style throughout this beautifully landscaped seaside vacation town. We used to love coming here for two weeks every summer; it was tradition. I'm not sure why we stopped. Maybe life got in the way—who knows. My brother and I had planned to continue the tradition until things changed.

Being twins, my brother and I were remarkably close and planned a lot to do together. I would never have imagined that I would be coming here to kill him. Just the thought of that caused my stomach to start roiling; I felt like someone just hit me with a wrecking ball. Suddenly, I was in denial about this. I started telling myself this was just some bad dream that I would wake up from any minute. Sadly, that minute never came.

I reached the top of the hill that overlooked what was once this place full of life, color, and laughter. Once, I would have been greeted by the smell of food grilling in the large picnic area that sat close to the volleyball court. I glanced over to that picnic area, but I wasn't greeted with the smell of food or the sound of people playing. Instead, there was only the smell of death and the screams of people who are trapped under the burning rubble of stone and wood. I tried to help them—I ran over as fast as I could, but it was too late; their screams came to an end by the time I reached them. The picnic tables were broken and the trees surrounding them lay on the ground, ripped from their roots. *How could my brother do this?* I asked myself. I stood on the hilltop for what seemed like hours, but in reality, only a few minutes had passed. I started my way up the grass hill toward the highest point of Mount Levier.

The thick dark smoke made it hard for me to see. My eyes began to water, and I started to cough, but I pushed myself forward. Buildings and cottages were still burning around me, but I could not stop—I had to get to the top of this mountain and end this once and for all. *How could this have happened?* I asked myself again in disbelief. Four years ago, the only problems my brother and I had in life were starting our sophomore year of high school and everything else that went with being teenagers. Now, I was making my way to him so I could kill him to save the world from all of this atrocity.

So much had changed in four years that I felt my eyes water again and knew it wasn't from the smoke this time. *Do I have the strength I need to face him?* So much depended on me succeeding, which was a lot to comprehend. I was only twenty years old, and life for the past four years had been full of enough pain and suffering to last a lifetime. I knew I was being selfish, but this wasn't how it was supposed to be.

Was it wrong to wish that we were just normal kids again? If I could go back, would I change anything? So many questions, but not enough answers. Suddenly, I felt myself stop; I reached the entrance to where he was. I looked straight ahead and saw an enormous, stunning temple sitting at the edge of the mountain top. I knew it didn't belong here, but I couldn't help but stare. This was it—there was no turning back. I took a deep breath and made my way inside. What other choice had he left me with?

Chapter One

It was a warm night in a little town called Arcadia. The sun had just set, and the children were still playing outside, enjoying the remaining weeks they had off before going back to school. The smell of backyard grilling filled the air. Sara, a beautiful, petite woman in her late thirties, was sitting on a patio swing, her smooth skin radiating the last of the sun's warmth as she slowly swung back and forth.

The warm summer air blew through her wavy brown hair that fell slightly past her shoulders. She smiled, deep dimples emerging on her cheeks that matched the smaller one on her chin. This swing meant a lot to her, and over time, it had become her favorite place to go and think. She bought it from a garage sale a few summers back, and while her kids thought it was a waste of money, that swing lasted longer than any of them expected. She always found it to be soothing and, on evenings like today, luxuriously relaxing.

Sara had begun to reminisce about the time when she found out about this incredible other world that existed and how things had changed since her eyes were opened to what really was out there. She was twenty years old when she met Gabriel. He was a year older than her, and she had been instantly attracted to him.

He was a slender but muscular man, with spiked-up black hair and the most amazing smile Sara had ever seen. Based on how he was dressed, she knew that he took good care of himself. He wore an expensive buttoned-up gray shirt with dark jeans, a black belt, and freshly polished shoes. Somehow, he was approachable yet had a mysterious presence to him.

Sara was beautiful in her youth as well; she had a runner's body, which she had earned in high school when she competed on the track and field team. Gabriel instantly noticed this as he began to walk her way.

"Hi," he said as came up to her, his eye contact strong. He barely blinked.

"Hi." Sara beamed, an effusion of warmth rushing over her.

"I don't mean to bother you, but you are the most beautiful woman I have ever seen."

"Thank you. You're sweet." She could feel the heat on her face rise as Gabriel stared at her. Sara didn't believe in love at first sight, but that moment changed her view of that.

After that night, things moved fast between the beautiful young couple. A year after they met, Gabriel decided to tell her he was a wizard. She, of course, found that hard to believe because things like that didn't exist, she thought. But she was wrong; he proved to her that everything he told her was the truth in an amazingly simple way: by making a rose appear out of thin air before her eyes. He thought it would impress her, but it only freaked her out.

Sara refused to take any of his calls for a while, but that didn't last long; Gabriel's charm was intoxicating. Eventually, they made their way back to each other, and Sara soon came to grips with what he had told her. After that, things were going really well between them. She even met his father, a tall, handsome man himself named Darwin. Soon after that, things started to change. Sara noticed a change in his attitude and how easily he got angry at the simplest of things.

When she realized she was pregnant, she put off telling him for a few weeks, worried about the man he was becoming. He wasn't the same man he was when they started dating, and that concerned her. Sara knew she couldn't keep the news from him much longer and decided that it was finally time to tell him. Unfortunately, the time would never come; Gabriel disappeared, and she never heard from him again. She had no idea what happened to him.

Suddenly she was overwhelmed by the thought of going through this alone. She didn't drink or eat for days. She continuously woke up in the middle of the night shivering and sobbing uncontrollably. Days went by like this, and after she put together the shattered pieces of her once happy life, she needed answers.

She sought out Darwin, but he avoided her calls like she was a pesky salesperson. Sara was angry, not knowing where he went or why she didn't hear from him, but that anger quickly turned to happiness after she found out she was having twins.

A few months went by before Darwin decided to finally tell her what happened to his son. When he got to Sara's house, he couldn't help but notice how much her stomach had grown.

Sara cradled her stomach. "It's Gabriel's," she said before Darwin could say anything. "And I'm having twins."

Darwin took the news better than expected. He finally told her everything that happened with his son—how he had killed countless people in his quest for power. Sara was shocked and didn't believe what Darwin was telling her about the man she loved. It took her a while to fully believe what Darwin had told her, but when she came around to it, Sara was suddenly grateful that Gabriel was gone.

As time went by, Darwin helped Sara out a lot, both financially and emotionally. He supported her in every way, and Sara was grateful for it. On one of Darwin's visits, he suggested Sara move to a little town called Arcadia. He also told Sara about his daughter Elizabeth who lived there with her daughter Bianca. "It's a great place to raise kids," he had said.

Sara liked the idea of her children being close to family, which meant a lot to her since she was an only child and her parents had died a month before her eighteenth birthday, so she decided to go visit this place and to meet Darwin's daughter, Elizabeth. When they got there, Sara instantly fell in love with the small town. When they arrived at Elizabeth's house, her young daughter opened the door. Darwin immediately embraced her and swung her up in the air.

Coming from the family room, a woman who couldn't have been much older than Sara greeted her. "This is my daughter, Elizabeth," Darwin said.

Elizabeth extended her hand. "Family calls me Liz."

Sara was overwhelmed. She suddenly didn't feel so alone. "Hi. It's great to meet you." Soon after that, it was decided. She picked everything up, moved to Arcadia to a house Darwin purchased for her and her kids, and it was a decision she had never regretted at all.

Sara got up from the swing and made her way toward a group of kids sitting at a gazebo, which was shared property amongst the rest of the homeowners in the little subdivision called Rivertowne. She saw her two boys, who were fraternal twins but looked alike all the same and who some people couldn't tell apart. They had the same thick, light-brown hair and brown eyes, but to those that knew them, they could see the differences, like how Andrew had his mom's smile or that Adrian was slightly taller. Both were handsome in their own way. Sara approached the gazebo about halfway from the house.

"Dinner in ten minutes!"

"Ok!" they both replied, in sync with one another.

"Are you staying for dinner, Chloe?" Sara asked Liz's second daughter.

Chloe leaped to her feet. "No, Mom said I have to get home and eat dinner there. She's constantly on me, saying she forgets I live there with how little I've been home. So, thanks for the offer, Aunt Sara, but I have to pass."

Ever since the start of summer, Chloe and her cousins had been almost inseparable. Adrian thought it was because she had a crush on Collin, Andrew's best friend. Chloe, a year younger than the twins but who had skipped a grade, was a pretty young lady herself. She had short blonde hair, beautiful skin as smooth as a baby's bottom, and the bluest eyes anyone had seen. She believed they came from her father's side of the family, but she didn't know for certain; she never knew him.

Even though Chloe grew up with her cousins and sister, she was very independent, preferring to do things for herself whenever she could. She was very athletic and preferred to hang out with guys instead of girls. Since she naturally gravitated toward the opposite sex.

Andrew and Adrian said their goodbyes to their friends but gave Chloe a hug and headed to the house. They both walked without saying anything to each other, but when they reached the front door, the smell of freshly made garlic bread filled the air and they knew exactly what was for dinner.

Andrew was the first to pass the threshold. "Smells good, Mom!" The twins went upstairs to wash up. Adrian finished first and went to help his mom set up.

"Why four plates?" he pondered.

Sara hesitated for a moment. "Grandpa is going to be joining us."

Adrian didn't know what to make of that. His grandfather rarely visited, and when he did, he always made him, and his brother, feel like they had done something wrong even though they hadn't. "Oh, ok."

Sara turned to grab the bread so Adrian wouldn't see the worried look etched on her face. Sara knew why Darwin was coming. She wished this day would never come, but nonetheless she tried to prepare for it. No matter how hard she prepared, though, she was never really going to be ready for it. How does one prepare to tell their kids that they might be wizards? Just the thought of that seemed ridiculous. She shook her head as if to clear the thoughts away and turned to finish setting up the table. Andrew came down and noticed the fourth plate as well, but before he could ask about it, the doorbell rang.

Sara reached across the table to set down the cutlery in her hand. "Andrew, can you go let your grandfather in?"

Andrew looked at her with surprise. Darwin came by occasionally but never joined them for dinner, so when Sara said that as if it was something normal, it caught him off guard. "Yup, we're pretending that's normal," said Adrian, reading his expression.

Andrew looked at him and laughed because dinner with Grandpa wasn't something they ever did. In fact, they only saw him once or twice a year. He would call them often, though, to check in. Andrew enjoyed those conversations more than Adrian.

Andrew opened the door and before him stood his grandfather, Darwin. He was a tall, handsome older man with shiny white hair neatly combed to the side. He wore half frame glasses connected to a silver chain around his neck. He had on a neatly ironed dark-blue vertical pinstripe suit, which Andrew thought was weird given the warm summer night they were having.

"Are you going to invite me in?" asked Darwin in a deep voice, the kind of voice that commanded authority and gave you goosebumps when you heard it. Andrew invited him in as Sara and Adrian joined in from the dining room.

"Hi, Grandpa," Adrian said as he took Darwin's coat. Sara followed with a hug and a soft kiss on Darwin's cheek.

"Nice to see you again, Darwin."

"Thank you for inviting me." He looked at the twins with amazement and wonder. "You boys got big!"

Sara led them all to the dining room. Darwin looked around as he made his way to his chair. He noticed all the little charms that were still in place, right where he left them. He pulled out his chair and sat down. "Smells delicious." Sara went into the kitchen to grab the main course and came back with a steaming pan in her hand, placing the lasagna on the table.

"Wow, Mom, that looks great!" Andrew noted as he sat down.

Before Adrian sat down, he immediately went for the bread. "I'm starving!"

Sara took her place opposite Darwin and waited for everyone else to serve themselves. "How was your trip, Darwin?"

Darwin took the salad. "Bit rough, but fine." A few minutes of awkward silence went by before Adrian decided to say something.

They begin serving themselves and chatted about light things—Darwin's trip, the boys wanting to go to the mall. Darwin took this opportunity to ask them what they were doing for their birthday since it was only a few weeks away.

Adrian took a sip of his soda and said, "Having a party. Nothing big; just having a few friends over."

"Sounds fun!" replied a smiling Darwin. He looked at Sara, whose worries were expressed clearly on her face, but before the boys could notice, she grinned and helped herself to some more bread. The look etched on Sara's face was a reminder that for the longest time Darwin had had an inability to join in any family activities, which was why he avoided visiting for extended periods of time. He felt guilty that the boys didn't know their father. Being around his family was always a stark reminder of his failures from years past.

The rest of the dinner went on with conversation about the little things going on in the family. Adrian and Andrew sensed something was going on but, as all teenagers do, they just finished their food quickly and excused themselves from the table. They clutched their dishes and put them in the kitchen, then ran upstairs like they were in a race. Darwin and Sara sat motionless until Darwin reached for his drink.

Sara! Darwin said, his voice deeper and with an echo that sent chills through her body. "What are you doing?" she blurted aloud.

Darwin gave her a little smirk. *I don't want the kids to hear this long overdue conversation we have to have.*

Her volume lowered. "You could have given me some warning before you barged into my head like that, you know."

I thought I did when I said your name.

"Not so subtle, if you ask me."

Given the sensitive nature of the conversation, shouldn't you be thinking what you want to say?

You're right, Sara thought begrudgingly.

I know how difficult this might be for you, but I can assure you, if they are wizards, we will teach and educate them on everything they need to know.

Sara sat there in complete silence; she knew what being a wizard could do to a person and the stress that it could cause. For her, it wasn't about her kids being "different"—it was about her kids being safe. She knew the kind of dangers that went along with having power. She wanted her kids to have normal lives, but she knew that if they were wizards, it was in their best interest to have Darwin teach them those ways. Life would only be harder if they didn't fully understand what they were.

I know you will, Darwin. I'm just worried that this will be difficult for them.

Darwin took a sip of his drink. *Completely understandable, my dear.*

A few minutes went by before either of them thought or said anything. Darwin knew how hard this was for Sara, given everything that had happened to her in the past. Darwin stood up and started to clear the table. He picked up a few of the dishes and as he went toward the kitchen, Sara rose from the table. "If they are, they will need to know the truth about their father."

Darwin was as still as a person could be, statue-like. Not even a breath escaped his mouth as he was utterly terrified at the thought of Adrian and Andrew finding out the truth.

"I know," was the only thing he could say before all that tension was interrupted by the doorbell.

"I got it!" Andrew yelled while racing down the stairs. He opened the door to let his best friend, Collin, into the house.

"Hi, Ms. S," he greeted Sara with a grin.

The corners of Sara's mouth moved upward. She said hello as she started to clear the table. She offered Collin some food but as always, he was already making his way toward the breadbasket before she could finish her sentence. Collin had always been like part of the family ever since he met the twins back in second grade. As she watched Collin and Andrew laugh and joke around, she couldn't help but feel sad—sad that what her sons had come to know as "normal" might change. How would they react to all of it? How would they take the news of their father? Before she could continue thinking about more and more scenarios that her boys might face, Darwin came back to the dining room.

"I should get going," he announced. They all said their goodbyes and Sara closed the door behind him.

Darwin strode down the driveway and crossed the street to the open field that led to the little pond in the middle of the subdivision. He turned to face the house he had just left and stopped next to a tall oak tree, placing his palm over his cane, gripping it firmly. He didn't need the cane to walk; it was more decorative than anything. He glanced up to a branch where a bird was watching.

"Keep a close eye on them," he commented as he stomped his cane on the ground. Within a few seconds, a bright-blue smoky light engulfed him, and he was gone. The only thing that remained was a beautiful white falcon perched on a branch in the tree he had just made eye contact with. The falcon leaped off the branch and soared high into the sky, letting the wind glide it to its destination.

It soared through the sky and once it spotted an open window, it shot down like an arrow to its target until it was safely inside. The falcon spread its wings as wide as they could go and morphed into a beautiful young naked woman in her early twenties with silky, bronzed skin. She had long straight brown hair with a braided blue streak in the center that came down to the middle of her back and striking hazel eyes. She snatched her purple robe that had been casually thrown onto her bed and put it on. She turned to close the window, but before she could close it, she had to take a seat on her bed to regain her strength.

She had been practicing magic ever since she was a child, but *morphing* took a lot out of even the most skilled wizards. At that moment, the bedroom door flew open and in barged Chloe.

"Bianca. Can't you hear Mom calling you?" Chloe snapped.

"Yeah." She took a deep breath. "I'll be right down."

Chapter Two

A few weeks had gone by since Darwin's visit, and the day of the birthday party had arrived. It was early in the morning and Sara was lying in bed staring at the ceiling, wide awake; she hadn't really slept. She groggily got out of bed and slowly made her way to her bathroom to put on some jogging pants. Her movements were sluggish and everything she did from brushing her teeth to putting her hair up was done with hesitation. She had been dreading this day for a while now. After all, today she would finally find out if her sons would continue to live the normal lives that they had grown accustomed to or if they would become a part of this new world. In a way, she felt guilty for how she felt about the situation because regardless, she would always love her children. Finally, she was ready to go run the errands she needed to before the party.

She barged into Andrew's room and attempted to wake him. "Andy, you have to get up soon to set up."

Andrew just turned over and mumbled something, but Collin, who was on the floor in a sleeping bag sat up and interjected, "I'll make sure he gets up, Ms. S." He yawned and stretched as Sara backed out of the room and headed downstairs.

She picked up her list of things to do and headed out to the garage. As she opened the overhead door, she saw Bianca walking up the driveway with her boyfriend. "Hey, Aunt Sara!" she said cheerfully.

"Hi, guys." She walked toward them and gave Bianca and Brad, Bianca's boyfriend, a hug. Brad's eyes were warm and welcoming to those he met. Everywhere he went, he was the life of the party. His good looks got him out of a lot of things. He was once able to convince one of his professors to extend a deadline for him, even though the syllabus clearly said no extensions.

Bianca was hard to win over for someone as overly confident as him, but the challenge was a welcome one. After he met her family, he took to them like bees to flowers.

"Mom said you might need some help," Bianca said.

"That would be great!" She explained what she had to do today, and Bianca informed her that she and Brad would pick up the party balloons, some water guns, and other water-related games since the sun was planning to unleash the hottest day, they had had all summer.

"It's going to be a hot day today, and every great summer party has an epic water fight!" Bianca beamed. Sara laughed as her car door shut. When Sara drove away, Bianca decided that it   would be best if she and Brad did the same because every time Brad was around the twins, they would behave like children, which Bianca knew would only mean that no work would get done. It wasn't even eleven a.m. yet and the sun was already as bright as it could be. Bianca knew it was going to be a beautiful yet scorching day.

*** * ***

BACK in the house, Adrian barged into Andrew's room and yelled at him to get up as loud as he could. "What the hell" Collin shouted, startled by the intrusion.

Andrew slowly rose and sat on the edge of his bed. "Really?" He grunted.

"Drew, we have to set up the volleyball net and tables!" Adrian quipped. Adrian was the only one who could call his brother "Drew" and get away with it, something he had done since they first started talking.

Andrew got up and based on the expression he had; Adrian knew in an instant that Andrew was in one of his famous crabby moods. He ignored it and told Collin to get up and make himself useful. Adrian headed out of the room and down the stairs. It didn't take long before Andrew and Adrian were arguing over who was doing the most and who was doing the least. These little arguments were not unexpected because at almost every party or family gathering, they always had to argue. Collin found the whole thing very amusing and just stood by laughing at them. Soon, they were both attacking

12

him—maybe because they knew Collin was right to laugh. After all, they were bickering like little children.

"Are you just going to stand there looking stupid, or are you going to actually help?" Adrian snapped.

"First of all, I'm doing you a favor. Second when you babies stop arguing maybe we could actually start, cause in case you haven't noticed, the only thing you guys have done is bring up the chairs and tables from the basement," Collin noted.

A couple seconds passed before they finally got to work. Collin brought up the volleyball net and headed to the backyard. Andrew followed with a table. Once they decided how they were going to arrange everything, the volleyball net was the first to go up. While Andrew and Collin worked on that, Adrian opened the tables and placed the chairs around them. A couple of hours went by before Bianca and Brad arrived with bags of water guns and other water-related items in hand.

"Hey guys, what's up?" Andrew rushed past them.

"Where's Adrian?" Bianca inquired. Andrew pointed toward the backyard as he rushed inside.

"Hi, cuz!" she called out. Adrian ran toward her.

"What did you guys get?" he exclaimed. Brad was already dumping everything onto the ground before Bianca could say anything. Collin ran up and the three of them started goofing around, energetic with excitement. Bianca smirked. Brad and Collin together were one of the best comedy duos she had ever seen.

"You guys are such little kids," she heckled as she turned back toward the house.

Brad blurted, "Don't act like you're not excited about the epic water fight we're going to have!" All three of them laughed as Bianca went into the house.

"So, Brad, did you tell her what college you were transferring too yet?" Adrian mumbled.

Brad shook his head. "Not yet." Brad decided he had enough of community college and was transferring to the University of Arizona and had decided to hold off on telling Bianca, who was going to a local community college for two years before transferring to a four-year program. Bianca had always known her plan ever since she started high school. She kind of figured that Brad was transferring schools, but it wasn't something that they spoke about. They both just wanted to enjoy the summer and not worry about everything else just yet.

Collin took the last of the water guns out of its package. "You better tell her soon." He examined the last gun and decided to keep that one for himself. "Because you only have a little over a month left."

After all the water guns were out of their packages, Brad got up, unable to settle in one place, and went inside the house. He marched into the house and saw Bianca talking to Sara.

With a pained stare toward Bianca he asked, "Did you want to go back and start getting ready? We have been here for a few hours already and don't want to be late coming back."

She grasped his hand, and they headed out.

✳ ✳ ✳

IT was almost three o'clock in the afternoon and the twins, Collin, and Sara were all finally dressed and done setting up. As expected, Chloe and Bianca were the first to arrive with their mother, Liz.

"Hey, Aunt Liz," Adrian and Andrew said simultaneously. She gave them both a hug and asked where Sara was. Liz knew Sara was curious to know what exactly was going to happen.

She walked through the sliding doors that led into the kitchen toward the marble island in the dead center. Sara was warming up the food and preparing the plates and napkins.

"Hi, Sara." Sara turned and gave her a warm embrace. She wasted no time asking Liz to go upstairs with her. Once they were in Sara's room and the door was closed, they knew that no one else could hear, so Sara asked the only question she had been waiting for an answer to.

"How will we know if they are…" Sara paused. "If they are, in fact, part of your world?" she asked with a bit of hesitation on the last few words. She didn't know if she offended Liz by the question or if she came off as ignorant. Liz didn't seem to notice; she answered right away.

"Bianca is going to do a little spell that will tell us for sure if they are or aren't."

Sara shrugged. "Oh, ok," she responded, not wanting to ask for specifics. She opened the door to go back downstairs, and Liz looked puzzled.

Sara glanced at her and could see she was baffled. "What is it?"

Liz spoke after a moment of silence, "I just thought you would have a lot of other questions." They both stared compassionately at each other and headed back to the party, where more people had arrived. The adults were outnumbered by the teenagers that were all there, but everyone was still having fun.

Adrian looked around, bouncing the ball up and down. "Who all wants to play volleyball?!" A mixture of adults and teens came up to him.

Andrew quickly added, "Adults against teens!" and the crowd seemed to surge with excitement. Bianca inched toward her cousins, but they both waved her off. "Sorry, but you graduated high school almost two years ago, so you are officially on *that* side of the net." Andrew pointed to where the adults were getting ready.

Bianca exchanged a knowing look with her cousin. "You've just made a *big* mistake!"

The teams were made up of Adrian, Andrew, Chloe, Collin, Lisa, and Dean on the teen side and Sara, Liz, Bianca, Brad, and a few other neighbors on the adult side. The teens, of course, had a bigger cheering section with the rest of the twins' friends standing around their side of the net.

The game was extremely competitive, the adults put in a lot of effort. Some had scrapes on their knees from diving too hard, others had to take a few breaks in between to catch their breath. They all went through a case of water faster than expected, thanks to the blazing sun beaming on them all, but in the end, the adults lost to the teens, thanks in large part to the twins and Chloe's athleticism thirty to twenty-six was the final score—not the correct score for volleyball, but it was just a fun game. After the game, Sara went into the house and asked Liz if Bianca had done what she was supposed to do yet, but was told no.

An hour passed and Sara decided that it was time for the cake. She decided to cut the cake inside the house since it would most likely melt outside in the ninety-degree heat. She told Andrew to start telling the rest of the guests to come inside and one by one, they all piled into the dining room. Andrew and Adrian took their places at the center of the table opposite each other while all their friends and other guests surrounded them. Sara was in the kitchen putting the finishing touches onto the cake before she was ready to walk it to the dining room.

"Are you coming?" Sara asked Bianca, who was standing in the kitchen. She was distracted with what she was doing. "In a minute!"

Sara continued to the dining room while Liz turned down the lights, and everyone simultaneously started singing "Happy Birthday." The lit candles, with the help of some daylight sneaking in through the partially pulled-down shade, were the only things lighting the room. Sara placed the cake down between her sons and joined in on the song. Back in the kitchen, Bianca stood by the sink, raised her hand in front of her, palm up, and let out a little chant. "*Invenio Occultus,*" she muttered, and a little ball of light hovered in her hand instantly. She pushed it forward and it quickly flew into the dining room. As Andrew came up from blowing out his side of the candles, he noticed the ball of light bouncing off the walls.

"What is that?" he questioned, and in that moment the ball of light flew by Adrian.

"What the—?" Adrian stammered as he dodged the light. Everyone was too busy clapping and were too loud to hear the twins saying anything. Liz turned the lights back on and noticed Sara looking at her sons; she was the only one that had noticed they saw something. Sara looked at Liz but before Liz could say anything, Sara returned her attention to her kids and began cutting the cake. Liz entered the kitchen and went over to Bianca, who was still standing by the sink.

"Well?" Bianca inquired.

"They noticed it," Liz revealed. Both were happy yet unsure of how to react.

People started making their way back to the kitchen to head outside. Andrew and Adrian decided to stay inside and sat at the kitchen table with a few of their friends. Liz saw this as a perfect time to go talk to Sara. She made her way to the dining room. Bianca joined her cousins to keep them from interrupting the conversation that was about to take place between her mom and aunt.

Sara was cutting the last few pieces of cake for the remaining people that still didn't have any. Liz joined Sara as the last guest made his way back outside. She stood in front of Sara, who didn't want to acknowledge her just yet.

Liz respected this and stood there in silence until Sara wanted to talk. Sara continued cutting pieces of cake and placing them on plates so people could help themselves to seconds or thirds. Suddenly, Sara stopped cutting and stood there motionless. Liz took this gesture as Sara asking what happened, so she came out and said what they knew.

"They are," she whispered.

Sara took a moment to take in the news and looked Liz in the eye. "Are you sure?"

Liz reciprocated her gaze. "Yes." Liz sensed Sara wanted to know how it worked and if it was, in fact, a dependable way of finding out. "There is energy all around us. It is how we are able to do magic." Liz flung the curtains open and pointed out the window. "From the trees to the grains of dirt beneath, everything that has this energy we can use, because that is where our magic comes from. Bianca channeled that energy into tiny balls of light that only those like us could see." Liz glanced at Sara to see her reaction.

"I'm sorry." Sara cupped her mouth. She wasn't hiding the fact that she wanted her boys to be "normal" that well. "You must think I'm a horrible person for the way I've been acting toward all of this."

"Not at all; I get it. It's a lot to process and I want you to know that I'm here, along with the rest of the family, to help you and them understand all of this," Liz reassured her.

Sara took in a cleansing breath and ambled to the kitchen to put the knife in the sink. She noticed Andrew and Adrian outside in the middle of a water fight with a bunch of their friends. In the midst of finding out that her kids were wizards, she must not have noticed the house was cleared out and that everyone was outside enjoying the party. Sara enjoyed seeing how much fun everyone was having and told Liz to let Darwin know.

Sara proceeded outside to join in on the fun while Liz called Darwin. Sara picked up a water balloon and threw it at Andrew, laughing and taking it all in. She wanted that moment to last because she knew everything was going to change—and soon. Bianca didn't know if Sara was putting on a brave face or if she really was ok with the news. *Maybe Sara is just stressed out not knowing, or maybe she doesn't want to offend me or Mom*, Bianca thought. Either way, Sara took the news better than they thought she would.

Bianca stood looking out through the sliding doors, waiting for her chance to go talk to Sara, but it never came; Sara was having too much fun. Liz got off the phone and made her way to the kitchen, but before she could say anything to Bianca, Brad was walking in too. He came in through the front door and Liz could feel the heat that followed him.

"Wow," Liz wiped the sweat from her brow, "did it get hotter out there in the past twenty minutes?"

"Hey." Bianca went to kiss Brad, hello. Liz navigated around the couple toward the sliding doors that led out to the backyard.

"We will talk later," she said as she passed Bianca. Bianca just nodded and waited for the door to close behind her mother.

Brad whispered, "Did you guys find out yet?" Ever since Bianca told him about all of this, he has been intrigued by her world.

Bianca snapped, "Shut up!" She knew that if her mom found out that she told Brad everything, she would be in a lot of trouble, no matter how much of an adult she thought she was. Brad just laughed and wrapped his arms around her.

"Everything will be fine." His lips slightly parted. "They are, aren't they?"

Together, arm in arm, they went outside to join the rest of the party and the water fight. A few hours had passed, and people started to leave while the friends that were staying the night were just sitting around the patio table laughing and talking about unimportant things. Sara started to clean up, and Liz got up and gave her a hand. They went inside and the two of them made small talk until Sara approached Liz.

She tilted her head to the side. "So, what happens next?"

"Well…" Liz took a few steps towards her. "Darwin will be here in a few weeks so you both can sit down and tell them."

"Oh. Ok." She gazed at Liz with sudden focus. "Why a few weeks?" Liz turned away. "He has some other things he has to take care of."

Sara continued cleaning without asking anything else. Not knowing what else she could say or do, Liz decided it was time to head home. She opened the sliding doors and told Bianca and Chloe she was leaving, but Chloe reminded her that she was staying the night and Bianca told her that she would just catch a ride home with Brad. She closed the door and turned to say bye to Sara.

"Ok, I'm going to get going." Sara dried off her hands and gave Liz a hug.

"Thank you," she whispered softly. Liz knew she wasn't just thanking her for helping with the cleanup.

"If you need anything or have any questions, please don't hesitate to call me." Sara smiled and led her to the front door.

Once the door was closed, Sara decided to go back outside. It wasn't that much cooler, but the sun was gone, and a nice breeze filled the air. She sat on the swing as a smile reached her eyes, glossy and bright as she watched her sons laugh and enjoy the night. That was the happiest she has been since Darwin's last visit, and it wasn't just because she finally had the answer but because she realized that her kids could handle anything that happened—because Darwin, Bianca, and Liz would all be there to guide and teach them. Sara's shoulders and torso slightly loosened as the tension started to fade away and she looked up to the sky, swinging gently and taking in the twinkling of the stars above her. Soon, she fell asleep.

Chapter Three

With a little more than two weeks before school started, Adrian and Andrew were getting more nervous and anxious about becoming sophomores—Andrew more so than Adrian, but that didn't come as a surprise to Sara. Andrew was always more reluctant to try new things than his brother. In fact, Adrian made Andrew join school activities and participate in sports. It wasn't that he wasn't good at those things, but just that he was shy. Andrew had always been that way ever since the first day of kindergarten, when he held onto Sara's leg and wouldn't let go. No matter what Sara tried to do, he simply wouldn't budge. It wasn't until Adrian came over and gripped his hand that Andrew finally let go of his mother's leg.

Adrian was always Andrew's protector. Even though they were only an hour apart, since that day, Adrian had always watched over his brother and made him do things that Andrew wouldn't do on his own. As Sara sat on her swing that she loved so much, thinking about the past, she was brought out of that peaceful moment by Adrian and Andrew barging through the sliding door asking for money for the mall.

"Oh, that's right, you guys are 'adults' now," she joked. Andrew and Adrian just laughed and asked what was in her cup. Sara shook her head in response and got up to go get her purse. She made her way inside the house as she yelled back to them, "What time will you guys be back?"

Andrew glanced at Adrian. "Probably around seven o'clock."

"Should I make dinner?" Sara came back into view.

"No, Aunt Liz said we will grab something to eat at the mall," Adrian answered.

"Wow, I have the day to myself, and I don't have to make dinner! Must be my birthday." Adrian and Andrew just laughed, hugged their mom goodbye, and went to the front of the house to wait for their aunt to pick them up.

"Are Dean and Lisa still meeting up with us?" Andrew asked as he closed the door behind him.

"Last text I got from Dean said yeah," Adrian looked at his phone, "so I'm sure they are."

"Chloe isn't going to like that, you know how jealous she gets," Andrew added. Chloe didn't really like Lisa all that much.

Adrian rolled his eyes. "Chloe should have just told Collin she liked him."

"That would have made too much sense. Besides, that's not why she doesn't like Lisa," Andrew sarcastically pointed out.

"Oh yeah, I forgot that's not it at all." They both laughed at Adrian's sarcastic retort and after a few minutes, Liz finally arrived.

"Collin made us run late," Chloe groaned as they got in the car. "Figures," Andrew smirked.

When they arrived at the mall, Liz parked in the first available spot. As they were getting out of the car, Chloe spotted Dean and Lisa making their way toward the car. She looked at Andrew, who simply said, "That's all Adrian!" and Chloe continued exiting the car.

"Hey, guys! Took you long enough," Lisa said while beaming. Chloe awkwardly smirked back, and they all proceeded inside. Adrian and Andrew could tell that Chloe was upset, but they didn't say anything to her.

Lisa looked Chloe up and down. "I like your sundress!" "Thanks."

Every time Lisa was nice, it made it harder for Chloe to hate her. After all, it wasn't her fault Collin liked her.

"Ok, guys, meet me in the food court at three o'clock," Liz told them as they went inside. The mall had two levels with many stores in it, and everyone had certain stores they needed to stop in. Bianca and Liz went off in one direction, the kids in another.

As the kids made their way toward the first store, laughing and talking, up on the second level was a tall, dark man with spiked black hair dressed in black slacks and a gray dress shirt watching them. His eyes were intensely focused on Adrian and Andrew in particular, watching their every move. As the twins and their friends went in and out of stores, the man followed, never losing sight of them. A few hours had gone by when Adrian stopped to tie his shoes. As he began to tie them, he glanced up and made eye contact with the man.

"Adrian!" Dean shouted.

Adrian turned. "Hold on." When he looked back up to the second level, the man was gone. Adrian shrugged it off and rejoined his friends about thirty feet in front of him. He double- checked to see if he could spot that man again, but he was nowhere to be found.

"It's 2:50, guys. We should start heading over to the food court," Chloe suggested. They all agreed and turned around toward the food court. Along the way, they bumped into some other friends.

"Hey, Clo, are you coming back to class? We all miss you," someone said.

Chloe looked around until she found where the mysterious voice was coming from. "Yeah, I go back when school starts. I had to take the summer off." They laughed and said their goodbyes to the three other friends they bumped into.

"Oh, you're still in Tae Kwon Do?" Lisa questioned.

"Yeah, but I needed a break, so decided to take the summer off."

"Wow, you have been in that for a long time! That's really cool."

"Yup." Chloe was desperate to avoid any other small talk that Lisa might have wanted to have. Lisa had always been overly nice to Chloe, as if she knew Chloe didn't like her.

Andrew wanted to break the awkward tension, so he chimed in with, "You've been in that for, like, *ever*, right?"

Chloe sneered at Andrew *why would he keep pushing us to talk*, "Since I was six years old."

They made their way to the food court and Bianca and Liz were already sitting down. They all dispersed to the various places they wanted to eat from, and it came as no surprise to anyone that both Adrian and Andrew made their way to the pizza stand. The twins were picky eaters and usually ate pizza or some kind of pasta and occasionally chicken. Liz noticed them and commented to Bianca, "Remember how Sara and I would have to cut everything they ate into the shape of chicken nuggets?"

Bianca raised her eyebrows as she stared at the twins' amused'. "God, they weren't the brightest kids were they."

✻ ✻ ✻

ONCE everyone was done eating and ready to get back to shopping, Dean told them he had to get home so that he could get ready for work. Since Lisa's mom was his ride, she would have to leave as well.

After they all said their goodbyes, Bianca and Liz decided to stay with the twins, Collin, and Chloe since they only had to go to a few more stores. As they made their way to one of the stores Andrew and Collin wanted to go to, Liz's nerves suddenly tensed up. She glanced around, looking over her shoulders, but didn't see anything suspicious. Once they reached the store, Liz and Bianca decided to wait outside.

After a few minutes Liz was looking around, trying to suppress that feeling, when she saw a perfume kiosk that she wanted to check out. As she was looking at all the different perfumes that this kiosk had to offer, that feeling rushed over her once more. She looked around from where she was standing and again didn't see anything, so she went back to looking at and smelling the perfumes. One by one, the aroma of each was better than the last. As crowds of people were walking past the kiosk, she spotted a dark figure from the corner of her eye. As more and more people passed, she saw the figure get closer. Chills ran through her as the figure approached.

Liz turned slowly toward the man she saw, and it was exactly who she expected. The only thing that was separating her from the same man that was watching the twins earlier were the groups of people going in and out of stores, oblivious to the danger around them. Liz backed away from the kiosk and looked directly into the man's eyes; they were familiar to her; someone she knew all too well.

She called him by his name, "Gabriel! What are you doing here?"

His lip curled and a smirk appeared on his face as he moved toward her at a slow pace.

With every small step he took toward her, she inched back, her breath quick and shallow.

Gabriel noticed and stopped. "Is that anyway to say hello?" She swallowed the knot that formed in her throat before she could say anything.

"What…" She gulped. "What are you doing here?" She tried her best not to let him hear the unease in her voice. They both stood where they were, motionless and focused intensely on one another, for what seemed like an eternity. He took another step toward her, but this time she didn't move, and finally they were standing a few feet from each other.

"You didn't think that I wouldn't come see them, did you?" She looked at him, but before she could say anything, he continued, "I've been locked away for sixteen years and now I'm finally out—thanks to the council, of course god knows the family didn't bother to help."

Liz thought to herself, *that must be why Darwin went to Avalon—to try and stop his release. How could he be granted freedom for what he tried to do? And why hasn't dad called or sent word that he was out?*

"The council voted earlier than expected, and Darwin's vote really wouldn't have made a difference," he said as if he had read her thoughts. Gabriel looked over to the store that the twins were in. "They turned out to be handsome boys, didn't they?"

"You should leave now Gabriel."

He didn't take that tone of hers too kindly and moved closer to Liz, to the point where she felt his breath coming out of his nose. "You can't keep me from my boys, Liz."

Before another word could be spoken between them, Liz's voice was loud in Bianca's head, *Get the twins and your sister out of here NOW!* Without hesitating, Bianca ran toward her cousins.

"You should leave now, Gabriel," she repeated, only this time the people all around them stopped moving as if someone hit the pause button on a remote control.

Gabriel smirked and repeated himself as well. "You can't keep me from my boys." He turned to walk toward the store the twins were in and saw Bianca running toward them through the window, grabbing Chloe along the way. Gabriel raced toward the entrance of the store, but before he made it inside, Liz flung her hand through the air, tossing Gabriel into a nearby kiosk on the other side of the walkway. With another wave of her hand, the people that were frozen around her were pushed out of the way with care so they wouldn't get hurt. They remained frozen, motionless as Gabriel cleared off the pieces of the broken kiosk and products off from his body.

Back in the store, Bianca yelled at Adrian to come to her and ran toward Andrew.

Adrian and Collin were confused but listened and moved quickly toward her.

"Grab onto my arms, all of you!" she ordered as she was holding Chloe's hand.

Chloe shrieked, "You're squeezing my hand really hard!" but Bianca ignored her. "You guys have to hold on very tight!" Terrified, they listened. Right before they teleported, Adrian noticed all the people that were in the store with them weren't moving, but before he could point it out to the others, they were all gone.

"Just so we're clear, you attacked me first." Gabriel rose from the ground. "You didn't leave me much of a choice, did you?"

Gabriel once again made his way toward the store the twins were in and noticed that they were no longer inside. He marched past a mall patron, his fists so tight that his fingernails began biting into his palms. Her hand was suspended midair as if she was about to move a piece of her hair away from her face when Liz cast a spell that left her, and the other people frozen where they stood.

Gabriel fumed. "Do you really think that you can keep me from them?" His voice was thick with frustration. He looked at her with hatred in his eyes as he called for his wand. With a wave of his hand, a black wand with gold trim appeared in it. Before Liz could react, he shouted, *"Inhabilitare!"* and she stiffened where she stood then fell to the ground, hitting it like a sack of bricks being tossed from a high perch. As he made his way toward her, he saw every muscle in her body cramping up. He boastfully observed, "That looks painful."

Liz couldn't speak; it felt like time had stopped. The pain was visible from the tears flowing down the side of her face. She couldn't help but be reminded of the time when she and Gabriel were younger, and he showed her this very spell that left her in agonizing pain. She had just turned sixteen years old and was learning all about her newfound powers and Gabriel was eighteen.

He called her to the backyard of their house where he was playing with Gunther, the family's German shepherd. It was a large dog with brown fur and black spots and had been the smartest, most playful dog they ever owned. Gunther ran over to Liz right when he saw her.

Gabriel asked her if she wanted to see something; like all kids, she was curious and said yes.

He held out his hand and his wand appeared. He grinned at her, clutched his wand, and pointed it directly at Gunther. He called out, *"Inhabilitare,"* and the dog went down. She looked on as the dog stiffened and collapsed to the ground and noticed all the muscles in his body began to cramp up as if he was turning to stone. She slid to Gunther's side and began sobbing, begging her brother to make it stop. He just laughed and told her it would be alright because it didn't last that long. She hoped the same could be said for today.

As the spell started to wear off, she was able to speak, but instead of screaming out in pain, she yelled out, *"CONFUSA!"* Gabriel jerked his head back and began to walk in circles, dropping his wand in the process, which gave her enough time to stumble to her feet. She was still in excruciating pain and wanted nothing more than to run away, but instead, she held out her hand and summoned her own wand and it appeared instantly. It was beautifully carved out of dark brown oak and was twelve inches long. She pointed it at Gabriel and shouted, *"TRANSPORTA AD CAVERNA!"* and Gabriel flew toward a display window, but before he hit it, he was gone. The only thing remaining was the sparks and smoke hovering slowly over the floor where he had stood.

Liz glanced around to make sure the spell she casted on the mall patrons was still active. She hobbled in pain toward the broken-down kiosk and pointed her wand at it. *"Figere ut,"* she panted, and the kiosk began to repair itself piece by piece, the merchandise that was scattered all over floated back to its original place. She leaned against a pillar for support, realizing that even after all these years, Gabriel was still much more powerful than her.

Once the kiosk was back up, she ran over toward the elevator while waving her hand and muttering words in a whisper. Group by group, everyone was soon back in motion as if nothing had happened. She was still in agonizing pain when she pushed the elevator button and got in, but before the doors could close, she was sucked up into what seemed like an invisible vacuum, teleporting out of the mall.

At the twins' house, Bianca was the only one standing as they teleported in. Collin fell to the floor while Chloe fell on the reclining chair, Adrian and Andrew fell at Bianca's feet.

"Sorry, the teleporting can be a bit rough for first timers," Bianca advised while trying to think of how she could explain what just happened. As she looked down at the twins, Andrew leapt to his feet and rushed to the bathroom. Teleporting must not have agreed with him since Bianca could hear him, vomiting. The others tried to ignore it, but it didn't seem to be possible, so Bianca thought she was doing them a favor by waving the door closed. That wasn't how the rest of them took it, because as she looked at her sister—who Adrian was now standing by, helping Collin to his feet—she noticed the fear and puzzled looks etched on all of their pale faces.

She stood there awkwardly, not moving until they all heard keys opening the front door. It was Sara coming home from her jog.

"Hi, guys," she said as she turned to close the door behind her. She placed the mail that was in her hand on the table before she realized that no one had replied to her. She looked over at the three pale-faced kids and realized something was wrong.

"Oh my god, what happened?" Sara rushed to Adrian's side, her gaze watering. "Where's Andy?" she asked frantically, but before anyone could answer, he emerged from the bathroom looking sickly and just as pale as the other three. "What happened?" Sara repeated.

She looked at Bianca. "Um…" Bianca breathed heavily. "I don't know. Mom yelled at me to get the guys and Clo out of there." She leaned against the wall. "So, I did. Mom looked frightened, so I didn't hesitate and did what I needed to."

"Where's Liz now?" Sara demanded to know, but Bianca had no idea. She was still a little winded.

"At the mall still, I think." Sara sprinted over to her purse that was sitting on the table against the stairs and frantically searched for her cell phone.

"What's going on?" Adrian yelled. That question stopped Sara dead in her tracks. She had no idea how to reply to it; she was always planning on telling them, but this was all happening too fast. She felt a heavy hollowness in her chest as she looked up at Adrian and had no clue how to respond.

This isn't how this was all supposed to happen, she thought to herself, *and what happened in the first place that made them ask that question? Was it even related to magic, or something else?* She had no idea.

"Adrian, I'm going to call your aunt to see if she's ok," she calmly told him.

Chloe was puzzled. "Can someone just say how we went from the mall to here in a second?"

Collin put his face into the palms of his hands. "Yeah, and when does the room stop spinning?"

Sara slowly brought the phone down to her side; she finally had an answer to her own question. She took a small step forward and looked at Bianca, who confirmed that they did indeed teleport home.

She looked back at Adrian, who whispered, "Mom?" Collin decided to sit down because standing was proving to be much more difficult, followed by

Chloe who let her legs give out and stumbled to the floor beneath her. Suddenly, Liz appeared in the dining room.

"Oh my god, are you ok?" Sara asked as she rushed to her side.

"I'm fine," Liz said, looking over to Chloe and Bianca so they wouldn't worry. Sara pleaded, "What happened?"

Liz looked Sara in the eyes. "Gabriel." That was all she needed to say for Sara to become more worried. Not only did the twins get shocking news like this, but the man she hasn't heard from or seen in sixteen years was back.

Not concerned with who Gabriel was, Adrian demanded to know what was going on.

Sara was relieved not to have to explain who Gabriel was just yet. Bianca answered before Sara or Liz could, "I teleported us from the mall." Chloe, Collin, Andrew, and Adrian slowly turned their heads toward her.

Puzzled, Andrew leaned in. "Teleport?" he repeated, as if he wanted to make sure he heard her right.

"Is that what you just did?" Chloe asked while pointing at her mother.

"Yes," Liz answered as the lingering effects of the spell Gabriel cast on her finally went away.

"How is that even possible?" Adrian questioned; his voice shaky.

"Because Mom and I are witches," Bianca answered quickly. Suddenly, it became awkward. Bianca lowered her gaze from the wondering eyes of her cousins. Liz, too, avoided meeting their stares. Suddenly, an unexpected outburst caught the attention of the room.

"That's freaking *awesome!*" Collin cheered, still woozy. The moment passed quickly, and silence once again fell over the room.

Finally, Andrew cleared his throat. "I take it you knew about this?" Sara just nodded at her boys. Chloe was still looking at her mother, her nostrils flaring. Liz couldn't bring herself to acknowledge her daughter's cold stare, knowing all the questions that must be going through her head. In that moment, Adrian, Collin, and Andrew looked at Chloe.

They must think that Chloe is a witch as well, Liz thought. They could all see Chloe's face was puffy and her eyes appeared red; she was taking it just as badly as the twins. Bianca rushed over and placed her hand around her sister.

"You, ok?"

Chloe turned toward her and asked the question on everyone's minds— well, the boys, at least. "Am I a witch too?" she sounded hopeful.

Bianca looked at her mother, who then approached them and said, "No, sweetie, I can't get into why now, but I promise we will talk about it." While She embraced her daughters. Chloe looked somewhat upset yet relieved at the answer. She had so many questions racing through her mind but couldn't bring herself to ask them.

"Andy, give me a hand," Collin said while extending his arm up to meet Andrew's.

Andrew helped him to his feet while Adrian, seeking answers, looked at his aunt.

"Witches? They exist?" he asked, still in disbelief. Liz couldn't speak; too much had happened for one day. Sara looked over to her boys and realized that now was the time for her to tell them. Today was the day she finally had to explain to her boys what was about to happen and who they were.

She cautiously approached them while Liz and Bianca looked on. Sara extended her hands to grasp theirs. She pulled them to the couch, sat them down, and took a seat between them.

"We need to talk."

Chapter Four

Sara sat between Adrian and Andrew in silence, trying to figure out the right words to use. In her mind, she was going through countless ways of saying what she needed to tell them, but she was ultimately left speechless. Chloe and Collin were just looking on as the three of them sat on the sofa in silence. Liz and Bianca asked Collin and Chloe to give them some privacy.

Chloe got off the floor, frustrated, and stormed out to the kitchen and out the sliding door.

Bianca followed Collin into the kitchen, where he turned around rapidly. "How could you guys keep this from her?" He leaned on a chair, clutching it tight. Bianca was surprised to see how upset Collin was over this—how defensive he was over Chloe. "She's your sister, and for both of you to keep something so important from her is just wrong!" Collin was visibly angry.

Bianca just looked at him, knowing full well he was right. "It's complicated."

"That's right, drop a bomb that witches or whatever are real on all of us and expect to not to have to explain it. I can see why Chloe is pissed off." He pushed the chair into the table and stormed outside, slamming the patio door hard enough to knock over the paper towels from the counter. That was out of character for Collin; he was always so respectful and courteous to people and always found a way to make everything positive. Liz and Bianca were thrown off by his actions and looked at each other, puzzled over what they had just witnessed.

Collin made his way over to Chloe, who was just lying in the middle of the trampoline that Sara bought the twins as an eighth-grade graduation gift. It was perfectly centered below the stars that were visible in their tiny, light-polluted town.

"Mind if I join you?" She was silent; there was too much to process. He pushed aside the black netting and slid next to her. They both laid there together, and after a few moments of silence, Collin glanced over at her.

"This is…" he searched his thoughts for the right words. "Unbelievable" not exactly what he wanted to say in that moment, but it was too late to take back.

Chloe couldn't take her eyes away from the stars illuminating above. "That's one way to put it. Another is crazy. Crazy that my mother and aunt could keep such a huge secret from us. Like we wouldn't find out. Don't they know that's the problem with secrets?" She looked over to Collin. "They always find a way to come out and leave nothing but destruction and despair in its path."

Collin was back to not knowing what to say. The only thing he could do was reach for her hand and hope it would comfort her. To his surprise it did. Chloe's heart began to race and for a split second, she forgot about what was going on back in the house.

"Wow. Andrew is loud" Collin noticed after he heard his muffled yell coming from inside.

✳ ✳ ✳

"MOM," Andrew yelled again to get Sara's attention. Adrian added, "What do you need to talk to us about?"

Sara sat there with her hands folded into her lap. She knew this was going to be hard for them to hear, but she knew she had to tell them. If only she could find the right words already and just say it.

"Are we like Aunt Liz and Bianca?" Adrian asked, holding his breath as he waited for an answer. Sara looked at them quickly, not surprised by the question but relieved that the burden of bringing it up first was gone.

"Yes."

Adrian sat there wrinkling his brow. He looked at his brother for comfort, but it never came. Andrew got up from the sofa quickly, raced over to the bookshelf that was against the wall, and stared at the bookends he bought for his mother at this antique store she loved going to. He remembered the day he got them for her. How could the same person keep something so important from them?

He turned so his gaze met his mother's. "Are you serious?" His voice was shaky. Sara stared into his eyes, hers filling with tears. "Yes."

Andrew stood there; his legs planted widely. Adrian got up to join his brother. "How could you keep this from us?" He went to his brother's side, nearly knocking Andrew down in the process.

"Were you ever going to tell us?" Andrew demanded to know, adrenaline starting to course through him.

Sara got up and went toward her boys, but they backed up. She realized how they felt and stopped from approaching them. She knew they didn't want her comfort but an explanation. "Please let me explain…"

"Explain what? The fact that you have been lying to us?" Andrew scolded, his voice cracking.

"Were you ever going to tell us?" Adrian yelled, his tone and volume rising with each word. Sara lowered her head as she appeared to shrink.

"Yes, but—"
"BUT what, Mom?!" Andrew interrupted; his body visibly trembling. "But you forgot? Or did you not think it was important enough?" The sarcasm in his voice was obvious.

Sara turned around with tears streaming down her face. She knew how betrayed they felt at that moment, because she had been there herself with Gabriel. She turned back to face her children who were now standing firmly in place, visibly upset.

"Go easy on your mom," Liz said as she came into the room, leaning on the wall. The spell Gabriel cast on her still had lingering effects. Everyone seemed startled by her reappearance; for a second, they forgot she was still there.

Adrian pinched his lips together. "Shouldn't you go talk to Chloe?" He pointed to his aunt. "But what do I know? I'm just assuming this all comes from our dad's side of the family, since Mom isn't telling us anything."

Liz looked at Adrian. "I will talk to Chloe later. There is a lot that you don't understand—"

But before she could continue, Andrew cut her off by yelling, "Don't you think you've waited long enough?"

Silence fell over the room. Liz stared at Andrew. "I know this is a lot to absorb and that you boys are angry, but you will show me and your mother respect and not shout at us."

Andrew and Adrian seemed to take her words seriously and went from standing firmly in place to plopping down on the sofa, exhausted. The anger was boiling in both. Adrian especially. But he knew he had to get his anger under control. Andrew meanwhile rolled his eyes and sat down and crossed his arms. Why should they show them respect after this he thought to himself.

Sara looked to Liz. "Have you talked to Darwin?"

"I called, but no answer." Liz glanced at her phone to see if he had called her back.

Sara looked over at her boys, sighing. "I know you have a lot of questions, and I will answer them in time, but we must wait for your grandfather. He can explain all this much better than I can."

Andrew and Adrian didn't say a word, but they didn't storm off either. Sara knew they were ok with that decision.

"Liz, can I have a word with you?"

"Yeah, of course." Sara led the way up to her bedroom for some privacy.

Andrew and Adrian looked frustrated but didn't argue, opting to just sit there in silence. After all, they had a lot going through their heads. Bianca was leaning against the wall staring at them, not knowing what to say.

She saw the pain and anger in their eyes, but she had no idea how to comfort them.

Bianca then turned her head to look out the dining room window into the backyard where she saw Chloe and Collin lying on the trampoline. She knew it was going to be harder to explain things to Chloe, and yet still had no idea what her or her mother were going to say to her.

✳ ✳ ✳

UPSTAIRS, Sara was sitting on the edge of her bed trying to absorb every word Liz told her about her confrontation with Gabriel. But the only thing she wanted to know was why— and how—he was back. Before she could say anything, Liz blurted out the exact thing that was on Sara's mind: "Why did the council let him out of the Tower?"

"The Tower?" Sara had never heard of that before, but then again, she didn't know much about that world at all.

Liz looked at her and explained to her that the Tower of Avalon was an inescapable two-hundred-foot tower made of solid stone. It was a place only the evilest of wizards went. There were no windows and magic could not be used inside. It was a place where the inmates were taken in shackles that suppressed magic no matter how powerful the person was that was being taken there.

"So… he's legally out." It was obvious Sara was terrified of this Tower she had never heard of. That was when Liz had an epiphany. She took a seat on the recliner that Sara had next to her bed, mumbling underneath her breath, "That's why he made it clear that I attacked first.… Why did I attack him?"

Sara was quick to chime in, "You were protecting the kids. I don't know anything about wizard law or why they let him out, but I do know what he did before, and so do you. That's why you attacked him." Sara gave Liz a reassuring nod and a comforting pat on the shoulder.

Liz finished telling Sara what happened and after she took it all in, they decided it was best to go back downstairs. As they were walking down the carpeted stairs, a gust of wind went through the air and Darwin appeared before they reached the bottom step.

He looked through the top of his half-framed glasses to the sofa where Andrew and Adrian were sitting and asked if they were ok. No matter how mad they were, Darwin was still intimidating to them, his voice still so deep that it gave them chills. They quickly responded yes, which made Bianca look at them in disbelief over how calm they were talking to their grandfather, after just moments ago they were yelling at their mother and aunt. Darwin glanced back at Sara and Liz and told them to follow him so they could talk.

The intimidation that Andrew and Adrian felt just seconds before quickly faded away; they could feel their skin warm as their temperatures rose. Before Darwin could lead Sara and Liz off to the kitchen, Andrew stood up and demanded to know what was going on.

"We deserve to know the truth," Adrian added, joining his brother. Side by side, they stared Darwin down. They were still intimidated by him, but it wasn't showing. Darwin took a deep breath and sauntered over to them.

"I'm terribly sorry for the way you boys found out about this; I really am. But I need to talk to your mother and aunt right now."

"But—" Before Adrian could finish his sentence, it was too late. Darwin had already left, taking Sara and Liz with him.

*** * ***

DARWIN stood in the Council Chambers trying to convince the rest of the members of the council that Gabriel couldn't be released, arguing that the fact that it was even a possibility was utterly ridiculous and outrageous. He had noticed that not one of the twelve council members were interrupting or adding to his testimony and suddenly knew something was wrong. He glanced around the room filled with throne-like chairs and noticed that Genevieve's chair was empty.

He looked over to Barnabas, the head of the council and the chancellor of Avalon.

Barnabas wasn't as powerful as Darwin but had still been elected Chancellor over him by the citizens of Avalon, and the council affirmed his election after Gabriel killed his predecessor. Barnabas wore a black robe with gold stripes on the arms and had long dark-gray hair.

"The council and I have already agreed to release your son." His raspy voice echoed around the room. Darwin was outraged and began to speak, but Barnabas just spoke louder, cutting him off. "GIVEN that he is your and Genevieve's son, we decided that it would be best if you didn't have a vote on the matter!"

Darwin fumed but didn't say anything. He just looked over to Adele, who carried a lot of influence over Barnabas and who he suspected of working for Gabriel. However, he had never mentioned his suspicions, as he didn't have the evidence to back up his theory. Not until now.

Curious after hearing his tale, Liz asked, "Do you think Adele played a role in his release?"

Darwin nodded. "No matter what part she played in Gabriel's release, he isn't allowed to visit the Sapien world."

Sara didn't know if she heard him right. "Sapien?" she murmured.

"That's what we call any place outside of Avalon. It stands for humans and where they live," Liz answered.

"So, you refer to us non-magic people as sapiens, and our society as 'the Sapien world'? Are you serious?" She couldn't help but laugh. "Ok, then, continue."

"If he's not allowed here, does that mean they will revoke his freedom once they find out he came here?" Liz questioned, hopeful that it would be that easy to rid the world of him again.

Darwin informed them that he would most likely get a warning and be told not to come back again. Not too sure if that would keep Gabriel away, Sara came to the decision to take the kids somewhere far away, but they convinced her it was best to keep them home given how much had already changed for them. Sara was hesitant but agreed and wanted reassurance that Gabriel would stay far away. Darwin told her he would take care of it. Once that was all situated, Darwin noticed Chloe and Collin lying on the trampoline.

"Were they at the mall too?"

"Yes," Liz informed him, bowing her head in anguish. She was reminded of the reality that was facing her and couldn't bring herself to look at her daughter.

"Take them home and mind wipe them," Darwin ordered as he led them back downstairs.

Liz or Sara didn't seem too surprised at what Darwin instructed them to do. They knew that Chloe wouldn't be able to handle the truth, especially after what had happened.

Liz called for Bianca and headed out the sliding door onto the patio. "Chloe, Collin!"

They walked over to her, "We are leaving Chloe."

Chloe was in disbelief. "Leaving? Shouldn't we talk about what is going on?"

"We will but after we drop Collin off." Liz wanted Chloe not to say anything else and just do what she was told. What was coming was hard enough without Liz feeling more guilty about it.

"Collin is a part of this too and…" Before Chloe could finish, Collin interrupted.

"Chloe it's fine. This is clearly a family thing and I'm fine going home so you all can talk." Collin was noticeably upset but didn't want to argue. Collin and Chloe headed to the car because they didn't have any other choice. Liz followed closely.

As Collin and Chloe got into the backseat of the car, Liz summoned her wand, got into the front seat, quickly turned to face them, and pointed the wand at them while saying, *"OBLIVISCI!"* With that, Chloe and Collin's heads fell back on the headrests, as if they had simply fallen asleep. Bianca looked at her mother, who could see the guilt displayed on her oldest daughter's face, but neither said anything and they drove off.

✳ ✳ ✳

BACK inside, Andrew and Adrian joined Sara and Darwin at the kitchen table.

"So, where should I start?" Darwin placed the palms of his hands on the table in front of him, as if bracing himself for impact.

He started to tell the twins about his side of the family and the history of the magical world. How magic comes from the world around us, from nature and energy, so to speak, energy that is unseen but can still be felt by gifted individuals. How those individuals have the ability to manipulate that energy.

They listened for hours as he went on and on. They were both fascinated with what they heard.

"Why did you keep this from us?" Adrian looked over to Sara.

Before she could answer, Darwin replied, "Because we had to be sure, so we agreed to wait until your sixteenth birthday, when most wizards and witches come into their power."

They looked satisfied with the answer they received. Andrew asked Darwin how they "did magic," to which he simply laughed.

"I will teach you."

"How do we even know we have powers?" Adrian asked, worried over the possibility they might not have those special abilities.

"Yeah, I don't feel any different," Andrew added, looking to his brother.

Darwin looked at Sara, who gave an approving nod as if giving him permission to do something. She excused herself from the kitchen to go make a phone call. Darwin got up and told both twins to clear the table as he searched the desk area that Sara had set up in the kitchen to do her bills. He held up a pen victoriously.

"Here we are." He made his way back to the table, placing the pen at the center of the round table. Next, he held his hand up as if to catch something and within a second, the pen flew into his hand. He held it up, showing it to the twins, and placed it right back down in the center of the table and looked over to Adrian.

"Now you try."

Adrian looked over to his brother, who was staring intently at him, then looked back at the pen and concentrated on it. His eyes began to squint, and his head started to shake.

36

"Ugh, I can't!" He slammed his hands against the table, frustrated at how stupid he felt.

"You're putting too much thought into it." Darwin leaned a little closer toward Adrian. "Clear your mind and concentrate on the pen coming to you."

Adrian tried again, He put all his focus on the pen, the plastic coating around it. It couldn't have weighed much, so he pictured it beginning to float, hovering midair, until it started to make its way toward him. No matter what he imagined, though, the pen didn't budge. "This is pointless!"

He got up from the table, the chair falling behind him. Andrew decided that it was his turn to try, so he looked at the center of the table and held up his hand. As he did, the pen slowly started to float, then rapidly flew toward his hand like a dart to a board. Adrian stared on in disbelief.

"How did you do that?!"

"I don't know, I just did what Grandpa said and…"

Holding up the pen, Andrew displayed it to his brother like it was a prize won. Adrian was annoyed. He was always better than Andrew at everything they did, and he couldn't let that change. He picked up the chair off the floor, snatched the pen away from Andrew, and slammed it into the middle of the table again. He focused, stared at it without blinking, and held up his hand, Adrian felt some kind of energy rushing through him. It worked—the pen flew toward him in a mere second. They both started laughing, excited over what had just happened. It was like the anger from just a few short hours ago had never happened.

Sara was watching them from the dining room, hopeful and happy that they were embracing who they were. Happy that the anger had faded from them.

"Ok, guys, I'm going to bed."

Too excited over what just happened, the twins didn't seem to hear her. "What else can we do?" they both asked their grandfather.

Not wanting to rush them into anything too big, Darwin held up the pen and said, *"PIGMENTUM GREEN!"* and the pen changed from black to green. Adrian and Andrew looked on with amazement.

Adrian snatched the pen from Darwin, he wanted to beat Andrew to it. He held it up at an arm's length away and said *"PIGMENTUM BLACK!"* The pen returned to its original color.

After a few hours of going over other little basic spells and magic, Darwin saw that it was going on two o'clock in the morning.

"Oh my, look at the time!"

Adrian and Andrew both looked at the clock above the stove and couldn't believe how late it was. Darwin stood up, grabbing his cane. "Now, boys, I have to get going, but if you want…" he fell silent for a moment, contemplating if what he wanted to say was a good idea.

"If you want, you could come to my home for the next few weeks before school starts, and I could teach you how to control and use your new abilities."

Andrew beamed. "Yeah! We will talk to Mom in the morning about that."

Darwin nodded and headed for the front while the twins followed. Before he reached the door, he turned around and looked them in the eyes.

"Now boys, I need you to promise me something before I leave."

"We won't do any magic unless we are around you or Aunt Liz," Andrew assured him, anticipating what his grandfather was going to say.

Darwin affectionately looked his way. "That's a good idea, but not what I need you to promise." He put one arm around them and leaned in closer, his glasses becoming nonexistent from that angle. He lowered his voice so as not to wake Sara. "I need you both to promise you won't tell your cousin Chloe about any of this."

They both looked stunned at what he was asking. Surely Chloe would want to know about being a wizard as well, and isn't that what Liz and Bianca took her home for anyway? To explain all of this? That was what they thought, at least. Then it hit them—Chloe was only fifteen years old, so she still had a year to go before getting her powers.

Adrian added, "I'm sure Chloe will be ok with waiting a year before she gets her power," thinking that Darwin thought she would be jealous.

Darwin stood back up. "That's not why you can't tell Chloe." He knew they would want answers, so he escorted them back into the kitchen and out the sliding doors. He paced back and forth calmly, searching for the words to say. It shouldn't be hard, given everything he had told them so far, but this was different. This was something that he dreaded telling them more than anything.

"Ok, what I'm about to tell you has to stay between us."

They both nodded in agreement, and he pointed to the swing that Sara loved so much, gesturing for them to take a seat. Darwin exhaled a deep breath.

"Chloe and Collin had their minds wiped of the incident at the mall and the events that took place when you all got back home."

Suddenly, the twins felt that anger again that they almost forgot about as it washed over them.

"Why would Aunt Liz do that?" Andrew demanded to know. "Because I told her to."

Andrew got up, letting his anger take control of him.

"Why would you tell her to do that? Just so she can go through the shock next year?" Adrian asked while looking over at his brother. "I'm sure she would rather want to know the truth now than have it all thrown at her once again later."

Darwin was silent for a minute or so. "The thing is, Chloe isn't going to be a wizard."

"How do you even know that if you weren't sure about us?" Andrew shouted.

Darwin hesitated for a few seconds before he answered. "Because she is adopted."

The twins fell back and sat on the swing, their legs giving out. How could that be?

Andrew's anger became sympathy for his cousin. She had no idea the terrible news was waiting for her. They didn't know how to respond to the insight Darwin just leveled them with.

"It isn't my place to tell you this, so I won't go into detail. I just need you to promise that you won't say anything to your cousin; it's up to Liz to decide if and when to tell her."

Andrew and Adrian still couldn't speak and just looked up at Darwin, exhausted f r o m   everything they had experienced that day. It was so much information to take in—such a burden to know something they couldn't share with the one person closest to them.

"Promise." Darwin's voice was even deeper and more commanding than usual.

"Promise," they both answered hesitantly.

Andrew stood up, looked at his grandfather, and shook his head. "This isn't right." He marched into the house while Adrian stood up and looked over at Darwin.

"I'll talk to him," Adrian reassured his grandfather. He followed his brother inside.

Darwin stood there for a few more seconds, looking at the house as all the lights went off. He tapped his cane on the patio floor and the blue smoky light engulfed him once again, then he was gone.

Chapter Five

Adrian and Andrew still hadn't slept since Darwin left. How could they after everything they have been through in a single day? They were filled with so many emotions—anger, shock, and finally, sadness. They spent the rest of the night in Andrew's room talking about everything that happened to them and if they should keep this secret from Chloe.

"I don't…" he trailed off. "I don't think it's fair that we keep this from Chloe."

"Drew, I know it's going to be hard, but if we tell her…" Adrian hesitated, still not believing it himself. "If we tell her what we are, we will have to tell her why she isn't like us. And Grandpa is right about it not being our place."

It was hard for them to come to an agreement on what to do, but they eventually agreed to keep this to themselves. By then, it was nine o'clock in the morning when Andrew looked at his alarm clock. "Wow, I'm not even tired!" Adrian wasn't either.

As they lay there, they both smelled the whiff of pancakes. They didn't realize how hungry they actually were until that aroma seeped in from under the door.

Adrian asked, "Did you hear Mom get up?"

"No." Andrew breathed in the delicious aroma.

Andrew leapt off his bed and helped Adrian to his feet. As they both headed toward the door, Adrian suggested they apologize to Sara for how they talked to her yesterday, and Andrew a g r e e d . When they opened the door, they were greeted with intensely bright sunshine sneaking through a window that sat above the stairs. They hadn't even seen the sun rise because Andrew had his windows blacked out with layers of curtains. Adrian looked over to Andrew.

"What? I hate the light!" Andrew blurted.

He knew Adrian was going to comment on how he slept. They both laughed and proceeded downstairs where Sara was in the kitchen with Liz.

"Morning, Mom, Aunt Liz," they both said.

They approached the table Sara already had set up for them. She was obviously trying to make things right with their favorite breakfast food.

"We wanted to say sorry for how we talked to you yesterday." Adrian said remorsefully as he looked over at his mom and aunt. They both knew how sorry the twins were. Adrian looked on, mournful, hoping they would forgive them.

"It's ok." Sara told them.

Liz glanced at both of them tenderly. "Yeah, we understand why you two were upset."

Sara gripped the plate of stacked pancakes and strode over to the table. As she set it down, Andrew told her that Darwin invited them to his house for the next few weeks before school started so that he could teach them more about their magic. "Is that something you want to do?" Sara looked over to her beaming children. "If that is what you want to do, then I am more than happy to let you." A smile was fixed on Liz's face. They were embracing who they were, and that pleased her.

"You guys are going to love Avalon."

"Avalon?" Andrew and Adrian always thought their grandfather lived in Arizona. They had never heard of Avalon.

"Yes." Liz forgot that there was still so much that they did not know.

"Should we get plane tickets?" Andrew mulled over the thought as he pulled out his phone.

"No," Liz replied, amused by the question. "Avalon is a wizarding country where the magical can live freely without fear of being seen or made fun of. A beautiful place that is unlike any other."

Adrian and Andrew looked at each other and couldn't contain their excitement. They were more eager than ever to go to their grandfather's house but decided they should try getting a few hours of sleep beforehand since they hadn't slept since the night before the mall. Sara told them that she would call Darwin later. They excused themselves and headed back upstairs, not realizing how tired they really were until they both reached their beds. A second after their heads touched the pillows, they were out.

Downstairs, Sara and Liz sat at the table talking about Avalon. Sara had always heard about it but had never seen it for herself since humans—or, as they would say, sapiens—didn't really go there. "Avalon is the safest place for them to learn about magic. It is, in fact, the best place for them to learn who they are and where they come from." Liz looked at Sara and could tell she was worried. "They can practice in the open and will never run into Gabriel. Dad won't allow it." Sara realized that Avalon was where Gabriel was, but what Liz had just said helped reassure her.

Sara got up from the table and rushed over to her phone that was charging at her desk in the kitchen. She dialed Darwin's number. It rang once, and on the second ring, Darwin pressed i g n o r e and it went straight to voice mail.

* * *

DARWIN placed the phone back in his pocket and looked directly in front of him where a large mansion sat on top of a curved stone walkway. The mansion was made of brick, like all the homes in this part of Avalon. He made his way to the front door. Atop the entrance of the doorway was a big circular balcony with two big stone gargoyles perched on each side. Darwin looked up and noticed Gabriel staring directly at him. Without hesitation, Darwin teleported from where he stood and before the smoke cleared from the door below, he appeared on the balcony behind his son. Gabriel turned and they stared intensely at one another before Gabriel finally spoke.

"Hello, Father. How nice of you to finally visit." Gabriel said, his palms sweaty.

Darwin just stared at him, not saying a word. No one would be able to tell how much this worried Gabriel, because what Darwin wasn't saying vocally, he said with his piercing blue eyes that were staring without so much as a single blink at Gabriel. Gabriel didn't let his fear show and continued to speak. "So, you come all this way just to stare at me? Do you really think that makes a difference?"

Still, Darwin didn't say a word. Gabriel started getting frustrated and began pacing back and forth, letting his years of resentment toward his father consume him. Darwin just watched as his son began to let his anger out.

"You can't keep me from my children!" Gabriel clenched his fists.

Finally, Darwin answered, "But I can," with his all-too-familiar voice that sent chills through even a powerful wizard such as his son. Gabriel stopped and turned to face his father, now more frustrated than scared.

"Can you?" A vein in his forehead started to pulse.

"Given your past, Sara doesn't want you anywhere near her children, so yes, I can, and I will."

"They are *my* children, so I don't see any harm in visiting and getting to know them! Sara has no right to keep me from them." Gabriel placed his arms behind his back, gripping one wrist with the other hand. How dare Darwin think he could still treat him like he was his lesser?

"But there is harm in seeing them, Gabriel. You're not supposed to leave Avalon, or do you not remember the terms of your release?"

"The council already gave me a warning about leaving Avalon, and once again, Father, they didn't feel the need to consult with you on the matter."

Darwin stared at him coldly and moved closer to his son, getting within an inch of his face. "Regardless of what the council says or if you choose to obey them is irrelevant, because the boys and Sara are under my protection, and I will do anything and everything to protect them."

Gabriel didn't like being threatened and backed away from his father. "YOU ARE NOTHING AND YOUR DAYS ARE NUMBERED! SOON…!" He paused for a second to calm himself down. "…soon you will see that it was a mistake to threaten me."

Gabriel quickly reached out his hand and his wand appeared in his closed palm, but before he could summon a spell, Darwin disarmed him and flung him to the nearby wall without much effort. "To draw your wand on a council member is a great offense, son. Surely, you know that."

He slowly approached Gabriel, who couldn't move even though he was trying.

"Now, where were we?" Darwin asked as he put his hand on Gabriel's chin. "Oh yeah.

Stay away from the boys and stay away from Arcadia." He leaned in closer to Gabriel, who was now trembling because of how much he was trying to move, but he still couldn't. Darwin looked at him over his half-framed glasses and whispered in his ear, "Besides, we both know why you truly asked to be released."

Darwin quickly turned away and strolled toward the banister of the balcony, waving his hand and releasing Gabriel, who fell to the ground. Darwin turned to face his son, who was on his hands and knees staring with so much rage directly into his father's eyes, but before he could do or say anything, Darwin growled, "This is for Liz."

He summoned his cane and pointed it at his son, yelling, *"Inhabilitare!"* Gabriel felt the same pain he inflicted on his sister just one day before tenfold since it was cast by a wizard whose power was unmatched. Gabriel collapsed to the ground, stiffened and unable to speak.

Darwin could see every muscle in his son's body firm up and flex uncontrollably. Darwin gave him a wink before he was engulfed in his trademark blue smoke, teleporting off the balcony.

❋ ❋ ❋

SINCE there was still daylight out, Darwin decided it was best to teleport directly into Sara's home so that the neighbors wouldn't see him. He forgot, however, Sara wasn't that familiar with seeing that herself, so of course he startled her.

"Sorry!" Darwin chuckled, but Sara just laughed it off.

"The boys are still sleeping," Sara informed him while taking a sip of her tea.

"That's fine. It's not like we have a flight to catch or anything." He looked on playfully at Sara, who found that joke amusing.

"Would you like some tea or something else to drink?"

"Yes. Coffee, if it isn't too much trouble. Thank you."

Sara lifted the pot and poured the steaming hot coffee into a mug. She handed it over to Darwin, who seemed to really enjoy the aroma of it. Sara took a seat at the table with him and asked, "What are you going to be showing them?"

Darwin took a sip of his coffee, steam fogging his glasses in the process, and set the cup back down. He knew that Sara was curious about what he had planned for her boys and felt obligated to tell her to ease her mind, if nothing else.

"I will be teaching them the basics of magic, the things that come naturally to most wizards."

Sara was intrigued, because she didn't really know much about the magic world apart from the things Gabriel had told her.

"What kinds of things come naturally to them?"

"Things such as telekinesis and teleporting. Those things will be taught first, followed by the basic understandings of potions and spells."

"Spells and potions? Are they dangerous?" This concerned Sara. Mixing things and casting spells left her feeling uneasy. Darwin looked at her and saw that she was worried, but he wanted to be honest with her. After all, she did deserve it.

"Some can be dangerous, but I can assure you, I will be there every step of the way."

Sara didn't seem to like that answer; she got up from the table and walked over to the kitchen sink to drink some water. Darwin quickly followed and put his arms on her shoulders, hoping to comfort her.

"Everything is going to be alright. I won't let them try anything I don't think they are ready for. I know this is hard for you, but it is better that they learn from me than on their own. Magic is a tricky craft that can be dangerous if the person doesn't have the proper training or understanding of it."

What Darwin said seemed to ease her mind a little—not much, but enough for her to feel comfortable with them going to study with him.

"Thank you," she said as she turned around. Darwin smiled and went back to grab his cup of coffee off the table. "Is two weeks going to be enough time to show them everything?"

"Everything young wizards need to know, yes, but *everything?* My dear, I've been around a long time and still don't know everything myself. That is what makes magic so incredible; it is ever evolving."

"I would need them to come over on weekends once school starts—if they want to, of course. There is just a lot to educate them on."

Sara poured out the rest of her tea. "As long as it doesn't interfere with their schoolwork and they want to go, that shouldn't be a problem."

Darwin looked pleased with her response and went back to drinking his coffee. Sara decided it was time to wake the boys, so she excused herself from the kitchen and went upstairs.

As always, she went into Andrew's room first and sat down on his bed. "Andy, sweetie, it's time to wake up." She patted him lightly on his back. He started to move and when he opened his eyes, he was still not fully awake.

"What time is it?" he asked groggily.

"Three o'clock, I wanted to let you both sleep as long as possible." she answered. She got off the bed and went over to Adrian's room, which was down the hall on the opposite side. She slowly opened the door but saw Adrian was already awake, stretching and yawning.

He looked at his mom. "Is Grandpa here?"

She nodded yes. She leaned on the door for a second as if taking a mental picture of her son, wanting to take in that moment for just a bit longer.

"Mom? Everything ok?"

"Yes." She got off the door and started to close it behind her. "Make sure you pack your toothbrush."

Adrian rolled his eyes at the thought of his mother thinking he was a child that needed to be reminded of basic hygiene. "I'm sixteen, you don't have to remind me to pack a toothbrush!"

"Ok, I'm sorry, my mistake. I forgot that has never *ever* happened before." Sara closed the door of his room. As she was walking downstairs, the doorbell rang, and when she opened it, she saw that Bianca was standing on the other side.

"Hey, what are you doing here?"

"Grandpa said I should come with," she answered as she let herself in.

"Oh, what a great idea!" Sara said.

"I thought it would benefit the boys to have someone there who went through the process not that long ago." Darwin took a few steps towards them. Sara led them into the living room to wait for the twins, who were still packing upstairs.

"Did you tell Chloe where you guys were going?" Sara inquired.

"No. She wasn't home when I left, but Mom said she will tell her when she gets back."

Sara was concerned over the fact that now everyone in the family would be keeping this secret from Chloe. "Does Liz really think keeping this from Chloe is the right thing to do?"

"I agree, secrets tend to do more harm than good." Bianca looked over at Sara. "When will she tell Chloe about all of this?" Sara asked.

"I'm not sure she will. When I asked Mom, she snapped on me and told me she doesn't want to talk about that right now."

As they continued to wait on the boys, Sara noticed that what was once a sunny afternoon was now filled with clouds that blocked out the sunlight. The wind began to pick up and thunder could be heard in the distance. Sara looked out the window and saw that it was still dry out. She looked up to the sky.

"Looks like a storm's coming in. Does this affect your travel arrangements?"

"No, but it's still best that we get going soon." He then joined Sara at the window. "You have to admire how unpredictable the weather is here," Bianca chimed in.

Sara beamed and proceeded to go up the stairs but before she reached the first step, Adrian was already making his way down, followed by Andrew.

"Sorry, forgot to pack after breakfast!" Adrian blurted out as he rushed past her to the living room.

Adrian and Andrew both had identical black duffel bags hanging over their shoulders that seemed to be over packed. Darwin led them into the kitchen and out the sliding glass door into the darkened backyard. The sound of thunder still filled the air, only this time it was accompanied by a flash of lighting raging throughout the sky. Sara hugged her boy's goodbye and gave them each a soft kiss on their foreheads.

"Pay very close attention to everything your grandfather shows you and listen to everything he and Bianca tell you."

They nodded in agreement with their mom. She went over to Bianca and gave her a hug and a kiss as well. Finally, she was in front of Darwin. She reached up on her tip toes to give him a hug and whispered, "Thank you for all of this."

Darwin embraced her tight, knowing that she was trusting him with the only two things that mattered to her in this world. "No need for thanks, my dear."

Sara took a step back and crossed her arms to try keep from shivering as the approaching storm made the temperature drop a little cooler than normal for the month of August. Darwin instructed everyone to hold hands. Since they were traveling a greater distance than Bianca normally did, he decided it was best to take them all.

"Everyone ready?"

They all nodded in agreement and Darwin gave a last look over to Sara, accompanied by a comforting wink, and within a second, a small swirl of glowing blue smoke started circling their feet, growing thicker as it rose higher and finally engulfing them when it faded, they were gone. Sara looked up to the sky and the wind started picking up more speed. She decided it was time for her to go back inside and when she did, the doorbell rang. She wondered who it could be since she wasn't expecting anyone. She slammed the sliding door and locked it as the doorbell rang again.

"Coming!" she yelled out as she made her way to the front. As she opened the door, Chloe and Collin let themselves in since the winds were making it harder to stand outside without their hair getting messed up.

"It's crazy out there!" Chloe whined. She turned and looked out of the thin window next to the double doors that led into Sara's house.

"Chloe, not that I ever mind or that you need a reason to come over here, but I wasn't expecting you."

"The idiots and I had plans to watch a movie and hang out." She said jokingly.

Sara didn't know how to respond to that, so she just told Chloe the truth. "I'm sorry, sweetie, but the boys and Bianca went to Grandpa Darwin's for the next two weeks." Chloe and Collin looked at each other, not knowing what to say. Chloe squinted her eyes like she normally did when she was frustrated.

"Why would they go to Grandpa's house, and more importantly, why wouldn't I be invited too?" Chloe was confused and a bit hurt.

Sara quickly responded, "Your mom said you didn't like flying, so you wouldn't want to go."

Chloe stood there and thought for a moment. "Ok, but that doesn't explain why they didn't tell me they were going to visit him," she said with the same squinting eyes and confusion expressed on her face. She looked over to Collin, who was just standing there in disbelief. "Did Andrew or Adrian tell you they were going to visit our grandfather?"

Collin shook his head.

Chloe is asking the same questions I would have asked myself, Sara thought. After all, the twins and Chloe were very close and told each other everything. Andrew would have even told Collin if it had been planned, but since it was a last-minute thing, they probably didn't even think about it. Still, Sara was a little frustrated that the twins didn't at least text one of them not to come over, so it didn't look like they were blowing them off.

Sara looked at Chloe and Collin as they just stood there. "Well, you guys are more than welcome to stay here and watch a movie anyways."

Before Collin or Chloe could answer, they heard the sound of raindrops hitting the roof at a rapid pace and saw the windows covered with thick waves of water courtesy of the rain running down the side of the house. Collin looked away from the window. "Sounds like a plan, Ms. S."

Chloe seemed to agree even though she didn't say anything; instead, she just kicked off her shoes and walked over to the sofa to sit down. Collin followed, removing his shoes and sitting on the bigger sofa right next to Chloe on the other wall.

"Good! Go ahead and pop in your movie and I'll make you guys some popcorn," Sara told them as she left the living room.

Chloe looked over at Collin. "I can't believe those little shits didn't tell us they were leaving for two weeks." Chloe had to act as if she was frustrated by it. But her cousin's being gone gave her some alone time with Collin, which she was incredibly happy about.

Collin looked at her, agreeing with her statement. "What jerks!" Collin wasn't really upset about it but felt like it was the only thing he could say at that moment.

"I'll get the movie ready," Collin ran upstairs to grab the movie that was already pulled out from the shelf and sitting on Andrew's dresser, then ran back downstairs. Collin put it in the DVD player and waited for the TV to go on before going back to sit on the sofa. Once everything was ready, he seized the remote and planted himself on the bigger sofa in the exact same spot he was in before. After a few minutes, Sara came back in with a transparent glass bowl of popcorn and handed it to Chloe.

"Thanks, Aunt Sara."

"You're welcome, sweetie. I'm going to start dinner in a few, so don't fill up on popcorn!"

Collin got up from the sofa once again, this time to sit next to Chloe who had the popcorn further away from his reach if he were to stay where he was. As he sat down, his arm brushed hers and a smile came to her face instantly. Collin didn't notice because he was too focused on the TV, but she didn't mind. *Maybe it's a good thing the twins left.*

Chapter Six

Adrian, Andrew, and Bianca teleported to Darwin's estate. Adrian and Andrew both stumbled to the ground when they arrived, still not used to traveling that way. Andrew once again cleared the contents of his stomach, only this time all over the freshly cut grass they had just appeared on. Adrian was the first to notice the many acres that surrounded them along with all the trees that lapped around the entire estate like they were providing a barrier to the outside world.

The trees were thicker and taller than the ones back home; the air was fresh, and a light breeze cooled the air to a rather comfortable temperature. However, Adrian couldn't take in the remarkable scenery for too long because he too, decided the trip was too much and joined in on his brother's recent activity. Bianca couldn't help but laugh at her cousins who were finally making their way back to their feet. Her laughter didn't go unnoticed by Darwin.

"Well, at least you two didn't faint." That comment quickly put an end to Bianca's laughter. Darwin winked at her as he helped them up.

The boys were finally able to stand without falling. Once they were able to fully see what was around them, they noticed that only a few hundred yards away was an enormous French château mansion made entirely of brick with highly pitched roofs. The towers that were on each end made it look like a castle. Darwin led them toward his home and as they made their way over a small hill, they noticed two sets of horse stables off to the side before the main house. As they came closer to the front of the house, the door flung open and out came a short, stocky bald man dressed in what looked like a butler uniform who seemed to walk with a little bit of a limp.

"Hello, Master Darwin!" he rejoiced. His thick British accent was hard to miss.

"Hello, Nigel."

Adrian, Andrew and Bianca stopped right before reaching the front of the house. The entrance was gargantuan and had four huge pillars leading into two double doors that were already opened. The twins had never seen a house this big and were still admiring the outside design.

Darwin gushed, "This is Adrian and Andrew, my grandsons, and you remember Bianca," as he pointed to each one of his grandchildren individually.

"So happy to meet you both, and lovely to see you again, Lady Bianca," Nigel beamed. "Please, let me take your bags."

Before any of them could object, Nigel waved his wand and all three of their bags vanished from their shoulders.

"Wow, Grandpa, this is a big house!" Andrew scoped out the land all around him.

"Thank you. It's been in our family for years."

The boys found that hard to believe; from the stunning bricks it was made from to the modernized look, they didn't think it could be more than ten years old.

"Shall we go inside so I can show you to your rooms?"

Darwin took a step up the single stair and into the house. Adrian and Andrew followed Darwin and Bianca inside and saw that the inside was just as beautiful as the outside. The entrance to the house had high ceilings with a large crystal chandelier hanging in the center of the room and a soaring staircase that split into two different directions halfway up. The living room had elegant sofas and chairs upholstered in silk with beautifully polished wood frames and carved legs. The drapes that hung over the window were made of heavy velvet in other dark shades. There was beautifully painted artwork on almost every wall, and every room they were shown had vaulted ceilings. The dining room had a long, thick oak table that seated fourteen people, a stunning hearth fireplace, and another crystal chandelier. The boys were amazed at how stunning Darwin's home was.

As he continued to show them around, they came into an impressive gourmet kitchen and saw an older woman with dark-grayish hair wearing a black dress with an apron who was preparing what seemed like dinner. The smell of pizza filled the air and both Adrian and Andrew's mouth moistened.

"Why, hello there! I hope you are hungry, because dinner is almost ready," she announced as she paced back and forth between the stove and counter.

"Smells delicious, Hekabe," Darwin praised. Even though Hekabe worked for Darwin, they were more like family by this point.

He escorted them upstairs and asked if they wanted their own rooms or to share one. At first, they didn't know how to respond. When they reached the top of the stairs, they both agreed that separate rooms would be better, and Darwin agreed with them.

"I'm going to get washed up for dinner." Bianca headed down a different direction in the hall.

They followed Darwin and he stopped at the first door on the left. He tapped the door with the top of his cane three times and then turned the doorknob.

"Dibs!" Andrew shouted.

Adrian didn't seem to like that one bit. The room was as big as both of theirs at home combined and had its own balcony and bathroom.

"Wow…" was all Andrew could say.

"Get washed up for dinner, Andrew" Darwin ordered.

He then led Adrian out of the room to show him his own a few feet down the hall. They reached the doorway and Darwin repeated the same tap three times, then opened the door, only this time Adrian caught a glimpse of the room transforming itself into a new design than it originally was.

Darwin paused. "Didn't have time to prepare the rooms before I left." Once it was completed, it looked similar to the room his brother had and Adrian seemed pleased.

"I'll let you get washed up too and see you downstairs in half an hour for dinner." Darwin then left Adrian to enjoy his room.

Adrian strolled over to his bed and leapt on it. He gazed around the room; it was somewhat familiar to him but new all the same. The bedding matched the ones from his room back home. Some posters of his favorite athletes hung on the wall. Andrew may have gotten his own balcony, but Adrian got a better view of Darwin's massive estate.

A half hour went by and one by one, Adrian, Andrew, and Bianca met in the huge, long hall.

Bianca displayed a wide grin. "You guys have no idea where to go, do you?" "You know how Drew is with directions," Adrian teased.

"Yeah, Andy is bad with them." Bianca nodded in agreement.

Andrew rolled his eyes, "Adrian just because you think you are better than me at everything doesn't mean you would be able to find your way downstairs."

"I don't think, I know I'm better than you at everything" Adrian added with a laugh.

Andrew grabbed Bianca's arm to keep her from moving. "Ok then. Lead the way. Mr. I-know-everything." Adrian stood there, trying hard not to smile.

"Ugh. Come on boys" Bianca said as she brushed off Andrew's hand.

As they made their way to the dining room, they saw Darwin was already seated. "This house is amazing, Grandpa!" Adrian took his seat.

Darwin smiled as Nigel bought a sizable pan of homemade four-cheese pizza followed by Hekabe, who had a basket of fries and thick, golden-brown deep-fried mozzarella.

"Forgive me if it's not good; I've never made this kind of food before." Hekabe set down the steamy dishes in the center of the table.

"Are you kidding? That looks amazing!" Adrian shouted. Bianca and Andrew nodded in agreement.

Hekabe raised her chin, exposing her neck when she heard the praise. She then headed back to the kitchen, confident that she had done the recipe justice. Nigel poured them all drinks and they began to eat.

"Tomorrow, we will go into the capital so I can give you a tour and pick up a few things," Darwin said.

"Can I stop in the potion shop?" Bianca asked.

"Of course."

The twins still weren't used to being waited on or being in such a large house with massive rooms. They found it a little strange that this was their grandfather's home, but they felt excited all the same.

Andrew pursed his lips and tilted his head sideway. "What's the capital?"

"It is where all the shops are located and where the official business of the magic world takes place."

"Official business?" Adrian leaned forward; eyebrows squished together.

"Yes, where the council meets and where the chancellor of Avalon is. You know, the people that oversee our world." Bianca's voice was muffled by the pizza she was chewing.

Adrian was still confused but decided he would ask more questions tomorrow; the pizza was too good to let it get cold.

During dinner, both Andrew and Adrian's phones beeped, showing a text from Sara. She told them that they forgot to tell Chloe and Collin they were going to be gone for a couple weeks. They both leaned their heads back in shame at blowing off the two people closest to them.

"I'll call Chloe before bed, it was my idea to come so I'll take the heat for this," Adrian said and Andrew, of course, would call Collin.

After dinner, they decided that they wanted to go check out the stables and the rest of the estate. Bianca told Darwin she would give them the tour of the grounds and Darwin decided that while they explored, he would go off to his office to finish some work.

As Bianca and the twins made their way outside and closer to the stables, they could start to smell the manure of the horses that were kept there.

"Ok, I'm going to give you a tour of the grounds, but it will have to be on horseback since it is a lot of ground to cover. But I should also warn you that these aren't your typical horses," Bianca gushed.

Before either of them could ask what, she meant, they reached the first set of stables and saw three beautiful, majestic white horses with wings. Adrian and Andrew were astonished by what they saw.

Amazed at what he saw before him, Adrian wondered, "Are these unicorns?" Bianca stared at him. "Unicorns? Are you serious?" she chuckled. "Unicorns don't exist. At least not that I know of."

"Oh, sorry, that's crazy of me to even ask. How *dare* I ask such a crazy question like that? These are just horses with wings!" It was a new level of sarcasm for him, and Bianca couldn't help but be amused.

"These beautiful creatures are Pegasi."

Andrew and Adrian glanced around as if looking for more details.

"You know, Pegasus, the flying horse? Well, they exist, and there's not just one," Bianca informed them. She then pointed to a spot next to herself and added, "Ok, guys, stand over here."

Like in most things, Adrian was first to give this mythical beast a chance. Nothing really scared him. Andrew always envied that about his brother and wished that he could be more like him. But he couldn't be. Andrew was always cautious, and this time wouldn't be different. After Andrew saw it was safe, he did the same thing and stood next to his brother, glancing over for reassurance that they would be ok.

Bianca walked over to the wall and gave both a saddle, instructing them just to hold it and stand still. They didn't know why they had to do that, but since they were new to all of this, they listened.

"Once they see that we want to ride them, they have to pick us."

Adrian understood, so he just stood there, but Andrew was still confused until he saw one of the Pegasus walk toward Bianca. He sniffed her hair and face and after a few seconds, he galloped over to the boys. After a few more seconds, the Pegasus went back toward Bianca and spread his wings, which spanned twelve feet from side to side. That was how Bianca knew it was ok to put the saddle on. As she did that, the other two Pegasus picked out their riders. Once they were saddled, Bianca led the way out of the stable to the open field a few feet away.

"You guys seem to know what you're doing," she observed, and they both just laughed. "This isn't our first time on a horse," Andrew gushed.

"Oh, that's right; Aunt Sara made you take lessons with Chloe."

"So how many Pegasi does Grandpa own?" Adrian wanted to change the subject, hoping to never be reminded of that summer.

"Six altogether."

All three Pegasi made their way slowly toward the center of the field, and the one Bianca was riding gave a nod to signal it was ready to take off. Bianca looked back at her cousins. "Are you guys ready?"

"What are their names? I figure since I'm putting my life in their hands, so to say, I should know their names," Andrew questioned.

"This is Azbo," Bianca answered as she gently petted Azbo's hair. "The one you are on is Gizmo, and Adrian, yours is called Rizzo."
"Hello, Gizmo, I'm Andrew. Please don't let me fall off," he whispered in Gizmo's ear. He petted the top of Gizmo's head. "Please."

Adrian looked at his brother and laughed, but afterwards, he whispered the same thing to Rizzo. Bianca exchanged knowing looks with them at how scared they both seemed to be. She turned back and gave her Pegasus the signal to go and one by one, all three Pegasi began to run. Once they picked up enough speed, they spread their wings and were off the ground, soaring through the sky. After a few minutes, Adrian and Andrew started to get the hang of it and got over their fears. They flew all over the estate and got high over a beautiful pond that each Pegasus glided lower to so they could get closer.

"This is where you guys will be training at," Bianca yelled over the sound of the hooves grazing the water below.

Confused, Andrew asked, "In water?"

"No, over there!" Bianca yelled while pointing to the field directly next to the pond.

They saw what looked like obstacle courses and excitement rushed through them. They couldn't wait to begin learning how to use their powers. They flew over the grounds for two hours while Bianca called out certain areas, she thought they would like to know about. Once they started to head back, they saw other houses miles apart from one another.

"Does everyone here have big estates like Grandpa's?"

Bianca looked on lightheartedly. "Well, this is Southport, the wealthiest city in all of Avalon—well, besides the capital, of course."

When they started to descend, both Adrian and Andrew braced themselves for what they thought was going to be a rough landing, only it wasn't—each Pegasus landed softly and they did so effortlessly, which the twins found fascinating. Once they were on the ground, they led each Pegasus back into the stables, removed the saddles, and brushed and fed them. After all, they wanted to show them how much they appreciated the ride.

The sun had finally set in Southport and Bianca decided it was time to leave the stables and go back in the house. During the walk back, Bianca told Adrian and Andrew how riding the Pegasus was a form of bonding and how each one belonged to them now. They both seemed to enjoy the news that Bianca had just told them; who wouldn't want to own a majestic creature such as a Pegasus? They finally made their way inside, where Hekabe had made cookies and had them set up on the table with three empty glasses alongside a jug of milk.

"Thank you, Hekabe," Bianca told her on behalf of all three of them.

"No need to thank me! It's a pleasure having Darwin's family here. Now if you'll excuse me, I think I'll retire to my room now."

As she left the room, Adrian asked, "Does she live here with Grandpa?"

"Yes, she and Nigel live in the west wing of the house."

They started to eat the snack that Hekabe left out for them. Each cookie was still warm and melted in their mouths.

"Wow, these are SO good!" Adrian said as he munched happily.

"So can I ask you a few questions, Bianca?" Andrew inquired while taking a big gulp of milk.

"Sure."

"Why does Grandpa live here by himself? I mean, this house is huge and seems like a lot for him."

"He doesn't live here alone. Three people live here, and up until a few years ago, he lived here with Grandma. Besides, it's his family home; he grew up here. So why would he leave?"

"Grandma, the lady who sends us birthday cards every year?" Adrian asked sarcastically. They really didn't know her; they barely knew Darwin, at that, but at least saw him every once and a while and spoke to him more.

"Yes." She couldn't help but laugh over what he said.

"I didn't know she was a witch, too," Andrew interjected.

Adrian and Andrew both looked puzzled because they really didn't know much about their grandmother and had never really felt the need to ask until now.

"She's a powerful sorceress and a wonderful woman," Bianca informed them. Andrew was surprised by how she said that.

"A sorceress?"

"Yeah. It's what we call lady wizards who are equally as powerful, if not more, than their male counterparts," Bianca answered.

"I thought you were witches?"

"We are it's just Grandma is older and more powerful than most of the population on Avalon." She laughed at how confused her cousins looked. "Some even say she and Grandpa are the most powerful magical beings in Avalon. And we are their heirs, so we have a lot to live up to. No pressure, though." She smiled over at Andrew and Adrian, who didn't know what to say. "She is also a council member."

They both sat there wondering if they would see her since they would be going to the capital in the morning, but neither one came out and asked. After a few hours in the kitchen, Bianca decided it was time for her to go to her room. She was exhausted after the busy day they had, and she needed her rest since they had another one lined up for tomorrow.

"Goodnight, guys." Bianca headed upstairs.

The twins were also tired and decided it was time for them to go to their rooms as well. When they reached the top of the stairs, they said goodnight to one another and went off to their own rooms. However, Adrian and Andrew didn't want to sleep—Andrew, because he was thinking about Chloe missing out on all of this and how he didn't like having to lie to her. This reminded him that he had to call Collin, so he picked up his phone and dialed Collin's number.

Collin didn't answer, but Andrew left him a voicemail explaining to him how sorry he was for not telling him he was leaving town and to call him back. After a few minutes, he heard a knock on his door. When he opened it, Adrian came walking in.

"Chloe is extremely upset with us," Adrian shouted as he barged into the room. "I don't blame her."

They both decided that they would make it up to her when they got back home. For now, though, they were going to enjoy the next two weeks.

"I'm not tired," Andrew told him.

Adrian felt the same way. It was hard for them to sleep in a place like this. They both decided to go sit on the balcony outside Andrew's room and talk for a bit about everything that was going on in their lives.

"I still find all of this shocking," Adrian said as he looked out at the field in front of him.

Stars were much more visible here than back home, the sky less polluted. "Same here." Andrew agreed with a glassy stare.

"Do you think we should tell Chloe?" Andrew asked, joining his brother in basking in the incredible view.

"We promised we wouldn't. Plus, there is more that goes with telling her this."

Adrian has always been the voice of reason and probably the only person Andrew listened to, so he agreed once again not to tell their cousin. As they sat there looking out into the distance toward the trees, they wondered how they would keep this secret from those close to them and if they would be good at being wizards. What Bianca told them about their grandparents didn't really help either. Despite their excitement at this whole new world, they were thrusted into, they both had doubts. They didn't know much but knew that if both Darwin and their grandmother were council members, they had a lot to live up to. They also realized that their aunt and Bianca had to be good at this stuff too.

"Do you think we're cut out for this?" Andrew wondered.

"I don't know, but this is our life now, so we have to give it a try."

"Do you think Dad was any good at this stuff?"

"I'm sure he was. I mean, this is his family," Adrian said.

"I wish we got a chance to meet him." Andrew's tone was a little off.

They both just sat there, thinking about their dad they never met who they were told died in a car accident before they were born. On the other side of the double doors that led out to the balcony in Andrew's room stood Darwin. He had come in to say goodnight to his grandchildren and overheard them talking about their father—a father he knew was alive and dangerous. He realized that Adrian and Andrew would need to know the truth soon but didn't want to ruin this moment for them. Darwin turned and exited Andrew's room, closing the door gently behind him so the boys wouldn't know he was in there.

He went over to his own room a little bit further down the hall and up one level, then opened both doors with a wave of his hand. As he came in, they shut right behind him. Darwin leaned his head against the door and thought about how to tell his grandchildren about their father.

Back on the balcony in Andrew's room, Adrian and Andrew continued to sit there and wonder what their father was like. Neither one said much to the other but didn't want to leave each other just yet. When they were upset about something, all they needed to do was sit with each other and that made them feel better. They always had a strong bond between them; it had always helped them before, and it was helping them now. They never thought about their dad as much as they had now, and it was really getting to them. Andrew regretted bringing up their father but knew that it was inevitable and something that he thought would benefit them.

Andrew interrupted the silence between them, "We should ask Grandpa what he was like,"

Adrian didn't acknowledge what he heard at first but looked at his brother with a somber expression. "I'm going to bed before we stay up all night again." He went back inside Andrew's room.

"Night, Adrian."

"Night, Drew!

After a few minutes, Andrew's eyes started to feel heavy. No matter what he wanted, his body was telling him it was time for bed.

Andrew stumbled off the balcony, closed the doors behind him, and lay in his bed. Once again, he was out as soon as his head hit the pillow.

The next morning, Bianca woke up Andrew and Adrian to get ready for their trip to Polaris, the capital of Avalon. Despite their meager few hours of sleep, both felt fully rested and excited about the day's activities.

Once they were downstairs, Darwin, who was with Hekabe eating the delicious breakfast she had made for the family, said, "I should have you kids over more often, because she never cooks like this when it's just me." They all laughed and proceeded to eat the omelets that awaited them on the kitchen table. Once they were finished, Darwin handed Adrian and Andrew a small clear vial each that had a purple liquid inside.

"What's this, Grandpa?" Adrian inquired. Andrew looked on, waiting for an answer as well.

"They are for you to drink before we leave. Since we are teleporting, this will help with the nausea and vomiting you two seem to experience afterwards."

Bianca looked on and once again laughed at her cousins, only this time Hekabe joined in, "You young wizards are so delicate nowadays." Even Darwin couldn't keep from laughing.

Adrian and Andrew were both hesitant to drink the purple liquid and each dared the other to go first. That didn't really seem to work so well, and Darwin suggested that they could just teleport and hope for the best. Andrew didn't want to take the chance, so he popped off the little cork and swallowed it in one gulp. Adrian quickly followed so Andrew's reaction wouldn't discourage him from drinking his own—which was a great idea, since the purple liquid left a bitter and salty taste in their mouths.

"I think the vomit would have left a better taste," Andrew moaned as he gagged, almost vomiting. Adrian rushed to the sink and quickly drank some water.

"Excellent. Shall we go now?" Darwin asked as he led them outside to the backyard.

While Darwin was leaving, Bianca looked over at her cousins, who were still having difficulties from the potion they had just consumed.

"Oh, come on, you big babies!"

As the twins followed Bianca they saw her teleport, and as soon as they both grasped their grandfather's arm, they teleported as well. Hekabe, who had now made her way to the door, watched them leave and went back inside the house. She looked around at the mess the kids and Darwin had left behind.

"What would Darwin do without me?" she wondered to herself, placing her hands on her waist.

She summoned her wand and it appeared instantly. She waved it gently in the air and said, *"Mundare et dimittere!"* Within moments, everything from the kitchen table to the dishes were cleaned and put away by the time she put her wand down by her side. "This is the easiest job I have ever had" Hekabe amused herself.

Chapter Seven

They soon arrived at a designated teleporter landing right across from the main entrance into the heart of Polaris. The potion that Darwin gave Adrian and Andrew must have worked, since neither of them were nauseous nor pale. Adrian was the first to approach Bianca, who arrived a few seconds before they did.

"I can't believe it!" His mouth dropped open. "Drew, do you see this?" The sky was full of what looked like miniature funnel clouds soaring through the air in an assortment of colors.

"Seeing? Yes. Believing, no."

Adrian pointed to the sky. "Grandpa, what are those?"

"Ah, those are turnabouts. That is how most people choose to get around."

"Wow." Andrew was memorized by the multiple colors gliding through the air.

The windy conditions made the smell of freshly baked bread and cookies fill the air, which was alluring to Andrew, who had a sweet tooth. Polaris came alive with the sounds of its inhabitants dashing up and down the sidewalks, going from store to store. The concrete sidewalks were wide with not one piece of trash on them. The buildings all looked modern but each one different and they were made of brick and stone; the tallest one they had seen so far was six stories high. It was the cleanest city Andrew and Adrian had ever seen.

"Grandpa, where are the streets?" Andrew noticed there were only wide sidewalks.

"No one in this country owns a car."

Andrew looked at Adrian, who found that to be surprising as well.

"How do people get around, then?" He wasn't sure how people could function without automobiles.

Darwin raised his eyebrows. Something that was so normal for him was positively exhilarating for his grandchildren; he couldn't be happier to share this experience with them. He pointed to a pinkish turnabout coming directly towards them. "Like that." A woman with a pink coat landed right in front of them, stamping her walking stick on the ground. "And by teleporting of, course." They were stunned at what they just saw and finally understood what Darwin meant.

"Wait…" Andrew paused, intrigued. "People can fly?"

"Not really; they use a spell to manipulate the wind around them to carry them from place to place."

They both thought they had seen it all but finally realized that Avalon was full of surprises. The lady in pink bowed her head at the sight of Darwin. "Sir."

Darwin bowed back. "Hello."

As they strolled through Polaris, all the people that passed Darwin did the same thing the lady in pink did, and he just returned a small bow of his own. Adrian noticed that all the people they had passed so far had on long elegant coats or robes of countless assorted colors and suddenly felt underdressed. They reached the end of the sidewalk and Darwin stopped to talk to a person that asked for a moment of his time. As they waited for Darwin, before them stood the tallest building in Polaris. It was nine stories high, beautifully designed of stone and marble and surrounded by an eight-foot-tall black metal gate. Adrian and Andrew looked on with amazement at this building, intrigued by what could possibly be inside.

Bianca stepped between them. "That's where Grandpa and Grandma work, along with the rest of the council members and their staff. And where the chancellor of Avalon's office is."

Andrew was fascinated. "They're pretty important people, aren't they?" Bianca smiled sweetly in response.

"Can we go inside?" Adrian asked right as Darwin rejoined the group. "Not today. We have a lot to do." He placed his arm around his grandchildren.

As he led them in another direction toward the business district, Andrew finally saw the bakery where that remarkable smell that greeted them upon arrival was coming from. Bianca decided to go off and explore some stores on her own. The twins and Darwin arrived at the front of this store named Adrasteia's Shop and went in.

The sound of a bell jingled as Darwin opened the door and they passed the threshold into what seemed like a high-end boutique. Adrian and Andrew were once again amazed at the sight of the shop. It had an elegant look, from its high ceilings and big chandelier that illuminated the entire shop to the tall shelves that spanned as high as the ceiling, stocked with all kinds of books and items they had no idea about and aisles of beautifully designed crystals and amulets.

"Darwin!" yelled a beautiful woman who had to be a few years younger than him.

She had long, curly red hair, white skin, and spoke with a thick Scottish accent. "These must be yer grandchildren ye hev been goin' on aboot!" she added as she made her way toward them. She quickly embraced Adrian and Andrew as if she had known them for years. "C'mere!" She pulled them closer to her. "So nice to finally meet ye wee lads! Darwin can't stop talking aboot ye boys."

They both stared at each other, dazed, as she turned and hugged Darwin. "Boys, this is Adrasteia, a good friend of mine."

"Youse boys go hev a look aroun' and help yerself to anything 'at catches yer eye. I hev to talk to Darwin for a minute."

As she and Darwin made their way to the back of the shop, Andrew noticed a small vial that had a glowing thick blue liquid inside it and just one word on the label: Eagle.

Adrasteia wasted no time. "So, I heard Gabriel wiz released from the Tower," she mentioned as the drapes they entered through came back together behind them.

"Unfortunately," Darwin snarled, "yes—yes he was."

"Do ye think he'll continue on 'is quest 'at got him sent to the Tower in the first place?"

"I'm sure of it."

"An' how was he even allowed oot?"

"I believe Adele convinced Barnabas to grant his release."

Adrasteia slammed down the trinket she had in her hand. "Are ye telling me their courtin' was a sham since the beginnin'?"

They both had a laugh. Ever since it was announced that Adele—a gorgeous tall woman with caramel-brown skin and captivating aqua eyes who dressed in nothing but the most lavish outfits—and Barnabas were dating, Darwin and a few other council members thought it was purely for personal gain on Adele's part. Since it could never be proven, the topic was never bought up again. However, it wasn't long until Adele was positioned as the chancellor's number two in the council. Still laughing over her comment, Adrasteia went over to a cabinet and pulled out two small boxes for Darwin.

"Thank you so much for putting a rush on these, my dear. You're the best in the business." He took the beautifully hand-carved boxes from her.

"Oh, please, Darwin, no need fer thanks."

As they stepped out from behind the drapes, both Andrew and Adrian were holding a few things in their hands while still looking around.

"Boys, come here," Darwin called out.

As they made their way to him, Bianca came walking in with two bags full of things that she probably had no need for.

"I want you to have something." He handed them the small boxes. As they opened them, they both saw a chain that was attached to what looked like an eye, only the eye had diamonds going all around it and a sapphire pupil.

Andrew held open the lid. "Wow, this is really nice!"

"Yeah, I don't wear jewelry," Adrian teased.

"Guess you guys are officially part of the family," Bianca boasted. She held her necklace up for them to see. Hers was the same eye, only she had an amethyst pupil. "It's kind of our family thing."

"Thanks, Grandpa."

Darwin smirked at their appreciation and said, "We should get going now. We still have a day of training to get to."

Adrasteia escorted them out and once again embraced each of them. "Don't be strangers!" she said, then back inside her shop she went.

"Oh! We forgot to pay for these." Andrew held up the items he had taken from the shelf. "Don't worry, she'll send me the bill," Darwin noted with a wink.

As they made their way back to the designated teleporter area, Adrian and Andrew were both fascinated at how breathtaking the capital was and how amazing Avalon was. They finally reached the area they came from and ran across the walkway. As soon as she could, Bianca was the first to teleport. Darwin turned to face the twins with his hands raised and asked if they were ready. They both took hold of one of his arms, and they teleported back to his estate. As they appeared back at Darwin's estate, they were greeted with the aroma of freshly baked garlic bread that they knew must be part of an incredibly delicious meal that Hekabe prepared for them.

"We will begin training after lunch," Darwin told them as they came inside. "Welcome back!" Hekabe greeted.

Adrian, Andrew, and Bianca said hi and looked around to see that lunch was in fact laid out on the kitchen table.

"Do you guys ever eat something that isn't made in tomato sauce?" Bianca rolled her eyes at their lack of taste.

"Hush now, Bianca, I made you something else," Hekabe playfully said. She pointed next to the stove, where a mouthwatering steak sat on a plate with mashed potatoes and corn.

"Now *that's* a good lunch!" Bianca blurted out as she went upstairs to get cleaned up.

Adrian patted his stomach. "We are going to gain twenty pounds before we leave here."

Andrew laughed and the boys went upstairs to wash up as well. Darwin rejoined them after lunch with a small black rectangular box. "I hope you boys had enough to eat, because you're going to need your energy."

He placed the box in the center of the table in front of the twins. Bianca sat silently, already knowing what was in the box and how important this moment would be for the twins. Darwin took off the lid to reveal two beautifully crafted wands. One was made of oak, the other of willow. Adrian and Andrew were stunned at the sight of the wands and didn't take their eyes away, even as Darwin tried to get their attention.

"Who wants to pick first?" Darwin wondered. Neither of them answered but knew which one they wanted, and luckily it wasn't the same one. Each of them picked up a wand and felt a strange current coursing through their bodies. They felt, for the very first time, the power that was inside them.

"Shall we begin?" Darwin stood up and they followed him outside with Bianca.

"Now, the fun begins!" Bianca shook them both, excited at what the rest of the day held.

Their Pegasi were already waiting for them on the small hill by their stables.

"Do you know where the training field is?" Darwin asked as they each got on their Pegasus.

"I showed them already." Bianca leapt onto hers.

And with that Darwin summoned his cane and pointed it to the ground. The wind began to pick up speed around him. "Excellent. Let's go then."

Within a second, the wind formed a turnabout the length of his body and he was airborne. All three of their Pegasi galloped at a rapid speed until they, too, were airborne. These majestic beasts were fast and caught up to Darwin rather quickly. However, none of them were airborne long since they reached the training field within ten minutes. Adrian was the first one to see that new obstacles were spread out on the large field next to the pond that Darwin chose to land by.

Darwin soon landed, followed by Bianca and then the boys, who still had their wands in their hands. As soon as they could, Adrian and Andrew got off their Pegasi and told them to go back to the stables. They listened and followed Bianca's back.

"First things first: teleporting," Darwin stated, wasting no time. He took a few steps and pointed. "Do you see that orange wall on the other side of the pond?"

Adrian and Andrew both looked across the pond and saw what he was referring to. "Andrew first," Darwin instructed.

"I don't even know what to do."

"Teleporting, like moving objects such as pens, comes naturally to a witch or wizard." Darwin got a bit closer to Andrew. "I want you to close your eyes and visualize the orange wall in your mind."

Andrew closed his eyes while Adrian and Bianca looked on. When he opened them, he was standing next to the orange wall with Darwin and Bianca.

"Holy crap!" he shouted and noticed Adrian still on the other side.

Adrian quickly closed his eyes and remembered Darwin's instructions, and when he opened them, he had joined his brother next to the orange wall.

"This is so beyond cool. And much easier than making a pen fly" Adrian stared across the pond where he was just standing, shaking his head.

Darwin and Bianca teleported back to the place they started from. This time, Adrian was quick to follow, then Andrew.

"As you get used to it, you won't have to close your eyes to visualize a place; you would just have to simply think of it," Darwin informed them.

They continued teleporting all over the field for an hour or so, getting used to it. Andrew even went back to Darwin's house to grab a piece of garlic bread leftover from lunch.

Darwin was amazed by how well they were doing. Being new to this world he didn't think they would grasp it this fast. But it reminded him of Gabriel and how naturally magic came to him. He didn't want to think of his grandchildren in the same way as his son. Darwin hated failure and felt like one when it came to his own son, so he didn't give it much more thought. "You boys are picking this up fast!" The excitement in his voice was contagious; Andrew and Adrian both started to feel better about belonging to a powerful family. "Ok, now on to some basic spells."

Bianca summoned her wand and stood twenty feet directly across from Darwin while the twins looked on.

"Shielding spells are important to know. This way, you can fend off an attack or simply block an object from hitting you," Darwin told them. All of a sudden, Darwin's cane was gone, and he was staring at Bianca. "Notice she is going to use her wand."

When they looked at her, she quickly pointed it at Darwin and a dark-green sphere of energy shot at him from the tip of her wand. *"Tutor Scutum!"* he shouted and a clear glowing, shimmering barrier formed in front of him, protecting him from impact, but it was gone as soon as the sphere hit it. Bianca let her wand hand fall back to her side as Darwin looked at the boys "Ok, now I'm going to use my wand."

His cane appeared in his hand, and he let Bianca know he was ready. Once again, she quickly pointed her wand at him, and the same dark-green sphere of energy shot out at him. He pointed his cane up and shouted, *"Tutor Scutum!"* and once again, a clear glowing barrier formed in front of him, only this time it was bigger and didn't vanish on impact. Instead, it sent the sphere back toward Bianca rapidly and hit her, pushing her back two feet through the air.

"Wow!" Adrian exclaimed while Andrew took a step back, inhaling a quick breath.

"You see what happened? The wand made the shielding spell stronger." Darwin stood up tall. "You see, a wand amplifies a wizard or witch's power, which is why it's a powerful tool to have at your disposal."

Darwin went on to say that some wizards and witches didn't even like to use wands because of how complicated they could be. This made both of the twins question if they would be able to use them, but Darwin quickly reassured them they would be fine. Adrian and Andrew spent the next few days training during the day with Darwin and Bianca, and occasionally Hekabe would join them. During the nighttime hours, Adrian hung out with Bianca while Andrew read the different books Darwin had in his study.

One night when Adrian and Bianca decided to go out on their Pegasi, Andrew declined to join them because he was captivated by a certain book Darwin recommended to him. After reading a few pages, he was able to find out what the vial he obtained from Adrasteia's shop had in it—a potion that transformed a person into whatever animal hair they mixed into it. In this case, it was an eagle. He was fascinated by what he just read and wanted to try it. He ran out of his room to Darwin's study and asked him if he could drink it. Darwin asked to see the vial.

"If you want to, I don't see why not." "But will I stay that way for a long time?"

Darwin took off his glasses and came from around his desk over to Andrew, sitting him down on a brown leather chair that was part of a pair in front of his desk. Darwin took a seat on the other one and asked to see the vial again. After Andrew handed it to him, Darwin held it up to his face to closely examine it and said, "This is a morphing potion, and what's great about these is it lasts for days—"

Before he could continue, Andrew interrupted, "Days?!"

Darwin chuckled. "As I was saying, what's great about these is they last for days and allow the drinker to morph into whatever animal they picked, whenever they want."

"What happens if it runs out? Do they stay that way?" Andrew asked, thinking about how life as an eagle might be.

Darwin chuckled. "No. After the last morph—usually around the fourth day—the drinker won't be able to change back into the animal until they make more of the potion, which is quite easy."

"Can you morph into another human? Or does it have to only be animals?"

"There is a potion that allows people to morph into other people, but it's quite painful and nobody does it." He was excited over Andrew's questions. He was finally able to share with them something special.

"Painful?"

"You see, in order for a person to morph or change into someone else, all their bones need to break and shift, and their skin needs to transform into whoever they picked, which is why nobody does it."

Andrew sat there, terrified at what he was hearing. "Is that how it is turning into an animal?" he quickly asked, regretting wanting to try this potion.

"Not at all. I can't explain why, but what I can tell you is it takes a lot of energy from a person when they change back to human form. No pain, just energy."

Andrew placed the vial in his pocket. "Ok, I'll just hold onto this, then," he murmured, kind of shaken up and nervous over what Darwin told him.

✳ ✳ ✳

IT was now a day before they were to leave back home and Darwin wanted to see everything they had learned from their visit, so he took them to the training field. It had been cleared of all the obstacles and only had a flag on a pole that Bianca was standing in front of.

They were a good distance away from where Bianca was standing and Darwin asked, "Do you see the flag?"

"Yes," they both answered.

"Excellent. Take it from her."

Adrian and Andrew were a little confused; it seemed like something extremely easy to do. "This isn't going to be fair for her." Adrian was confident. "Not fair at all."

"Yeah, it's two of us against one of her, Grandpa!" Andrew shouted.

Darwin grinned. "I think she'll be alright." They both laughed and Darwin asked if they were ready.

"Yes!" they answered at the same time.

Darwin pointed his cane directly ahead and a streak of light came out of the tip and sailed across the field. The field started shaking and five eight-foot-tall brick walls emerged from the ground. Each spread across the field while at the same time a steel tower emerged from the pond. Adrian and Andrew stared at it as water poured down from the top until the tower came to a stop. It must have been thirty feet tall, and water was still raining down from it, mimicking a waterfall as Darwin teleported to the top. Adrian and Andrew regained their focus and took cover behind the wall closest to them.

"Ok…" Adrian was breathing heavy. "Now what?"

"Now we get the flag!" Andrew summoned his wand and raised it in the air. "*Ignis Draco!*" he yelled, and three bursts of fire came out of the tip.

Bianca looked up and saw all three of the fire bursts merges together to form a dragon. "Impressive," she mumbled to herself, summoning her wand.

"When in the hell did you learn that?" Adrian stepped back from him. He needed a moment to process what just happened.

"It's called reading a book. Now let's get closer to her!" Andrew rolled his eyes towards his brother.

As she was distracted, they made their way closer as Darwin watched from the tower. As the dragon flew down directly at Bianca, she pointed her wand at it and said, *"Stinguo!"* A blast of water shot through the air, and all that remained was the mist from the extinguished fire dragon.

That was weak, cousin. Her voice was piercingly loud in Andrew's head. He just laughed, knowing it served its purpose.

"Ok, my turn." Adrian lifted his wand in hand.

He raised it to the sky and said, *"Aculeus globulos!"* and hundreds of miniature electrified orbs shot out of his wand and over the wall toward Bianca.

She defended against it by saying, *"Tutor scutum!"* but a few of the orbs managed to find her and sent little shocks through her body before the protection barrier was fully up. Bianca was stung, but not in pain.

Andrew looked at his brother but didn't say a word. Adrian looked back at him and said, "I read, too." Adrian squinted and a hard smile came to his face. Andrew wasn't amused.

Everything comes naturally to him. It's so annoying he thought.

Bianca quickly teleported to the wall Adrian and Andrew were hiding behind but before they noticed, she flung their wands out of their hands with a wave of hers and both wands floated toward her. As soon as she caught them, she teleported back to the flag, and at the same time Adrian and Andrew teleported too. She twirled her wand in her hand and pointed it in their direction when she saw them, quickly jerking it to the left. Suddenly, the boys were airborne, having been thrown easily against one of the eight-foot walls that spread out on the field. Adrian and Andrew fell to the ground, but both managed to get up rather quickly and ran to take cover behind another wall that was a bit further back to regroup.

"What now?" Adrian was breathing heavily.

They both were a little winded and surprised at how good Bianca was with magic. Adrian could see from the look expressed on his brother's face that a light bulb had just gone on and now he had an idea.

As Andrew reached in his pocket, he told Adrian, "Get ready to grab the flag."

Adrian didn't question him and positioned himself at the corner of the wall, ready to run.

He glanced back at Andrew, who was now drinking a glowing blue liquid from a vial he just pulled from his pocket. Within a few seconds, his clothes fell to the ground as he morphed into a beautiful bald eagle that flew four feet from the ground behind all the walls to avoid being seen. Adrian bolted out toward the flag, casting spells with his hand that Bianca easily deflected. But as she was distracted, Andrew swooped down, wrapped his talons around the flag, and soared high in the sky before Bianca could react, dropping the flag at Darwin's feet up in the tower.

Bianca and Adrian stared at him as he landed on the railing in front of Darwin.

Darwin couldn't contain his delight at what he just witnessed, yelling out, "That was terrific—simply terrific!" He waved his cane at the field and just as quickly as the walls came up, they vanished. The tower even started to submerge itself back in the pond while Darwin teleported off. Andrew once again soared up to the sky and as he was coming in for a landing, he morphed back into himself while Adrian watched, shaking his head at what his brother had just done. Darwin handed Andrew his own robe off his back before he fully morphed so he could cover up.

"You both did amazing out there," Darwin grinned. "Yeah, you guys did," Bianca agreed.

All of them teleported back to Darwin's house and when they got there, they talked and laughed over everything that just happened.

"Well, back to reality tomorrow," Bianca uttered. Adrian and Andrew both sighed at the thought of having to leave.

"You boys can come back any weekend you want. Just call me and let me know so I can come get you right away."

After a few sips of water, Adrian and Andrew ran upstairs to pack up their belongings to go home and prepare for school, which was starting when they returned after the weekend.

Bianca's eyes widened. "They're both better than I thought they would be."

Darwin grinned and wrapped one arm around Bianca. "All my grandchildren are amazing."

Chapter Eight

At 5:45 in the morning on the first day of school, Adrian's alarm clock buzzed as loud as it could. He reached over and slammed his hand against the snooze button, almost knocking it off his nightstand in the process. He turned around to try to get a few more minutes of sleep and once again the alarm buzzed—now, it was six a.m. and he had to get up for school. With all that was going on in his life, he forgot to start going to bed early so he could get his body off of the summer hours it had grown accustomed to. He lay there but didn't move. He knew he had to get ready, but he just wanted a few more minutes of uninterrupted sleep. Unfortunately, that wasn't going to happen, because Andrew was now banging on his door.

"GET UP!" His voice was muffled by the thick wood of the door.

Adrian finally sat up, his eyes still closed and head barely able to stay up on its own. He rose from the bed and stumbled out of the door. When he reached the bathroom, his eyes finally opened and adjusted to the light.

"How are you going to bang on my door to get up but hog the bathroom?" he asked his brother, who was brushing his teeth. Andrew rinsed his mouth out and looked at Adrian.

"It's going to be really weird with Chloe today."

Adrian rolled his eyes and let out a heavy sigh. "Are we going to have this conversation once a day now?" He didn't like being reminded about Chloe not knowing.

Andrew stepped out of the bathroom and turned around, but before he could say anything, the door slammed in his face. Andrew rubbed the back of his neck and continued to his room to get dressed.

Sara came out of her room wearing a black skirt and blue blouse. While putting her earrings in, she asked, "Are you guys going to need a ride to school, or are you taking the bus?"

"Collin is picking us up!" Andrew shouted.

"Nothing wrong with riding the school bus!" she yelled back.

Andrew didn't reply, and she went downstairs to make her morning coffee. After a few minutes, Adrian came out of the bathroom and Andrew was once again asking the same question.

"Oh, come on, I'm standing here in my towel! Can I at least get dressed before you ambush me?" He slammed the door to his bedroom shut.

Andrew gave him a few seconds, then barged into the room. "I know we talked about it, but how can we keep all of this from her?"

"Look, I know it's going to be hard, but we can't tell her. End of discussion."

Andrew realized there was no point in arguing so early in the morning and conceded to his brother's argument—for now, at least. He headed back to his room to grab his backpack and go downstairs. Before he reached the stairs, Adrian yelled out, "Do you think we can stop somewhere for breakfast?" Andrew turned around and looked at Adrian standing in his doorway.

"Yeah, in the kitchen," Andrew replied.

Adrian was already dressed and had his backpack swung on one shoulder. "I'll see you at school!" and before Andrew could object, Adrian was already gone. Andrew annoyed him into teleporting to school so he wouldn't have to sit in the car watching Andrew sulk over not telling Chloe.

Andrew flapped his hands at what his brother just did but continued to walk downstairs. The doorbell rang and Sara rushed over to open it. Andrew reached the bottom step as Colin and Chloe were walking in.

Collin greeted her in his normal way, "Hi, Ms. S." Sara said hi and bye to both and kissed Andrew on the forehead.

"Where is your brother?"

"He left a little early."

Sara glared at him and already knew that he had teleported to school. Andrew could tell his mom was angry. "Tell Adrian I want to talk to him after school," she ordered, then stormed out of the door to begin her day, slamming it shut.

"Why didn't he wait for us?" Chloe wondered.

"It's probably because he doesn't want to get yelled at by you," Collin joked. Andrew just turned and headed for the kitchen to hopefully avoid the conversation.

"So, how was Grandpa's house?" Chloe chased after him, not really wanting an answer. Before Andrew could respond she interjected, "How come I wasn't invited? And don't give me that 'because you're afraid of flying' crap."

"Sorry." He placed his hand on her shoulder. "And why aren't you taking the bus?" he asked, hoping that question was enough to change the topic.

"Collin said I could ride with you guys, and since it's his car and he was the only one to take driver's ed over the summer, I didn't think I had to clear it with you." She marched out the front door, slamming it in the process. What Andrew had hoped would change the topic had only agitated her.

"Well, at least she's not hounding you about going to your Gramps anymore," Collin teased. He couldn't help but laugh at his own joke.

"Let's get going." Andrew rolled his eyes.

They both left the house and headed to Collin's car, where Andrew noticed Chloe had already made herself comfortable in the front seat. Andrew climbed in the back and Collin drove off. Chloe and Andrew didn't say much to each other on the fifteen-minute drive to school, but he did notice how Chloe and Collin were joking and talking in a way they never had before.

Given how she was mad at him, he decided that it would be best not to say or ask any questions. When they arrived at school, Adrian was standing in the parking lot talking with some other friends.

"Hey, cuz-o!" he shouted as he saw Chloe get out of the car, but she just gave him one of the most evil looks imaginable in return.

Adrian, of course, laughed and put his arm around her. "Come on, you can't be mad about us visiting grandpa." He glanced back and said bye to the friends he was with.

Chloe proceeded to punch him in the gut—not too hard but hard enough so he felt a little pain. "You could have let me know."

"Sorry," was all he could say. That punch caught him off guard. They finally decided to walk toward the school. Chloe, however, had to go to another building and Collin had to get a copy of his class schedule from the admissions office. Since they were headed in the same direction, they walked off together. Andrew took the opportunity to walk alone with his brother to tell him that he shouldn't use his power if he didn't have to. Adrian told him to lighten up and they made their way inside.

"I'm serious, Adrian. We told Grandpa that we would be careful."

"Drew! I *was* being careful. No one saw me." "Adrian grew frustrated over being questioned.

That didn't matter to Andrew, who still wasn't letting it go. "We can't just go around using our powers just because we can."

"Why? Because you say so?" Adrian stopped to look at his brother as he tried to come up with an answer. Andrew couldn't answer at first because Adrian was right; neither Darwin nor Bianca had said they couldn't. But then it came to him.

"Out of respect for Mom who, by the way, wants to talk to you after school."

Adrian just shrugged his shoulders without saying anything and stormed off. He knew his mom wouldn't want them using their powers without Darwin or Liz to supervise them. They were just beginners, after all, and still had so much to learn. When they got to their lockers, Dean was waiting for Adrian.

"Hey. Where have you been?"

"Sorry. Been busy with family stuff."

Dean could see that Adrian was annoyed but didn't ask why.

Adrian went on to tell him that they were visiting their grandfather at the last minute and didn't tell anyone. Dean really didn't care; he was just giving Adrian a hard time and was only waiting for him because they had their first period together. As the first bell rang, Adrian and Andrew took the books they needed, and Andrew was the first to lock his locker and walk away. Before he got far, Adrian looked over to his brother.

"Drew. Just relax already will ya? Stop worrying so much."

Andrew just nodded and they both went off to class. While all the students were making their way to class before the second bell rang, a voice over the intercom was informing all the   students about an assembly after second period in the main auditorium to meet the new principal. Andrew thought that was good news, because that meant third period would be canceled for the day and since second period was a free period for him, he had an easy day ahead of him.

Once the bell rang after his first class, Andrew went back to his locker to exchange a few things and to grab another book he borrowed from Darwin's study he had wanted to read since they arrived home. Once he had the book, he went to the library and sat way in the back where he knew he wouldn't be bothered. He reached into his backpack and pulled out the thick olive-green book that was quite heavy.

The cover was so faded that he couldn't make out the symbols on the front; when he opened it, he was sure to be careful. It looked like everything was handwritten on what felt like old sheepskin parchment. He examined each page carefully and saw a few things such as spells and ingredients for potions that got his attention. He wasn't able to read everything, so he just turned the pages and was fascinated by the images he saw next to the writings.

He came to a page titled "The Three Crystals." He turned the page to read on, but it appeared that those pages were ripped out. This only made him more curious about the crystals, so he flipped through every page hoping that he would come across some kind of information   about them, but unfortunately, he didn't. Before he could give the crystals any more thought, the bell rang, and he packed up his bag to get to the assembly.

Adrian and Andrew arrived at the auditorium at the same time. As they headed inside,   they saw Chloe and Collin along with some other friends sitting together beside two open seats they must have been saving for them. As the rest of the students and teachers piled into the auditorium, they talked and joked around with their friends. A woman from the admissions office took her place behind the podium set on the stage.

"Good morning, students and faculty," she announced as silence began to fall over the crowd. "We don't have much time, so let's get right to it," she added affectionately. "Please welcome to the stage the new principal of Arcadia High: Dr. Adrasteia McKenzie."

As the twins became more focused on the stage, they saw Adrasteia— whom they met in Avalon—walk up the stairs to take her place behind the podium. Her long curly red hair looked a little shorter than when they last saw her and she was wearing a gray pantsuit with a black blouse, both surely made by a designer from Avalon. Andrew and Adrian glanced at each other with puzzled expressions but didn't say a word; they couldn't, with Chloe sitting right beside them.

They turned their focus to the stage, where Adrasteia just introduced herself to the students and faculty, and everyone seemed to be surprised by her Scottish accent.

As Andrew looked around the room, students seemed to be captivated by her voice.

Chloe even whispered, "Cool accent," in Andrew's ear; she must not be mad at him anymore, he assumed. Adrasteia continued talking about her experience, her qualifications, and her plans for her new position as principal.

'Ello, boys, Adrasteia said, startling both Andrew and Adrian. They looked up at the stage and saw her still addressing the crowd. *Dinnae worry, you won't miss much,* she spoke to them again. Adrian and Andrew stared at each other for a few seconds and realized they could both hear her. *Aye, boys, keep lookin' at the stage.*

They both obeyed the command at the same time.

I just wanted to tell ye why I'm here. Darwin thought it would be a good idea to 'ave someone 'ere to watch over youse boys. Now, before ye say anything, he doesn't think ye need a babysitter; he simply wants ye to hev someone here that ye can talk to if you hev any questions. Besides, it gives me a chance to get to know ye two a wee bit better!

Adrasteia saw them both nod their heads in acceptance of what she told them. However, her stomach felt hard because she knew what she just told them was a lie. Even though she didn't agree with Darwin about concealing the real reason she was there, she followed his instructions after Darwin reassured her that he would eventually tell them about their father. But until then, she would be there to keep them safe while they attended school.

Adrasteia thanked everyone for coming and dismissed them all a few minutes before the bell rang, then made her way off the stage. After fourth period, Andrew met Adrian, Dean, and Lisa by his locker, and they went to lunch together. Once in the cafeteria, Adrian noticed Chloe and Collin, who happened to have the same lunch period as them. They were already a few people ahead of them, but as Adrian waited in line, he noticed how friendly they were and began to wonder if something happened while he and Andrew were at Darwin's.

"Drew, did you see that?" he asked while staring at them. Andrew glanced towards Chloe and Collin.

"Yeah, I noticed that on the drive this morning but didn't ask because Chloe was still mad at me." Adrian didn't say anything else as they finally arrived at the food station where they only had three options to choose from:

pizza, burgers, and a variety of sub sandwiches. As always, they picked the pizza with a side of fries and a bottle of water to wash it down with.

They took seats at the table their friends sat at and began to eat.

"The new principal is *hot* for an older woman!" Dean said randomly. Everyone laughed at his outburst and continued to eat and talk among themselves.

Once the bell rang, everyone got up from the table. Chloe ambled off in the opposite direction from everyone else.

"Chloe, wait up!" Adrian called out while trying to catch up with her. "What's up?"

They made their way to the garbage cans to throw out their trays. "I'll see you guys later!" Andrew shouted as he casually passed them. He didn't want to stick around and deal with whatever Adrian needed to talk to her about. He loved Chloe, but he had other things on his mind.

"So, is there anything you want to tell me?" Adrian inquired. Chloe was caught off guard at the question.

"What are you talking about?" They started walking through the crowed hallway and Adrian saw Collin talking to some friends by the lockers.

"You and Collin seem closer, and I was curious to see if anything happened while we were gone."

Chloe started to blush, her face feeling warm, and butterflies began twirling around in the pit of her stomach. "Nothing out of the norm." She tried to ignore the feelings coming over her. She turned her attention to Collin, who had just been joined by Lisa, gently stroking Collin's arm and laughing flirtatiously. "Besides, he's interested in someone else."

Adrian saw what she was talking about and felt awkward about bringing it up. "Sorry, you guys just seem to have gotten closer in the two weeks we were gone…"

"We have! He's a good friend." The butterflies and rosy cheeks were gone. Sadness came over her at how chummy Lisa and Collin were with each other.

Adrian looked on compassionately and they parted ways. The second bell rang soon after and the hallways were cleared of students, now all in class. That is, with the exception of Andrew, who made his way to the head office, where the principal was located. He came in and asked to see Dr. McKenzie, and the assistant told him to have a seat. After a few minutes, Adrasteia came out and was surprised but happy to see Andrew was the student wanting to see her.

"Please, come in!" She stood clear of the door, making room for Andrew to pass, then closed the door behind them. She took a seat at her desk while Andrew sat in the chair directly in front of her.

"Sorry to come unannounced."

"Don't be foolish, boy, no need to apologize; my door is always open fur ye and yer brother."

Andrew was enthusiastic and began to tell her why he came to see her. He told her about the book that he borrowed from Darwin and that while he was looking through it, he came across a page that said "The Three Crystals" but the pages after that were torn out. While he was explaining that to her, she already knew the book he was referring to as well as the fact that Darwin wouldn't have let him borrow it. Adrasteia didn't say anything about him taking it without Darwin's permission, since it would most likely cause Andrew to get nervous and not say anything else. Besides, she wanted him to know that he, along with Adrian, could trust her.

Once Andrew finished telling her about the book, she looked deeply into his eyes. "So, what do ye want to know, dear?"

Andrew sat silently for a few seconds before asking, "What are the three crystals?"

Adrasteia thought for a minute on how to address his question. She decided she didn't want to lie to him and proceeded to tell him the story she had heard when she was a child.

A very long time ago, thar was a man from a small mountain village who started to realize he was different from the other people around him because of 'is abilities. He was able to do things that at the time were never heard of or done because no regular person was capable of such things. After a few months of learnin' how to use and control 'is abilities, he set oot on a quest to see if other people like 'im existed. He went from village to village but didnae find anyone.

It wasnae long before he started gettin' discouraged from continuin' on what he thought was a hopeless quest. Wan night on his way oot of the last village he searched for, he noticed a bright green light flash in the sky and doon into the woods. He rushed into the woods in desperation, hopin' it was someone like 'im. He came to the spot where he saw the green light land but didnae see anythin' in the darkness.

He cast a spell 'at brought light to the surroundin' area around 'im, and as he looked around, he noticed two men lookin' at 'im from behind a tree. He asked them about the light he just saw and if they knew what it was. One man came from behind the tree and said it was 'im while the other man looked on. After a few minutes, they started to talk and show each other what they could do and became instant friends.

Years went by and they each grew more powerful and started callin' themselves Wizards.

They became like brothers to one another and 'oped to find others like them as the years went on, but they never did. The three of them eventually started families but lived close to each other so they could remain in each other's lives. Over time, they noticed 'at they weren't agin' like the other people in town.

Wan by wan, their families died aff an' they would live on. When the first wizard outlived 'is third son, he decided he didnae want to go on in life after losing all those he 'eld dear, so he tried killin' 'imself—only it didnae work. He talked to the others aboot what he did, and they decided 'at they, too, wanted it to end. Once they realized it was their power 'at was grantin' them longer lives, they came to the decision 'at they didn't want 'em anymore.

So, they set aff oan a quest together to find a way to take away their powers so they could live out the rest of their lives like normal men. On 'at quest, they came across an old lady whose specialty was makin' crystals. They were fascinated by 'er creations and asked 'er many questions about 'em. She explained to 'em 'at the crystals were an energy force 'at could bring prosperity and peace to their lives. They asked 'er if she could make 'em each a crystal, and she agreed.

After a few weeks, she delivered 'em each three different beautifully designed crystals.

They accepted 'em and thanked 'er for 'er work and went back to the little mountain village they lived in. Once thar, they came up with a spell 'at would transfer their powers safely into the crystals. The three of them agreed 'at wud be the best thin' to do since they each so desperately wanted to live normal lives again.

On the night they cast the spell, each crystal absorbed the energy from their bodies, and they became normal. They tested themselves by castin' spells with their wands, but nothin' 'appened. They were beyond excited 'at it actually worked, so they buried their crystals in a safe place and went back to their homes. Unfortunately, they didnae realize 'at by removin' their energy or powers, they took out the one thing 'at gave them life, and each passed away in their sleep 'at very night.

"Now, o' course, none of this 'as been proven to actually have happened. Many believe it to be a myth."

Andrew was hanging on to her every word, fascinated by what he learned. "What do you believe?"

Adrasteia was cautious with how to answer him. "It was a good bedtime story me dad told me, so I never really gave it any more thought." Before

Andrew could ask any other questions, the bell rang and Adrasteia stood up. "Now get to class, my dear. Can't have ye missing all yer classes yer first day!"

She led him to her door, and he thanked her for her time. Adrasteia looked on warmly and closed the door behind her as she made her way back to her desk.

✳ ✳ ✳

AFTER the last period of the day, Chloe went to her locker to gather her belongings so she could meet the twins and Collin in the parking lot to go home. When she closed her locker, she noticed Adrian walking toward the west entrance of the school that went out to the football field and not much else. She thought there was a miscommunication about where to meet, so she followed him and called out his name, but he couldn't hear her over all the noise coming from the other students. Chloe started to go a little faster toward Adrian, who was now at the first set of doors leading outside. As she made her way toward him, she bumped into a few other students, slowing her down a little. She picked up speed and ran toward the doors Adrian had just exited out of.

When she got through the second set of doors, she turned to her left and saw Adrian walking toward the trees that were located across the football field and at the end of the school's property. But before she could yell his name, he disappeared. She stood there, motionless and in shock, not knowing what to think about what she just saw. After a few seconds, other kids came through the doors behind her, which startled her out of her catatonic state. She slowly paced toward the doors of the school, looking back a few times in disbelief at the spot where she just saw Adrian vanish.

Chapter Nine

After taking a few months off for the summer, to relax and not have to worry about competition, Chloe was back in her Tae Kwon Do class. It was only her third class back, but her sparring partner was getting the best of her and threw her to the ground a lot easier than normal. After seeing his best student taken down so easily, her sensei decided that class was over.

Usually after class, the students went to their locker rooms to change, but this time Chloe just plopped herself down on the mat and began taking off her sparring equipment. Her sensei could tell she was obviously distracted by something, so he approached her to see if he could do anything for her.

"Chloe, is everything alright?"

She looked up at him. "Yeah, why do you ask?"

He crossed his legs and sat down in front of her. "Well, it isn't like you to be taken down so easily." He laughed a little, so she knew he wasn't really criticizing her. Chloe opened her mouth as if she were about to speak, but then just closed it and continued removing her gear.

After a few more seconds of silence, she decided that she had to say something to satisfy his curiosity. "I just have some stuff on my mind; I'll be better next time."

It had been a few weeks now since she had seen Adrian disappear from across the football field. She hadn't told anyone about it or really seen the twins since that day because she figured it was best not to talk about something she still couldn't believe happened.

"Anything you want to talk about?" her sensei asked her. Chloe just shook her head no and packed away her sparring equipment. Even if she wanted to talk about what she saw, how could she without people looking at her like she was crazy? Besides, she had always been loyal to her cousins and wouldn't risk anything by talking about them to people they don't know.

"Distractions are a test your mind puts your body through," he told her. Chloe looked a little puzzled, but then he explained himself. "Look at what happened in class: someone who you are better than managed to get you to the ground without so much as breaking a sweat. No matter what is going on, you must stay focused and clearheaded."

"I'm not going to lie, sensei, it's hard to not be distracted right now. I have some stuff going on in my life that I can't make sense of."

"I believe we are never given things we can't handle, so whatever was thrown at you must have been put in your path for a reason."

"Why is that?"

"I'm afraid that's not for me to answer; it is something you must figure out on your own." He got up from the ground, smiling warmly at her. "If you ever need to talk, I'm here."

Chloe was pleased and stood up to thank her sensei for his input, throwing her bag over her shoulder. She decided to walk home in her *gi* instead of changing to avoid any more unsolicited advice, no matter how comforting it was. On her walk home, she kept visualizing what she saw Adrian do repeatedly, trying to make sense of it. Unfortunately, she couldn't seem to understand how something like that was even possible. Initially after she saw Adrian disappear, she tried convincing herself it was her mind playing tricks on her and that it didn't really happen. However, that didn't last long.

When she arrived home, she hesitated to go in after she heard Adrian and Andrew's voices inside. She paused but knew that she couldn't keep avoiding them. She looked to the living room and saw both of her cousins sitting on the sofa talking to Bianca.

"Hey, cuz-o!" Adrian yelled out.

"Hi." She took off her gym shoes and rushed upstairs to her room without saying another word. Andrew, clearly frustrated that she kept avoiding them, decided to follow her upstairs.

When he got to her doorway, he saw that she was putting her stuff away. "How was class?"

"Fine," she responds coldly. "Is something wrong?"

She quickly looked up to him, forcing herself to answer, "What are you talking about?" She didn't want to let on that she was weirded out by what she saw.

"You haven't been coming over, and in school we barely see each other. Adrian and I thought you might still be mad about us going to Grandpa's."

She went over to her closet and took off her karate gi top to throw it in the hamper followed by her pants.

Andrew noticed that she was wearing the pink princess shirt with matching short shorts that his mom gave her this past Christmas and said, "You should go to school in that tomorrow; *that* will get Collin's attention."

Chloe laughed but knew she had to reassure him she wasn't mad at them or avoiding them in any way so they wouldn't suspect anything—at least not until she figured out what was going on and if Andrew even knew about Adrian. When she got back to her bed, she told Andrew, "I have just been so busy with school and Tae Kwon Do that I haven't had time for anything else."

Andrew went over to her bed and sat down next to her. "Why haven't you at least driven to school with us?" Chloe looked at Andrew, thinking of what to say.

"I have been going to school early to run a few laps around the track. I figure since I didn't really stick to my workout routine during the summer, I would get right back to it since school started." This really wasn't a lie, because she had been going to school early to run laps to clear her head. "Tell you what—I'll skip Monday and catch a ride with you guys to school," she offered, hoping that he would drop it.

"Cool, see ya then!" Andrew could still feel like something was off with her but got off her bed and went over to the door. He glanced back at her to give her a wave goodbye before closing the door behind him to rejoin his brother downstairs. Chloe was relieved that Andrew believed her, and as she got up from the bed, she saw her black recorder she used for school on top of her backpack. That voice recorder was a gift from Bianca w h o   knew that Chloe would rather record her lectures than handwrite everything the teacher said.

Chloe stared at it for a while as if thinking about something, then placed it back in her backpack. She heard her cousin's saying bye to her mom and snuck over to her bedroom window that overlooked the backyard. She looked out and saw both Andrew and Adrian looking around, so she quickly hid on the side of the window to avoid being seen. After a few seconds, she peeked through the blinds of her other window and saw both of her cousins disappear. She quickly backed away from the window; even though she had seen that before, seeing both of them do it simultaneously caused her to lose her balance. Luckily, her bed was there to catch her.

The next morning, Chloe awoke and called Andrew to see what they were going to be doing that day. After Andrew told her that they were going by Collin's house, she decided to go visit her Aunt Sara. She waited until she knew the twins were gone before walking over. On her walk to their house, she thought about reasons the twins could possibly have for keeping such a big secret from her. After all, they were all really close and told each other everything.

When she reached the house, she called Andrew again to make sure he and Adrian were, in fact, gone. As she put her phone back in her pocket, she approached the door slowly to give her enough time to come up with something to tell Sara why she was there. She rang the doorbell and after a few seconds, Sara opened it.

"Hi, Aunt Sara." Chloe stepped inside. "I know the twins aren't home, so I figured I would use the silent house of yours to catch up on some reading, Bianca has friends over so too much going on over there. If that's ok," she added while holding up a book.

"Of course that's ok." Sara led Chloe back toward the kitchen. She was a little nervous but didn't let it show.

"Can I get you something to drink?"

"I can get it, thanks." Chloe told her.

"I'm making pasta for dinner if you're planning on staying that long."

"Not staying long. I'm just going to read for a few then go back home. This is a nice little break for me, but Ma is making steak and mashed potatoes."

"That sounds delicious."

"Yeah, the twins really need to get a broader palate," Chloe said and started to laugh.

Sara looked at her tenderly and Chloe went upstairs to Andrew's room. When she walked into his room, she reached into her pocket and pulled out her black recorder, looking around the room for a place to hide it. She saw a bookshelf made from wood leaning against the wall and glanced up and down trying to figure out where to hide the recorder. When she saw the top had a flat surface, she decided that was where she was going to place it.

She took Andrew's chair and rolled it from his desk to the shelf so that she could reach the top. Before she stepped on the chair, a big olive-green book that was between some other books caught her eye. She let go of the chair, grabbed the book, and sat down. Chloe had never seen this book before and when she opened it, she saw that on the inside cover there was an engraving that said *Property of the D.G. Estate.* She didn't give the engraving much more thought and continued flipping through the first few pages. She stopped at a page titled *History of Wizards* and began reading. It wasn't long before she realized what the twins were.

"Wizards…" she whispered to herself. Before she could continue reading, she heard footsteps climbing up the stairs and quickly put the book back, threw herself back in the rolling chair, and let the momentum guide her to the desk. As soon as Sara came in, Chloe pretended to be reading the book she bought over.

"Andrew and Adrian are coming back here because Collin's game system froze up on them or something," Sara told her.

"Ok," Chloe replied as Sara left the room. When she heard Sara back in the kitchen, Chloe quickly rolled herself back toward the bookshelf, stepped on the chair, and placed her recorder at the very top. She hit the red Record button and climbed down to put the chair back at Andrew's desk. She gathered her things and went back downstairs.

"I'm going to get going now. I really need to get this reading done and when the twins get back, I won't be able to."

"Oh, ok sweetie. Do you need a ride home?"

"No thank you, I don't mind the walk." She gave her aunt a hug goodbye, then turned and rushed out of the sliding door in the kitchen to not bump into the twins on her way out.

On her walk home, she couldn't help thinking about what she had just read. She had so many questions going through her head, yet she didn't have anyone to answer them. For a split second, she even thought about talking to her mom about all this but knew she couldn't. *She wouldn't believe me anyways,* she thought to herself. When Chloe finally arrived home, she ate dinner, took a shower, and went to bed. It was early, but Chloe didn't care; sleep had always been her way to escape reality.

In the morning, Chloe got up and quickly got dressed to go over to the twin's house. It must have rained the night before because the sidewalk was wet and little puddles lined the streets.

She arrived at the twins' house, let herself in, and shouted, "Guys, I'm here!" Adrian came in from the kitchen to greet her. "Hey, cuz, long time no see."

"Really, Adrian?" Chloe was unamused by his snarky comment.

"Well, I was starting to think you didn't like me anymore," he said, teasing her.

"You guys need to stop being so sensitive."

"WOW, ok then. I made some eggs—do you want any?" He turned back to walk toward the kitchen.

"No, I already ate."

Adrian didn't reply, so Chloe took the opportunity to go upstairs and retrieve her recorder. When she reached the top of the stairs, she noticed that Andrew was in the bathroom. She went over to say hi and asked him if she could borrow a DVD. Of course, he said yes. She raced into his room, rolled his desk chair to the bookshelf, and swiftly collected her recorder. She was able to put the chair back before Andrew was done in the bathroom and went back downstairs. When she reached the bottom step, she noticed that Collin had just arrived.

"Hey, stranger," Collin playfully joked. It sounded almost as if Collin missed her.

"Hey, sorry, I have been busy the last few weeks." The way Collin was acting made her nerves fire all at once; it gave her hope again that he felt the same way about her. Seeing Collin always made her happy, like nothing else mattered.

They both looked intently at each other until they were joined by Andrew, who was now ready. All of them left the house while Andrew locked up and Chloe took her place in the back seat of Collin's car. When they were all in the vehicle, Chloe connected her pink earphones into her recorder.

"What you listening to?" Andrew, who was also in the back seat, asked. "Mr. Moreno's lecture. We have a quiz today."

"Well then, I'll leave you to it." Andrew rejoined the conversation Adrian and Collin were having up front.

Chloe forwarded every ten seconds until she heard Adrian saying he wanted to go back in a few weeks. Since it appeared that Chloe forwarded it too much, she rewound the recorder until she heard Adrian coming into Andrew's room. She couldn't help but stare at her cousins, who she couldn't hear, but whose voices were coming in loud and clear on her recorder. She overheard them talking about going back to Grandpa Darwin's, but that wasn't what got her attention. It was what they said about Bianca that made her sit up in the back seat and listen intently, her heart racing rapidly, making sure not to miss a single word. She heard Andrew say, "Maybe this time we can beat Bianca," to which Adrian replied, "Yeah, she's really good at all that stuff." *Could Bianca be like them?* she pondered. *Could I be like them?*

The recorder didn't help like she wanted it to; instead, it just added more questions to her ever-growing list. Chloe practically jumped out of the car when they arrived at school. She just wanted to get away from her cousins as fast as she could. By the time everyone else got out of the car, Chloe was already entering the school. "She's in a hurry," Collin guessed. Andrew was worried. He knew something was wrong but couldn't do anything about it now, because school was about to start.

When Chloe reached her locker, she leaned against it. She watched other students pass her by to get to class, but she couldn't even get herself to put her things away. She felt her chest getting tighter and her limbs felt like lead. She had this feeling before at one of her Tae Kwon Do competitions; she was having a panic attack. She stood there, closed her eyes and started to count to ten.

The first bell rang, then the second, and still there was no movement from her. She finally turned to open her locker but hesitated again to put her things away and grab the book she needed for first period. After a few minutes, she decided school was too much for today; she had to know if Bianca was like her cousins. She slammed her locker shut, storming off to the nearest exit, looked around, and then left school.

When she finally arrived home, she saw that no one was home, as expected. Chloe barged into her house and dropped her backpack at the foot of the stairs as she rushed to Bianca's room. She didn't even know what she was looking for but continued to search the room. The first thing Chloe looked for was books like the one on Andrew's bookshelf, but nothing turned up. She checked in Bianca's closet but the only thing in there were the totally normal clothes and shoes that Bianca owned. *If Bianca does have anything, she hides it well*, Chloe thought to herself.

Chloe sat on her bed and stared at some poster of a rock group that Bianca had hanging on her wall. Chloe got up from the bed to examine the poster. She felt the wall around it and behind it, but there was nothing. She turned her head and saw another poster of some actor that Bianca was in love with, which brought a smile to Chloe's face because they were both fans of his movies.

However, the smile quickly turned into curiosity because this poster was different—this one was in a thick frame hanging on the wall. Chloe tiptoed over to the wall and removed the poster to see that behind it sat a shelf.

Chloe reminded herself to breathe because the sight of all these little vials left her breathless. She took a deep breath and inspected all the vials. The ones on the top shelf had a white piece of tape that said *Falcon* on it while the others all had different names.

Chloe took a step back to realize what she had just learned: Bianca *was* like her cousins. She hung the poster back on the wall, shaking a little in the process as her nerves got the best of hers, and left the room.

She approached her mother's bedroom door, uncertain to go in out of fear of what she might find. It all started to make sense to her though: the twins were at Darwin's, Bianca had these little vials hidden in her room, so it would make sense that if her mother's side of the family were wizards, she would be one, too. She went in hoping to find something to prove that it was only the twins and Bianca that had been lying to her and looked around.

Chloe stood in the middle of her mother's room, frustrated; she couldn't find anything. The only place she hadn't looked was in the closet, so she quickly went toward it and opened it. It was a bigger walk-in closet than Bianca's, so she was optimistic that she would find something to prove her case. Behind some luggage that accidentally fell over when Chloe stepped on it to reach a top shelf, sat a three-drawer file cabinet. Chloe tried to open it, but it was locked. She searched around franticly for a key but couldn't find one.

Then she remembered there was a key sitting on her mom's nightstand she just saw.

She raced out of the closet, dashed over to get the key, and returned to her position in front of the filing cabinet. As she inserted the key, her heart began to beat faster, but she stalled on unlocking it.

What if Mom is like Bianca, Andrew, and Adrian? What if I *am like them?* she thought to herself. Not stalling anymore, she unlocked it and pulled it open, only she didn't find magic books or vials of strange liquids; all she found was a thick manila envelope. She sat down on the floor in front of the filing cabinet with the sealed envelope in her hand, a little confused, but opened it anyways.

As soon as she opened the envelope, she wished she hadn't. All the information inside was about her. Chloe was devastated, and with everything that had been going on in the past few weeks, she broke down, tears flowing down her cheeks. She decided she couldn't continue reading and put everything back in the envelope, back in the file cabinet, locked it, and put the key back where she found it before she ran to her room, where she paced back and forth.

This was all too much for one person to take in, and she needed someone to talk to too. She sat on her bed, pulled out her phone, and texted the one person she felt she could talk to. Collin was at lunch by the time he received Chloe's text but didn't hesitate to skip the rest of the school day and go to her. He just had to think of something to tell Andrew and Adrian so they could find another way home. Once Collin told Andrew his excuse, he quickly left the school, hoping he wouldn't get caught by any of the three security guards patrolling the campus.

Chloe was sitting outside waiting for Collin and finally saw him turn down the street. She ran over to the curb where the mailbox was located to meet him. When he pulled up, Chloe got in. He could see that Chloe had been crying because her eyes were red, puffy, and still watery from the many tears she shed.

"What's wrong?"

"Can we just get out of here now?" Chloe replied, her voice shaky. Without wavering, Collin drove off, not saying anything until Chloe spoke. "Thank you for coming." She looked at Collin, the only person she trusted in that moment. Even though she was devastated over what she found out, Collin still managed to make her feel happy, like a ray of sun breaking through a cloudy day.

"Don't mention it."

Chloe loved his smile, and just seeing it made her feel a little better. If Collin only knew how much showing up meant to her. *Would he be flattered or freaked out?* she thought to herself. She wiped the remaining tears from her eyes and saw Collin pulling into a park.

"This is where I come when I feel like crap."

Chloe looked out over the playground area where she and the twins used to play all the time. When things were simpler. "I haven't been here in a while."

Collin glanced over to her. "You'll be surprised at how comforting the swings can be."

They both got out of the car, and went for the swings, each taking a seat. Both began swaying back and forth, enjoying the sun beaming on their faces. The air was cool, but the sun warmed them. The leaves were starting to change colors, the signal that fall was upon them.

"This day would be perfect if I didn't find out I was adopted," Chloe said bluntly, still staring off into the distance, not making eye contact with Collin. Collin placed his feet firmly on the wood pellets beneath him, stopping him from swaying. He looked at Chloe, dumbfounded over what she just blurted out. She finally returned his glaze, forcing a smile on her face.

"Wow—this is surprising to hear. How… how did you find out about this? Did your mom tell you?" Collin was caught off guard.

"Nope, I found out all on my own." She looked at Collin but quickly returned her gaze back into the wide-open space in front of her.

Collin didn't know how to respond so he stood up and extended his hand to her. "Come here, I want to show you something."

She looked down at his hand and her stomach started to spin, heart started to race—it felt like her insides were vibrating, yet she took his hand without hesitation. He led her off the playground and into the field.

"Where are we going?"

"You'll see in a minute."

In that moment, they reached the top of the grassy hill that overlooked a pond. The way the sun hit the surface made the water mirrorlike, reflecting the multicolored trees around them. Chloe was hypnotized by the beauty of it all. "It's so beautiful…"

"It's amazing how something so simple can really brighten someone's day," Collin told her, grasping her hand tighter.

"Thank you for this."

"Look." He turned to face her. "Chloe, I don't know how it would feel to find out what you did, but what I do know is, you have an amazing family that cares about you. I'm also sure your mom would have told you eventually."

"You can't know that. My mother would have told me by now if that was her intention. I'm not going to lie, finding out I was adopted is tough and something I will be dealing with for a while, but that isn't the only bombshell news I found out Collin." She looked at him. She then started to tell Collin everything, from seeing Adrian teleport to what she found in Bianca's room. Collin was speechless; it was a lot to take in.

"I can see that no one told you, either." Chloe was surprised, trying to see how the news made him react. She thought Andrew's best friend he would have known. Collin let go of her hand and ran down the hill a little, then looked back at Chloe, who was relieved that he didn't know.

"Are you joking?" But from the look on her face, Collin could see that she wasn't.

However, he was feeling, Collin knew that Chloe felt ten times worse. He calmed himself and turned toward her.

"This explains why Andrew thinks you have been acting weird," he told her. "Wouldn't you?"

Collin always the glass-half-full guy. "If you think about it, it's kinda cool." His words didn't reflect the scared look etched on his face. Chloe looked at him sweetly; no matter what, Collin always found a way to make something negative into a positive. *Who knows? Maybe this is a good thing,* she thought. Still, finding out about being adopted was the hardest to digest. She wondered if she did the right thing by laying this all on Collin. He looked panicked and scared. Chloe looked at him. "Are you ok?"

Collin looked at her then towards the ground. "I don't know. It just all seems so unreal, you know?"

"Tell me about it" Chloe looked at the time. "Can you take me home?"

"Wow, it's already five o'clock!" Collin mentioned while looking at his phone.

"How time flies when your world is thrown upside down…" Chloe reached for his hand. Now she was comforting him.

As they walked back to Collin's car, Chloe saw that he was still processing everything. "Sorry for laying all of this on you."

"It's ok. I'm sorry that you have to be going through this."

Chloe knew he was as shocked as she was about what the twins could do, but she also knew that he wouldn't say anything because he wanted to be there for her. This only made her feelings for him grow. They soon reached his car, got in, and drove off.

When Collin pulled up to Chloe's house, they saw that Sara's car was parked in the driveway. "Are you going to be ok?" Collin once again took her hand in his.

"Yeah, venting to you helped," she replied as she gripped his hand tighter. She didn't want to let go. She felt her feelings for him getting stronger. He was kind to her, and she wanted to reach over and kiss him but didn't.

"Anytime," he said warmly.

Chloe got out of the car, leaned into the window, and thanked him once again for being there for her. When she made her way inside, the smell of chicken filled the house.

"There you are! I was just about to call you." Liz trekked toward her. "Go get washed up for dinner. Aunt Sara brought chicken."

Chloe peeked around her mother and saw everyone sitting down for dinner. "Ok," Chloe said and made her way upstairs.

When she got to her room, she became upset again. *How can they act like everything is normal?* She paced back and forth rapidly, squeezing her hands together, then violently letting them fall back to her side. That was it—she was consumed with anger, and Collin wasn't there to calm her. She rushed to her mother's room, snatched the key that was sitting on her nightstand, took the manila envelope, and went downstairs. She plodded threateningly and slowly into the dining room where everyone was serving themselves and talking, keeping the envelope hidden from view. When she looked at everyone, she became frustrated once more. *That's it.* She threw the envelope in the center of the table. Silence fell over the room. Liz was the only one to look in Chloe's direction. Tears filled her eyes as she looked at her daughter; she knew exactly what was in that envelope.

"The magical power, I'm guessing, comes from *your* side of the family, Mom," Chloe fumed, looking at Liz. Everyone was now staring at Chloe, some in shock at her discovery, some remorseful for not telling her sooner.

Chapter Ten

Chloe stared at Andrew and Adrian, who didn't seem shocked at what she just blurted out. "I guess I shouldn't be too surprised that you two wouldn't tell me. I mean, you kept the wizard thing from me, so what's one more lie?" Chloe could barely get the words out. Feeling betrayed by those close to her ripped her apart inside. Tears began flowing down her face; saying it out loud had made it all that much worse somehow. Chloe raised her hand to her mother, who was getting up to walk toward her. "Don't come near me. All of you, just stay away from me!"

She stormed off upstairs to her room, where everyone could hear the door slam shut. The twins, as well as everyone else at the dinner table, were stunned. Each one of them was internally trying to figure out how she knew everything she did. No one could be more upset than Liz, however, who now had tears in her own eyes over the hurt her baby girl was feeling.

"I could mind wipe her again," Liz suggested, wiping her tears. Everyone's attention now focused her way.

"NO! So, what, are you going to erase her memory every time she finds out?" Andrew felt that same anger he felt when he found out about what he was. Liz just sat back in the chair, not knowing what to say.

"Andy, that's enough!" Sara shouted, hoping to calm her son down.

"No, Mom, Drew is right. We can't just keep lying to her. We tried it Grandpa's and Aunt Liz's way, and she still found out!"

Sara didn't object; she knew her sons were right. The lies had to stop.

"Mom, they're right," Bianca agreed and looked at Liz, who was just sitting there rubbing her brow in disbelief that Chloe found out this way. She agreed with everyone else.

"No more lies."

Sara didn't want to overwhelm Chloe by staying there and adding to the conversation, so she pushed her chair away from the table and stood up. "We will leave you guys alone to deal with this." She gestured to her boys to clean up their mess. She walked over to Liz and leaned down to her. "If you need anything, don't hesitate to call."

Liz just nodded her head and Sara led Adrian and Andrew out the door. The walk to the car was silent, Andrew and Adrian both tormented with guilt for not telling their cousin. Sara could see that they were upset but didn't press the issue.

The entire ride home was just as silent. No one even bothered turning the radio on. When Sara pulled into the driveway, she turned off the car and looked at her boys. "You guys didn't do anything wrong by not telling Chloe. You were both doing what you thought was right and what you were told to do. Chloe is mad right now, but she will forgive you."

No matter what his mom said, Andrew always knew it hadn't been the right thing to do.

Chloe is part of this family and deserved to know the truth, he thought. Neither of them responded to Sara's comment and exited the car to go inside. Andrew went up to his room and Adrian followed.

"Do you think she'll ever talk to us again?" Andrew asked as Adrian as he flopped down on his bed.

"I honestly don't know. If I was her, I wouldn't want to talk to anyone ever again." Adrian said.

They both sat there for a few minutes, not saying a word. When things went wrong or something bad happened, they always found comfort in just being in the same room with each other. A bond close brothers have, but even more so for twins.

Andrew agonized over all this. "I hope she forgives us…" he said, putting his head down. As exciting as it was for them to be experiencing this new life, Andrew couldn't help but feel like he had lost his cousin. He felt helpless, lost, at how things would never be the same.

"We have to actually apologize for her to forgive us, which brings us back to the 'her not talking to us' subject." Adrian placed his arm around his brother. He felt the pain Andrew was in and wanted to make it go away.

"She'll talk to us again—she has to. We go to the same school, so she won't have a choice—we'll just corner her," Adrian stated, in denial now about what the fallout could be. He was consumed with guilt over the thought of her not talking to them. Andrew laid back and just stared at the ceiling in his room, giving Adrian enough time to realize how stupid his last comment was. *An ambush is* exactly *what we need to get Chloe to talk to us again,* he thought sarcastically.

"Maybe that wouldn't be a good idea," Adrian reflected, realizing how stupid the thought was.

"There it is." Andrew was relieved that Adrian reached the same conclusion.

✳ ✳ ✳

BACK at Liz's house, Bianca was sitting at the dinner table with her mom thinking of a way to approach all of this. Liz wanted to rush up to her room and comfort Chloe, but that wouldn't be smart. After all, Chloe made it clear that she didn't want anyone to follow her upstairs.

Bianca knew what her sister needed. "Let's just give her some time, then go up to talk to her."

Liz agreed and both sat at the table thinking of what to say to Chloe when they talked to her. Bianca picked up her plate from where she was sitting before all of this happened and started eating again. Liz slowly turned her head her way, mouth slightly open.

"What? I get hungry when I'm nervous!" Bianca mumbled. Liz couldn't help but be amused. Seeing Bianca eat gave her an idea—she got up from the table, grabbed an empty plate that was meant for Chloe, and started putting food on it. When Bianca looked at her, Liz looked back. "She has to eat, right?"

She put a chicken breast—Chloe loved white meat—mashed potatoes, coleslaw, and a biscuit on the plate. As she made her way upstairs, she mumbled, "*Calesco,*" and steam started coming off the plate as if it was freshly delivered moments before. She knocked on Chloe's door, but there was no answer. Liz let herself in anyways and saw Chloe lying on her bed. "Here, you should eat." She set the plate down on Chloe's desk. "When you're ready to talk, your sister and I will be right downstairs waiting." She left Chloe's room, closing the door behind her.

Chloe waited a few seconds before she got back on the phone she had hidden under her pillow when Liz knocked on the door. "Hey, Collin, sorry about that. Liz brought me a plate of food."

"Don't be like that, she's still mom to you" Collin said, his voice loud in her ear. Chloe lowered the volume on her phone.

"I know, it's just SO frustrating. I hate being lied to."

"Well, you could continue pouting in your room, or you could go talk to your mom. You're mad that no one told you anything, yet you stay in your room talking to me, telling me things I'm sure I'm not supposed to know."

"You're right. I should go talk to them and finally get some answers."
"Good. I think that would smart." Collin agreed.

"I'm going to eat first. I can't absorb any information about this fake magical family of mine on an empty stomach."

Collin laughed at her comment, causing a rippling effect as Chloe started to chuckle too. After a few seconds of laughter and saying goodbye, Chloe pushed end on her cell phone, threw the phone across the bed, and took hold of her plate of food. As she started eating, she started thinking about what to ask. She didn't want to ask about her real parents; that would probably hurt Liz. She did, however, want to know why Liz didn't tell her sooner.

Once Chloe was done with her food, she left her room to go downstairs, where Bianca and Liz were still waiting in the kitchen. Bianca casually smirked at Chloe; she returned it with a dry, barely visible grin of her own. Bianca took that as a good sign. *Maybe Chloe will overcome this and move on.*

Liz was the first to greet her. "Let me take that," she said, taking the plate from Chloe's hand. Liz saw that most of the food was eaten, which was good news for her. Chloe went over to the small rectangular table that sat three in the center of the kitchen. The tips of Bianca's fingers hitting the table at a rhythmic rate was the only sound.

"So, the magic thing—how long has that been going on?" Chloe asked. The sound of Bianca's fingertips rattling against the wood table suddenly stopped. She hadn't thought this was going to be the first question Chloe asked. Liz approached the table and took a seat.

"Magic has been in our family for generations."

Chloe was thrown off by her response, so much so that she tweaked her neck at how fast she looked toward her mother. She hadn't expected Liz to admit it right away, and from the look on Bianca's face, neither did she. Most people would deny stuff like that without any proof; after all, Chloe didn't have any hard proof beyond what she saw Adrian do, which she didn't tell anyone at the dinner table about.

"Oh," was all Chloe could bring herself to say. Liz and Bianca got a little chuckle out of it. "Why didn't you tell me I was adopted?" The chuckles and smiles died out instantly. Things were serious again.

"Before your dad died, we had a conversation about when the best time for us to tell you was, and he said when you turned eighteen. I didn't agree with him at first and we argued a little over that, but he died soon after, so I decided to wait until you turned eighteen."

Bianca looked at her mother, clasping her hands together. She knew that Chloe wouldn't be told the whole truth today. It was always said that their dad and the twin's dad died in a car accident a few months before Chloe was born, but Bianca knew the truth.

Mom, we shouldn't keep lying to her, Bianca's voice was piercing. Liz squinted and turned her head at how uncomfortable she felt.

Not now, Bianca.

"Oh, ok," Chloe scoffed.

"Sweetie, this doesn't change anything. You're still my daughter." Liz gripped her hand, but Chloe pulled away.

"Yeah, you will always be my annoying little sister," Bianca added as she reached for the other hand.

Chloe leaned back in her chair. "It changes the fact that I will never be like you guys." She looked at both of them. "Or that I can't trust a thing you two say."

"You can trust us. I did what I thought was best. It wasn't the right choice but a choice I made." Liz tried to reach for Chloe's hand again, but she pulled it out of view.

"This is a lot to process. Everyone gets to go to Grandpa's, and I'm left here to figure things out for myself. It isn't fair." Chloe told her mother.

Liz knew that not being like them would affect Chloe. "I know, sweetie. But think of it this way: You know all that Tae Kwon Do stuff, right?

"Yeah," Chloe answered, frowning. Why her mother would bring that up at this crucial time didn't make sense.

"We don't know any of that stuff," Liz said, gesturing between Bianca and herself. Chloe just stared at her mom like she had just said something incredibly ridiculous. "Hear me out," Liz muttered, seeing the frustration in her daughter's face. "You know how to do some amazing things that we don't have a clue how to do, and we can do some amazing things that you can't do."

Bianca thought it made sense; she just hoped Chloe would see it the same way.

"Chloe, you and your sister are my whole world, which will never, ever change." Liz said while opening her palm, hoping Chloe would take her hand.

"I can't. I just can't. You lied to me about so much. This feeling doesn't just go away because I hold your hand mom." Chloe stared at Liz, like she didn't even know who she was.

It got late and Chloe had to get ready for bed. Just because her entire world had stopped didn't mean the rest of the world did. School still started at eight o'clock in the morning and she would rather have been there than see her mother. Liz told her that she could miss the next day because of how late it was, but Chloe ignored her and wanted to be anywhere else but home.

Besides, she had already missed an entire day before. Being at school would also give her the distraction she needed. Chloe left her house not knowing if things would ever be the same again. She felt more alone than she ever had before.

Over the next few weeks, Chloe kept to herself except for talking to Collin and a few of her other friends from time to time. Every time she saw Andrew or Adrian, she would turn to walk the other way. Andrew didn't push the issue and knew that eventually Chloe would start talking to them again. Adrian, however, didn't feel the same way as his brother.

When he would see Chloe avoiding them, he would yell out to her and say something sarcastic loud enough for her to hear. One time, he even teleported right in front of her when she turned away from them. Luckily, no one was around when he did that. Chloe just went around him as if nothing happened, keeping her smile hidden so he wouldn't see.

When she arrived home one day, Bianca, who Chloe had barely spoken to, asked her if she and her cousins were talking again. Bianca already knew the answer, but it was a great way for her to start the conversation. Bianca told Chloe that she needed to start talking to them again because they were going through a lot, and it would be nice if their cousin was there for them. Plus, Thanksgiving was in a week, and nobody liked awkward dinners. Chloe knew Bianca was right. Even though she wanted to say something to her sister about it, she couldn't; Bianca's boyfriend was at the door.

"Just go talk to them already," Bianca told her as she got up to let Brad in. Chloe didn't respond but agreed, planning to say something to them tomorrow at school.

"Hey! I missed you so much." Brad embraced Bianca, lifting her off the ground in the process. They hadn't seen each other for a few months since Brad had gone off to school.

Luckily for Brad, Bianca took the news of his transferring to a university better than he thought she would. They talked almost every day over the phone, but Bianca was still excited to see him.

"I'm so glad you're here," she told him as he set her back down to her natural height, leaning in for a kiss at the same time.

"Hi, Brad," Liz said as she came in from the kitchen. "How's school?" "Hi! It's great. A little hard at first, but great now."

"Are you both staying for dinner?"

"No, we're going out to eat."

Even though Liz had made enough food for all of them, she understood they wanted to spend time alone.

"Remember what I said," Bianca told Chloe before she and Brad left the house.

Liz looked over at Chloe. "Come eat."

"I missed you so much," Bianca said while wrapping one arm around him and pulling herself into his body, her grip tight around his waist. Brad looked over to her, kissing the top of her head.

"I missed you too."

"So much stuff has changed since you left that—"

"Shhh, none of that matters. Tonight, it's just you and me. College, family drama—all that stuff doesn't exist tonight," Brad declared. Bianca was beyond thrilled over that idea. She leaned more into him as they got to the car, delighted that he was back.

✱ ✱ ✱

THE next morning, Chloe woke up an hour before she normally did, anxious to get to school. She got dressed, gathered her belongings, and headed out the door. It was a chilly winter day, but she still decided to walk. Adrasteia, who had been waiting for Chloe to leave so she could talk to Liz, slumped down in her car, turning her head away from Chloe to not be seen. She waited until she was sure it was clear before she got out of her car. With Chloe now a good distance away, she headed toward the front door.

The sun was just starting to rise, the neighborhood silent. The only thing that could be heard was the clicking of Adrasteia's pumps hitting the concrete beneath her feet. When she got to the door, she rang the doorbell. After a few minutes, Bianca opened it, still dressed in her pink-with-white-polka-dot shorts and black crop top that she slept in, her hair unkempt.

"Adrasteia, what are you doing here?" Bianca asked as she stepped aside so Adrasteia could pass.

"I'm here to talk to yer mum."

As Bianca closed the door, Adrasteia went to take a seat in the family room to wait for Liz. After a few minutes, Liz was walking down the stairs, tying the strings of her long black silk robe that swayed side to side an inch from the floor, Bianca right behind her.

"Hi, is everything alright?" Liz questioned as Adrasteia stood up to greet her.

"So far, aye."

"Please, come, I'll start a pot of coffee." Liz led the way into the kitchen. She pushed a button on a black coffee pot, took two cups from the cabinet above the counter, placed them a few inches from the coffee pot, and went to take a seat at the kitchen table where Adrasteia was already sitting. Bianca leaned against the wall, wondering why Adrasteia was there. Adrasteia wasted no time telling them, "Darwin sent me a message. He thinks it's a good idea if he retrieves the Alexandros crystal an' moves it somewhere else," Adrasteia informed them. She had no idea that Bianca didn't know the crystals existed. Bianca quickly got off the wall.

"Wait, as in the crystal from wizard mythology, that mom and Grandma told me wasn't real?" Liz and Adrasteia didn't reply. "Mom, that's real?"

"Yes."

"How many lies can one family have?" Bianca said. She pushed herself back against the wall. "And Grandpa knows where it's at?"

Liz didn't want to explain this to her daughter, not yet at least. "Bianca, don't you have a class this morning?" Bianca knew that was her mother's way of telling her to leave, and she didn't like it.

"Whatever, I'm out of here." She stomped out of the kitchen, letting out one last frustrated breath as she passed her mom.

"My apologies. I assumed she knew since everyone was on high alert since yer brother's release."

Liz stood up and made her way to the counter. "It's alright. Why does he think he should move it?"

"He didnae elaborate, but he did mention 'at Adele was lookin' into the council archives."

"I thought there wasn't any information about the crystals in the archives. I thought Barnabas's predecessor removed all of it?" She started pouring the steamy, freshly made coffee into the coffee mugs.

"I wasn't able ter ask; Darwin 'as been busy with council matters and tryin' to appeal Gabriel's release, but Adele keeps shuttin' him doon by way o' the chancellor. And you know yer father—he suspects somethin' is going on, so he's hopin' fer the best but preparin' fer the worst." Adrasteia took a sip from the cup Liz placed in front of her.

"Ok, thank you for telling me." With that, Adrasteia let herself out and went back to work, taking the coffee that Liz poured into a travel mug for her to enjoy.

Bianca came downstairs, didn't say anything to her mom, and stomped out of the house. She wasn't going to class, though; she was going by Brad's house. Missing class really wasn't a big deal for her. She was getting good grades so far in the four classes she was enrolled in and since Brad was only here for a little over a week, she wanted to spend as much time with him as possible, especially after the morning she just had.

✳ ✳ ✳

STUDENTS started making their way into the building where Chloe had been waiting for Andrew and Adrian by their lockers. She looked frantically through the hordes of students and teachers now filling the halls that had been silent and empty just a few seconds before. She saw them then— Andrew, Adrian, and Collin walking side by side talking, laughing, and each eating an egg sandwich they must have just picked up. Each wore black jackets with three small green letters to the left, *AHW*, which was a reference to the Arcadia high wrestling team. They must have joined in the past few weeks when she wasn't talking to them.

"Hey, guys," Chloe said as they approached her.

"Can we help you, miss? Are you lost? The advanced nerds building is that way," Adrian joked while pointing to another part of the campus. Collin, Andrew, and Chloe laughed.

"Really?" Chloe pinched her lips together.

"Can you get away from my locker, stranger?" Andrew teased.

"Ok, I get it. Are you done now?" She wasn't at the point where she wanted to joke with them. But she knew that was their way of dealing with things.

Andrew's smile faded away quickly "Sorry. We are just glad that you acknowledged us."

"I know. It was just too much to process, and I couldn't bring myself to talk to you right away.

"I have to get to my locker. Chloe, I'll see you by my car after school?" Collin asked, pointing at her.

"Yeah." It had been a while since Chloe had taken a ride home with them and she was excited for that because she hated taking the school bus. Chloe stepped aside to let her cousins get to their lockers. "I was wondering if you guys want to hang out this weekend?"

Adrian and Andrew just looked at each other. They had already made plans to go to Darwin's with Bianca for the weekend. They didn't know what to say next, because since they hadn't spoken, they never got the "wizard talk" out of the way.

"Guys, that whole *W* thing is no big deal anymore. It is strange and weird, but I know this is all new for you guys too."

"We're going to Grandpa's this weekend with Bianca," Adrian finally said, holding his breath in anticipation over her reaction.

"You should come," Andrew added. Andrew didn't know how she would take the invitation.

Is it too soon to show her that world? Would she be able to handle everything that comes with visiting Grandpa? he wondered.

To his surprise, she responded, "Sounds fun, but are us normal folk allowed over there?" Adrian and Andrew just stared at her with grins on their faces.

"All members of our family are allowed over there." Adrian said as he glanced at Andrew.

Andrew slammed his locker shut. The first bell rang, so Adrian closed his locker and they all started walking to get to their classes. When they reached the first hall that led to the south side of the school, Adrian said goodbye.

As Andrew and Chloe walked on, he told her, "You were always allowed to come to Grandpa's. He was just waiting for Aunt Liz to tell you everything."

"Cool, then it should be fun." Andrew was happy with her response; he had hated not speaking to Chloe for the past few weeks. When he reached the hall that led to his first class, he leaned in and gave Chloe a hug, squeezing her tight.

"I'm glad you know everything. I'm just sorry you had to find out that way. How did you find out about *us*, by the way?" he asked, backing away from her.

"I saw Adrian disappear. Don't be sorry; I know it must have been tough for you guys too." Chloe was trying her hardest to at least get back to normal with her cousins. She knew deep down that none of this was their fault.

Andrew told her that he would call Darwin after school to tell him about the coming weekend. Chloe was excited about finally going to Darwin's house. She had always wondered why they didn't visit him or where he even lived; the only thing she knew was it was an airplane ride away. As she got to class, she was happy for the first time in weeks. Even though she found out some tough news, things were starting to get back to normal. As normal as they could get for her, at least.

Chapter Eleven

It was a chilly, wet day in Polaris. Rain had been pouring down for most of the past two days. Adele was sitting in a big leather chair at her desk located in her office inside council headquarters in the capital. Her desk was big and made of glass. She sat quietly, listening to Barnabas go on about a weekend getaway he planned for the two of them. She looked around her office, eyes glazing over a long black leather sofa and two matching single seating chairs against the left wall, thinking of a way to get him to leave.

"Barnabas, I really need to get back to work now." She stood up from her chair and slowly made her way over to him.

"You're right, I believe I've taken up enough of your time." He got up and returned her gaze. She was irresistible and gave him a flirtatious look, to make up for the rudeness she hoped he didn't notice, as she placed her hand on his back to guide him to the door.

"I will see you later," she teased him, opening the door so that he could leave. When he departed, she closed it quickly and that endearing look that was displayed on her face quickly changed to one of annoyance. She sat down on the sofa to take in the sound of the rain hitting the window. A few minutes went by before she looked down at her watch. It was time to go, so she dusted her clothes off to get out the wrinkles and headed over to her desk, grabbed her briefcase, and teleported from her office.

Even though teleporting was against the rules in the capital outside of the designated areas, council members were immune to such rules and could come and go any way they wanted from their offices.

Gabriel was standing in a room of his mansion staring out of a tall window cascaded with the heavy rain that had been pouring down on Polaris all day. The rain almost blocked his view of his backyard, but he still stared. The room was large with a marble oval table in the center surrounded by throne-like chairs, reminiscent of the ones in the council chambers.

There was a knock on the double doors. "Come in," he said, still mesmerized by whatever he saw out of the window. As her heels clicked against the cold floor, he greeted her. "I was wondering when you would come." He didn't even bother to face her.

"Hello, Gabriel." Adele stood at attention, like a soldier waiting for orders. Still not looking at her, he instructed her dully, "Go on."

Adele proceeded to tell Gabriel about accessing the archives of Huckabee, the old chancellor, and learning about an assignment he sent three wizards on. She informed him that the wizards were never mentioned by name, nor does she know what the assignments were. From the notes, not even the three wizards knew about each other.

"What is the relevance of this information?" Gabriel tapped his foot. The thought of hearing something that didn't concern him wasn't the best way to start a conversation.

"Every single council meeting and assignment since the start of the council are detailed in the archives except those particular ones."

"Three wizards?" Intrigued, he now turned to face her.

"Yes, and Darwin was mysteriously gone for five days the same time those assignments took place."

"Do you think he was one of the three assigned?" He stared directly into her eyes, waiting for her answer.

"I don't like to assume, but Darby confirmed that Darwin knows about the Alexandros crystal." Gabriel was captivated; he finally had a link to the crystals and their existence.

Before he could respond, an attractive young woman came through the double doors. She had long black wavy hair with burgundy highlights, an olive complexion reminiscent of someone of Mediterranean descent, and she wore dark low-cut jeans along with a long black military style coat. "The others are arriving," she informed them.

"Thank you, Isabel." Adele took a seat at the oval-shaped table. "Show them in."

One by one, eight other wizards came in and took their seats after greeting Adele and Gabriel. Each one of them had on long dark coats, almost matching one another. Gabriel finally took his seat directly across from Adele where he could see Isabel standing slightly to the left behind her. No one said anything; they sat patiently until Gabriel started speaking.

"Adele has told me some interesting things that she has found out." He flicked his gaze at everyone around the table. No one muttered a word, intimidated by him.

"I may have uncovered some information regarding the crystals," Adele informed them all. As she looked around, she could see that some are annoyed. They were hiding it well, but some were still annoyed at the purpose of this meeting.

It had been sixteen years since any of them had seen Gabriel, and a lot of them didn't feel as strongly as he did about finding these crystals. The last time they started this quest, it ended with their leader being captured and all of them losing almost everything they had in the process. Sure, Gabriel didn't name his accomplices, which they were all grateful for, but this crusade had always ended with nothing. They didn't even have proof that the crystals ever existed in the first place, but no one would ever dare speak out against Gabriel.

"What information?" asked Sophia, an elegant-looking woman with blonde hair who looked to be a little older than everyone else there. Adele told all of them the same thing she told Gabriel, only this time she left out the information her source confirmed about Darwin. When she finished explaining, some were still annoyed, and others were curious.

"Is it possible that these wizards know where the crystals could be?" asked Gavin, a well-built, handsome man who had been Gabriel's friend since childhood. He was very loyal to Gabriel and would follow him anywhere, which left a lot of people in the organization wondering why he wasn't Gabriel's number two over Adele. But Gabriel was the best strategist and knew Adele would get further in the Avalon government to be of some real value.

"It is," Adele responded.

"I need you all to combine your resources or whatever it takes to find out the identities of these three wizards," Gabriel ordered. He looked around the room at each of them. "This takes priority over anything else."

"With all due respect, sir, I don't think it's wise for all of us to make the crystals a priority. After all, we do have our covers around Avalon to keep up with. I, for one, think it will be too great a risk, especially with your father trying desperately to revoke your freedom," replied Elias, a heavyset older man with a British accent.

"Are you questioning my leadership, Elias?" Gabriel bristled at his comment, annoyance coursing through his veins.

"No, sir, I simply think it's ill-advised to put all of our resources into something that hasn't been proven to exist."

"Well luckily for us, we didn't ask your opinion," Adele smirked. Everyone could see the anger in her face.

The room was silent for a few seconds before Gabriel added, "That sounds like you are questioning my leadership." He stood up from his chair, sending a squeaking sound echoing around the room from the legs sliding on the floor.

"Not at all, sir," Elias trembled, his voice a little shaky now. Gabriel slowly started to walk around the oval table, placing his hand on everyone's chair as he passed, making the entire group feel uneasy.

"I founded this organization for the sole purpose of finding the crystals of the Elder Wizards, and I admit we hit a bump when I was imprisoned in the Tower." He slowly placed his hand on Elias's chair, each finger casually sliding down to the next one, while still pacing around the table. "And I know that over the past sixteen years, the search has stalled a bit. Of course, there have been those who continued to be loyal to me, while others continued to live their lives like nothing happened. Forgetting about the sacrifices I made in order for you to continue living your worthless existences." He stood behind his chair, staring at Elias.

"Sir—"

"I don't believe I was done talking, Elias!" He pushed his chair violently into the table.

Elias sat there quietly looking at Gabriel, sweat forming on his forehead.

Before anybody could react, Gabriel pointed his wand that he summoned while walking around the table directly at Elias. A burst of purple light hit Elias in the center of his chest, his face slamming down on the marble table. No one moved or said a thing as the *thud* of Elias's lifeless head echoed in the chamber. Elias' death rattle coming out of his mouth served as a reminder at how short-fused Gabriel was.

"Is there anyone else who thinks I'm not leading to the best of my abilities?" Gabriel asked as he looked around the room, hoping to make another example out of someone, yet no one replied to his question.

"Anyone else think it's *ill-advised,* finding the crystals that could benefit us all?" he repeated, clenching his wand in his hand. Still, no one replied. "Good."

The steam coming from Elias's pores on his face and the back of his neck told everyone the spell Gabriel cast on him. It was the blackest of magic, a spell that caused the person's insides to boil and melt. Soon, the rancid smell coming from Elias's body filled the room. It was unbearable, but still none dared to move.

"Adamaris!" Gabriel called out while looking directly at a man who was no doubt the largest man in the room, only he wasn't fat. He was very muscular and had a scar over his left eye. He was the most intimidating of all Gabriel's disciples sitting around the oval table.

"Sir," Adamaris answered, his voice deep, so deep that it echoed around the room. "Get rid of that." Gabriel said, gesturing to the body.

Adamaris pushed away from the table, got up, and strode over to Elias's chair. He pulled out the chair with one hand, picked up Elias's body as it slumped down, almost falling to the floor, and with one hand flung the body over his shoulders. Body in tow, he started to walk toward the double doors that Isabel opened for him.

"Adamaris!" Gabriel called out one more time.

"Yes?" He turned to face Gabriel, Elias's body just dangling from his shoulders. "Make sure his family joins him."

Adamaris simply nodded and smirked. It gave him something to look forward to. He continued to exit the room. When he passed Isabel, she got a mouthful of the rancid smell coming from the body. She gagged a little but turned to face the doors so no one could see. Everyone else waited for Gabriel to dismiss them, and when he did, he realized something. Adele noticed his expression and asked, "Is something wrong, Gabriel?"

"You and Isabel stay behind."

"Of course," Adele replied, always an obedient servant.

DARWIN was walking through the council building in Polaris listening to the voicemail Adrian left telling him about this coming weekend visit. Darwin was pleased with the news that Chloe finally knew the truth about the family.

He placed the phone in the breast pocket of his jacket and ascended the spiral stairs that led to his office with a grin, happy that Chloe would finally be coming to visit. When he reached his office, he was stunned at what he saw. He never thought Gabriel would have the nerve to come to the capital, let alone the council building and his office.

Darwin's anger was clearly expressed on his face. He wanted nothing more than to summon his cane and cast the most horrific spell he could think of, but he didn't—he couldn't.

After the way the chancellor had been acting, it wouldn't be wise on Darwin's part. Before Darwin could speak, Gabriel got out a few words.

"Out of your entire collection, I've always admired this piece," Gabriel said while looking at a painting. It showed a black-and-white tiled floor with a man standing next to an empty frame that was missing the bottom half, pointing at something, but he had no arms, and the frame was hanging on a grayish wall that the man was standing in front of. It was a unique painting that Darwin had chosen to frame and hang on his wall.

"What are you doing here, Gabriel?"

"The missing piece," Gabriel responded, still looking at the painting. "What are you doing here?" Darwin repeated, his voice deeper and louder.

"Can't a son come visit his father at the office without getting the third degree?" Gabriel turned to face Darwin. He was no longer intimidated by his father.

Before Darwin could respond, Isabel appeared right behind him, reaching for his arm.

She spun him around, pointing her wand at his chest. Darwin raised his hand, and she flew against the wall. As Darwin turned back quickly to look at his son, it was too late—Isabel had served her purpose. Darwin was distracted long enough for Gabriel to shoot a paralyzing spell at him. Darwin fell to the ground, unable to move.

As he lay there, he saw Gabriel walking toward him. He knew he wasn't able to move or speak, so he waited; he knew this was his end. He let Gabriel get the best of him and now he was going to pay for it. Gabriel didn't waste any time. "Did you really think I wouldn't figure it out?" he asked as he bent down close to Darwin. Isabel was now getting up from the corner where she fell after hitting the wall.

"For sixteen years I have been locked away, referred to as the 'crazy boy' in the Tower who was locked away for believing a 'child's fairy tale.' Meanwhile, my own father knew all along that the crystals were real yet didn't do anything to help me. YOU LET THEM LOCK ME AWAY! Your own son." Gabriel stood up. He raised his wand and said, "LOCANT QUOD EST OCCULTA!" and a white foggy cloud materialized in front of the painting. It took the shape of an old lady with long hair but no eyes and long nails wearing a raggedy cloak that floated in the air.

It stared intensely at the painting hanging on Darwin's wall and then floated around the room, scanning each item one by one until it came to Darwin. The foggy lady was now face-to-face with Darwin, her body of fog parallel to his. Her lifeless eye socket started with his head, then slowly began floating down, scanning his body. She stopped at his chest, opened her hand, and his button-up silk shirt tore open. The white fog positioned her hand over his chest, slowly moving it side to side about an inch away from it. Her corporeal hand reached into his chest, his body tensing up in the process. Darwin was in agonizing pain, but she still dug in, sensing that the thing being looked for was close. She removed her hand and an X appeared in the center of his chest.

Gabriel was excited; he knew he had found the missing part of the painting. Within a few seconds, the foggy lady was gone. Gabriel touched the tip of his wand on the freshly carved X and said, "REVELARE!" What looked like a big chunk of flesh from Darwin's chest started to emerge, the exact shape of the missing piece from the painting floating in the air. It wasn't skin and bone, however; it was a piece of old parchment. Gabriel pointed his wand toward the wall, and the painting was complete. The man's arm in the painting was now pointing to a mirror in what was once an empty frame.

Isabel looked on, a little confused. *Did Gabriel really go through all of this for a painting?* She thought. She heard footsteps coming her way, and then, a voice familiar to her. "Sir, we have to go." Gabriel seized the painting off the wall. He turned to face Darwin.

"Until next time." He stared at Darwin with a mischievous grin that would send chills down a normal person's spine. As soon as Darwin's office door opened, Gabriel and Isabel teleported away.

"Oh my god!" yelled Adrasteia, her Scottish accent a relief to Darwin, who still couldn't move or talk. She knelt down beside him and intuitively knew what spell was cast. "Go get me a healin' elixir!" she yelled to a capital guard who ran quickly out of the office. She rubbed Darwin's thick white hair and told him it was going to be ok. Within a few seconds, the guard was back and handed her a small vial with a neon-red liquid inside that she made Darwin drink. "LEAVE!" she yelled to the guard.

As the door closed, Darwin regained movement in his arms and legs. Then he was able to speak. "He knows."

"Shhh, let's get ye aff tha floor." Adrasteia helped Darwin up and moved him to a sofa in the corner of his office. "What does he know?" she asked as she took a seat next to him.

"That the crystals are real."

"But 'ow?"

"I don't know, but the painting Huckabee gave me must have something to do with it," Darwin said. Adrasteia looked at Darwin, not knowing what to make of what he was saying.

"What does the paintin' hev to do with the crystals?"

"It's a map to the crystals!" Darwin mumbled, remembering something crucial that he and Huckabee talked about, but the more he tried to remember, the fuzzier the memories became. "Huckabee told me that for security reasons, I wouldn't be able to remember where I hid the Alexandro's Crystal. So, I allowed him to mind wipe me after he made the map and after he implanted the missing piece inside me. He knew that would be the safest way to keep the information out of the wrong hands."

"I dunno why he didnae just destroy the damn things," Adrasteia yelled, angry at how irresponsible it was of the former chancellor.

Darwin winced. "Ugh…" He needed to catch his breath. "He believed the crystals were the reason magic existed and if they were destroyed, our world wouldn't exist."

"Well, he was an idiot."

"Still, a lot of the people in our community believe our power comes from the elders as well."

"What now?" Adrasteia wondered aloud.

"Now I need to recover the memories Huckabee took from me."

"A recovery spell is tricky." Adrasteia said.

"I know, but we must. We don't know how long it will take Gabriel to read the map."

Adrasteia was uncertain of this course of action. "What if he can't? It would then be useless fer him."

"Gabriel is very determined. He'll figure out a way." Darwin couldn't waste any more time. "Gather what we need. The sooner I can recover what was lost, the sooner I can go get the crystal."

"Ok, I'll come to yer house once I 'ave everythin'."

"My grandchildren are coming over this weekend, so it's best that we meet by your place. I don't want them to know about any of this."

"Maybe it's time to tell 'em the truth about their father," Adrasteia suggested as she came to the door.

Darwin didn't respond, but he knew she was right. With Gabriel one step closer to finding a crystal, he knew the time had come to tell Adrian and Andrew the truth. Darwin knew that they were bound to hear about Gabriel. After all, last time Gabriel was on this quest, he sent all of Avalon into a panic. Now that he had proof, they existed, it was only a matter of time before gossip spread across Avalon and the twins would hear the truth from someone else.

How should I tell them? He thought to himself. He would have to talk to Sara first, of course, and explain to her what had happened. He decided to invite Sara to Southport this weekend as well so that they could talk about the best way to tell the boys about their father. Darwin got up from the sofa, still feeling the effects of what transpired, stumbled over to the window, and stared up into the sky at the multiple colors flying through the air.

He decided against telling anyone, especially the chancellor. Adele was too close to him and could manipulate what action, if any, he took against Gabriel. Besides, Darwin and Barnabas had never really gotten along over the years, and that wouldn't change. So, at that moment, he decided that telling Sara about what had happened would be best. He limped over to his desk, picked up his cell phone, and dialed her. When she answered, he hesitated at first but proceeded to tell her everything that happened. Then came the hard part—the part that now was the time to tell Adrian and Andrew the truth.

Sara didn't like being forced into telling her kids the truth but agreed with Darwin. Andrew and Adrian finding out from them was a lot better than the alternative. Sara told Darwin that she would accompany Liz and the kids this weekend to Southport, where they would sit down and talk to both. The thought of telling them made Sara nervous. They were just starting to get back to normal with her, and now more lies were to be revealed.

Chapter Twelve

A gust of wind caught Adele's attention. She was still in Gabriel's mansion sitting at the oval table. She looked to the side, where she now saw Isabel and Gabriel standing and holding a painting that she had seen before. She was happy they were successful, considering Darwin wasn't an easy target to get one over on. She pushed the throne-like chair back, got up, and casually made her way to them. Before she got close to them, Gabriel was already setting the painting down on the table. Isabel looked at Adele with a little bit of confusion but didn't say anything. Gabriel was studying the painting, almost like he was hypnotized by it.

Adele stood nearby, waiting for him to speak; she knew from experience how much Gabriel hated being interrupted. He raised the bottom of the painting, gently gripping the corners as the top still rested on the table. He examined it very vigilantly, bending down to see the back of the canvas, and then gently placed it back on the table. He paused for a second, then strolled up a set of curved stairs that led up to a loft where rows of bookshelves are. He approached the second row, scanned each book with his hand, and went for the one that was in the middle, one that was black with gold lines and very thick. He paced back down the stairs to the table, placed the thick book down, and took a seat. Gabriel began flipping through the pages, scanning every page that he thought could be relevant to what he was looking for. Adele glanced over at Isabel.

"Is Darwin dead?"

"Not sure. I heard that annoying shopkeeper's voice, so we left."

"Adrasteia?" Adele asked. Before Isabel could answer, Gabriel finally spoke.

"She most likely got him an elixir before the spell could kill him." He didn't look away, still flipping through the pages. Adele looked concerned over Gabriel's response. She paced over to Gabriel and placed a hand on his shoulder.

"We should take the painting to a safe location. Darwin will most likely be coming here with guards to arrest you."

Gabriel glanced up at her and agreed. He summoned some of his personal guards that were standing outside the room by the door. He instructed them to pack all the books and take them to the Azazel estate. They bowed their heads in obedience and ascended the curved stairs to the books.

"I want you to go back to your office and keep me informed of what actions they are taking against me," Gabriel instructed as he looked at Adele. Adele nodded and teleported back to her office. Upon arriving, she quickly left her office and rushed to the chancellor's. She passed his secretary without saying a word, going straight into his office.

Barnabas was startled. "Dear god, what is it?" he asked as he held a pen in his hand, ready to sign some paper.

"Um," Adele hesitated. *Why doesn't he know about what just transpired?* "I wanted to know if you wanted to grab dinner. I finished up my work for the day and I'm absolutely famished."

"I would love to, my dear, but unfortunately I can't."

"Why?" She wondered if Darwin had in fact told him about what Gabriel just did. Adele took a few more steps closer to his desk, anticipating his response.

"With Genevieve on assignment, Darwin suggested that we adjourn any sessions until after the holidays, which I agreed to, and now I must get a lot done before this day is over." Adele was a little surprised by what Barnabas just told her; after all, if Darwin already spoke to the chancellor and neglected to tell him about Gabriel, it must have meant he was going to handle it himself.

But on the other hand, Gabriel wasn't officially in any trouble. Nonetheless, she was surprised but, in some ways, relieved. Adele was sure that Gabriel would be delighted to hear that neither the council nor the chancellor were after him.

"Very well, then."

She left Barnabas's office to go back to hers. The entire walk back, she was curious about Darwin's motive for not telling the chancellor. After all, he had been trying desperately to get Gabriel back to the Tower, yet when he finally had a chance, he didn't say anything. When Adele reached her office, she closed the door and leaned against it. She realized that not only was Darwin going to retaliate but that he was going to kill Gabriel for his actions.

That is the only reason Darwin would keep this from the council and the chancellor. Adele knew that she must warn Gabriel to stay in hiding, because as powerful as he was, she knew that he was no match for Darwin. Not until they obtained the crystals, at least. Adele strolled over to her desk to retrieve her personal belongings, then teleported.

✳ ✳ ✳

IT was finally the weekend, and Sara, Liz, the twins, Chloe, and Bianca all teleported together to Darwin's estate. The potion that Liz made Chloe drink must have worked, because she wasn't pale, white, or sickly looking. She was simply amazed at the sights she was seeing for the first time. She quickly released her mother's hand and stepped away from her. Things were still a little cold between them. The twins must have been used to teleporting by now, as neither one of them drank the teleporting potion to travel. As always, Nigel was there to greet them, only this time he bought along Hekabe.

"Great to see you again!" Hekabe shouted as she sauntered toward all of them with her arms open, as if she could give them all a hug at once. She saw Sara standing behind Liz, still holding Andrew's hand. "I'm so glad you're here," Hekabe told Sara, who smiled widely at her. Sara had met Hekabe once before a very long time ago, but she still remembered her.

As Nigel led the way inside, Chloe looked around and is still entranced at how green and colorful the surroundings were. She looked over to the stables and saw what she thought was a horse only, it was spreading its wings wide and standing on its two hind legs, excited at the sight of her owner, Bianca.

Chloe slowed down a little, fascinated. Adrian rushed to her side, put one arm over her shoulders, and whispered, "Amazing, isn't it?"

Chloe just grinned from ear to ear and before she could say anything, Andrew added, "Later, we will introduce you to them!"

"Them?" Chloe replied, the excitement in her voice obvious. Bianca couldn't help but smile over her sister's excitement. It brought some much-needed ease to her because for a few weeks now, things had been a little weird for Chloe, which made Bianca worry. But now, seeing her sister smile brought joy to Bianca.

As they went inside, Chloe still couldn't believe how gorgeous Darwin's house was. She looked around and smelled the delicious meal that was being prepared for them; she didn't realize how hungry she was until that aroma reached her nose. Hekabe led Liz, Sara, and Bianca into the kitchen while Andrew suggested that he and Adrian show Chloe their rooms. Since Andrew's room was the first one, they reached, they went in there first. Chloe was instantly shocked at how big it was and that he got his own balcony.

She slowly paced around the room, examining everything she could touch. The twins looked on and couldn't help but let their happiness consume them. They couldn't be more overjoyed that they finally got to share this part of the family's life with their cousin that they trusted and talked to about everything. Chloe made her way to the balcony but didn't go outside.

"Do I get my own room too?"

"Of course, you do," spoke the familiar deep voice of their grandfather. They all turned around, surprised that he was behind them. Chloe was astonished; she really hadn't been expecting to get a room at her grandfather's house, but the surprise was welcomed. As she went to hug her grandfather hello, he told her how happy he was that she was there. This helped Chloe feel truly welcomed and calmed the nerves she had been feeling about this trip. When Chloe backed away, Darwin extended his opened hand and told her, "Let me show you your room, my dear."

Chloe took his hand and they proceeded to exit the room, the twins following behind. As they moved down the long hallway and came up to a dead end where they could only go left or right, Darwin asked Chloe where she would like her room as he looked down both hallways. She pointed to the right and they all went that way, Darwin still holding her hand with the twins looking on with joy. They knew that Darwin giving Chloe a room would make her feel like nothing had changed since she found out she was adopted. They came up to a set of great big white double doors and Darwin asked Chloe, "What is your favorite color, dear?"

Chloe thought for a second and then answered, "Black and pink." Darwin looked on cheerfully at her, tapped his cane on the door twice, and waited a few moments before opening it. Chloe and the twins could hear things moving around inside, which only made Chloe's excitement grow. Things finally came to a stop and Darwin let go of Chloe's hand, turned both knobs, and pushed the doors open.

Chloe's mouth slackened at what she saw before her. The room was the same size as Andrew's, her walls painted pink with white borders. Along the walls were black dressers, one long and one tall, against opposite walls. There was a black chaise lounge chair draped with a pink silk blanket in the corner wall closest to her bed. The bed itself was queen size with black and pink linens with a bonus surprise in the middle: a black kitten with a few white spots under its chin, fast asleep. Chloe still couldn't speak; since they had arrived a little bit ago, it had been surprise after surprise, and she kept thinking she couldn't get happier. She turned to Darwin, hugged him tight, and thanked him for her room.

"No need to thank me, my dear," Darwin told her while letting out a deep breath. The impact of her hug almost knocked the wind out of him. "Well, I suppose I should go say hi to your parents." Darwin turned and left, leaving Chloe and the twins in her room. As soon as he left, Chloe rushed to the bed to greet the kitten that had just woken up from her little nap.

"This is amazing." Chloe was beyond excited. "This place is amazing!" She gently ran her hand over the kitten's back.

"What are you going to name her?" Andrew asked while taking a seat on her bed.

"I don't know." Chloe started contemplating what name would be fitting for this little kitten.

"How about Lucy?" Adrian suggested as if a light bulb went off in his head. Chloe agreed.

"Lucy it is!"

✳ ✳ ✳

DARWIN joined Liz, Sara, and Bianca at the table in the dining room. Hekabe brought him a cup of tea and went back to making dinner a few feet away. He explained to them what happened before their arrival. Sara already knew about a few things from when she spoke to Darwin during the week but she, along with Liz and Bianca, seemed concerned, not surprised.

Bianca asked, "Why not tell the chancellor?"

"Because with Adele right by his side manipulating him, I can't take the chance that he won't believe me."

"Do you think he will still try to contact the boys?" Sara interrupted, her nerves very much on display.

"I think that was all meant to be a distraction so I wouldn't figure out how much he knew about the crystals."

"We should have known that Gabriel didn't care to meet the boys. It was all part of his plan for those damn crystals!" Liz slammed down her cup of tea, causing some of it to leap from the cup onto the table below.

"Why don't you just go get the crystal and keep it here?" Bianca wondered. "Because I don't know where it is."

Bianca was a little bit confused. "Aren't you the one that hid it?" she asked, a little perplexed about her grandfather's reply.

"Yes, but Huckabee told me before the mission that he would erase the memory of where I hid it after I was done. But not before he made a map of its location, of course."

"Who's Huckabee?" Sara asked, oblivious to this new world she had been thrust into not too long ago.

"The old chancellor," Liz interjected. "Adrasteia said that you told her that the best thing to do would be to move the crystal," she added.

"Yes, I thought I would have time to find it and move it, but unfortunately I underestimated how much Gabriel knew."

Liz was growing impatient to know what the plan was. "So, what now?"

"We have to find out as much as we can about the missions Huckabee assigned and who carried them out," Darwin replied. "The Alexandros crystal should take priority right now, though, since we know Gabriel has the painting."

"Well, he has a great head start on finding it," Bianca noted.

"I'm sure Gabriel hasn't figured out how to read the map yet. Huckabee wouldn't make it that easy; I'm sure of it."

Darwin glanced at Hekabe. "Did he ever mention anything to you that could be relevant to us now?"

"My brother never mentioned council matters to me. He was very secretive about what went on there. I wish I could be of more help. I'm sorry." Hekabe said.

"It's ok." Just then, the muffled sounds coming from the balcony above the open window caught his attention.

Chloe and the twins leaned over the rails of her balcony, looking toward the stables.

Chloe was anxious to go meet those beautiful creatures she'd seen on her way inside the house.

Andrew looked over to her and noticed her staring at the stables. "You know we can go see them if you want?"

"Now? Can we? Chloe asked, a little uncertain.

Andrew extended his hand for Chloe to take. "We can do anything you want." She gripped his hand and they all teleported to the side of the stables, where the Pegasi couldn't see them since they startled easily.

"How long does that potion or whatever my mom gave me last?" Chloe asked, referring to the elixir she drank that made teleporting easier to take.

"For a while," Andrew said.

As they approached the front of the stables, they realized that they had been spotted by Rizzo, Adrian's Pegasus. Rizzo rushed to his side in excitement and brushed its head against Adrian's face. Gizmo did the same to Andrew while Chloe looked on.

"Oh my god, that is super adorable."

"Come stand over here," Adrian instructed her, pointing next to him. As Chloe strode to his side, she asked, "Why do I have to do this?"

"Because that's how they choose you!" Andrew informed her while walking up to Adrian. It didn't take long for a white female Pegasus to walk up to Chloe, who was just letting it do what it had to in order for her to feel comfortable with her.

It bowed its head at Chloe, who asked, "Why is she doing that?"

"Because she chose you. You're now the proud owner of your very own flying horse!" Adrian grinned. Chloe was amused, the feelings she had just days before about being an outsider quickly snuffed out like a candle being denied oxygen.

"I'll say it again. This is amazing!" Andrew strolled over to her to show her how to put on the saddle and she climbed on top of it.

"Her name is Zoe!" Adrian called out while walking over with his saddle. "How do you know?"

"They each have names over their stall," he answered. As he put the saddle over Rizzo, he looked at Andrew, who was finishing up with Gizmo, and told him to show Chloe the basic instructions of how to ride Zoe. Once they were all ready to go, Adrian led the way and the other two followed.

Chloe was a bit nervous but excited as well and held on tight to Zoe as she saw Adrian and Andrew take flight. It wasn't long before she, too, was up in the air. The sun had just set, but there was still a hint of daylight in the air as they soared.

She looked down and noticed that they were way higher than she thought they would go. It felt as if she was riding a roller coaster. Her heart was racing—the height these majestic beasts could soar to was exhilarating. She was scared, yet felt safe, like she somehow knew Zoe wouldn't let anything happen to her.

Zoe sensed that Chloe was nervous and descended a little to ease her mind. Chloe appreciated that gesture and patted Zoe on the head, her suspicions confirmed. Andrew slowed down so that Chloe could catch up and he could point out the different things on the estate.

When Chloe got next to him, he pointed down to the field by the pond to tell her that was where they trained last time they were here. Adrian looked back to see Andrew pointing at the field and decided to land. Andrew and Chloe landed a few seconds after Adrian and as soon as they climbed off their Pegasi, Andrew was bragging about beating Bianca and Adrian in capture the flag.

"You got lucky!" Adrian said as he playfully pushed Andrew. "Yes, 'lucky.' Lucky that I read and study."

"Sorry I didn't spend my first night here reading so many books!" Adrian replied. He wasn't used to coming in second to his brother.

"Amazing. Guess not everything comes so naturally to you, then, huh?" Andrew quipped. Adrian just ignored him, and they both began to tell her about the last time they were at Darwin's, showing her a few things, they learned by practicing at home. Chloe couldn't help but feel a little jealous. Instead of showing her jealousy, she nodded and listened intently to them; she didn't want to ruin anything. Chloe knew that in time, those feelings would pass, and they would be closer than ever before.

"We should get back," Andrew suggested.

"Yeah, we wouldn't want Hekabe getting mad at us for showing up to dinner late," Adrian stated. The three of them went back to the house to eat dinner with the rest of the family.

✳ ✳ ✳

"DINNER was delicious as always, Hekabe," Darwin said contentedly while staring down at an empty plate. Darwin glanced over to Sara, who glimpsed back at him, signaling that she was ready to talk to the boys. Darwin rose from his chair at the head of the table and asked the twins if they would come with him upstairs. He headed toward the kitchen stairs, since those led up to his study a lot faster, and the twins followed with Sara closely behind them. Liz and Bianca looked their way as they exited the dining room but went back to helping clean up once the twins and Sara were out of sight.

When they reached Darwin's study, Sara closed the door behind them. That was when the twins suspected that something was going on. They looked over at Darwin, who was sitting by the bookshelf where Andrew had taken the book without asking. Andrew wondered if that was why Darwin asked them to come with him. In the sitting area of Darwin's study, there were two single seats and a large sofa. Darwin sat on one of the single seats, waiting for everyone to sit down. Adrian took a seat on the sofa followed by Andrew and eventually Sara, who wanted to sit by her boys.

"Is everything alright?" asked Andrew, his heart racing. *Am I in trouble?* he wondered. "Yes, I just wanted to tell you both something."

"We both did," Sara added.

For about half an hour, Darwin's voice was the only one heard as he told the twins about Gabriel, covering everything from the first time he tried getting the crystals to his most recent visit to Darwin's office. The twins listened to his every word, captivated by the story they were hearing. Sara looked at both, once again worried about how they would react to this new information.

"Are the crystals you're talking about the elder wizard crystals?" Andrew asked after Darwin was done. Darwin was a little taken aback by the question, surprised that Andrew knew about the crystals.

"Yes. Yes, they are, Andrew," Darwin replied, curious as to how he knew that. Adrian looked a little confused because he had no idea what they were talking about.

Andrew sensed Darwin's curiosity. "I borrowed one of your books last time I was here. When I read through it, it mentioned something about the crystals, but Adrasteia filled in the rest. I hope that's ok?" Darwin didn't want to lose focus, so he told him it was fine.

"Ok. This guy sounds dangerous, but why are you telling us about him?" Adrian asked.

"Because he's your father," Sara admitted. Andrew and Adrian quickly looked her way, confused and shocked about what they had just heard.

"What…" was the only thing Adrian could say before silence fell over the room. Sara put her hand on Adrian's shoulder to comfort him, but he quickly stood up.

"You told us our dad died in a car accident with Chloe's dad," Adrian spat. He raised his voice a little louder, pacing back and forth.

"I know, but only to spare both of your feelings. How would you feel knowing who your dad really was?"

"Probably the same way we feel now. Betrayed, angry, frustrated," Andrew added as he stood up to join his brother. Once again, they had been thrown information they were not expecting.

"It was my idea not to tell you who your father was. We couldn't. We didn't even know you two were going to be wizards, and telling you about him would have been foolish," Darwin added. The twins were stunned at his excuse; Darwin was acting like he didn't do anything wrong by keeping this from them. Sara was a little shocked by the way Darwin justified his reason.

"Then why didn't you tell us when we found out we were wizards?" Adrian fumed. The pain and hurt he was feeling was reminiscent of the day they found out who they were.

"Yeah, this is something we should have known," Andrew added, agreeing with his brother. Darwin was once again speechless; he knew that they had a point.

Sara got up and strode over to her boys, who were now standing side by side, and told them, "There was just a lot going on. You boys had just found out you were wizards, and that Chloe was adopted, and I thought telling you then about who your father was would be too much for you guys to handle."

"Lies! That is all this family is about," Adrian shouted as he pulled away from his mother and stormed out of the room. Sara tried to stop him, but Andrew blocked her.

"I'll talk to him. You guys did enough." Andrew was frustrated. *How many more lies do we have to hear?* He looked at Sara and Darwin in disgust.

When Andrew left the room, he slammed the door behind him, leaving Sara and Darwin wallowing in their choices.

"They'll be alright. They just need time to process what we told them," Darwin told Sara, hoping it would reassure her.

"Will they? They spent their entire life thinking their dad was dead and now they know he's alive—not just alive, though, but this evil, disgraceful person." She sat back down and put her head against both of her palms. She just wanted to make her boys' pain go away. For a split second, she wished Gabriel was dead.

Darwin knew Sara was right; finding out about Gabriel might be too much to handle.

Sara glanced up to look at the door, wanting nothing more than to chase after her boys, but she knew that wouldn't be a good idea. Even Darwin wanted to go check on them, but he, too, knew that he was the last person they wanted to see right now.

"I know that right now might not be the best time to say this, but you have done an amazing job raising those boys," Darwin said as he stood up to go over and sit next to her. "I promise you; I will not let Gabriel hurt them," he added as he put one arm around her to comfort her.

"Thank you," Sara replied, resting her head on his shoulder.

They both sat there in silence, hoping that Andrew and Adrian would forgive them for this. Even though Sara and Darwin believed they were doing the right thing, they knew the boys might not ever see it that way. Down the hall, Andrew chased after Adrian. When he spotted him, he shouted for Adrian to wait. Adrian turned around to see Andrew running up to him.

"I keep forgetting how big this house is. I think I just ran a mile," Andrew panted, hoping to lighten the mood. It seemed to work because Adrian laughed. "Before we go downstairs, can we talk for a minute?"

Adrian agreed and they headed toward Andrew's room.

Chapter Thirteen

Andrew closed the door behind him as Adrian went directly out to the balcony, which had become their go-to place to talk. It might have been because the stars shined brightest at night on Andrew's side, or perhaps because the view was a little bit better here than in Adrian's. Either way, it was a calm and soothing place they liked to go.

"You know, the last time we were out here, we were talking about what kind of person our dad was. I guess now we know," Adrian said. He sat down on one of the outdoor lounge chairs they "borrowed" from Darwin's patio.

"Yeah, I remember. You know, Adrian, I kind of get why they didn't tell us about him," Andrew said as he sat down on the other "borrowed" chair.

"Are you actually saying you're ok with them lying to us?" Adrian asked.

"No. I'm not ok with them lying; I just mean that I get it."

Adrian didn't like what he was hearing and went back to looking up at the night sky. A few colorful turnabouts flew by, which he watched until he saw them shoot down over at the Hacker estate. *Must be Mr. and Mrs. Hacker coming home from a night out*, he thought to himself.

"Seriously, what does finding out about Gabriel change?" Andrew asked, hoping to engage his brother.

"I don't know," Adrian replied, still looking out into the distance. "Maybe hear him out. There are always two sides of a story".

Andrew looked at his brother like that was the most foolish thing he had ever heard. "Look, to me, our dad died years ago. This Gabriel person doesn't matter to me; from what they told us, he is evil," Andrew told him as he slouched back down against the built-in pillow on the lounge chair that was extremely comfortable for patio furniture.

Adrian stared at Andrew. "Evil doesn't just happen, Drew. Don't you want to at least hear his side?"

"You can't be serious. Did you hear about everything he has done? This guy is bad news! And maybe you're right, evil doesn't just happen. But from what we just heard, he's not someone we want to run into."

Adrian knew Andrew was right. But even after hearing about their dad, he had hope that maybe there was still good in him. Adrian decided to drop the subject for now. He just couldn't believe that their dad was alive.

They heard someone come into Andrew's room, but they didn't move. They assumed it was their mother or grandfather coming in to make sure they were ok. They were both relieved to see that it was neither; it was Chloe coming to check on them. She had figured something was going on after she saw Darwin and Sara both leave to talk to them.

"You guys ok?" She walked out in front of them and leaned against the railing. Andrew halfheartedly smiled at her and told her they were fine. Naturally, she didn't believe him and pressured them to tell her what was going on. It didn't take long before Andrew told her everything that Darwin told them. Chloe was dumbfounded, to say the least, because that brought up questions about her own father's death as well.

However, that wasn't something she could think about now; she had to be there for her cousins. After hearing everything Andrew said, Chloe sunk down until her butt met the cold concrete beneath her feet and leaned her back against the banister. Adrian tossed her a pillow from the lounge chair that she placed under her.

"Wait, what are those elder crystal things that you were talking about?" Adrian wondered, remembering that he wanted to know more about them when they were mentioned.

Andrew then proceeded to tell him and Chloe the story Adrasteia told him about the crystals. Chloe and Adrian hung onto his every word like they were being told a bedtime story. When Andrew was done talking, he noticed that Chloe and Adrian hadn't blinked. It was so quiet that they could hear the wind chimes from the back door ringing. A few minutes passed and finally Chloe was the first to break the silence.

"Do those crystals exist?"

"Apparently, they do," Andrew informed them. He was reminded of the answer he received when he asked Adrasteia the same question. He hoped she was honest with her answer; he couldn't take it if someone else he thought he could trust lied to him.

Adrian decided that he had had enough for the night and went back to his room; after all, there was only so much life-changing news a person could take. As soon as he stood up, Chloe jumped in his chair.

"Wow, these are very comfortable," she said, looking at Andrew, who was now entertaining himself by making the pillow Chloe had been sitting on float in the air. Andrew just sat there with his arm extended, resting it on his knee, and slowly moved each finger.

"That's so cool." He glanced at her warmly and crossed his arms, sending the pillow back to the ground in the process. Hoping to change the subject, Chloe asked him what else he had learned to do. He answered her earnestly, but she had no idea what he was talking about, which amused them both.

"You must have questions about your dad," he told her, knowing that if his father didn't die in a crash, hers most likely didn't either. That, or he did, and his mom just used that tragedy to say their dad died as well. Either way, he knew that Chloe had to be thinking the same.

"No, not really. I'm guessing he did die in a car accident and our moms thought it best to say your dad was with him."

Andrew nodded, then turned his head to look out into the distance. Chloe sat there and wondered if what she said could be true. She hoped it was because it would make things so much less complicated. She didn't let herself think about it anymore. She knew that Andrew needed her, so she just sat with him until it got late enough, and they both fell asleep nestled in the chairs.

* * *

THE next morning, Chloe and Andrew woke up on the balcony to discover someone must have come in and covered them with a blanket while they slept. Chloe stood up and stretched by reaching her arms over her head and arching her back, took a deep breath of air, and hit Andrew on the head as she passed him to go inside. Andrew wasn't expecting that but still acted like it didn't faze him as he got up and closed his balcony doors. As he started getting out his clothes for the day, there was a knock at his door.

"Come in," he called out, and in came Bianca.

"Hey. Your mom told us what happened. Are you ok?"

"Yeah, I'm fine." He told her that he would see her downstairs after he showered, so Bianca left his room. She could tell that he was still upset, but she didn't want to push the issue.

When Bianca went downstairs, she saw that Adrian was already walking into the kitchen, where Hekabe made something for everyone. Pancakes for the twins, eggs and bacon for Chloe and Bianca, omelets for Sara and Liz, and soft-boiled eggs for Darwin—his favorite—and a mountain of toast to go with everything.

"Are there any biscuits?" Adrian asked. Hekabe didn't have to say anything for Adrian to know that there weren't any biscuits; her facial expression said it all. "Sorry for asking," he said with a smirk as he passed her.

Bianca laughed because even though the twins were both in a lot better shape since joining wrestling, they continued to eat like pigs. That thought gave her the opportunity to talk about something other than Gabriel and the drama that went along with him.

"How's wrestling going?"

"Good. Drew, Collin, and I have this competition going to see who could get the most pins the fastest."

"That sounds fun."

"It's the only way to make it fun. The coach works us very hard, so instead of quitting, we figured why not use this as a way to better one another? Also, I think I'm in better shape than the both of them." Adrian lifted his shirt to show his cousin his newfound abdominal muscles.

"But yet you still want biscuits," Hekabe said unexpectedly, causing Adrian and Bianca to burst out laughing.

"She has a point, fat ass," Bianca teased while looking at Adrian's stack of pancakes on his plate. Adrian just laughed it off and headed to the dining room table.

"Dear, can you take him the syrup?" Hekabe asked Bianca as she extended her hand to give her the syrup.

"He doesn't like syrup." Hekabe paused for a moment.

"Well, can you just place it on the table for the normal people, then?" she said, smiling. Bianca took it, which was nice and warm, and walked into the dining room, placing it on the table. She could sense the tension in the room between Adrian and Sara, who had just come down for breakfast. Any other person would think they didn't know each other at all the way Adrian ignored her. Instead of making it more awkward, Bianca just said good morning and told Sara that the food was in the kitchen. Bianca looked at Adrian. She wanted to say something, but she knew that it wasn't a good time, so she just headed back into the kitchen to grab her food. Soon, everyone else was sitting at the table eating the delicious food that Hekabe prepared. The only conversation taking place was between Chloe and Bianca; Liz was still getting the cold shoulder from Chloe.

Andrew would chime in with a joke here and there, but for the most part, it was silent.

Chloe and Bianca were the first to excuse themselves; they put their plates in the dishwasher and went outside through the back door. The cool fresh air was a relief, the birds chirping in the distance, the sky once again filled with those colorful turnabouts that Chloe still was mesmerized by.

"How do you like it here?" Bianca asked after she saw her sister looking at the people most likely making their way to work.

"It's an amazing place. I would have never in a thousand years thought a place like this existed."

"I just wish that there wasn't so much tension inside," Bianca sighed, looking back at the door.

"Well, what do you expect when its lie after lie with this family?" Chloe added. They both made their way toward the stables.

✳ ✳ ✳

BACK inside, the twins were back in Andrew's room trying their best to avoid their grandfather and mother.

Andrew looked at Adrian. "We're going to have to talk to them eventually." He was fully ready to move on and forgive them.

"I know."

"So, what do we do?" Andrew asked. Neither of them knew what to say. Suddenly, there was a knock on the door. They both looked at each other and stood motionless, as if that would tell the person at the door nobody was there. However, they forgot that the door wasn't locked, and after a short moment it was pushed open.

Liz peeked her head in. "Mind if I come in?"

"Not at all, Aunt Liz," Andrew was quick to answer. Liz closed the door behind her, went over to the twins, and took a seat on Andrew's desk chair.

"I know you both are angry, and that it's not ideal, but when you guys are parents, you will understand why they lied to you." Adrian and Andrew sat there in silence. They knew their aunt had a point.

"They were smart to send you in," Andrew told her, to which she just laughed.

"Yeah. That was pretty smart," Adrian added.

"It wasn't their idea. Dad suggested that we have Thanksgiving dinner tomorrow before we leave since he won't be able to make it next week. Which I thought was a great idea since I have some stuff to do as well. Besides, how much fun would Thanksgiving dinner be with all that tension going on?" she added, hoping it would ease her nephews' feelings. Andrew and Adrian agreed and went off to talk to Sara and Darwin.

When they arrived at Darwin's study, they both stood there, hesitant to go in. Adrian finally opened the door, catching Darwin and Sara off guard. "Do you guys have a minute?" Adrian asked.

"Of course," Sara added, happy to see them.

Adrian led the way to the same sofa they had sat on before. The awkward silence didn't help things, yet none of them knew what to say. Finally, Darwin spoke.

"I am deeply sorry to lay all of this on you. I know it seems like we are only telling you things when it is convenient for us, but I can assure you that is not the case. Keeping this from you both was something I felt we needed to do." Darwin got up and sat between them, taking their hands. "I am truly sorry, boys. I really am."

"It wasn't all his fault. He is being kind by trying to take responsibility for it. Look, boys, you must understand that finding out everything that I have learned about your father was overwhelming for me. So, I agreed with Darwin. I never thought that Gabriel would be released from the Tower."

"So, if he wasn't released, you both wouldn't have told us?" Adrian asked. Silence fell over the room again. "I thought so."

"Adrian, stop! I want to move on from this!" Andrew shouted.

"Fine. Let's move on." Adrian's tone was sarcastic.

"Sweetie. What can I do or say to show you how sorry your grandfather and I are?"

"It's not that, Mom. I just wish you had told us about him. Maybe if we had visited him, things could have been different."

Hearing Adrian say that left Sara with a pit in her stomach. She looked over at Darwin, whose eyes were widening, his mouth falling open. Darwin knew instantly that Adrian was somehow blaming himself for what Gabriel had become.

"Adrian. Nothing would have changed the man Gabriel has become. His thirst for power consumed him long before you were born." Darwin gripped their hands tighter. "You boys have made me so proud. The compassion and empathy you showed Chloe when she was going through everything, she went through proves to me that you are better off not knowing him"

"I couldn't agree more with your grandfather," Sara said as she looked at her boys.

After a few hours hugs were shared, tears were shed, and in the end, they all wanted to move on from this. Andrew made them promise to not lie or keep anything from them anymore, and Sara and Darwin agreed.

Before Darwin went to bed that night, he told the twins that he wanted to see how much, if any, they had improved on their magical skills. He told them that they would be going to the training field, along with Bianca, for another challenge. They were excited yet nervous over that idea.

The next morning, Sara was in the kitchen with Liz and Hekabe drinking coffee when Darwin marched in through the back door. His hair was a little tousled, presumably from the windy conditions that went along with flying in a turnabout over Southport.

"Where have you been?" Liz asked her father after she noticed that he had on his beautifully handwoven dark-blue cashmere robe.

"Setting up the training field for the boys and Bianca."

After he told them what he had planned for the boys, they all told him that they would like to watch. Darwin was, of course, fine with that idea. Sara was excited, yet nervous; apart from the occasional floating items or teleporting, she hadn't really seen her boys use their magic.

Darwin took Sara's hand and teleported to the field, followed by Liz and Hekabe, while the twins, Chloe, and Bianca decided to take their Pegasi. After all, they did enjoy riding them as much as the Pegasi enjoyed being ridden. When they were close enough to see the field next to the pond, they saw a huge metal globe-shaped arena wrapped in what looked like a chain-link fence. The tower had already risen from the pond, and they assumed that was where Sara and the rest of the group would be watching them from.

As they came closer to the field, Andrew decided that he wanted a bird's eye view of the new arena, so he flew directly over it. Adrian, Bianca, and Chloe followed. What they saw was amazing—there were three different levels, all with walls and other kinds of bunkers for cover, and the center of the arena was open space. If you were standing on each level, you could see the one directly below you just by simply looking over the side. After soaring over the new training arena, they all descended one by one to the green field below.

Adrian was beaming. "Wow, Grandpa, this is amazing!" He leapt off Rizzo and petted her, then sent her back to the stable with the others.

"Oh, it gets better," Darwin replied while looking at the arena, where three big metal balls with four spikes protruding from all sides began floating around the arena, each on a different level while one ball circled the flag.

Sara stared at the arena and worry began to set in. She looked over at Darwin, who gave her a reassuring look and told her that they would be fine, but that didn't seem to make Sara feel any better. Liz looked over to Sara and told her, "Darwin wouldn't put anything in there that would hurt them." That seemed to comfort Sara a little more. Liz then reached for Sara and they both teleported to the top of the tower.

"Alright, Bianca, since you are the most experienced, I want you guarding the flag, which means that you can start on whichever level you want," Darwin instructed. She didn't waste any time teleporting into the arena where she knew the twins couldn't see her.

Darwin huddled with the boys. "Both of you have to start on the third level and make your way down." Adrian and Andrew both grew anxious to start. "Make sure you both start on opposite sides of each other," he added before he went to join Sara and the others up in the tower.

"I call left!" Andrew told Adrian. Before Adrian could respond, Andrew was already in the arena.

"Yeah, that's fair," Adrian said to himself before he teleported inside.

A few minutes passed before a loud horn sounded, signaling that the training session had started. Andrew, the better strategist, waited patiently for Adrian to make the first move, which didn't take long. Andrew peeked out from behind the wall and saw Adrian running to the ledge right across from him and jumping off. However, he didn't quite make it to the level below because Bianca fired off a stunning spell that hit Adrian midair, sending him back to his starting point. Andrew's patience paid off, as he saw where Bianca was hiding and pointed his wand at her rapidly. He fired off the same stunning spell that pushed her into the fence on the edge of the arena, giving him enough time to float to the second level.

"Did he just float?" Liz was stunned at how effortlessly he did it.

"That's very impressive." Darwin was surprised by what he had just witnessed.

Meanwhile, Adrian was finally back on his feet. He ran over to the other side of the third level where Andrew started from and looked around until he saw the spiked ball coming his way. He waited and then leapt onto it, sliding off the side a bit, but he quickly grasped one of the spikes and pulled himself into a sitting position. All that weight training must have been paying off; he was perfectly hidden behind the ball as it circled the arena. Adrian was perfectly still, holding onto the spike as the ball circled around, grateful that he had put more time into core training lately. Adrian noticed another ball coming his way, circling the arena counterclockwise. He timed his transition perfectly and let go of the spike that he had been holding on to, dropping effortlessly onto the second-level spiked ball and getting into the same position to remain out of view.

As Adrian circled the arena, he could see that the flag was right below him. He looked around, making sure that no one saw him, and positioned himself to make one final leap, then released his grip so he could drop down to the spiked ball on the first level, the same one the flag was located on. As he positioned himself, once again letting his chin rest slightly over the spike sticking out of the big round metal ball, his arms began to jiggle, undoubtedly tired from supporting all his weight as he jumped from ball to ball. Adrian realized that he wouldn't be able to hold on much longer; he released his grip one last time and dropped down to level one.

Bianca spotted him and tried to teleport but was blasted back into the fence. She smirked, knowing instantly Adrian had spotted her and cast a defensive spell prohibiting her from stopping him.

"HA! Didn't expect that, did ya?" Adrian shouted.

"Oh, ok. I see you're overly confident in your abilities now. Maybe Andrew being better at magic is making you up your game a little, huh?" Bianca regained her footing, started running, and leapt off the ground, trying to catch the metal ball circling the first level, but it didn't work for her like it did Adrian; she jumped too soon and hit the ball, quickly falling back to the ground. Andrew saw what was going on, decided to cast his own turnabout spell, and flew around the arena, taking cover behind one of the metal balls so that no spells could hit him.

Adrian was still trying to figure out how to remove the flag from its protective shield when he saw that Andrew had made it to the same level. Andrew looked Adrian's way, giving him a condescending smirk, and ran behind a wall for cover. Andrew looked at the flag and noticed it was placed behind a protective shield. He looked over to where he saw Adrian but couldn't see him anymore. He glanced back at the flag, but before he could do anything, Adrian was behind him, pointing his wand and yelling, "*LANUAE MAGICAE!*" teleporting Andrew back to the level they started on.

Adrian ran toward the flag, pointed his wand at it, and yelled "*DIMITTAM!*" The protective shield shattered, and he claimed the flag, looked up to the tower, and waved the flag in the air, declaring victory. Unfortunately, he didn't see Bianca coming, who snatched the flag from his hand while riding one of the metal balls that had proved to be extremely useful. As Adrian watched his cousin circle the arena, he couldn't help but smile at his defeat. Bianca jumped off the ball and ran toward her cousins who were now by each other, and the arena started disappearing around them.

Sara and Chloe looked on in amazement at what they just witnessed. For them, this was all new, but Sara was proud. She looked at her boys, encouraging them to continue. Adrian was the first to notice, followed by Andrew who looked up at her, glad to see she was happy.

However, Darwin noticed that Chloe's smile was dry. He could sense she felt left out. He reached out his hands so Chloe and Sara could hold on to him and teleported back to the field next to the twins and Bianca.

"That was impressive! All of you were very impressive," Darwin said, and Liz nodded her head in agreement.

"I'm starving," Adrian blurted out, surprising no one.

Darwin glanced at everyone. "I suppose we should get back for dinner now. I'm sure Hekabe cooked up a feast worthy of the holiday."

They teleported back to the house, Sara and Chloe grabbing on to Darwin once more.

Back at the house, everyone smelled the food that Hekabe had prepared. The twins and Chloe all ran upstairs to get cleaned up and changed for dinner.

"Adrasteia called. She said to tell you she has what you need," Hekabe informed Darwin while Sara, Bianca, and Liz looked on.

"What does Adrasteia have?" Liz inquired.

"She has the ingredients for a recall spell." Darwin told her.

"I heard those spells are dangerous. Don't they cause people to have mental breakdowns and suffer from really bad headaches?" Bianca chimed in.

"They could be, but Adrasteia is an expert at potions—more so than I am—so I'll be ok," Darwin reassured her.

"Is it worth the risk?" Liz asked.

"I have to do anything I can to prevent Gabriel from locating the crystals. But I need to know where to look. And since Huckabee made sure I wouldn't remember, a recall spell is the only option, I'm afraid."

No one said another word since Adrian was the first downstairs. Everyone started making their way to the dinner table to enjoy the beautiful, delicious Thanksgiving dinner Hekabe made for them. They feasted on turkey, stuffing, yams, sweet potatoes, and, of course, pasta for the twins. After dinner, everyone was sitting at the table, too bloated to move, when Darwin said, "Chloe, can you follow me, my dear?" He pushed his chair from the table and stood up, waiting for her. She got up and they both headed upstairs to his office.

"I know that this might be a lot to take in, or that you might feel left out. But I want you to know that you are a big part of this family, no matter what," he told her as they entered his office. "Please take a seat," he instructed as he reached over his desk to grab something.

"Grandpa, I promise I'm fine," she said, hoping that would keep him from seeing that she was a little jealous.

"Nonetheless, I wanted to give you something." He handed her a box. "What is this?"

"You have to open it to find out, my dear."

Chloe opened the box to see a necklace similar to the ones the twins and her sister had, only hers was pink. "Wow. This is beautiful," Chloe marveled, still looking at it.

"It's our family crest, so to speak. We all have one," he said while pulling his out from under his robe.

Chloe looked at him, tears starting to well in her eyes. She was overcome with joy knowing that her grandfather was doing all he could to make her feel like she belonged. "Thank you, it's beautiful."

"A family is more than just flesh and blood. It's heart that makes us a family, and you take up a big spot right here," he said as he pointed to his chest.

Chloe leaned over and gave him a hug. "Thank you." She wiped away tears from her eyes.

Together, they went back downstairs to rejoin the family.

Chapter Fourteen

It was a cool, crisp night and Brad strolled up the path to Bianca's door. He rang the doorbell and patiently waited for someone to let him in.

"Can someone get the door?!" yelled Bianca from her bedroom. Chloe took her time to get to the front door.

"Hey, Clo." Brad entered the foyer and, like always, found himself waiting for his girlfriend.

"She's still getting ready. I swear, she's acting like it's your guys' first date or something."

He went over to the couch after realizing it would still take a bit longer for Bianca to come down, but he prepared for that by telling her to be ready at an earlier time so they could actually be on time. After all, ever since Brad and Bianca started dating, she had never been on time for anything.

"We haven't seen each other in a while. And it took me a while to get ready, too," Brad joked, giving Chloe a wink.

"Hey, sweetie!" Bianca raced down the stairs to greet him.

She looked stunning, as always. Dressed casually in dark jeans and a gray sweater with her hair down, just like Brad liked it. He met her at the bottom step and gave her a peck on the lips.

"Hi, babe," he whispered softly. Chloe just stared at them.

"You know you guys saw each other, like, four days ago, right?" heckled Chloe as she brushed by them, making her way up stairs.

Bianca wasn't amused. Once Chloe was out of sight, Bianca turned to Brad and kissed him. The kiss was passionate, but they were interrupted by Liz.

"What do you guys have planned tonight?"

Brad quickly stepped back, wiping his lips. "Movies and then back to my place for dinner."

"I forgot to tell you!" Bianca stepped down the last step to get her keys and glanced over to Liz. "I'm just going to stay at Brad's tonight, Mom."

"Ok, *be careful*," Liz mouthed as she took a magazine from the coffee table. Brad and Bianca sauntered hand in hand out the door toward his car.

"UGH. She acts like they never see each other," Chloe grunted as she barged into her room. She looked out of her bedroom window with her phone in her hand.

"Aww, young love," Collin's voice echoed from her phone, sounding staticky as he mocked them. "You can't make fun of them for that."

Chloe jumped on her bed and looked directly into the phone. "I didn't know you were the romantic type." A sarcastic grin surfaced on her face.

"As much fun as video chatting with you is, you caught me at a bad time. I have to go help my mom with something." Collin informed her.

"Oh, well, here I thought you were going to tell me some love stories," Chloe jokingly said, giving Collin a dazzling stare.

"Bye, Chloe," Collin replied.

Chloe, radiating joy, softly replied. "Bye, Romeo."

Collin and Chloe had been talking a lot more over the past few weeks, something that Chloe really enjoyed. She never thought they would have gotten to be such good friends, but Collin had been the one person she could talk to when she found out everything about herself and her family. He was compassionate and sweet toward her after the news, which only made her feelings for him intensify. Chloe knew they wouldn't be more than friends, but she was surprisingly ok with that. She pointed her remote at the shelf across the room and music began to play.

THE next day, Andrew and Adrian made plans to hang out with some friends and were at home waiting for Dean, Lisa, and Collin to arrive.

"Tell Mom we need milk!" Andrew shouted from the kitchen. As Andrew rushed toward Adrian, who just hung up the phone, he questioned his brother, "Did you tell her?"

"She heard you," Adrian responded. "So…" he added, looking at his brother. Andrew wondered what his brother had to tell him. "Go on."

"I've been practicing moving things in the woods. It started with branches and other small stuff, but yesterday I moved this big boulder that was blocking a path. It was awesome," Adrian told an annoyed-looking Andrew.

"Adrian, you're not supposed to be doing that out in the open! What if someone saw you?" Andrew chastised, a little more irritated with his brother's disregard of the rules their mom and grandfather asked them to go by.

Adrian bellowed, "Relax, Drew, no one saw me! Besides, where else are we supposed to practice and get better?" Now Adrian was starting to get annoyed. He knew there was a reason he had been hesitant to tell his brother.

"That still doesn't change the fact that it's risky for you to do that in the open! Besides, we practice at Grandpa's, not here where people could see us. At home we are supposed to read the books Grandpa gave us," Andrew stated. *When did I become the more responsible one?* he wondered.

"Oh my god. That's your problem—you never have any fun or take any risks. It's always about reading and following the rules." Adrian rolled his eyes and started walking toward the window to see if their friends were there.

"Yeah. That's it. You know—" But before Andrew could say anything else, Adrian cut him off.

"Save your lecture, DAD! They're here."

Andrew's face reddened as he rubbed the back of his neck. They wouldn't be able to finish their conversation today, but knowing there wasn't anything he could do now, he simply ran up the stairs to grab his jacket while Adrian let their friends in. As they made their way inside, Collin let Adrian know what the plans for the night were.

"We decided to go to Francisco's for dinner. Are you guys ready?"

"Yeah, Drew is just grabbing his jacket."

Collin nervously suggested, "Call Chloe and tell her to come with! We could pick her up on the way."

"Ah, so you and Chloe, huh?" Adrian joked.

"Shut up. We just got closer as friends." Collin's cheeks turned a slight rosy red and he playfully pushed him, hoping that would make Adrian back off.

"Guys are so scared to tell a girl how they feel," Lisa teased, mocking the two of them.

"Whatever," was all Collin could say, hoping that would be the end of it. Fortunately for him, Andrew came back down, so they were ready to leave. As they approached Collin's car, Adrian called Chloe to invite her out to dinner. Naturally, she said yes, and they picked her up.

Francisco's was a little busier than normal, so the wait for a table was going to be twenty to thirty minutes. No one seemed to mind the wait, though; Francisco's was the best Italian restaurant in town. The walls were made of brick all around and had elegant paintings from Italy hanging on them. The booths were black leather and lined the walls on both sides. The tables in the middle of the restaurant were covered in cream-colored tablecloths with black leather chairs surrounding them.

The lighting was dim, and the restaurant was filled with background noise of all the patrons having conversations with one another. Knowing that the wait was going to be a while, Collin walked over to Chloe, who was conversing with Adrian.

"Hey." Collin looked to Adrian. "Sorry to interrupt you guys, but I was hoping I could have a few words with Chloe." He soon realized that asking her to talk by themselves wouldn't help keep Adrian off his back about his feelings for her. Collin looked at Adrian, who just nodded and stared at the two of them, finally turning to join his brother.

"He's so immature." Chloe blushed.

"How you holding up after the long weekend at Hogwarts?" he teased. Chloe let out a chortle, thrown off by his bluntness.

Chloe lowered the tone of her voice to a whisper. "Good. It was a lot of fun. A little weird to see what they could all do, but still fun. It's just a little hard to get used to the fact that a world like that exists."

"Yeah, tell me about it. I'm still trying to wrap my head around all that." Collin looked over to the twins, who were having their own conversation.

Chloe affectionately stared at him. She had to tell herself over and over that he was just a friend, but Collin was making it hard for her by being dependable and extremely nice. She even thought, just for a second, that maybe he was developing feelings for her as well. However, that was quickly squashed when Collin had asked about Lisa the other day.

Chloe and Collin continued talking until Andrew informed them that their table was ready. As Chloe inched closer to Collin, he put his hand on her arm to let her go by first. That simple soft touch sent chills coursing through her body. She led the way, imagining what kissing him would be like. After all, her imagination was all she had since she knew they would never be anything more than friends.

✳ ✳ ✳

THE next day in Polaris, Darwin was casually strolling through the streets of the capital, saying hi to those who recognized him as he passed. The people of Avalon, with a few exceptions, were very polite in that way. He continued on his way until he reached that familiar street with the delicious-smelling bakery on it. He headed in the direction of Adrasteia's shop but was called into a small walkway squeezed between two buildings by a short, stocky older man.

"Alistair! How are you, my old friend?" Darwin inquired as he looked over his shoulder to make sure no one saw where he went. Alistair made sure it was all clear before he spoke.

"Word is Gabriel is having a difficult time finding out how to read the map," Alistair replied, his voice hoarse,

A feeling of hope started to rush over Darwin. "Good. Hopefully, that will buy me enough time so I can get to it first."

"I don't understand why you don't take this matter to the council," Alistair questioned.

"Because Adele has Barnabas wrapped around her pretty little finger. And the council members that aren't afraid of her won't do anything without hard proof showing that Gabriel is, in fact, after the elder crystals."

"Makes sense, I suppose. I still find it hard to believe that Adele could be working with Gabriel without there being any proof of the matter." Alistair glanced over to Darwin, hoping he would reveal any kind of evidence he may have had.

"Yes, I know. They do well to cover their tracks. And like I said before, I can't go accusing the chancellor's number two of anything without hard evidence. But we can worry about that later; the priority right now is stopping Gabriel from getting the crystals," Darwin replied cautiously, glancing over his shoulder once more.

"Very well. Good luck, old friend. I will keep you posted on what I find out," Alistair quipped before he teleported out from between the buildings.

147

Darwin exited the walkway the way he entered and continued to Adrasteia's shop. He finally arrived in front of her building, opened the door, letting himself in. The bell on top of the door rang and brought Adrasteia out of the stock room.

They met at the counter and Darwin was the first to speak. "Were you able to find everything I need?"

"O' course," Adrasteia replied, her words muffled by the banana muffin she was consuming.

"Great, thank you for acquiring these items for me. It's greatly appreciated."

"I suggest ye think long an' hard aboot doing it. Now, before ye get all huffy wi' me, I'm not here tae tell ye what to do or try tae talk ye oot of it; I just want ye tae be careful. This spell is very risky, even fer a skilled wizard such as yerself." Adrasteia stared at him before going into the stockroom. Darwin thought about what she said as she disappeared into the back.

After a few minutes, she came back out to the counter holding a black box in her hand.

The box itself was pure iron and appeared to be heavy. As she set it down on the counter in front of Darwin, it made a loud *thud* and she thought the weight of it would surely go right through the counter. She made sure it was secured, then placed her hand on top of it.

"Thar is only enough fer one try, so ye have tae get it right the first time."

"I intend to," Darwin replied as he looked from the box back to Adrasteia.

A few seconds passed before that familiar sound of the bell ringing echoed through the shop. Darwin and Adrasteia looked over at the same time to see who it was. Darwin's expression changed to that of aggravation at the sight of who entered. The way the light from the chandelier hanging above hit her face magnified her beauty. He could see why Barnabas was so infatuated with her. There Adele stood between two council guards with a smug look on her face, as if she knew Darwin was doing something he shouldn't be.

Darwin grew more frustrated. "What brings you here, Adele?" The authority in his voice sent chills through the guards; they did not want a confrontation with him.

Adele slowly strolled across the shop, casually glancing at the shelves. "Something was brought to my attention —" she stared directly at Darwin"— so I figured I would look into it."

"I see." Darwin met her glare with one of his own. "You took it upon yourself to investigate something that the council guard could easily handle themselves?" Darwin stared at her with a condescending expression. "How very astute of you," he said, knowing full well that she knew of his plan. Darwin was going over the people in his mind who knew about his meeting with Adrasteia but could not pinpoint the source of the leak. After all, everyone he told, he trusted. This puzzled him, but he couldn't do anything about it. Now, he was more concerned with how to get out of the mess he was soon to be in. Should he teleport out of Polaris and run from the council, or should he stand by and see how it plays out? He couldn't decide; both ways could produce bad outcomes, so he stood where he was and waited for Adele to show her hand.

Adele gave her own condescending stare right back. "I wouldn't be in the position I'm in if I weren't so astute, Darwin. So, what's in the box?" Adele interrogated as she inched closer to the counter.

In that moment, Darwin knew exactly why Adele was there. He also knew that if he ran, his entire family would be targets of the council guard, and he couldn't afford that—not now.

Darwin's frustration was obvious. "We both know the answer to that question already," he spoke unflinchingly "so let's not play this game." He glanced directly at Adrasteia.

Adrasteia, I need you to do something else for me. We don't have much time, so I have to be quick, Darwin thought so only Adrasteia could hear.

What do ye need me tae do?

First, go to my house and check for bugs or any listening devices. If you find any, destroy them. Then go to Liz's and tell her what has happened and help her scan her house for bugs as well.

Are ye sure 'at is the right thing tae do? Shouldn't I go directly tae Liz so she can start the process tae get ye oot of the Tower? Adrasteia asked, her strong Scottish accent echoing in his mind.

There will be time for that later. I have a feeling none of that will matter anyway, because Adele will make sure I'm kept in the Tower long enough for Gabriel to find the Alexandro's Crystal.

Then why not just take care of these guards an' teleport oot of here? It's not like anybody in this room can keep ye from leavin', Adrasteia told him as she got into a defensive stance. Such a loyal friend to Darwin, ready to do battle for him and the greater good.

Doing that will cause more problems than my family needs right now. Besides, I have a feeling Gabriel isn't any closer to figuring out how to read the map, so I think I have some time to see how this goes.

Very well. I will do what ye ask.

And Adrasteia, if you don't find any bugs, that means they are getting their information elsewhere. Darwin tilted his head and made strong eye contact with her. He knew as well as Adrasteia that Gabriel was getting his information from somewhere or someone, but who?

Unfortunately, he didn't have time to dwell on that question much longer.

Adele marched up to the counter and opened the box without saying a word. When the contents of the box were revealed, she simply smiled and turned to face Darwin. In the box was a substance that was illegal for anyone to have. "Are you going to come willingly?" she inquired as she summoned her wand she desperately wanted to use.

Darwin looked at Adrasteia, who already had her wand hidden behind her back as if she were preparing to use it.

"Can you hold onto this, my dear?" Darwin asked her as he handed her his cane.

Adrasteia took it with her free hand and didn't say a word.

I still say ye wipe tha floor with this bampot an' get the heck oot of here, Adrasteia thought as she glanced at Darwin, who just winked at her.

"Guards. Take him to the Tower," Adele ordered. She was thrilled.

As the guards escorted Darwin out of the shop, Adele stayed back. "I can't wait for the day ye get what's coming to ye," Adrasteia told her. Adele just smirked and left the shop.

Adrasteia quickly ran to the door before the bells could stop ringing and locked it. She stood there watching as Adele led the guards toward the Tower. This angered Adrasteia; Adele could have easily teleported him to the Tower, but what fun would that have been when she could make Darwin suffer the embarrassment of all the stares from the onlookers he was surely going to pass?

Adrasteia rushed back to the counter, grabbed Darwin's cane, and teleported from her shop in a hurry.

Chapter Fifteen

drasteia teleported inside Darwin's home, startling Nigel, who happened to be cleaning up and dropped the dishes in his hands. "Dear god, woman! Are you trying to give me a heart attack?" His voice trembled and his body shook as he asked.

"My apologies, Nigel," she told him as she went to the chimney to grab two handfuls of leftover ash.

Dumfounded, Nigel inquired, "What exactly are you doing?"

Moving around frantically, Adrasteia was barely paying attention to him. "I…" She glanced around. "I—I need tae check for bugs."

"I can assure you, madam," Nigel said as he stiffened up and placed his hands behind his back, insulted over what he just heard, "that you will not find any bugs in this house. I clean daily, and—"

"Ugh, listening bugs, ye bampot!" She interrupted him before he could finish his sentence and kept fidgeting with her ingredients.

"Listening bugs? Do you really think someone would dare put such things inside Darwin's home?" Nigel moved cautiously back a few steps, glancing around the room. Listening bugs were the most unpleasant things to see. They oozed a nauseating green slime as they moved around. They were about an inch long and wide, purplish, and resembled a caterpillar with little ear-like arms protruding down the spine of their back.

She began to tell Nigel what happened to Darwin and why he asked her to come to his home. Nigel began to stutter; he was having a difficult time trying to find the right words to say. Darwin being taken like that was the last thing he ever thought would happen.

Adrasteia rushed into the kitchen and went directly to the counter. She opened the cabinet, shoving things to the side until she spotted what she needed. She snatched a small, faded black mixing bowl made from clay and put the ash inside. She slid over to another cabinet, running her fingers through a wide variety of items, grabbing the other ingredients she needed to add to the ash. She mixed it all together with a spoon and marched to the center of the sitting room.

She began to pour the contents in a circle around her until the bowl was empty. She sat on her knees in the center of the circle and mumbled a few words. Not even Nigel could hear what she was saying, and he was standing a few inches from her. Before long, the circle of blackish ash turned an aqua blue and began to rise from the floor. It moved and expanded slowly and went right through Nigel, who was just watching it. As it expanded through the length of the house, it extended through the walls and outside. The circle rose up the sides of the house until nothing, but air was inside the circle, and then it disappeared. Back in the house, Adrasteia looked directly at the spot in front of her.

"Nothing." She let out a sigh. It would have been a gross sight if listening bugs were found, but she still wished for it, as the alternative was much worse. "Nothing at all."

Nigel stared at her. "Isn't that good news?"

"No. Unless there's a bug at Liz's place, he is getting his information from someone," she whispered as she leaned on a chair. The thought of someone betraying Darwin rattled her.

"What now?" Nigel asked, similarly concerned over someone being disloyal.

"I have te go te Liz's and do the same thing." She stood up straight, realizing she had to be quick.

"What can I do?" Nigel asked.

"Tell Hekabe that I need te see her as soon as possible." She rushed out the front door. "And don't repeat anything 'at happened here te anyone!" she added as her voice started to fade from earshot. Adrasteia liked teleporting outdoors, feeling it was more respectful.

"I'm not a gossip," Nigel told her with a bit of hostility in his voice. He didn't like being told the obvious.

Adrasteia teleported away then, leaving Nigel standing there with a suspicious look expressed on his face. A few minutes later, Adrasteia appeared in her office at the school and took out a vial from her desk. As she made her way around the empty school, she poured little drops from the vial where she had cast protection spells. The first drop lit up and disappeared as soon as it touched the floor, indicating that the spell was still working. She rushed to each other spot to do the same thing, and when she got to the last one, the drop from the vial didn't disappear when it hit the floor. She dropped another one, and still nothing happened.

A noise caught her attention, and she summoned her wand. She slowly inched toward where the noise came from, cautiously investigating each doorway until she reached the end of the hall. She put her wand away when she realized that no one was there, returning her attention to the last protection spot to recast the spell. When she turned the corner, she was hit by a stunning spell that threw her sixteen feet down the hall. She quickly recovered and yelled out, *"Tutor Scutum!"* and a transparent purple shield deflected another spell that was about to hit her.

"Only three o' youse?" Adrasteia cautiously approached. "I'm insulted 'at Gabriel would think so little o' me!" she called out as she saw three wizards walking casually toward her.

"I personally think this is overkill, but who am I to argue with the boss?" said one overconfident wizard.

"Momento Mortis!" Adrasteia shouted as she pointed her wand directly at the mouthy wizard, who fell to the ground, dead, and instantly started decaying. The other two wizards shot spells at her that she quickly defended against. Before they could fire off anything else, she flung her wand right and left quickly, sending the remaining wizards to opposite sides of the wall. One quickly got back on his feet but was sent down again by the same spell that got the first wizard. Now two bodies lay on the floor, decomposing.

As the final wizard got up, Adrasteia stunned him, sending him flying through the side doors of the school. She quickly teleported to where he landed and watched him try to crawl away while pleading for his life.

"Dinnae worry." She casually approached. "I need ye tae give Gabriel a message fer me," she told him as they both stopped moving.

The man was in excruciating pain. "What message?" he asked her, his voice trembling in fear. *Why did Gabriel only send us three? She's too strong!* he wondered.

"The school is aff limits! Now get oot o' me sight!" she said forcefully as she pointed her wand at him, teleporting him away from the school.

Adrasteia raced back inside the school, waved her hand, and the two bodies moved toward each other. Pointing her wand at the lifeless corpses, she yelled, *"Transporta!"* and the bodies were gone. She breathed a sigh of relief. "I'm gettin' tae old fer this," she muttered, sounding winded.

✳ ✳ ✳

THE next morning, Adrasteia went to see Liz and told her everything that had happened yesterday, which shocked and angered Liz.

"Why would Gabriel risk killing you? He must see you as a threat."

"I'm no threat te Gabriel. That was Adele's doing, just like what is going on with Darwin."

"I will ask for a special hearing to get him out. I don't even know how the rest of the council is letting Adele get away with these things," Liz said.

Adrasteia moved closer to Liz. "She 'as the chancellor wrapped 'round her pretty wee finger."

"I wish Mom were back already. She has been unreachable for the past few months." Liz pushed her hair behind her ear. She always did that when she was stressed, and not hearing from her mother left her worried.

Adrasteia looked at Liz. "Negotiating treaties and protecting our interest abroad is time consuming"

"Yes. Adele planned all of this very well." She perked up then, her heart beginning to beat faster. *Could something have happened to Mom?*

"Do ye think ye could get Darwin oot soon?" Adrasteia wondered, seeing how worried Liz looked. She hoped her question would bring her back to the task at hand.

"Those laws haven't been enforced on council members for years, so I'm hoping that I can explain that to the magistrate," Liz answered, slowly focusing again on what was going on with Darwin.

"Well, they wanted Darwin oot o' the way, and they found oot a way tae do it." Adrasteia felt uneasy about the entire situation. She, too, is worried but doesn't allow herself to focus on that.

"We need to find out how they are getting their information, and soon," Liz stated.

Liz packed her bag and headed to the capital for Darwin's hearing. She would be the one representing him since it was an emergency. Besides, she wouldn't trust anyone else with   something as important as this. Adrasteia wished her luck, and off she went. When Liz arrived at   the high court building, she was met by Adele, who greeted her warmly. Liz was quickly aggravated by the sight of her but didn't let it show.

Adele now walked side by side with her. "I guess Darwin was investing in his future when he sent you to law school. Are you sure you are up to date on Avalon law?" Adele questioned in a condescending tone. She hated outsiders and Liz was one, no matter her lineage.

"Oh, please, Adele." Liz tried to get ahead of her, speeding up to a brisk pace. "We both know these charges are ridiculous and without merit and will not hold up. I'm sure whoever is arguing this case for you knows that and will just give him a fine and let him go," Liz snapped at her, brushing her off like she didn't matter.

"I can tell you right now that the only thing I know is that Darwin broke the law, and I will be sure to point that out to the magistrate." This caused Liz to stop in her tracks.

Liz shouldn't have been surprised that Adele would be the one handling this case. She simply went into the courtroom, not showing that she was bothered by what Adele just blurted out. The Avalon courts somewhat resembled the courts back home, which comforted Liz since it had been a while since she was in an Avalon court. As she entered the courtroom, she was met by one of her former classmates sitting at the magistrate's bench.

"Calvin," Liz asked, surprised to see him sitting there. He hadn't been the brightest student back in school.

"Liz." Calvin looked surprised to see her. "How nice it is to see you after all these years!" He glanced over and saw none other than the vice chancellor. "And Lady Adele, did I read the brief right? Are you arguing on behalf of the nation of Avalon?"

"Given the nature of the offense, the chancellor thought it best if I handled this case."

"Ok. Shall we begin, then?" he questioned as he took his seat. The charges against Lord Darwin are a little bit of a stretch. Aren't they?" Calvin wondered as he flipped through the parchment in front of him. He was surprised at the fact that it was even brought to his court. "Hmm…" Calvin stared intently at the charges. "I suppose it is against the law for council members to possess certain ingredients—" He finally looked up at them.

"Your Magistrate, that law has never really been enforced. I feel that Darwin is being treated unfairly and therefore should be released immediately. After all, those ingredients could have been used for other spells as well. Did you ever take that into consideration?" Liz asked as she glanced over at Adele.

"Council Member Darwin is a high-ranking official who has been on certain assignments that unfortunately required precautions to be taken in order to ensure secrecy. Furthermore, he has signed agreements to that effect," Adele stated firmly as she approached the desk and handed Calvin the proper documents.

"I need to see those and confer with my client," Liz interjected as she watched the magistrate look over the stack of parchment given to him.

"We will gladly wait for Ms. Gabarra to do that. We only ask that Lord Darwin not be released in the meantime," Adele demanded. She didn't care about the process; she just wanted Darwin out of the way.

"Ugh. WOW!" Liz couldn't believe the outrageous request that she just heard. "That is low, even for you. There is no reason why my client shouldn't be released from the Tower. What Lady Adele is requesting is ridiculous. The charges do not call for that level of punishment," Liz responded, boiling with anger that her father was taken to the Tower over charges that had no merit.

Adele sensed that Liz was proving her point effectively and spoke more firmly, "Lord Darwin's skill level and this vendetta he has toward his son makes him a risk to be let out." Feeling that she was losing, she was left with no choice. "The chancellor also requests that you take into account his position on this matter." Adele slowly looked over to Calvin, hoping that would nudge him in the right direction.

"Which is?" Calvin inquired, surprised the chancellor had an opinion on the matter.

"That…" Adele glanced between both the magistrate and Liz. "That he should be kept in the Tower."

A few seconds went by before Calvin issued his ruling.

"Lord Darwin will remain in the Tower," Calvin ordered hesitantly. The magistrate wouldn't think of going against the chancellor of Avalon. Adele was right to bring that up.

This angered Liz, but she knew she couldn't do anything about it. She looked over to Adele, who was already walking out, and knew that this was going exactly how Gabriel wanted it to.

Liz quickly packed up her belongings, rushed toward the exit, and asked the guard to have Darwin waiting in a consultation room for her. Before she left, she went to file paperwork necessary to speed the process along so that they could get a trial date set. Liz couldn't help but think that this was the perfect way to keep Darwin out of Gabriel's way. She didn't want to admit it, but she felt very strongly that she wouldn't succeed in time for Darwin to be let free to deal with her brother.

Once the paperwork was filed, Liz teleported to the gates of the Tower. Since no one could teleport directly into or out of the Tower proper, that was the furthest she could go using magic. The enchantments used to make sure that couldn't happen were extraordinarily strong and no wizard, not even the chancellor, could get through that. As Liz went from the gates to the entrance, she kept asking herself why Darwin didn't just teleport from Adrasteia's shop knowing all that he did.

She was taken directly to where Darwin was waiting and instructed the guard that there were to be no interruptions during her visit. The guard agreed and closed the door behind him.

Liz sat directly in front of her father. "Dad. I'm sorry to say that I don't come with good news." Liz couldn't look him in the eye. "This plan of theirs is working perfectly for them."

Darwin was upset, but he had expected as much. "That isn't important right now." He reached for Liz's hands. "These charges won't hold," he reassured her. "I need you to find Huckabee's vice chancellor, Lester Sterling. He might know or have information about where that map leads. The only thing we have going for us is that Gabriel is having trouble reading it."

Holding her father's hands, Liz wondered, "Why didn't you just run from Adrasteia's shop?" She was annoyed that she got bested in court today.

"Because they would have gone after the family. I couldn't have that." Darwin squeezed her hands tighter, trying to comfort her. "Everyone has been through so much as it is. Besides, I have faith in my people to find it before they do."

Liz was hesitant to feel as confident as Darwin; if it was so easy to find Huckabee's number two, he would have done it himself. They talked for a few more hours and he instructed Liz not to rest until Lester was found.

Darwin told her that he was a hard man to track down but that there were a few spells that might help with that. They both knew, however, that Lester was an immensely powerful wizard and had stayed hidden for so long because those spells didn't work.

Neither of them wanted to admit defeat before they even tried, so both sat there in silence waiting for the other to speak, but that time never came, as it was time for Liz to leave. They exchanged hugs and Liz went on her way.

The next day, Liz met with Adrasteia in her office at the school to tell her what she and Darwin talked about.

"Lester is a powerful wizard, dear. Finding 'im willnae be easy. After all, the locater spells that I would use, he invented," Adrasteia told her. She felt it in her gut that they would not succeed, but she didn't want to say it out loud. Liz was already overstressed.

"There *has* to be a way to find him. Maybe family members or something?" Liz asked, hopeful that Darwin's faith in them wasn't ill-conceived.

"Only family he 'ad was a mother and sister, who were both killed."

Adrasteia didn't have to tell Liz who killed them; Liz already knew, though it was never proven. They sat in silence for a few minutes, each thinking of a way to try to find him.

Unfortunately, they both had no idea how.

"Well, we have to start somewhere. I'll get Bianca on it as soon as I get home," Liz finally replied.

"Good. Ye need tae focus on gettin' Darwin oot o' the Tower."

"Easier said than done. I have to admit, Adele planned this out perfectly."

"An' o' course, yer father is too noble o' a man tae have run away."

"He didn't want to put the family at risk by running." She agreed Darwin should have fled when Adele showed up to the shop.

"Oh, please. Adele would 'ave nothin' tae come after youse with," Adrasteia told her.

"Why couldn't he just kill Gabriel when he had the chance?" Liz looked at Adrasteia, who was caught off guard by what she heard. As evil as Gabriel was, he was still Liz's brother. Surely Liz had some feelings for him deep down inside. The bell rang throughout the school, signaling that the halls would soon be full of students.

As Adrasteia stared at Liz, she realized Liz had no regrets over her statement. She could see the anger and sadness expressed on her face along with frustration. Adrasteia sat there a few more seconds, searching for the right words to say. After what seemed like an eternity, she finally said, "Fer the same reason he didnae run from Adele. It's not in 'is character."

That seemed to be the right thing to say, because Liz half smiled, and they both got up at the same time. As Adrasteia led Liz out into the hallways filled with all the students making their way to their next classes, they saw Adrian and Andrew looking over in their direction. The twins decided to go toward them, squeezing their way through the crowded halls until they were in front of their aunt and Adrasteia.

Andrew was surprised to see his aunt. "Hey, Aunt Liz! What are you doing here?"

"Just visiting," Liz replied, giving him a hug.

"Yeah. Don't buy it," Adrian teased, the lies becoming easier and easier to spot. Andrew quickly looked at his brother, wondering why he said that, but before Andrew could say anything, Liz asked them to go into Adrasteia's office. As Adrasteia and Liz followed them in, they exchanged a look with each other, silently agreeing that they had kept too much from them already.

After Liz filled them in on everything that had happened, Andrew and Adrian just sat there, not knowing what to say. Adrasteia saw that they looked worried and regretted letting Liz tell them. She came around her desk and got down to eye level with them. "Dinnae worry aboot Darwin. Yer aunt is an excellent lawyer an' will 'ave 'im oot soon."

"I didn't tell you to worry you both; I told you because we have kept a lot from you, and you deserve to know the truth. But please, do not worry. I promise all will be fine," Liz added.

"How is Bianca going to find this Lester guy? I mean, if he's so hard to find, how could she find him?" Adrian questioned. Bianca wasn't much older than them; how could she do something not even Liz or Adrasteia could?

"There is always a way. It will joost take a wee bit of thinkin' on our parts," Adrasteia replied, hoping to reassure them.

"Is there anything we could do?" Adrian asked, eager to help.

"Yeah. You both can get back to class. I will keep you guys updated throughout all of this, I promise," Liz told them, ushering them toward the door.

Adrian and Andrew exited Adrasteia's office and headed to class, but first they had to go to the student office to get passes for being late. Liz and Adrasteia looked on, both feeling bad for how much they were going through at such a young age.

Adrian, don't react, Andrew thought

Good god, Drew! You know I hate when you do that.

I might know of a way to find this Lester guy.

They just told us to stay out of it. Adrian thought.

Now you want to start listening to them? Didn't you tell me that I don't take any risks?

Andrew thought, remembering the conversation they had had the other day.

This is different. It's not practicing in the woods, Drew, it's serious.

Aren't you tired of being treated like kids? I'm not saying let's go break Grandpa out of the Tower. I'm simply saying I might know a way to find that Lester guy.

As they both stood at the counter waiting for their passes, they stopped talking for a minute. Andrew was just waiting for Adrian to say something.

How? Adrian finally thought.

There is this book in Grandpa's study that I saw. It had banned spells in it, and I remember seeing a section on finding lost things. Might be worth a look, Andrew thought.

Banned spells? That sounds safe. Adrian looked over at his brother incredulously. They were still new to this world, and casting spells from a book called "Banned Spells" might be a bit much for them.

Let's just go to Grandpa's after school and take a look. If we don't find anything, we can go back home and wait for Bianca to come up with something. Although, I'm sure she doesn't know about Grandpa's book.

He let out a frustrated grunt. *Fine,* Adrian reluctantly agreed.

"Here you boys go," said a front office employee handing them their passes.

As Adrasteia and Liz looked at them, they continued feeling bad. Liz finally said she had to go and hid behind Adrasteia's door before teleporting away. Adrasteia went back to watching the twins go toward their class until they were out of view.

THE clicking of her stiletto heels hitting the ground echoed as Adele made her way down the marble corridor toward her office in the capital building, her assistant walking fast to try and keep up with her. Adele commanded authority everywhere she went, and this was no different.

Employees of the capital building stayed clear of her; some were scared of her; some just chose to not come in contact with her. As Adele reached the staircase that led to her office, she stopped, turned to face her assistant, and told her she wasn't needed for the rest of the day, sending her on her way.

As Adele ascended the staircase, she knew who was waiting for her on the other side of her door. As she reached her office door, she hesitated for a second, looking around and making sure no one was close by. She opened her door and came in to find Gabriel sitting at a chair in front of her desk. She locked the door behind her and made her way to him.

"You know people already suspect we are working together." She strode to her desk. "Are you sure it's wise for you to be in my office?" Adele muttered as she took a seat, crossing her long legs.

"I couldn't wait to hear the news," Gabriel replied. He didn't care about how things looked. He was overly confident about what he could get away with.

"Darwin won't be a problem." Gabriel tried to hide the relief he felt. He couldn't show that he feared his father; after all, Darwin was possibly the strongest wizard of his time—with the exception of his own mother, of course. Showing any kind of fear was pure weakness.

"Excellent. Now I can continue my search without any interference from the old man," Gabriel, relieved now, stated, hoping he wouldn't have to kill Adele for noticing his moment of weakness.

"I'm assuming the shop owner is dealt with?" Adele inquired.

"Not quite, but I'm sure she won't be a problem," Gabriel reassured her.

"Not quite?" Adele repeated quizzically, confused at his reply. She thought Adrasteia would be dead by now.

"Oh, please. She is nothing and won't be a problem," Gabriel explained, aggravated over Adele's expression. *How dare she question me?*

"Adrasteia isn't nothing, Gabriel." Adele tried to regain his focus. "She could be a threat—that is why we agreed it was best to eliminate her."

Gabriel's anger at his number two consumed him. He hated being questioned. He contemplated the repercussions of killing Adele, making a pro and con list in his head. *She's a powerful ally—pro. Her position as vice chancellor has gone to her head. Hmm… what to do?* In the end, it was more beneficial to keep her alive.

It took him a bit of time to finally speak. "I can't spare any more men right now." This was incidentally also the reason he hadn't killed Adele in that moment.

Adele didn't quite understand what he meant. "What happened to the men you were going to send in the first place?" She knew they had failed but wanted him to confirm it. Even though she feared him a bit, she liked testing the limits.

Gabriel stood up; his anger noticeable over the questions Adele was asking. Perhaps it was because he felt foolish for having underestimated Adrasteia, or maybe because he felt that he didn't have to explain himself to Adele. Either way, Adele took that as a sign to stop asking questions.

"Good job with Darwin. I will keep you posted on my progress locating the crystal," Gabriel said, reminding himself that Adele was too valuable to kill. Adele just nodded and Gabriel teleported from her office.

Adele sat at her desk, worried over the possibility of Adrasteia becoming a problem. She knew that Gabriel always underestimated people because, according to him, no one was better than him and no one would ever be.

Chapter Sixteen

I t was a cool, crisp evening in Southport. The moon illuminated the dark sky, the trees swayed back and forth as the wind blew through the air, and Southport's unique citizens were flying through the skies to whatever destination they were headed.

"I don't think I will ever get used to seeing people flying in tornados," Andrew mumbled.

He chuckled over his own joke as he and his brother stood on the grounds of Darwin's estate. They had just convinced their mom to let them spend the weekend there.

"Drew, do you want to keep looking up at the sky, or can we get inside and get started on what we came here for?" Adrian was still frustrated with his brother's "rules" for how he should use his magic.

Without saying a word but while giving his brother a look of annoyance, Andrew led the way toward the front door of Darwin's house. When they reached the front door, they decided to ring the bell even though they both had keys so they wouldn't seem rude by just walking in. A few seconds went by before Nigel opened it.

"Hello, young masters," Nigel said as he stepped aside to let them in.

"Sorry for just showing up unannounced, but our visit was sort of last minute," Andrew informed him.

"Nonsense. No need to ever be sorry for coming to your home away from home."

"I thought I heard familiar voices," said an enthusiastic Hekabe coming into the foyer, grinning ear to ear. She gave both boys a warm embrace. "You must be famished!"

"No, you don't have to cook anything for us. Just pretend we aren't here," Adrian stated.

"Nonsense, boys, and it isn't up for debate. Besides, it won't take me more than thirty minutes to prepare some pasta with garlic bread," she told them as she pulled them into the kitchen.

Neither Andrew nor Adrian argued with her. They were quite hungry, and the thought of Hekabe's homemade pasta and bread made their stomachs growl. As they made their way into the kitchen, they took their seats at the counter while Hekabe gathered the items she needed from the cabinets.

"I placed some fresh towels on your beds," Nigel said as he went back into the kitchen.

He then proceeded to grab two cups from the cabinet above the sink. "What can I get you to drink?" he asked as he placed the cups in front of the twins.

"I got it." Adrian got up and headed over to the fridge. He and Andrew weren't used to getting waited on; that was probably the one thing they wouldn't get used to when they came to visit.

Once Hekabe had dinner prepared, she did something unusual for her and sat down with Adrian and Andrew to eat. That was the first time that she had ever joined them at the table since they had been coming to visit their grandfather. The twins were both surprised, but they seemed to enjoy the thought of having dinner with her. They asked Nigel if he was going to join them, but he decided against it and took his plate of food to his living quarters and ate it by himself.

"As always, Hekabe," Andrew said as he stared at the meal in front of him, "the food looks great."

Adrian nodded in agreement, for his mouth was already stuffed with Hekabe's delicious garlic bread.

Hekabe served them both a big plate of pasta and looked over at them like they were neglected puppies waiting at the pound for a warm home to go to. Adrian and Andrew, both played it off like they didn't notice. Their sole purpose for being there was so that they could get into Darwin's study and find the book they needed for the locator spell. The faster they ate, the faster they could get on with it. Unfortunately, Hekabe came right out with the question they knew was coming. They hoped it wouldn't come, but it did.

"How are you boys handling the Darwin situation?" she warmly asked.

"Ok, I guess. We know Aunt Liz will get him home soon," Adrian told her, fidgeting with his hands, avoiding eye contact. Even though Darwin told them that they could consider his home theirs, Adrian still felt like they were doing something wrong, being there under false pretenses.

"Well, if anybody can do it, it will be Liz. She is the smartest lawyer I have ever known," Hekabe said with enthusiasm. Andrew knew that Hekabe wouldn't just stop there. She would want to be certain that they were indeed ok and might find something else to talk about to keep them at the dinner table longer. He had to think of something fast to throw her off the "Darwin situation," as she called it.

"Do you think you could make us some cookies?" he asked, hoping it would change the topic.

"Of course, my young masters. I know the perfect ones, too! You finish up here and I will get started on them in a jiff," she told him as she got up from the table.

"Awesome. We will just go get cleaned up quick since we will be staying the night," Andrew said, but there was no point—Hekabe was mumbling to herself already what sounded like a list of ingredients as she rushed toward the cabinets.

"I wonder what kind she's going to make," Adrian wondered.

Andrew looked at him with frustration. *Hey, fatass, relax. Now we can go upstairs to get that book.* Adrian had forgotten for a second but got up from the table and led the way to the stairs.

"You know," pushing Adrian forward, Andrew looked up at him, "you keep eating like that and it will only be a matter of time before you lose your abs and need insulin injected into your veins. I'm sure coach wouldn't appreciate that," Andrew stated as he followed. *How can he eat so much?* he wondered.

Adrian glanced back at his brother. "You're such an ass." He placed his hand on his stomach, needing to reassure himself that he hadn't grown a belly.

They reached Darwin's study to find it was locked. Andrew placed his hand over the lock. As it clicked, he turned the doorknob and opened the door.

"Why can't we just teleport in?" Adrian inquired.

Andrew removed his hand from the lock. "Because this door blocks people from doing that. You think Grandpa would allow just anyone in there?"

"Oh!" Adrian was stunned but inquired further. "Isn't the plan to keep lookout and speak louder so you can teleport out?

"Ugh." Andrew hated being the one to pay attention to things. "It's ok to teleport *out*, idiot." Andrew glanced back at Adrian. "Because the spell doesn't work once inside. You really need to read the books Grandpa recommends." Andrew wasn't used to being the one in charge when it came to him and Adrian, but it was something he could get used to. Finally able to surpass his brother at something made him feel more like an "alpha," as Adrian would say. "Now keep lookout," he instructed Adrian as he entered Darwin's study. As he looked at his brother, he could tell Adrian was nervous. "Can you relax? It isn't like we are breaking into the Tower of Avalon or something."

"Just hurry up!" Adrian said.

Andrew closed the door behind him and paced slowly into the center of the room. He was always so fascinated by all the books that made a wall around Darwin's huge study. He went over to where he remembered seeing the book and ran his finger over each spine of the books, hoping to find the one he saw the last time he was there. As he passed from one to another, a feeling of anticipation rushed over him, for one day he hoped to read every single one of these books. He finally came across the one with the spell that he needed. He took hold of it with two hands; it was a little heavier than he remembered.

He returned to the door but before he could open it, he heard Adrian talking. The other voice was that of Nigel, who they thought had turned in for the night.

"You know, dear boy, you can go in if you'd like. I know it must be hard that your grandfather is locked in the Tower. He spent most of the time in that study of his," Nigel said, reminiscing about his master and how he missed him as well.

"Yeah. It is hard, but Aunt Liz reassured us that it was just some misunderstanding and that he will be out soon." Andrew knew Adrian wasn't just saying Liz would get Darwin out as a distraction, for Andrew felt the same way. They wanted to see Darwin really badly. That feeling just motivated Andrew to want to do the spell even more, as he knew that finding Lester would be a great help. He ran back to the center of the room as he heard keys shuffling in Nigel's hand. He knew that Nigel was letting Adrian in, so he quickly teleported out of there as soon as the door opened. Adrian was relieved that Andrew got out before Nigel could see him.

"Thanks, Nigel. Being in here does make me feel closer to him," Adrian told him as he looked around to make sure Andrew wasn't anywhere in there.

"I will leave you alone," Nigel said. He turned and left the room.

Adrian just looked around and saw Darwin's fedora hanging on the coat rack in the corner. He smiled at the sight of it. He didn't realize how much he missed his grandfather until that moment. That was when he realized that he and Andrew needed to do what they could to help Darwin get out of there, and the best way to do that would be to help Bianca find Lester as soon as possible.

After a few minutes, he barged into the hall, looking both ways to make sure that Nigel wasn't still wandering around anywhere. As soon as Adrian saw that the halls were clear, he rushed quickly to Andrew's room, knowing that was where his brother would be.

When Adrian barged into Andrew's room, he saw his brother standing at the center of the room by the round table Nigel always placed breakfast on. But instead of Hekabe's delicious, abnormally large waffles that Andrew would always ask for sitting on the table, there sat a big thick black book in its place. It looked as old, if not older, than the other book Andrew found on their first visit there. The cover was made from wool and had a weird gold symbol placed in the center, and the pages were crinkled parchment.

"Is that it?" Adrian asked.

"Yes." Andrew didn't make eye contact with him.

Andrew opened the book. The pages inside looked fragile, like they would crumble at the touch of a human hand.

"Be careful, Drew, those pages look like they aren't meant to be handled." Adrian's voice was a bit louder than his normal speaking volume. He didn't want to be responsible for destroying such an old book. But Andrew knew that the pages were ok to be touched because he had gone through that very book before. As Andrew carefully turned the pages looking for the spell he wanted, Adrian hovered over him in anticipation.

"Here it is!" Andrew caressed the pages gently.

"Can you read that?" Adrian asked. Andrew didn't say anything because he was making sure he could read it. He had progressed a lot faster in Latin than Adrian, and he was grateful Adrian wouldn't really understand it.

"Yeah, but you're going to have to go into the capital tomorrow and get some ingredients from Adrasteia's shop," Andrew informed him. He had to get certain items himself that he needed to be alone for.

"Why am I not surprised that Super Nerd would understand what it says?" Adrian joked. He always mocked his brother for being a nerd. Even when they had been in football together, Adrian would be joking with the rest of the team while Andrew was reading comics on the sidelines or talking to Collin about the latest comic book movie that just came out.

"Don't be mad because you're an idiot who doesn't utilize his visits here or study at home."

"Just make a list of what we need, and I will go tomorrow when I wake up. Now I'm going downstairs because those cookies are making me foam at the mouth." Adrian charged for the door.

Andrew shook his head over his brother's love of food. *How can he be in such great shape after the way he eats?* he wondered to himself again, smirking as Adrian left his room. However, that smile wasn't meant to last. He soon grew worrisome as he realized that this spell was not for beginners; the ingredients alone showed him that this spell might be difficult to cast. He doubted his and his brother's ability to cast such a spell, but he couldn't let the nerves get to him. He knew this spell had to work. He put the book under his bed and went to join his brother downstairs.

* * *

THE next morning, the sun was shining so brightly that it seeped through the small cracks of the black curtains that were closed shut on all the windows and patio doors of Andrew's room. Andrew smelled the breakfast that Nigel left on the table for him and hopped out of bed. It wasn't long before Adrian came barging in his room carrying his own plate of food.

"Good. You're up." Adrian placed his food down on the same table. He glanced around the room and saw a chair in the other corner of the room. With a quick wave of his hand, the chair glided over to him, and he took a seat. Andrew yawned and stretched sleepily, not saying anything, but eventually joined his brother at the table.

"Oh, before I forget," Andrew added, walking over to grab what looked like a sheet of paper from under the bed. "This is what we're going to need." He sat down at the table, handing Adrian the piece of paper. Adrian glanced over the list and placed it in his pajama pants pocket. They both started to eat their breakfast when Andrew noticed that they didn't have any syrup to go with the waffles Hekabe made. Adrian didn't mind since he didn't care for syrup anyways, but before Andrew could say anything, a warm steel bottle of syrup appeared in the center of the table.

"So, what will you be doing while I'm playing gofer today?" Adrian asked as he began cutting up his waffle.

"I have to go get a few things myself," Andrew informed him, hoping he wouldn't ask anything else. The two continued to eat their breakfast quietly.

A few hours passed after breakfast before Adrian was finally ready to head to the capitol. He walked over to Andrew's room and didn't see him but noticed that the patio door was open. He approached it to find Andrew reading the book that had the spell in it.

"That is a big book," he remarked to get Andrew's attention. Andrew held it up. "It weighs a ton."

"I'm about to head out," Adrian let him know as he glanced over to the stables that sat two hundred yards or so away from the main house.

"Ok. Meet you back here tonight," Andrew replied. A few seconds later, a gust of wind lifted Adrian off the balcony and toward the stables. Andrew went back to reading, internalizing the exact steps to complete the spell.

Over at the stables, it seemed Adrian still needed to work on his landing, as he stumbled to the ground. He quickly recovered and ran over to the stables. His Pegasus became overly excited as if he could feel Adrian approaching. The other ones just continued eating like nothing had changed since Adrian came in.

"Rizzo! How you doing, boy?" Adrian asked as he pet his Pegasus on the head and gently placed his own head on Rizzo's. "I missed you, boy." Rizzo whinnied and snorted in excitement.

After a few minutes of greeting each other, Adrian decided that he would ride Rizzo to the capital instead of teleporting. That way, he would get to take in the sights of this magnificent place from the sky. Adrian hiked over to the storage room and lifted the specially made saddle off the wall, which made Rizzo start rearing in excitement, his wings expanding as much as they could in the stable.

"Settle down, my boy!" He made his way back toward Rizzo. He unlocked the stable holding him and the Pegasus quickly galloped outside. Once Rizzo was out, he started rearing again, only this time expanding his wings as far as they could go as his forelock swayed from the strong breeze blowing through the sky. It was such a stunning sight to behold that Adrian almost forgot where he needed to go.

He took hold of Rizzo and made him stand on all four legs again. He put the saddle on, double-checked to make sure everything was secure—after all, the saddle needed to be put a little further back than that of a regular horse—and finally checked that the wings weren't blocked. Satisfied at what he saw, he quickly jumped onto Rizzo's back.

It wasn't long before Rizzo soared through the sky high above Southport, passing other wizards that were flying through the sky themselves, some on majestic beasts such as Rizzo and others in their own personalized colorful turnabouts. Adrian was glad in his decision to go to the capital on Rizzo because the sights were something remarkable to take in. Sometimes he still couldn't believe a world such as the one around him existed, but he was glad it was and that he got to be part of it. Southport was beautiful, but it was only a small part of the amazing country that was Avalon.

All of Adrian's happiness quickly dissipated when he saw the Tower of Avalon in the distance. He began to think about his grandfather and what he was doing in there. Knowing that there was a reason Gabriel wanted him out of the way made Adrian sure that casting this spell was the most important thing they could do to help find what Gabriel wanted so badly.

He signaled to Rizzo to speed up, and just like that, he was soaring even faster. Within minutes, they started to descend. You would think a big, majestic beast such as Rizzo would make a hard landing on the concrete below, but he didn't; the landing was soft and gentle, just like him. As always, the capital was heavy with wizard traffic as people quickly raced up and down the walkway. Adrian looked around for that temporary stable he saw the last time he was there so Rizzo could wait there for him. He finally spotted it and led Rizzo toward it, saying that he would only be a few minutes. He tied Rizzo to the pole in the corner of the stable.

"Looks like you have this place to yourself," he told Rizzo as he gently pets the side of his face.

Leaving the stable, Adrian leapt out onto the busy walkways of Polaris toward Adrasteia's shop. As he passed other wizards, he noticed that some bowed their heads to him in sorrow; others gave him a cold, hard stare, as if they all made the conclusion that Darwin was guilty and that was somehow inherited by Adrian. *Guess we know who's on Grandpa's side,* he thought to himself as he kept walking. The smell of the bakery signaled that he was close to the shop, and he made a mental note to himself to stop there after Adrasteia's. The familiar sounds of the bell ringing overhead greeted Adrian as he strolled in. He waited for Adrasteia to greet him like she always did, but he heard not a word. *Weird… she is always at her shop when school is out for the weekend.* Adrian assumed Adrasteia was busy in the back, so he started looking for the items he needed. Before he could take out the list Andrew gave him, he was interrupted.

"Can I help ye find anything?" spoke a voice in the background with a similar Scottish accent to Adrasteia's. It sounded like it belonged to a young man probably Adrian's age, if not older. Adrian turned around and didn't speak for a second.

"Um…" he fidgeted with his hands, not knowing what to do. "No, I'm good, thank you," Adrian said, a little flustered.

"Are ye sure? That's what I'm here fer!" the clerk replied with a soft smile expressed on his face as he slowly made his way toward Adrian. Adrian couldn't help but notice how he resembled Adrasteia a bit. He had a light skin tone like her; his curly auburn hair was a different shade of red than Adrasteia's but nice all the same; and his sapphire eyes were remarkable. It was also very obvious that he worked out. As he approached, Adrian began to fidget some more, not knowing what to say.

"I'm Tavish. My grandmother owns the place an' asked me to come in today because she couldnae make it," the clerk said as he extended his arm to shake Adrian's hand.

"I didn't know Adrasteia had a grandson. I'm Adrian." He grasped Tavish's hand to shake it.

"Ah. Yer Darwin's grandson." Tavish warmly stared at him. "I've 'eard so much aboot the grandchildren o' one o' the most beloved wizards."

Adrian stayed quiet for a second, mesmerized, it seemed, by Tavish's accent. "Yeah," he finally said.

"Yer one o' two, correct?" He flashed one of the most beautiful smiles Adrian had ever seen his way.

"Yeah." Adrian continued shaking his hand.

"Not much o' a talker, are ye, grandson of Darwin's?" Tavish asked winsomely as he continued to hold and shake Adrian's hand somewhat. A few seconds went by before Tavish finally let go. Adrian quickly wanted to say something, so he didn't look like an idiot in front of him.

"Yeah. Sorry, just have a lot on my mind." He felt a little nervous, which was unusual for him.

"I heard." Tavish stepped back a few inches. "But I'm sure Darwin will be oot soon."

"Yeah…" Adrian swayed side to side a little. "I'm sure he will." Tavish laughed and sauntered away but turned around to look at Adrian one last time before he turned the corner of the aisle.

Really? Adrian asked himself as he shook his head over how stupid he must have sounded. Adrian pulled out the list Andrew gave him and began walking around looking for the items on it. After a few minutes, he couldn't seem to find the remaining two ingredients and decided to go ask Tavish if he could help.

"I'm actually having a hard time finding the last two items on this list," Adrian informed him, putting the sheet of wrinkly paper in front of Tavish. Tavish just looked Adrian in the eyes.

"Wow!" He stared intently at Adrian. "Ye do know more than a few sentences!"

Adrian laughed at his remark but didn't say anything else while Tavish looked at the last two items on the list. He came out from behind the counter and closely passed Adrian, who began following him to an aisle.

"These are tricky tae find, so we keep 'em on the top shelf over here so we can say we have 'em in stock when someone comes looking fer 'em." He stepped onto a three-stair ladder and reached for a little black plastic bag on the top shelf, his shirt raising slightly above his waist, revealing his lower abs. Adrian just stared without saying a word.

"Here ye go." He tossed the bag at Adrian, who caught it right away. Tavish climbed down the steps and took a few steps to another part of the shop as Adrian followed. "Here it is," he said as he picked up a small vial of thick purple liquid and handed it to Adrian.

"Thanks." Adrian turned to head toward the counter as Tavish went back behind it, grabbed a pen and paper, and began to write up the items Adrian was purchasing. Adrian took out his wallet but was interrupted.

"No need. My aunt just bills Darwin at the end o' the month." Tavish's smile was infectious.

"Oh. Ok." Adrian stood there silently, not knowing what else to say, his heart beating a little faster.

"How often do ye visit our world?" he inquired, sighing as he continued writing what Adrian just purchased.

"Lately, every other weekend or so."

"And I'm just meeting ye *now*?" Tavish gushed. He continued writing down the items. Adrian took a deep breath.

"Usually, we just hang by my grandfather's house."

"Well,…" Tavish gazed into Adrian's eyes. "I guess I'm gonna 'ave to swing by next time yer oot here."

"Um…" Adrian stammered, taking a few steps back. "Yeah. That would be cool," he answered, his tone more excited than he had anticipated.

The sun was starting to set on Polaris and Adrian finally decided to get going. As Tavish packed up Adrian's items, Adrian searched for a pen from near the register and wrote down his number on a blank receipt sheet.

"Here you go. Give me a call sometime and next time I'm out here, we can hang," Adrian offered, his confidence finally coming back to him.

Tavish glanced down at the sheet he was handed. "Sounds like a plan." He handed him his bag of items then took the phone number and stuffed it in his pocket.

Adrian turned and hightailed it for the exit, but before he turned into the aisle that led out the store, he glanced back one last time at Tavish, who was returning the look. They both smiled as Adrian disappeared out of sight. A few seconds later, the familiar sounds of the bell ringing rang out, signaling that Adrian had left the store. Tavish gently laughed to himself as he approached the storage room of Adrasteia's shop.

✳ ✳ ✳

OVER on the edge of Southport, Andrew stood at the opening of a great big gate. He reached into his messenger bag and took out an orb, placed it directly in front of him, and let it go. Instead of falling to the ground, the orb became suspended in the air.

Andrew mumbled a few words, and the orb began to light up bright enough so he could see the pathway in front of him, but not bright enough that other people could see it. The only people in that part of Southport were buried six feet deep anyway. As the orb passed through the gates, it illuminated the words "Nottingham Cemetery" overhead as Andrew followed.

Andrew began looking around and saw all the tombstones on both sides of the walkway. He mumbled again, this time a little louder as he followed the orb. "*Invenies Sterling.*" The orb lit up a little brighter and began moving a little faster in front of him. Andrew started to walk faster and after a few minutes was brought to a stop in front of a mausoleum with the name "Sterling" carved into the stone on top. Andrew tried opening it, but not surprisingly, it was locked. He took a few steps back, made a pushing gesture, and something sounded like it hit the ground as the door opened.

As he went in, he noticed a piece of the wall where the lock met the door was missing, but he saw it a second later lying on the ground. He decided he couldn't focus on that now, so he entered the mausoleum. As he entered, he said a few words and the orb began to glow brighter until a few miniature orbs popped out of it and took their positions in the corners of the Sterling resting place.

They illuminated the room as Andrew paced around looking for something. As he flicked his eyes around, he closely examined the walls with what looked like four square stone drawers in them. He carefully looked at each name on the drawers but apparently couldn't find what he needed.

Around the corner, he saw two huge stone tombs sitting in the center of a large area with the same four stone squares on the walls surrounding them. He examined the first tomb, his face lighting up with excitement. It was the one he was looking for. Andrew tried sliding the cover off, but it was sealed shut. He tried making a pushing gesture like he did with the door, but it wouldn't budge. After examining the tomb's seal, he summoned his wand and tapped the cover while saying "Unseal," and to his surprise, it worked.

He sent his wand away and slowly raised his hand, and in that moment the lid began to levitate off the tomb. He gently placed the cover on the ground next to the tomb and looked inside, rather exhausted because the cover was a little bit heavier than what he was used to practicing on. He saw the remains inside and carefully reached in to grab them. They fell apart somewhat, but not as badly as he thought they would. Piece by piece, he placed them on the ground near the cover.

Once the human remains were exactly the way they were laid out in the tomb, Andrew slowly backed away while raising his hand once again. The cover was once again suspended in midair. Andrew took a deep breath, sighed, and the cover slammed down on the bones, crushing them until there was nothing left but dust. He gently placed the cover, shockingly still intact, back on the tomb, summoned his wand once again and said, "Seal," and just like that, it looked as though the tomb was never opened. He reached into his messenger bag and pulled out a small sack, a sweeper, and a piece of cardboard. He carefully swept up each dusty piece of bone and poured it into the sack, then placed the items back in his messenger bag and teleported out. As the smoke settled, the orbs started to dim until the mausoleum was once again surrounded by darkness.

Chapter Seventeen

Sticks and branches broke underfoot as Andrew and Adrian made their way through the woods behind the school. They came back from Avalon yesterday but couldn't get out here until now. They made their way deeper into the woods, trying to find the right spot. A spot where there was some kind of light so they could see what they were doing, and a spot that wouldn't be visible to the passing cars they heard in the distance on the other side of the woods.

"Drew. What's with the bunny?" He had been wanting to ask that question since he saw that Andrew had it.

"Shhh! We don't know if anyone is out here. Did you bring the poster board I told you to grab?" He knew full well Adrian had it but needed to ask something to avoid the question that was going to be answered very soon.

Adrian looked at the poster board that he obviously had brought, looking back at his brother, annoyed. "What is this?" He held up the poster board high enough for Andrew to see.

Andrew glanced back. "Ah. Ok. Sorry"

They continued their trek into the woods until the sounds of the passing cars from the nearby highway gradually faded away. "Here should be fine." Andrew gently placed the carrier cage holding the bunny against a tree. Adrian set down the poster board and the bag from Adrasteia's shop on the ground while Andrew reached into his messenger bag and took out the bone dust. Andrew then retrieved a medium-sized cauldron from a box he was carrying and placed it in the center.

Seeing what his brother just pulled out, Adrian teased, "Way to add to the stereotype, Drew."

Andrew chuckled but quickly started pouring the ingredients into the cauldron while chanting words repeatedly. Adrian looked on in anticipation as a green flame ignited from within the cauldron. Andrew then told him to grab the rabbit from the cage.

"Why?" Adrian stood there with one arm clasping the other at the elbow. "Why do you need the rabbit?"

"Because…" he trailed off. "Because this spell needs a sacrifice." Andrew couldn't turn to face his brother.

"Wait…" Adrian took a step back. "WHAT?! Are you serious?" Adrian started breathing heavily. He was disgusted by the idea of sacrificing a defenseless creature.

"Yeah…" Andrew finally looked to his brother. "I know it sucks—hey," he said, trying to make eye contact with Adrian to calm him down a bit, "but it's required."

Adrian paused for a few seconds; the green flame crackling was the only sound that could be heard. Andrew stared at his brother for a few moments before shouting, "Adrian!" He didn't want to shout, but they had to hurry.

Adrian hesitated but finally went over slowly to the rabbit, picking it out from its cage. He cradled it and petted its head, hesitating, but handed it to Andrew, who was holding a knife. Adrian just stared at him, horrified over what was about to happen. But at that moment, Andrew wavered. He looked at his brother. "I can't…" Andrew was dripping sweat.

"Can the spell work without it?" Adrian asked, hopeful that it would. The green flame started to die down.

"No," Andrew said, his hands trembling, voice cracking.

Adrian got on his knees in front of his brother, took the fussing rabbit and the knife from Andrew, and without any more hesitation, he cut the rabbit from neck to groin. The creature let out a yelp and convulsed profusely as its blood poured into the cauldron. The green flames rose higher until it was bright red, and the rabbit was dead.

"Now what?" Adrian asked, his chest rising up and down rapidly as he looked at the creature whose life he had ended. He gently placed the rabbit on the ground. He was breathing as if he had just run a mile as he stared at the lifeless body in front of him. Andrew didn't say anything; he just took the poster board and laid it on the ground. Then he went for the cauldron and threw the black ashes on the poster board like a pail of water onto a burning fire. The ashes spelled out one simple word: Trusdale.

"All that for a word?" Adrian was angry over what he had to do for such little in return.

Andrew rushed to a nearby rock and puked. The gore of the spell proved too much for his stomach to handle. "Pack everything up," Andrew said, wiping his mouth. He rolled up the poster and placed it in his messenger bag. He looked over at Adrian, who was digging a hole in the nearby dirt with his bare hands. "What are you doing?"

"I'm going to at least bury the little guy. Can't have wild animals defiling his corpse." Andrew didn't mock his brother but went over to help. He supposed it was the least they could do for the innocent creature they just killed. After the hole was deep enough for Adrian's liking, he got up to get the rabbit and placed it in the makeshift grave. Andrew and Adrian both stood up, looked down, and had a short moment of silence.

"Sorry, little guy." Adrian filled the hole with dirt and got up.

"Let's get going. Mom's probably going to get pissed if we get back late." Andrew clutched his brother's shoulder, replaying what had just happened over and over again.

"Drew. Next time, do you think you can fill me in on all the details of a spell we are doing together, please?"

Andrew let out a heavy sigh. "Won't ever be doing a spell like this again."

*** * ***

THE next morning, Andrew was wide awake in the bathroom brushing his teeth. Adrian entered, yawning and stretching without saying a word.

"Put on a shirt, will you?" Andrew demanded, annoyed that his brother's favorite thing to do was walk around shirtless.

"Don't be mad because you have to watch what you eat and work out daily for these while all I have to do is… oh yeah, nothing!" Adrian teased as he started slapping his stomach. Andrew was always kind of jealous of how in shape Adrian was without having to do that much work. He was able to eat like a pig, while Andrew had a daily routine he had to stick to stay in shape.

"You're such a tool."

Adrian began brushing his teeth as Andrew retreated to his room to get dressed. After a few minutes, Adrian came in and asked Andrew if Collin was still picking them up.

"No. He's getting us from Chloe's," Andrew replied.

"Oh." Adrian had forgotten overnight that they had to tell their aunt what they did. He really didn't want to be a part of that conversation, but what choice did he have?

Once they were dressed, they took hold of their school bags and teleported to their aunt's house to talk to her about what they found.

"Hey, guys. You're here a little early," Liz said to them. A few awkward seconds went by, and Adrian knew he would have to take the lead on this; Andrew was always the quiet one.

Adrian was apprehensive. "We have to talk to you." He looked his aunt in the eyes. "Ok. Well, let's go to the kitchen. I made cereal." Liz marched into the kitchen as the twins followed without saying a word. This worried Liz, but she didn't let it show. "What's up?" she asked them while grabbing a cup and filling it to the brim with freshly made hot coffee.

Andrew didn't say anything; he just reached into his bag and pulled out the rolled-up poster board. As he handed it to Adrian, Bianca came in.

"Good morning, all," she said and went straight to the cabinets for a bowl.

"Hi," Andrew and Adrian both said simultaneously.

"We think we found Lester Sterling," Adrian blurted out as he handed his aunt the rolled-up poster. Bianca and Liz quickly looked at each other, amazed at what Adrian had said.

"How do you 'think' you found Lester Sterling?" Bianca asked, confused since every locater spell, she had tried didn't work. Liz unrolled the poster board and instantly saw the burnt ashes cemented onto it.

"Trusdale?" Bianca got closer to her mother, looking at the poster.

"How did you boys come across this?" Liz probed, already knowing the answer. Before Adrian could answer, she interrupted, "You did a revealer spell," her nostrils flaring.

Bianca glanced at her cousins, then back to her mom. "Revealer spell?" She had never heard of that.

"Yeah. It's like a locater spell, only it requires certain ingredients," Liz said, looking from Bianca back to the twins, knowing full well what that spell required.

"We had to help!" Adrian shouted. "This was the only way."

"We told you we were handling it!" Liz couldn't help being a little angry at them.

Knowing that a sacrifice was required for this spell made her realize that the boys were getting ahead of themselves when it came to magic. *How would they even know what spell to cast?* she wondered.

"And how well was that working out for you, huh?" Adrian asked rhetorically, knowing that the attitude he just gave out couldn't be taken back.

"Do you have—" Before she could finish, the doorbell rang. It was Collin coming to pick the three of them up for school.

They could hear Chloe rushing in. "Hey, guys." She entered the kitchen and looked around, sensing she had stumbled into something unpleasant. "Well, this is awkward…"

"You guys get to school," Liz ordered. She was clearly not pleased with her nephews at all.

The twins were silent, and Chloe knew they wouldn't answer in front of her mother, so she dropped it like nothing was happening. Chloe took her bagel and proceeded to the front door to let Collin in. Andrew and Adrian followed closely behind her, leaving Bianca and Liz in the kitchen.

"Look into this." Liz handed the poster to Bianca. Liz seized her briefcase and headed to the garage without saying another word, and Bianca knew that she was angry.

"Let's just go." Chloe pushed Collin back outside. They exchanged glances at one another but didn't say anything. The twins were right behind them, closing the door to their aunt's house without saying bye.

"I wanted a bowl of your mom's homemade cereal," Collin joked, looking sadly back toward the door. Chloe did all she could to keep her teeth from showing and took her seat in the front, glaring out of the window so Collin wouldn't see how amused she was. Andrew got in the back with Adrian. He knew that they hadn't heard the last of their aunt being mad.

Before they went into the school, Adrian asked Chloe to wait for him while Collin and Andrew strolled ahead. "See you after school!" Collin grinned from ear to ear at Chloe when he passed her.

Chloe did, too, but was quickly brought out of it by Adrian, who started telling her what they did last night and why she had entered such a cold kitchen a little bit ago. She seemed a little perturbed over the whole rabbit thing, but she supported her cousins. "Well, they can't expect you guys to not do anything. They obviously weren't getting it done, so if you helped, I don't know what the big deal is." That made Adrian appreciate her more.

"I'm sick of them treating us like kids."

"Well, you're only sixteen, my dear cousin," Chloe teased as she put her arm around him. "Just put it out of your head and focus on school. I hear there is a pop quiz in anatomy." She knew that would put a smile on Adrian's face.

"Great. Just what I needed."

"If it's worth anything, I would have done the same thing you guys did." Her kind words were comforting to Adrian.

He looked at her warmly. "Thanks."

BIANCA sat at the computer typing "Trusdale" into the search engine, hoping that something useful would come up. She browsed the results, writing things down in a notebook she set beside her. After searching for another hour and writing down a few more things, she picked up her phone to call her mother. She explained to Liz that she had found two small towns that went by Trusdale in the states and two in Europe with the same name. Liz instructed her to go search the towns in Europe first since they were the farthest and more likely to be places that Lester might be hiding.

Bianca leaned back into her chair. "I know this is a long shot, but at least we have a lead." A few seconds of silence passed. "Mom?"

Liz cleared her throat. "It was very irresponsible for them to do that spell," Liz sighed. "What were they thinking?"

"Ugh." Bianca leaned forward, still staring at her screen. "There is no point debating what we can't change. We have the information now, and we have to use it." She was frustrated by her mother. "I agree with everything you are saying, but we have to focus. I plan on leaving after class."

"Don't you have class tomorrow?" Liz wondered. She didn't want Bianca failing.

"No, I'm off the rest of the week." Bianca switched hands, holding her phone. "I think I could find him."

Liz hesitated. "OK. I agree. Just please be careful."

"I will be."

"Keep me up to date with everything you find out. Love you! Bye."

"Will do. Love you too." Bianca set the phone down.

After class the next day, Bianca headed toward the library to do a bit of research for an assignment due in a week and a half when a familiar voice stopped her in her tracks.

"Hey, beautiful," Brad cooed, beaming her way.

"Oh my god! What are you doing here?" Bianca excitedly asked. She leapt into his arms for a warm embrace.

"I tested out early for the semester because I missed you."

"I didn't even know you could do that." She hugged him tighter.

"Me neither, but when I saw that it was an option, I took it, and it worked out well. Got 3 As and a B!"

"This is so awesome. I missed you." Bianca kissed her boyfriend as if they had been separated for years.

"Where are you going now?"

"I was going to the library, but now you are taking me out to lunch." Brad agreed and they went to a little sandwich shop on campus since Bianca still had an afternoon class to take.

"So, how's the family?" Brad placed the sub sandwiches on the table. Bianca told him how the twins were doing spells they shouldn't have been and how her mom was upset about it. But before she could continue, Brad interrupted her, "I meant with Chloe. Not that all the other stuff isn't interesting! I'm just curious how she's doing with everything."

"Chloe is doing great. I even think Collin has a thing for her." She loved how concerned Brad was for her sister.

"That's adorable. It's about time, too, because last time I was here, you could totally tell she had a huge crush on him."

"At least *someone* can have a normal life," Bianca mused, a bit envious of her "normal" sister.

"They're awkwardly cute when they're around each other," Brad added as he took a bite of his meatball sandwich.

"I know you were here not that long ago, but I'm glad you're back. You have no idea how happy I am to see you." She gripped his hand.

"I missed you too, babe," he answered as he gently rubbed his fingers against hers.

Bianca went on to tell him about how she had to go searching for a guy who might be able to help her grandfather out.

"Are you leaving? I just got here," he frowned.

Bianca knew he wouldn't like that and remorsefully explained, "I know, but this is important."

"Well then, can I go with you?"

"You want to go with me?" Bianca asked, surprised at the question.

"Yeah. It will be so much fun! We can look for that guy but also take in the sights."

"My mom would kill me if you came with me."

"She doesn't have to know. Besides, I came back to see you and don't want you to be away from me right now." Brad gripped her hand tighter.

"I don't know..." Bianca didn't know what else to say. What she was doing was important, not a vacation.

"Please?" Brad begged.

"Fine. It'll be fun having you come with me," Bianca finally gave in to Brad's request.

She could never resist his cute smile and charm.

"This is going to be so much fun. Just you and me together! Granted, you will be looking for some other guy, but whatever." They both laughed.

After lunch, Brad escorted Bianca to her next class. They parted with hugs and kisses, and he told her he would pass by her house later. She hesitantly broke free from his lips and said bye.

* * *

THE bell sounded and Chloe, as usual, was the first one out of her class since she sat in the front row, always a teacher's pet. She made her way to her locker and as she passed the other students, her mind wandered to how her grandfather might be doing. She missed him so much and had been worried about him since she heard he was taken to that Tower. She didn't want to bother anyone with her worries because she wasn't a part of that world, and she knew her mom was trying her hardest to get him out. She also knew that her mom tried to hide things so she or her cousins wouldn't worry, which was frustrating for Chloe because they weren't kids anymore. She finally reached her locker and switched out her books.

"Hi," Collin said, startling Chloe.

"Hey, yourself."

"How was class?" Collin asked as he leaned against the lockers.

"Good. How was yours?" Chloe continued grabbing the books she needed for her next class.

"Boring. "I was thinking… if you don't have plans already, I was thinking about checking out that new burger place on Main Street this Friday. I hear the burgers there are beyond good and wanted to know if you would like to join me?" Collin nervously gulped down the knot in his throat.

"Um. Yeah! I've been wanting to go there for a while now," Chloe answered, blushing in the process while her heart skipped a beat.

"Great! Cool. Alright. I'll see you after school." Collin turned and ran off. He was excited, yet nervous about the plans he just made.

"What was *that* about?" Adrian asked as he went up to Chloe's locker.

"I think Collin just asked me out on a date." Chloe's face was turning a bright red.

"Wow." Adrian glanced behind to see Collin turn out of view. "That's cool, but can I see your notes from last week?" Adrian asked as they walked to their next class together.

"Ugh. Maybe you should pay attention in class." Chloe riffled through her backpack, handing him her notes.

"Why pay attention when I have such an amazing cousin who takes AP classes with me and who does enough listening for the both of us?" He put an arm around his cousin and brought her in for a hug.

Chapter Eighteen

The familiar sound of the doorbell ringing brought joy to Bianca, for she knew who was at the door. She opened it to let Brad in and once again they hugged and kissed hello, looking madly in love. Bianca's heart always raced when she saw him; she knew from the first time they met that he would be the one. Brad obviously felt the same, his eyes glued to Bianca's every move like if he blinked, he would miss a crucial moment. Never had there been two people more in love than these two.

"Come in before my mom pulls up!" Bianca pulled him into the house. "Is she on her way back?"

"I don't think so, but who knows. Is that a big enough duffel bag?" she asked, looking down at the object that just slapped against her leg.

"I packed for both warm and cold weather. You never did tell me where our little adventure would be taking us!"

"Let me finish this note and we'll go." Brad sauntered toward her, leaned on her back, and put her hair to the other side as he gently kissed her neck. Bianca was brought out of her task at hand as she was thrusted into this hypnotic state, his lips so soft, so full of love. She quickly snapped out of it and continued writing her note.

"Thanks for letting me tag along. I would be so bored without you here."

"I'm glad you wanted to come." She went to grab her own overnight bag full of clothes. "This might be a little much the first time, so take this," she added as she handed him a small vial. Brad drank it, scrunching his face as it left a sour taste in his mouth. He took Bianca's extended hand and they teleported to the first destination on their quest.

ADRIAN and Andrew slowly approached their front door. They had a long day at school with weight and conditioning training in order to stay in shape for when the wrestling season started up again—something Andrew wanted to quit but Adrian wouldn't allow. The last thing they needed was what waited for them inside. As they went in and dropped their school bags and jackets in the closet by the front door, they heard whispers coming from the dining room. Adrian peeked his head into the dining room to get a look at who was there. He instantly became frustrated, immediately knowing this was the part where they continued to get yelled at.

Andrew looked at him and without Adrian having to tell him anything, he sensed the impending doom waiting for them in the next room. Andrew's stomach started to ache from the nerves pilling inside him. He didn't have Adrian's calm personality at all—another thing he envied in his brother. The closer they got to the dining room; the more nervous Andrew felt. A layer of sweat began to form atop his head as he saw the anger in his mom's and aunt's eyes.

"Sit down. We need to talk," Sara said sternly as she looked at both her sons. Liz crossed her arms and leaned back into her chair. She had to tell Sara. They needed to know what they did wasn't ok.

"Mom, before you say anything, I want you to know that all we wanted to do was help," Adrian said. He did what his mom asked and took a seat at the table.

"You were told that Liz and Bianca were handling it."

"Well,..." Adrian glanced at his aunt. "We helped more." Once again, Andrew's mouth dropped open slightly at how Adrian didn't seem to be feeling the same empty feeling in the pit of his stomach that he was.

"Do you know how dangerous that spell was?" Sara scolded, getting angrier at Adrian.

"Do you? I mean, you yourself don't know what kind of spell we did or how, so why are you yelling at us?" Adrian pointed out, shaking his head.

"I know you both are inexperienced and doing magic so dark that it required a sacrifice isn't something you should ever be doing. Do you have any idea how mad I am? At the both of you?" Sara fumed. "And for you, Adrian, to be so nonchalant with what you both did is disgusting."

"Well seeing as how you lied to us for years about who we are and our father, I think I know how you feel!" Adrian bellowed. He stared at his mother as if they were having a contest to see who would blink first. Andrew just sat there in silence, looking directly at the table in front of him. He couldn't believe what Adrian just said.

"Go to your room!" Sara yelled; her voice so loud that the dogs in the backyard next door started barking. Andrew was the first one up the stairs as Adrian tried winning the staring contest he had entered in with his mom. "I said *go*!" Sara ordered again. Adrian pushed himself off the table and marched to the stairs, slamming his feet with each step.

"Oh, before I forget, your grandfather wants to see you tomorrow," Sara added, hoping that would get the message across to her stubborn son of how much trouble they were in. Adrian stopped at the bottom of the stairs. For the first time since being home, he was finally feeling the pit in his stomach his brother felt without knowing it. He silently continued up the stairs to his room. A few moments later, he heard Andrew in his own.

He marched over. "Did you hear that?" Andrew's door was opened.

"Yeah." Adrian went back to his room and closed the door behind him.

✳ ✳ ✳

THE entire school day went by faster than any other this year. Maybe it was the universe punishing them for the spell they cast. The anticipation of going to see their grandfather made their hearts race all day. In what seemed like no time at all, the moment was finally here. The note they both received in third period from the principal to meet in her office after their last class had arrived. The walk to Adrasteia's office was slow and left them both with no saliva in their mouths. Adrian and Andrew came from opposite sides of the school but arrived at the same time. Both of them lackadaisically marched to the office, hoping that would make time stop so they wouldn't have to see Darwin. Unfortunately, it didn't work.

"You guys can go straight in," said the lady at the front desk.

As they went into Adrasteia's office, she quickly got up to greet them. Andrew closed the door behind them as she took their hands and teleported.

This was the one time they hated being able to teleport; they were at the entrance gates of the Tower of Avalon within seconds. They swallowed what saliva they had left in their very dry mouths as they were cleared by the Tower guards, who all wore black dress robes, to enter. Andrew and Adrian's hearts raced faster as they reached the enormous metal doors of the Tower.

They had to wait for the second pair of guards to clear them before they could open the doors. The loud squeaking sounds the door made as they opened only added to the fear they felt. As they headed inside, Andrew and Adrian felt different. They felt "normal," like something had been drained from them, but didn't feel tired. As Adrian tried to teleport back home in fear, he was reminded that no magic could be done inside the tower. No matter how hard he tried, nothing happened. As they followed the guard inside, Adrian wondered to himself again why Darwin would allow himself to be brought here. *Why not run, knowing that this place takes away our abilities?*

Adrian hated the feeling of being "normal," like this place robbed him of what made him special. Even though he hadn't been a wizard that long, he had grown accustomed to the feeling. The anger he felt toward this place, toward the Tower, distracted him from the nerves he felt about seeing their grandfather. The echo of the door in front of them unlocking brought his nerves back instantly. "Two at a time," the guard ordered. Adrasteia gave them an uncomfortable yet reassuring smile as the door closed behind them. In front of them was a long metal hallway leading to another big set of double doors.

The clunking of the guard's shoes hitting the steel floor was all that could be heard. For a second, Andrew thought he could hear Adrian's heart beating but knew that wasn't possible— perhaps his own, but not Adrian's. The walk to the doors seemed like an eternity. As they waited for them to unlock, Adrian and Andrew exchanged looks at one another and took deep breaths. They were led into another long hallway, a mirror image of the one they were just in, only this one had four or five doors on each side. And this time, instead of being led down another long hall, they were led to the first door on the left.

"Wait here for the prisoner," the guard demanded as he closed the door on them.

The prisoner… Andrew thought. Those words angered him—he knew his grandfather wasn't a prisoner. Adrian must have felt the same way, as he angrily pulled a chair out from under the table. Andrew took a seat next to him and they both waited in silence, looking around the room with no windows. The room was solid steel all around; even the floors were steel, making the room colder than it should have been. There were only three seats, which were uncomfortable, but why wouldn't they be? This place was designed for discomfort, after all.

They only had to wait a few minutes before they heard the footsteps of what sounded like multiple people heading their way. Both Adrian and Andrew's hearts raced faster again like they had just run a triathlon. The footsteps got closer, each step making the twins take deep breaths.

Finally, the footsteps stopped. The familiar sound of the steel door unlocking caused the loud breathing to stop. The door opened slowly, causing them to take one last hard gulp.

"Hello, my dear boys." Besides the black jumpsuit and matching open robe he was wearing, Darwin looked the same, his hair neatly combed and his gold glasses resting on his chest by the chain around his neck.

"Hi," they both said simultaneously.

Darwin went over and gave them both a big embrace, calming them in the process. The guards left the room and Darwin took his seat at the chair across from them, locking his palms together. "How's Chloe and everyone?"

"Good," Andrew replied. He was still anxious about the fallout from what he and his brother had done.

"Chloe says hi," Adrian added.

"Send her my best." His speech was unsettlingly calm.

"Look, Grandpa, we know that we shouldn't have done that spell, but we couldn't just sit back and not do anything to help," Adrian blurted out. He just wanted to get it out there already; he must have gotten his courage back after Darwin's reassuring hug.

"How did you even know how to do that spell?" Darwin quizzed, looking directly at Andrew. He already knew how but wanted Andrew to confirm it.

"I found it in one of the books in your study."

"You're the little knowledge seeker, aren't you?" Darwin asked rhetorically as he unlocked his palms and sat back in his chair. "I'm not mad at you boys. Not at all. When Liz told me, I was a little surprised that you would perform such a spell, but not mad," he told them. "I should have gotten rid of certain books from my study when you two started to visit."

"We wouldn't do those kinds of spells again anyways." Andrew hoped that would reassure him.

"It was only this one time because we figured it was worth a shot," Adrian wanted nothing to do with those books anyway.

"I understand, but there is a reason those spells aren't preformed anymore." Darwin leaned in closer to them.

"Why?" the always curious Andrew wondered.

"Because it's dark magic, as your aunt informed you." Darwin's tone became more serious. He needed them to know the severity of practicing dark magic. "Any spell that requires a blood sacrifice is dark magic. Even the most skilled wizards take precautions in casting those if they need to. I know it doesn't feel like it, but that kind of spell takes the most beautiful of things and turns it into something else. You guys are fine, but I can assure you that the area where you cast that spell has changed. That's why those spells are outlawed."

"We didn't know…" Adrian lamented. After all, this was all new to them no matter how fast they were advancing in their training.

"That's why your aunt and mom are so angry."

"We're sorry," was all Andrew could say.

"I know. But what's done is done. All I ask is you give that book to Adrasteia or Hekabe as soon as possible."

"Ok." But Andrew didn't want to; he enjoyed reading as much as he could.

Darwin knew his time was limited, so he used the next thirty minutes to tell them how the case against him was going and assured them he would be out soon. "Visiting time is over," said a guard walking into the room after their time had passed. The twins trekked over to Darwin, who now stood and towered over them as they gave him a hug goodbye.

"I will see you soon," he told them as he was led out of the room. Andrew and Adrian were happy to see him doing well and believed that he would, in fact, be out soon.

They both were then escorted back to a waiting area where Adrasteia sat. She was relieved to see them in much better spirits than when they first arrived. She picked up their coats and the trio left the tower. Once they passed the gates, Adrian and Andrew could feel their ability to teleport return if they wanted to, but they didn't have to; Adrasteia gripped onto their arms and teleported all three of them back to school, leaving only a fading green light. Back in her office, she asked the boys to sit for a minute before they said goodbye. Andrew and Adrian both knew she wasn't the type to yell, but they knew she had something to say on the matter, like their mother and aunt.

"I know it must be frustratin' tae be treated like wee children, especially after being thrown into this world ye ne'er knew existed. And fer all o' us adults tae tell ye tae stay oot of things mustnae help."

"A little," Andrew agreed.

"Ye both remind me o' Darwin when he was a wee lad."

"Really?" Adrian asked. He felt honored at the comparison.

"Oh, aye. He was always seekin' knowledge an' ways to contribute tae things goin' on around him. And ye know what?"

"What?" they both said at the same time, hanging on to her every word.

"He absolutely hated being told tae stay oot o' things. Now 'at was a long time ago—a very, very long time ago—but still, he 'ated it. Well, youse boys should be on yer way before ye keep remindin' me how old I am." She laughed.

Adrian and Andrew stood with pride after being compared to their grandfather. After all, he grew up to be a remarkably successful and influential wizard. This, along with seeing Darwin, made their day. They got up to leave but before they reached for their school bags, Adrasteia asked them for the dark spell book back. Andrew was surprised, she knew he had it and stood there for a few seconds before reaching into his bag for it. He wasn't mad that she was asking for it—just disappointed that he couldn't read through it some more.

"Just like yer grandfather," she repeated, bringing a grin to Andrew's face.

They collected their things, said goodbye to Adrasteia, and one after the other they teleported home, each arriving in their own room. Andrew smelled the chicken that Sara had in the oven and his stomach rumbled, reminding him how hungry he was. He could only imagine how fast Adrian would be running downstairs to eat everything in sight. When he left his room, however, he noticed Adrian was still in his. Then he remembered how he and Sara had last left things.

Adrian was hesitant to go down, but he was just as hungry as Andrew, if not more.

Andrew signaled for his brother to walk down with him, and Adrian followed. Sara was standing by the sink washing some dishes.

"Hey, Mom," Andrew greeted. "Hi."

"I'm sorry!" Adrian blurted out. The guilt was consuming him, and he just wanted it said.

"Thank you." Sara walked over to hug him. Andrew was happy at the sight of them hugging because he knew his mom was having a hard time with all this too.

"You are both grounded for three weeks still." She casually opened the oven to take out the chicken she was making.

"*Three* weeks?" Adrian shouted.

Andrew was hoping he wasn't included in that punishment, even though the spell had been his idea. "Both of us?"

"Yup. No magic, no Avalon, and no going out with friends. And do you know what the best part is?"

". . . what?" Andrew asked, concerned over how happy his mother looked. Sara retrieved a talisman from her pocket, and it started to glow.

"Aunt Liz gave me this nifty little thing to make sure you two aren't doing any magic! You see, it glows around wizards who have just performed spells and whatnot," she said with a smirk. "As you can see, it's working perfectly, and Darwin used this on Liz when she was younger. Wasn't often, but it worked then and works now," she added while staring at it. "Now wash up for dinner!" she told them with a grin.

✳ ✳ ✳

FRIDAY came so fast, Chloe thought as she opened her locker, getting ready to go home.

She made sure to only take the books she had homework in and leave the rest. High school books were big and bulky now, and yet the school officials wondered why more and more students were getting backaches. As Chloe gathered her things, Collin approached her and asked if they were still on for tonight, catching Chloe by surprise. She had tried going the entire day without seeing him, even ditching a class they had together and taking the bus to school just to avoid him.

She told him that they were still on, and he told her what time he planned on picking her up. As he turned away to leave, they exchanged smiles and Chloe went back to packing her backpack. She didn't mind seeing him for a few seconds. She had put a lot of thought into what she wanted to do today, and not having Collin see her until she was all made up was one of those things. Even though she saw him daily and they had hung out before, this time felt different. This time felt as though those feelings she had for him were finally being returned, and just the thought of that brought butterflies to her stomach—no, scratch that, they were more like bats.

Chloe snapped out of her daze and hurried to get to her bus before she missed it. The bus drivers were generally good at knowing when everyone was on their bus but since Chloe rarely took it, she might not be so lucky. She ran outside and thankfully; bus number seven was still there. The ride was quick, maybe eleven minutes tops before she was being dropped off on her corner. She ran home, heading straight to her room to get ready. Even though Collin was getting her at seven o'clock and she had plenty of time, she was in a rush. Liz heard the front door open and shut and Chloe's room door slam shut five seconds later. She laughed to herself, knowing exactly what was going on.

The doorbell rang, sending Chloe into a panic. She didn't realize how late it was and still couldn't decide on what shoes to wear. "Ugh! Why do I have all these shoes? Who needs five different pairs of the same color? Why?! After a few seconds of nervous back and forth, she decided to wear her knee-high purple dress boots to match her purple three-quarter-sleeve handkerchief-hem top she bought the other day. Her outfit was completed with dark skinny jeans along with her punk rock updo hairstyle. As she went down the stairs, Collin couldn't help but stare.

"Wow. You look very nice," he complimented her. He felt a strange feeling in his stomach—he was nervous again. He felt underdressed, as he wore a graphic tee, dark straight-fit jeans, and brand-new white sneakers.

"So do you," she reassured him. Liz was ecstatic as she looked on. She knew how long Chloe had waited for this day and was happy that her daughter was getting what she wanted.

"You guys have fun!" she couldn't contain her excitement, grateful at how normal this moment felt.

"Ok. See you later, Mom."

"Bye, Aunt Liz!" Collin joked.

As they drove to dinner, they talked about school and how things were going at home. When they pulled up to the restaurant, they saw that the parking lot was full but waited for a table anyways. This was their first time coming to this restaurant and when they went in, they were greeted by music and a friendly staff, the walls decorated with pictures of old movie stars and posters. The booths were lined up against the wall perfectly and tables took up all the other space. The servers all wore perfectly pressed identical uniforms.

There were a lot of people in there, but luckily for Collin, he knew the hostess. Once his friend Ruby saw him and Chloe, she called them over to her. They exchanged pleasantries and she took them to a table for two all the way in the back of the restaurant. "Is this ok?" she asked. The lighting was dim, and the music was soft, setting the mood for a romantic night, and Collin said it was perfect. Chloe thought so too, as they took their seats.

"Thanks, Ruby," Chloe expressed as Ruby turned to walk away. They sat down and looked over the menu.

"So far, I like this place!" Collin said, his nerves getting the best of him. He had to keep reminding himself that it was still Chloe.

"Yeah. And the food smells great," Chloe approved. She was calm—not nervous, but very happy.

They ordered their food and talked the night away. One would think two people who saw each other every day wouldn't have much to talk about, but somehow, they did. As the night started to wind down, their waitress brought over their check. Collin, the gentleman he was, paid the bill and escorted his beautiful date to his car. They joked and laughed some more as they made their way to Collin's car. Chloe couldn't help but think about how this night was going to end, which brought a smile to her face along with that familiar feeling in her stomach of riding a   roller coaster. As they approached and stopped in front of her house, both anticipating ending the night with a kiss, neither of them made a move. They just sat there awkwardly until Chloe broke the silence.

"Well… um… thank you for tonight. It was a lot of fun." Silence fell between them once more.

"Yeah, it was," Collin added, his heart beating faster. He just wanted to grab and kiss her, but he wasn't sure if he could. After all, she was his best friend's cousin. Plus, he had only ever kissed one other girl before at a party during a game of spin the bottle.

Chloe opened the car door and said goodbye. Before Collin could act, she was already halfway to her door. *Way to mess that up*, he thought to himself. Chloe looked back one more time before she went in and waved goodbye.

She couldn't help but smile and feel incredibly happy at how her date went. She knew Collin wanted to kiss her goodnight but like her, he was nervous. She ran up to her room with the excitement of knowing that he felt the same way she did, no matter how awkwardly it had ended.

Chapter Nineteen

Bianca and Brad teleported to the first of four stops on their quest for Lester Sterling. Brad stumbled upon arrival, not used to teleporting, and before Bianca could say anything, he vomited on the dirt road they stood on. Bianca was surprised; the elixir he drank should have worked. It was midafternoon, and the fresh air blowing through the area was so much different than being in a big city. Bianca told Brad to sit down as she looked around to see if there was any place, she could get fresh water for him.

Unfortunately, they had teleported to a very secluded area of this small town—in fact, it was the very edge of the town they needed to search. After a few minutes, Brad told her that he was ok to walk. Bianca rubbed his head then helped him to his feet. Before they started to leave, she asked him if he was really ok to move. He assured her that he was, and so they began their journey toward the town in the distance.

They hiked a couple of miles in, not knowing if they were in Trusdale, they came into what they were sure was the heart of the little village. The dirt roads were full of people strolling up and down with oversized baskets of what could only be fresh fruit in their hands. Kids played kickball in the open fields on both sides of them. Up ahead, there was a two-story building that was kind of run-down but had a homey feel to it. Bianca only understood the word "inn" on it. She marched toward it with Brad while telling him that they would get a room for the night.

At the front desk, the lady who greeted them was incredibly nice. Her words were hard to understand, but Bianca somehow managed to get her to understand that they needed a room for the night. In that moment, Bianca realized that looking for Lester in two foreign countries was going to be difficult. Not impossible—just difficult. Brad leaned on her while they waited for their key to the room. When the front desk lady came back, she had a bigger-than-normal key attached to an oversized rubber ball.

The clerk handed the key to Bianca and said two simple words: "Sleep tight!" Bianca glanced back and gave a wave, then she and Brad ambled up to their room. That was the easy part—all the rooms were numbered, so all Bianca had to do was match the number on the ball to a door they passed. Finally, they found a matching number. They entered the room, surprised by how clean it was and the amount of space they had. The freshly washed sheets filled the air with the smell of lavender. Brad was the first one to the bed and the first to feel how soft the king-size bed was. Everything was handmade, right down to the bed itself.

"You have to feel how soft this bed is, B!" Brad patted the bed and playfully winked at Bianca. "I bet this is what a cloud feels like." Brad bounced on the bed, hoping to get Bianca to unwind a bit.

"Ok, you rest up and I will be back." Bianca picked up the photo of what Lester would look like today, completely brushing off Brad's attempt to make her relax a bit before rushing off.

Brad leapt off the bed and glided to her side. "I could go with?"

"No. You need to rest up. Teleporting takes a lot out of regular people." Bianca left the room in a hurry. Any longer and she would take Brad up on his offer for her to rest her eyes. She also knew that she would do a better job looking for Lester without any distractions, and she had to face it: Brad would be a distraction. She reached the lobby doors and marched out with purpose. The sun was still out, but she didn't know for how much longer. Kids were still playing on the fields and people were still meandering up and down the dirt road.

The buildings all around her in this little town known as Trusdale were no taller than two stories and further apart than the ones back home in Arcadia. As she passed the countless people hurrying past her, she couldn't help but notice how friendly they all were. Everyone sent a smile her way as she passed, and one lady even offered her a piece of fruit. Bianca graciously accepted the woman's generous gift; after all, it would be rude if she didn't.

She got to a part of town where a church stood right in the center of the road. It was the tallest building and as she looked up, the sound of the bell in the tower of the church began to ring. She gathered there must have been some importance to it, because everyone around started navigating toward the big white church. Bianca decided to join the rest of them, and as she got closer, she noticed a priest standing at the doorway.

Must be time for a service or something, she thought, seeing how everyone started to pile in. She decided to see what all the fuss was about and went in as well and not surprisingly, people welcomed her even though it was so obvious she was an outsider. She looked up at the tall ceilings and admired the stained-glass windows all around her. Before the service started, she decided it was probably best to go explore the little village some more. As she headed toward another street, she was surprised that many people were still out walking around. *Guess not everyone goes to the church service after all.*

She came to a dead end and noticed a little café-like establishment to her left, and she decided to check it out. When she went inside, she saw people sitting down talking and laughing. Bianca couldn't understand anything anyone was saying but was still curious at the patrons as she passed by. She then took out the picture of Lester she made before her quest and asked the guy behind the counter if he had seen him.

She had trouble getting out the words but soon realized that this man spoke English—granted, not perfectly, but enough to get by if he ever decided to move to the States. Bianca felt heat on her face and knew she was blushing. The gentleman behind the counter offered her a cold beverage, telling her she shouldn't feel embarrassed. He then looked at the picture and informed her that he had never seen that man but would ask if anyone else had. He went around the cafe and began talking in his native tongue, showing the picture to the customers as he passed them.

Some people shook their heads while others said the word "no" and Bianca was disappointed. For a second, she let herself believe that this would be an easy task. She thanked the gentleman for his help and left a twenty-dollar bill on the counter. She decided she needed another perspective and headed back to the inn. When she arrived, she saw that Brad was asleep. She stared at him, envying the fact that he could sleep at that moment.

He looked so peaceful and comfortable that Bianca couldn't help but crawl into bed next to him—just for a few minutes. That few minutes turned into a few hours, and she woke up suddenly, startling Brad in the process. Bianca was relaxed but frustrated that she had lost so much time. She told Brad she would be back later as she drank a small vial she pulled from her bag. Before Brad could say anything, the door closed shut behind her.

When Bianca got outside, she looked around to make sure no one was watching and raised her palm. That same little ball of light that made her realize the twins were wizards appeared in her hand. With a quick gesture of her hand, she released it into the air. She found cover and removed her clothes from her body while watching the light ascend to great heights. As her top fell to the ground, she transformed into a beautiful white falcon with a blue streak weaving down its back. She soared high into the air and caught up to the little orb of light, still, as if it was waiting for her. The light then shot down and multiplied into hundreds of little lights that spread out within the village like a swarm of fireflies below as Bianca soared high in the sky looking down.

In her current state, her incredible eyesight allowed her to see everyone in the streets clearly. She began to glide down closer to the town as all the lights zoomed past the people below. No one noticed them, however, since the lights themselves were invisible to human eyes. Minutes passed and Bianca was still gliding through the night sky watching the lights below.

After a few hours, she decided that it seemed Lester wasn't in this Trusdale.

She flew back to where her clothes were and transformed back to her beautiful human self. When she got back to the room, Brad could see she was exhausted, so he told her to lay down. She took his advice and he lay next to her holding her tightly, and it wasn't long before they fell asleep.

Bianca woke up the next morning feeling relaxed and refreshed after a great night's sleep. *Brad was not joking about how comfortable that bed was.* After her shower, Bianca packed up the few items she took out and they were ready to go to the next Trusdale on their list. They dashed out the front door of the inn so they could be seen leaving and once they were clear of onlookers, she gripped Brad's hand and they teleported from that nice, quiet little village.

Brad bent over, closed his eyes tight, hoping not to let the dizziness win. "I don't think I will ever get used to that." They had arrived at the border of the next Trusdale to search. Bianca's eyes widened as she led the way into town. This Trusdale was somewhere in Italy and was the exact opposite from the one they just left; you could see the big, beautiful houses that lined the streets of this Trusdale from miles away. This town was similar to the suburbs they had back home, and with each step they took they noticed all the luxury cars that passed them by. *This must be the place Lester Sterling calls home,* Bianca thought to herself.

People they passed on the sidewalks didn't even acknowledge Bianca and Brad as they walked by. Bianca was worried they wouldn't find a place to sleep for the night. As they went further into town, they noticed signs that said, "Downtown Trusdale" and followed them. They were amazed at what was all around them—luxury hotels one after one another. Bianca felt relieved, and they entered the first one they came across. Once they were all situated, Bianca once again told Brad to stay in the room and said she would be right back. Brad wasn't too excited about that, as he wanted to spend time with her, but he knew he couldn't say anything since he wasn't supposed to be there in the first place.

A few hours later, Bianca came storming back in, not looking pleased. "Guess you didn't find him?" Brad wasn't expecting her back so soon and had just ordered food for himself.

"No," Bianca uttered as she slammed her bag down. She began searching her bag for something, she noticed Brad's annoyed expression.

"Something wrong?"

"Well, I was hoping that we could take a few hours for ourselves." A hopeful smirk came across his face. "We should enjoy this beautiful place. Maybe grab dinner?"

"Brad…" Bianca disregarded riffling through the bag for a second. "You know why I'm here. I told you this was important, so please don't make me feel bad for doing what I have to do." She rushed into the bathroom, grabbing her smaller bag she had placed in there earlier.

"I know." Brad quickly followed. "But we need to eat, so why not do it together?" he asked her as he brought her closer to his chest.

"You're right." Bianca paused. "We can go to dinner." Unable to resist his charm, she realized it wouldn't hurt to enjoy some time together when they could.

"Good!" Brad rushed over to the burger he had just ordered and placed it in the small fridge that was tucked away next to the wardrobe.

They decided that the restaurant across the street from the hotel would suffice. Once inside, they saw that reservations were required to eat there, so Bianca chanted a few words and her name suddenly appeared on the fifth line of the hostess's notepad. "Right on time!" the lady told them in Italian as she led them to their table for two. Bianca was never happier to have taken Italian throughout high school since now she was fluent in it. Searching for Lester would be that much easier with her actually knowing the language of this Trusdale.

Bianca and Brad took their seats and looked over their menus. Everything was expensive, which made them both want to try it all. After a few minutes, they ordered their food and Brad reached over, taking Bianca's hand into his. "This is nice," he said as he stared into her eyes.

"It is." She leaned in and gave him a gentle kiss on the lips. "Thank you for making me come out. I needed this."

"You're welcome," Brad said, happy that they had some alone time to try to enjoy themselves. Bianca, however, knew this dinner couldn't be all pleasure and cast her wizard finding orb spell again. She held out her hand and watched as the orb emerged from the center of her palm.

"What are you doing?" Brad asked, not being able to see the light floating in her hand.

Bianca said a few more words and the orb zoomed past Brad, who didn't even flinch. With another wave of her hand the orb multiplied into at least one hundred more and zoomed past every patron enjoying their meal. Not one person saw them and one zoomed past Bianca, who dodged it by moving her head like it would hit her.

Brad watched, amused. "What are you doing? You look ridiculous staring off like that," he teased.

Bianca monitored the room. "Just checking to see if Lester is in here." Her focus returned to Brad. "But he's not." As if it would be that easy.

Once she was sure that he wasn't in there, she chanted a few more words in Latin and the orbs disappeared just as fast as they had appeared. Just then their food arrived, and it smelled incredible. Bianca picked up her silverware. "Now, we can enjoy dinner!"

As they ate, they laughed and joked and no one around them seemed to exist; Brad could only see Bianca and vice versa. An older couple a few tables away nodded their way as if they were moved to see such a young couple in love. They even sent over a bottle of champagne for Brad and Bianca to enjoy. Bianca thanked them from her seat and went back to her night with Brad. A few hours later, the couple left the restaurant hand in hand and strolled across the dimly lit street back to their hotel. Bianca couldn't help but kiss Brad on the neck while he looked for the key card to open their door. Once the door opened, Brad returned the kiss and the door closed behind them as he led her toward their bed.

Bianca felt anxious throughout the night. She tossed and turned and only felt calm when she watched Brad sleep. He was her everything, and she couldn't be more grateful that he came with her. As soon as seven o'clock hit, she was up, showered, and ready to go. She hoped today would be different. She hoped today she would find Lester. This Trusdale was a luxury if Bianca ever saw it; it was full of wealthy people, and any wizard from Avalon would feel welcomed. So why wouldn't Lester be there?

She made her way out the door, but not before giving her sleeping boyfriend a kiss on the forehead. The sun was starting to rise, and the streets of downtown Trusdale had more people on them than Bianca expected. She took out that picture and showed it to people that passed her. Some looked at it and some blew her off like she was a homeless person begging for food.

Some even treated her like she had the plague. Bianca didn't let that faze her, though; she knew she had to stay positive, so she kept at it.

An hour or so passed and Bianca felt like she needed to get coffee, as she was starting to feel the effects of a sleepless night. She looked around and spotted a cafe across the street. She headed in that direction, still asking people if they had seen the man in the photo. Once inside the café, she knew the people here wouldn't be as friendly as the small village they visited a couple days ago. Bianca knew it was time for a break.

She sat down in a luxurious chair that had to be the most comfortable thing she had ever sat on. She didn't know if it was because she was incredibly tired or if this chair was, in fact, made of the most comfortable padding in the world. She set the picture beside her and looked over the menu. Like last night, everything was in Italian and Bianca was grateful she could read it. She took a few minutes, then the waitress came over to take her order.

"Signor Darling," the waitress mumbled while glancing at the picture on the table. Bianca didn't realize what she was talking about at first. It took her a few moments before she realized the waitress was talking about the picture.

Bianca quickly picked up the photo. "You know this man?" Bianca asked in Italian while tapping her finger on the picture of Lester's face.

"Si," replied the waitress. Bianca was uncertain, so she asked question after question, all of which the waitress had an answer to. The waitress told Bianca that she knew him as Benjamin Darling and that she remembered him because of his accent and how generous and sweet he was every time he visited. The waitress told Bianca he did not live in town but only visited when he was dropping or picking up suits from the tailor across the street. Bianca thanked the waitress and left a generous tip herself on the table, then bolted for the door.

As Bianca ran through the streets back to her hotel, she felt relieved. She still hadn't found Lester, but she felt closer than ever to finding him, like it was only a matter of time now. She barged into the room, waking Brad in the process. He was startled but already fully awake. Bianca tossed him a T-shirt and told him to get dressed and meet her in the lobby with their bags. She only needed her laptop bag and bolted out the door before Brad could respond.

Bianca went down to the lobby of the hotel to wait for Brad and to search the next two Trusdales for a "Benjamin Darling." She knew it was a long shot; a wizard as skilled, as smart as Lester wouldn't leave any trace that could lead to him. After searching for a few minutes, she found a hit for a Benjamin Darling from a local newspaper in Tennessee.   The article was titled "Generous Man Donates to Save School." It was written ten years ago and included no picture, but Bianca believed it was him.

Brad entered the lobby, scanning the room until he spotted Bianca. "You know we had Wi-Fi in the room, right?" Brad asked as he stood a few feet away from Bianca.

"Oh. I didn't know." Bianca stood up. "Are you ready?"

"Yeah," Brad replied, a little confused as to what the plan was.

Bianca packed up her laptop and gripped Brad's hand. Brad gave her a good morning kiss and Bianca looked at him for a lingering moment, feeling like she was the luckiest girl in the world to have such an amazing boyfriend. He didn't even ask why she was in a hurry; he just did what Bianca needed him to do. She smiled at him one more time, looked around to make sure no one was around as they turned the corner behind the building, and they teleported to what Bianca hoped was their last stop in the search for Lester Sterling.

Brad instantly vomited once they arrived. *He must have forgotten to take the anti- teleporting vial. I can't babysit him and make sure he takes it,* she thought. He

used a pole holding up a sign that read "Welcome to Jackson, Tennessee "
to keep him from losing his balance. Bianca asked if he was alright, to
which he replied a queasy, "Yes." He didn't feel quite like he did the first
time, but he still needed to lay down. She went into town with him and
given that they saw farms around them as they walked and a small town
square a few miles down the road, Bianca felt like it would be much easier
to find out if he was here compared to the other places.

Like the other two places before, the couple was easily able to find an inn
for them to stay in. Bianca sat Brad down on a nearby bench and made her
way inside the inn. She was greeted by a young blonde woman who checked
her in and gave her a room on the second floor. Bianca led Brad upstairs and
he quickly got into bed. This one wasn't as comfortable as the previous ones,
but it would have to do. Bianca told Brad that she was going to check out the
town and told him to drink the vial she left for him to help with the nausea.
She couldn't forget her useful picture of Lester that was a little crinkly now,
grabbing it swiftly then rushing down the stairs and out the front door to
begin her search. She saw a woman across the street cleaning the front steps
of a local grocery store.

Bianca rushed over. "Hi, miss." She waited for the lady to look at her. "I
was wondering if you have ever seen this man?" She held up the picture of
what Lester Sterling would look like now.

"No," the woman snapped sternly. Even with her welcoming Southern
accent, Bianca knew that the lady was aggravated with her.

"Ok. Thank you for your time." Bianca took a few steps back down the
stairs, feeling slighted. *I thought Southern people were supposed to be friendlier than
that.* As she hiked around the town square, she saw people talking and
laughing with each other. Bianca had always wanted to live in a small town
like this, where everyone knew each other and the only stores around were
owned by someone in the community, not those big-box stores that were
everywhere back home. The friendliness and closeness that she saw around
her made her feel warm and happy inside. There was just something so warm
and homey about the environment of a small town compared to somewhere
like Arcadia.

As she passed people in the street, she showed the picture and asked the same
question. Although they looked at the photo and simply said "no," saying it with
a rather rude tone, she kept asking. She came upon another store called Sandy's
Hardware and went inside. She went up to the lady at the cashier counter and

showed the picture to her. The lady looked at it and once again, the answer was no. Only this time, it was followed by, "If you're not buying anything, you need to leave." Bianca couldn't keep her aggravation hidden any longer.

"You know, I always figured a small town like this full of good people would be a little bit more friendly to visitors! I guess that old saying of Southern hospitality and being welcoming to outsiders is a myth."

"Look. Just go back to wherever you came from, darling, 'cause you won't find that man here. People in town have been telling you they have never seen him, so you need to get on now," the lady responded coldly.

"You're right. Sorry for wasting your time." Bianca left the store. She had a feeling this lady knew something. She had a feeling the whole town knew something, given that they obviously informed the hardware clerk of her search, but Bianca didn't let it show. She simply left.

She couldn't shake the feeling that the lady at the hardware store knew more than she was letting on. Suddenly, Bianca decided to turn around to watch her and see what she would do. But she couldn't watch her as herself, so she went somewhere safe to transform into her falcon form and soared high in the sky, circling the hardware store below. Bianca landed on a nearby roof and stared down at the entrance.

A few minutes went by, and she saw the lady locking up and rushing to her car. She took off rather fast from the parking lot and Bianca followed from above, flying a little slower so she didn't pass the car below. Bianca soared through the air effortlessly as the lady drove about three miles up the road. Bianca looked ahead and only spotted one farm by a giant house. The lady turned off the road down a dirt driveway that led to the house Bianca saw.

The car came to a stop. The woman from the hardware store got out and ran up to a man sitting on a rocking chair on the front porch. Bianca couldn't really make out what they were saying so she opted to circle the property as they talked. The lady only stayed for a few minutes before rushing back to her car and taking off, leaving nothing more than a cloud of dust that blocked Bianca's view for a few seconds. As the dust cleared, Bianca saw the man staring directly at her as she flew above the property. It was clear as day that she found Lester Sterling.

Bianca quickly traveled back to the inn to let Brad know she had found Lester. She saw the window to her room was open, flew in, and transformed back to her human self.

Bianca's bare feet pounded on the floor. "I found him!" She rummaged around for new clothes from her bag. "Did you hear me? I found him!"

Brad sat up. "Really?" He was surprised by how sure of herself she sounded.

"Yes!" Her heart was racing; the way Lester had stared at her gave her chills. Bianca had heard the stories of how powerful a wizard he was. Even though it didn't feel like it, finding Lester was the *easy* part. Talking to him might be difficult, if not impossible. *What if he blows me off or teleports away?*

Brad went to her side and caressed the small of her back. "You should go talk to him now before he runs again."

"I know!" Bianca turned to sit so she could put her shoes on. "I'll be right back."

"Take me with you," Brad rushed to get dressed as well. "Because the faster you talk to him, the faster we can go back home. I went to that store across the street for something to eat and everyone I passed looked at me like I had the plague or something."

Bianca sat there thinking. "Yeah, you're right. The faster we get answers, the faster we can go home. Grab the bags!"

Brad quickly packed the few items that were out and zipped up the bags. As he put them over his shoulders, Bianca gripped his hand and they teleported from their room. The teleporting potion must have helped a lot, because Brad was perfectly fine as they arrived in front of Lester's home. Bianca was surprised to see that he hadn't moved from the rocking chair she had seen him in before.

Bianca casually approached, gripping Brad's hand tighter. "Mr. Sterling. It's an honor to meet you." She stopped a little bit ahead of Brad.

Lester sat there, rocking yet motionless, staring at his uninvited guests. "Why, hello there," he finally uttered in a welcoming tone.

Bianca took a few more steps farther, releasing Brad from her grip so he wouldn't follow. "We don't mean to intrude. It's just—"

Lester interrupted, "You mean going around town asking every Tom, Dick, and Harry if they know who I am and then showing up to my home unannounced is you 'not meaning to intrude'?" He didn't expect a response and stood up from his chair. Bianca stopped moving. Her heart started racing, not knowing if he was going to attack her or what. Lester was obviously from the South as his Southern drawl quickly exposed. He had dirty grayish hair and hazel eyes and was of average weight and height with the exception of some padding around his midsection.

Bianca warmly stared at him. "I do apologize for the intrusion—I really do, but my name is Bianca, and this is Brad, and I need your help. My grandfather needed me to find you so I can ask you where the Alexandro's Crystal is hidden."

"Your grandfather…" Lester was bewildered. "Wait a minute, are you Darwin's kin?"

"Yes!" Bianca breathed a sigh of relief. "And Gabriel is looking for the crystals. Darwin would be here himself, but he's locked up in the Tower of Avalon on bogus charges."

Lester's tone quickly changed to a more welcoming one. "Why am I not surprised."

Would y'all like to come inside for some drinks?" He rose from the rocker and gestured toward the door.

"Sure." Bianca's heart is beginning to slow to a normal beat. She reached for Brad's hand and followed Lester inside. She was hesitant because she knew how powerful Lester was, but she didn't have much of a choice.

Lester held the screen door open for them. "Now, I left that world many years ago and want nothing to do with it, but Darwin was a friend back in the day, so I will answer what I can for y'all."

"Thank you." Bianca, feeling relieved over the warm welcome, led Brad inside.

Lester followed, brushing past the couple. "But let's try to make this quick so y'all can be on your way." Lester headed over to his kitchen to grab a couple of cups with ice then made his way back to the living room bar and poured Brad and Bianca some soda.

"Do you know where the crystal is?" Bianca asked as Lester gestured for them to sit down, handing them their drinks.

"Hmm…" Lester stood up straight, placing his hand on the back of his hips. "I'm afraid I do not, sugah."

Bianca looked disappointed. "Do you know how to read the map?" Bianca was hopeful that she hadn't wasted her time finding him.

"Huckabee was a very secretive wizard." Lester took a few steps back and found his seat. "That's why he didn't tell me much, and over time he lost his ability to trust anyone—even me. So, I knew there was a map, but I'm afraid I can't help you with that, either." Lester's eyebrows drew together.

Bianca let out a sigh. All this time looking for Lester to get his help was proving to be a waste of time. "Is there anything else you can tell me that could help us find the crystal before Gabriel does?"

"Hmm…" Lester thought. "Have you heard the story of the Elder Wizards?"

"Yes."

"Many wizards around the world believed—because of a prophecy or whatever nonsense went around back then—that an heir of Alexandro would reunite the three crystals and be made an immortal with unlimited power."

Bianca was puzzled. "Then why is Gabriel so determined to find it?" It sounded like it would be useless for Gabriel to get ahold of those crystals. Lester got up from his chair and paced to the table in the living room.

"You must not have known. How could you? Only Huckabee knew." Lester was distracted by the disheveled papers on the table. "Why do you think Darwin was the one selected to hide the crystal?" Lester turned to Bianca, who was standing up now. "Darwin is an Alexandro's heir, which makes Gabriel—"

"An Alexandro's heir!" Bianca finished Lester's sentence. Her heart began racing again.

Bianca was taken aback and looked at Brad, who had been listening intently to their conversation. This all had to be lost on him, but he was listening just the same. Bianca then went over to the window to get closer to Lester, who was now looking at her. They were only a few feet apart.

"How can Darwin find the crystal without the map?" Bianca asked, her breathing a little heavier. This new information was a lot to take in.

Lester looked at her. "The map alone is no good."

"Why?" Bianca was hanging on to his every word.

"Darwin's staff…" Lester was unsure if he should continue. "Well, his staff is the key to unlocking the place it's sealed in." Lester placed his left hand on his hip, leaning back.

Bianca felt relieved. The first bit of good news since they had found Lester, finally, and now she knew that they were a step ahead of Gabriel. It might not be a big step, but a step, nonetheless. *As long as Darwin's staff is safe, we don't need to worry*, Bianca thought to herself.

Lester took a step forward. "You know—" He didn't have a chance to finish his sentence as he was blasted in the center of his chest by a bright-red light and nothing but pink mist was left in his place. Lester Sterling, who had hidden successfully from every wizard in the world for years, was dead.

Bianca quickly turned in the direction the blast came from, summoning her wand in the process, and was stunned to see Brad pointing his wand at her. As he shot the same spell her way, she deflected it just in time, but the force of their spells hitting each other sent her crashing through the window behind her. Bianca landed on the floor outside, unable to move and as pale as a ghost. Brad climbed out of the window, wand in hand.

"Nice deflection spell. You're fast. Not how I wanted the spell to work, but it looks like the end results will be the same." Brad glanced at her inner thigh and saw a big piece of glass sticking out of it while blood slowly poured out. The glass must have hit an artery. He gently removed it so the blood could flow freely. "Thanks again for bringing me with you on this adventure of yours. It turned out to be very informative," Brad told her as he crouched down and stroked her hair. He then leaned in and kissed her on her forehead, a familiar kiss Bianca had felt so many times before. Bianca's eyes closed and her head tilted to the side as Brad stood up. He looked down one last time at his girlfriend, who was slowly dying, and teleported out of sight. Brad was gone.

Chapter Twenty

Brad teleported to a small town in Avalon called Brookshire where the majority of the council members along with other high-profile wizards of Avalon lived. He stared up the pathway to a sprawling estate that had to be the biggest one in the neighborhood. He approached the tall, thick wooden doors and rang the doorbell.

After a few seconds, a lady wearing a white skirt and top with a black apron tied around her waist greeted him. Brad told her he was there to see the lady of the house and she waved him in. As she accompanied him in, he peeked around and saw paintings on the walls and a grand staircase directly in front of him. He admired one painting in particular hanging on a wall by the doors.

He stared at it but not for long, as the lady who answered the door returned to tell Brad the lady of the house was on the back patio having brunch. He made his way to the back of the house where he saw a gentleman in a gray suit carrying two plates out of the opened double doors. One had eggs benedict with ham and spinach; the other had hotcakes, two slices of bacon, and fresh fruit. The sight of the food made Brad hungry, as he hadn't eaten at all yet. As the butler put the plates down on the table, Adele was surprised to see Brad standing in the doorw a y .

"Darby!" Adele called out Brad's true name as she placed her tea on the table. "What are you doing here?" This caught Isabel's attention, who was sitting across from Adele, and she quickly turned around.

Brad looked on coldly. "I'm done with my little experiment." Brad always loved Adele's accent and how it made her sound so elegant and authoritative at the same time. Brad glanced at Isabel, sending a flirtatious wink her way. Isabel turned back to her delicious breakfast that was sitting in front of her.

"Would you care for something to eat, Darby?" Adele gestured for him to join them.

Darby approached the table. "Yes, please. And I'm beyond happy to drop this 'Brad' name from my vocabulary." He looked over at Isabel again.

Adele waved her servant off and he went inside, probably to grab another plate of food for Adele's new visitor. Soon, Adele's servant made his way back to the table and set down a plate of eggs and bacon with a side of poached potatoes and toast in front of Darby. He began to ravenously eat with Adele and Isabel. After a few moments, Adele took a sip of her tea and sent both of her servants away so they couldn't hear what Darby was going to say.

"Delicious, isn't it?" Adele warmly smiled his way.

"It really is," Darby said, his voice muffled by the food in his mouth.

Adele glanced his way as she took a bite of her poached egg. "So, Darby…" She took a moment to swallow her food. "Tell us what you have found out." She took another bite off her fork, savoring it.

"I found out something that will for sure win me some points with Gabriel himself." Adele had never seen him so confident before. He continued eating but before Adele or Isabel could say anything, a voice sounded out from below the back steps that led to the acres of grass that was Adele's backyard.

"And what would that be?" Gabriel said as he ascended the cement steps, marveling at the beautiful bricks that paved the side.

Adele, Isabel, and Darby quickly rose from the table when they saw it was him. Darby gulped down the food in his mouth and moistened his lips. Neither he nor Isabel say anything; they simply bow their heads in his direction. His heart began to beat faster as Gabriel made his way to the table. "Well. Go on." Gabriel took a seat at the table, joining the three of them. "Please, sit down." He stared at Adele, implying that even in her own home, he was in charge. The three of them took their seats, but Darby couldn't bring himself to take another bite.

"Darby, is it?" Gabriel inquired, staring right at him as sweat formed just above his brow.

"Yes, sir." He could feel the sweat slowly running down the side of his face. "Darby is my given name, but your sister knows me as Brad." He could feel his palms begin to moisten.

"Please don't let me interrupt what you were going to say." He waved his hand over the empty spot in front of him. Instantly, a cup of hot coffee appeared before him. He poured some sugar into it and magically stirred it with a motion of his finger without touching a spoon or the cup it was in.

Darby went on to tell them about his trip with Bianca. He told them how they found Lester Sterling in a small, crappy hole of a human town in the South. He was quick to mention that Lester didn't know how to read the map or where that map was, but that the key to unlocking where the Alexandro's Crystal was hidden was Darwin's cane. Gabriel listened intensely to every word.

"You're right." Gabriel leaned back into his chair, taking a sip of his coffee. "That did win you some points," he affirmed, his tone genuine. He was truly happy over what he was told.

Darby breathed a sigh of relief. He thought Gabriel wouldn't like hearing that Lester didn't know how to read the map, but he didn't seem to care. Gabriel finished his cup of coffee while everyone else finished their breakfast. "I trust Mr. Sterling won't be sharing that story with anyone else." Gabriel looked at Darby.

"He won't." Darby puffed out his chest. "I killed him." He was confident now knowing he had done something no other wizard could do found and killed Lester Sterling.

"And the girl?" Gabriel asked—not out of concern for his niece, but to make sure she would not be a problem.

Darby paused. "I killed her too." He looked up, not knowing if Gabriel would appreciate that.

Gabriel leaned forward; his cheekbones raised prominently. This was the first time Adele had seen a smile on his face since he was released from the Tower. In fact, she couldn't remember the last time Gabriel actually smiled. After all, it's not like he was much of a happy person to begin with. Adele was thrilled that Darby was able to deliver this good news. She couldn't imagine what the outcome of Gabriel's visit would have been if he hadn't been there.

"Tell me, Darby—or do you prefer Brad?" Gabriel questioned him. "Darby is fine, sir."

"Tell me, what was it like killing a girl you were with for so long? I know Adele assigned you to spy for us, but after a couple of years of dating, I can't imagine it…" Gabriel trailed off. "I can't imagine it being so easy to kill someone you knew intimately." He watched Darby, standing there sweating, looking for any sign of weakness.

Darby picked up on Gabriel's test based on what he had heard about him. "It was very easy, sir. I knew that if I didn't kill her, she would take that information back to her mother. I knew you wouldn't want that, so I acted on instinct and killed her."

"No hesitation." Gabriel relished in his response. "That's good." He took another sip of his coffee.

Darby, still unsure if Gabriel thought he regretted his actions, was quick to point out, "Don't get me wrong, sir. I will miss the great time in bed I had with her, but other than that, I really didn't give it a second thought." He shot another pointed glance at Isabel. Gabriel was happy with him and placed his hand on Darby's shoulder.

"You did an excellent job." Darby sat up straight on full alert, reveling in a job well done.

Gabriel strutted toward the double doors that led back into the house, but before he went in, he looked back at Isabel. "Isabel, come. I need you to do something for me." He continued into Adele's house. Isabel stood up quickly and followed, but not without throwing her napkin on Darby's plate. He looked amused over how jealous she was as she stormed off.

"Don't worry about her. She'll be fine." Adele told Darby, whose amusement faded and quickly turned into annoyance over what Isabel just did. Adele caressed his face and gently turned it toward her. "You did well. I'm proud of you."

✳ ✳ ✳

"HEY, guys, wait up!" Andrew shouted to Chloe and Collin from across the crowded hallway of Arcadia high. Chloe pulled Collin to the side to wait for Andrew to catch up. "Have you or Aunt Liz heard from Bianca yet?"

"No. Mom said she might be a week or two."

The three of them began to walk down the hall again. Andrew looked disappointed over Bianca not calling yet. He was starting to think that the spell he and Adrian cast had been for nothing but was trying to wait to get conformation from his cousin that they failed in helping find Lester Sterling.

Andrew started to pay attention again to Chloe and Collin, who seemed to be in their own little world, laughing and giggling over inside jokes.

Andrew suddenly felt like a third wheel even though Chloe was his cousin and Collin, his best friend. He decided to let them go to class together and told them he would see them at lunch. Andrew turned and headed down another hallway. *They need to make it official already*, he thought to himself as he made his way down the crowded halls to his next class.

Collin and Chloe didn't even seem to notice Andrew had left and continued walking with each other. They reached Chloe's class and once again had a moment where neither one of them knew if they should kiss the other or not. Collin shook his head and patted her on the arm, telling her he would see her at lunch. He then continued down the hall to his class, disappointed at how he had just patted her on the arm. In that moment, he felt extremely stupid.

Chloe stared at him, laughing before heading into her own class. She took her normal seat in Mr. King's class, her favorite class of the whole day. The bell sounded and in came Mr. King. He told his students good morning and to take out their books and turn to page sixty-four. Chloe, being the good student she always was, already had her book opened to said page. Mr. King asked the class a question, and like always, Chloe was the one to answer it.

"Correct, Chloe," Mr. King told her. "Unfortunately, you didn't raise your hand, so you're going to have detention after school." Chloe and the rest of the class were amused at his comment, thinking it was a joke.

"Good one, Mr. King," Chloe said, giggling with the rest of her classmates.

"Don't worry, Chloe. It won't be a real detention because you will serve it here, with me. I could always use the help grading papers from other classes," Mr. King chuckled.

As he went back to teaching the class, Chloe and the rest of her peers realized that Mr. King wasn't joking. Chloe wasn't very happy about that, and it showed for the rest of class; she didn't answer any other questions, no matter if she knew them or not. Chloe stood in the lunch line after class still aggravated over what happened. The line moved at a slower pace than usual, adding to her aggravation.

She finally got up to the buffet table only to find that the cheeseburgers had all been taken. *This just isn't my day*, she thought to herself. Since there didn't seem to be a lot of options left, she settled for a chicken Caesar salad and a bottle of water. She paid for her food and searched for the cafe table where she and her cousins usually had lunch. The overcrowded cafe made it hard to see who was sitting with Adrian but as Chloe got closer, she saw her:

Lisa. Of course, Dean was at the table, too, but Chloe didn't care for Lisa ever since she had found out Collin had a crush on her.

"I can't believe Mr. King gave me detention for not raising my hand!" Chloe slammed down her tray.

"Yeah, I heard. That sucks," Lisa replied. She was always trying her hardest to befriend Chloe, but she didn't respond, even though she heard her. Lisa had tried everything to become friends with Chloe, but nothing seemed to work. Sometimes Chloe felt bad for how she treated Lisa—after all, Lisa wasn't to blame for anything—and today she decided to take a different approach.

Chloe started to empathize with her. "It does suck," she finally replied, causing Adrian to look over at her, his mouth slightly agape.

Lisa was caught off guard by it. "Well from now on, don't answer any of his questions."

"Yup," Chloe agreed cheerfully. "That's what I'm going to do from now on." Adrian couldn't believe that Chloe spoke more than two words to Lisa. "This day really sucks," Chloe added.

"I have days like that. Where one thing goes wrong and suddenly everything that can go wrong does. It's aggravating," Lisa said, jumping on her chance to have a real conversation with Chloe.

"Right!" Chloe agreed. That was how her day had been going, and it was extremely aggravating. However, all of that changed for Chloe in a second because Collin came to join his friends at the table and sat right next to her—he didn't even notice Lisa until she and Dean said hi. Collin quickly looked at Chloe and gave her an extra pudding cup he had. All the bad stuff that happened to her was instantly washed away by Collin's simple actions.

"I heard what happened in class." Collin squeezed in to make sure he was sitting next to Chloe. "I bet Mr. King just wanted his best student to help him with stuff after school." He winked at her. Chloe blushed and continued eating her lunch.

It was finally the end of the day and Chloe slowly started putting her books away in her locker. She looked at all the other students and a feeling of jealousy rushed over her—jealousy because the other students could leave for the day while she had to go sit in a room with her former favorite teacher. She put the books she needed to take home in her backpack so she could just do a grab-and-go once she was done with detention. Chloe didn't mind staying after school for student council or other activities, but detention? *That* she didn't like at all.

Collin was heading towards her. "Hey, Chloe." Chloe glanced up.

"Hey, you."

Collin now walked shoulder to shoulder with her. "How long is your detention?"

"I think an hour and a half."

"Ok. Well, call me when you get home or whatever."

"Yeah." That warm, fuzzy feeling she got around Collin started to rush over her. "For sure."

Before Collin met up with the twins, he escorted Chloe to Mr. King's class and gave her a hug goodbye—something she wasn't expecting. Once Collin left, she glided into the classroom with the biggest smile on her face. She took a seat at her usual desk and waited for her teacher.

Chloe started to get agitated after a few minutes because Mr. King hadn't shown up yet.

After what seemed like a long time, Mr. King finally walked in. Chloe looked back and saw him, then turned around to face the front of the class again. Mr. King entered the class, making sure to close the door behind him and lock it.

"Hello, Chloe," he said as he strolled by her to get to his desk.

Chloe didn't respond, hoping that would let Mr. King know that she wasn't pleased with him. Unfortunately, he wasn't fazed by Chloe's little attitude and continued to his desk and put down his bag. Chloe just stared down at her desk, hoping her favorite teacher would pick up on her attitude, but once again he just ignored her while grabbing an item from his desk.

"Chloe, we'll be working in the back of class today," he told her as he pointed to a desk in the back.

Without hesitating, she got up and started making her way to the back of the class. Mr. King quickly followed. Chloe wasn't happy that her favorite teacher wasn't even acknowledging her juvenile attitude toward him and decided she had enough. She turned around to confront him, which threw Mr. King off guard. He narrowed his eyes to a squint and stopped walking.

Chloe glanced down at his hand and back up to meet his gaze. "What's that?"

"Nothing. Back of the class, Chloe," he ordered. Chloe thought she saw a needle in his hand and didn't want to turn her back on him.

Chloe took a few steps back. "Why are we working in the back of class today?" She continued moving backwards and away from Mr. King as fear came over her.

As she slightly inched backwards, hoping to get a little further from him, Mr. King inched closer. His fists tensed up and his eyes focused on Chloe. Suddenly Mr. King lunged forward, trying to grab her, but she quickly dragged a desk into his path, making him trip and drop the needle. Mr. King pushed the desk out of the way, causing it to knock over a few others in the rows across the aisle. Chloe was now against the wall, never losing sight of him as he ran directly at her.

When he was close enough, Chloe front kicked him in the stomach, causing him to slouch over, and giving her a clear path to his face, which she instantly kneed. As Mr. King fell to the ground, Chloe ran over to the door, but it was locked. When she turned around, she saw him rushing at her again. She tried to dodge him and for a second thought she was successful, but he got ahold of her shirt and pulled her toward him.

He turned her around, so she was facing him and punched her two times in the face with each hand. As he went for a third, Chloe blocked another impact of his fist and spun into him, sending her elbow directly into his nose and breaking it. Her back was now against his chest and before his head came back from the blow of an elbow to the face, Chloe flipped him over her shoulders. His body made a loud *thump* on the ground in front of her as it fell. Chloe hopped over Mr. King's body and ran toward another door that led into the adjoining classroom next door.

Right as she got to the door, her body jerked forward, and she knocked her head on the wall in front of her. She was knocked unconscious by Isabel, who was standing behind her with her wand out above Mr. King, who was starting to get up.

"You had *one* thing to do!" Isabel put her wand away.

Mr. King was now standing and changing into something else—a morpher. A creature that looked like a normal human with two arms, two legs, and two eyes, but the similarities ended there. Their skin was rough and lizard-like, their eyes like those of a snake.

He brushed himself off. "I'm still getting paid, right?" His voice echoed with every word. Isabel rolled her eyes at the question. "Grab the girl."

The morpher reached down and picked Chloe up, throwing her over his shoulder. Isabel held out her arm and they teleported from the school.

COLLIN pulled up to the front of the school, hoping to surprise Chloe and give her a ride home. He waited ten minutes and still, there was no sign of her. He looked at his radio for the time and knew there was no way she got out early, and since this was the only entrance that was unlocked after normal school hours, there was no way he had missed her. Collin decided to park his car in one of the first spots in the faculty parking lot and ran inside the school. He passed the administrative office and saw a clerk at the desk. He paced down the empty hallway, passing a janitor sweeping the floor. They exchanged pleasantries and he continued down the hall.

He reached another hall on his right that led up a ramp connecting to a hall that went to Mr. King's classroom. He reached the classroom, but the door was locked, and the shade was down as well. He ran into the next classroom and went to the door connecting both rooms. When he got to Mr. King's room, the door was locked but he saw desks and chairs tossed on the floor and instantly knew something was wrong. He ran out of the classroom and zoomed past the same janitor he saw coming in. He frantically opened the office door, startling the clerk that was still working, and rushed up to the front desk.

"Ms. Simpson, something happened in Mr. King's classroom! My friend had detention with him, and I went to his class and desks and chairs were thrown on the floor," Collin said as he tried to catch his breath.

"Ok. Something the janitorial staff will have to clean up, I'm sure. You students and your pranks. What student was last seen in that class?" Ms. Simpson asked.

"CHLOE!" he shouted out so the clerk wouldn't refer to her as "the student" anymore. "She had detention with Mr. King, and now that room looks like something happened in it."

She looked up, startled by how loud he was. "You need to calm down."
"LOOK, YOU STUPID—"

Adrasteia came out of her office to investigate the commotion that was going on. "Mr. Lynch!" She waited until Collin looked back at her. "Please lower yer voice," Adrasteia ordered. Collin explained what he saw and how Chloe had detention and he thought something was wrong. Adrasteia didn't think twice before she told Collin to come with her. They quickly made their way to the classroom, passing the janitor who kept having to sweep up after them because their running was making the dust go everywhere. Once they reached the room, Adrasteia saw that something happened.

"Go back tae the front office an' tell Ebony tae call the police," Adrasteia ordered.

Collin ran back to the office again, frustrating the janitor in the process. He barged into the office, startling the clerk again, and told her to call the police.

❋ ❋ ❋

217

ADRASTEIA slowly looked around the classroom and sensed that magic was indeed used.

She teleported from the school to inside Mr. King's house so no one could see her. She was in the kitchen and spotted a flashing light coming from an answering machine on the counter by the microwave. She hit the play button and heard a woman's voice saying she was sorry she had missed him, and they got to Grandma's ok. She also said she would try calling again later. The woman ended the message with "I love you," so Adrasteia assumed it had to be Mr. King's wife.

The message ended and Adrasteia continued looking around. She got to the living room and saw Mr. King on the floor, dead. Adrasteia, shocked by what she saw, went back to the kitchen for a napkin and wiped off the answering machine's button she touched, then teleported back to Mr. King's classroom. As she was walking back to her office, she called Liz and told her to get to the school. By the time Adrasteia reached her office, the police were already there, and Liz was right behind them.

Adrasteia told Collin to take the police officers to Mr. King's classroom and let them know what was going on while she talked to Liz. She escorted Liz into her office and proceeded to tell her what happened and what she saw at Mr. King's house. Liz just mumbled, "Gabriel…" and teleported from Adrasteia's office.

She appeared moments later at the entrance to the Tower of Avalon where she was informed by the gatekeeper that the Tower was on lockdown. Liz argued with him but to no avail. Without the ability to teleport into the Tower, Liz had no choice but to go back to the school. When she got there, she yelled that Gabriel had gone too far and that she would find him and kill him. Before Liz could leave, Adrasteia placed her hand on Liz's shoulder.

"Ye can't go confrontin' him—not while he 'as Chloe. He obviously wants somethin' since he went through the trouble o' taking her. You need tae calm down an' think this through clearly."

"My daughter was taken, and you want me to calm down?" a frustrated Liz asked, pushing Adrasteia's hand away.

"Our world is different from 'is one. Ye need to play the part fer the police officers an' do as they say," Adrasteia demanded.

"Play the part?" Liz grew frustrated.

"Yes. They will most likely assign an officer to accompany ye back to yer house. Ye need to go with them an' not do anythin' else. We will find her an' get her back, but we need tae be smart aboot it. I'll go tae Avalon meself tae find oot what he wants, an' he willnae even notice I'm there."

As the police officers returned, Liz started to calm herself down. She knew Adrasteia was right; Gabriel would want something in exchange for Chloe, so she would wait to hear from him while Adrasteia began the search without Gabriel knowing. Like Adrasteia said, an officer was assigned to take her home. As Liz left the school, she decided to call Sara so she could get ahold of Adrian and Andrew to let them know what was going on.

✳ ✳ ✳

"DREW. I have to go to Ziggie's department store," Adrian said as he held up a bag of items he had to return as they made their way through the mall.

"I haven't been in there since they remodeled, so I'll go with," Andrew replied.

As they went into Ziggie's, Andrew saw a pair of shoes on the wall he wanted to check out. Adrian, meanwhile, went directly to the register so he could make an exchange. The young girl behind the counter saw him coming her way and she and her coworker started giggling.

Adrian knew them from school, and he also knew the girl he was about to talk to had a crush on him thanks to Dean, who always brought it up.

"Hey, Adrian," she said with a huge grin as he put his bag down on the counter.

"Hey, Chelsea." Adrian looked over at his brother, who was trying on the pair of shoes he saw.

"What can I help you with today?" Chelsea asked, not taking her eyes off him.

"I would like to return this or exchange it." He took out a shirt from the bag. He looked at her but noticed something was wrong—Chelsea and her coworker weren't moving. He looked at Andrew and began to back away from the counter. "Drew!" Adrian yelled loud enough so Andrew could hear him over the music playing in the background.

Andrew looked up from the mirror. "What's up?" he asked, finally looking in his brother's direction. That's when Andrew saw that the few people in the store weren't moving anymore.

Andrew was startled by his phone ringing and saw that it was his mom, but before he could answer, another voice that didn't belong to Adrian called out, "That's probably your mother or my sister calling to let you know Chloe is missing."

They both looked in the direction of the voice and saw Gabriel standing a few feet away.

Adrian summoned his wand, but Gabriel immediately sent him flying against the wall with a wave of his hand. Adrian knocked over multiple shelves, and clothes fell on top of him as he landed on the floor. Andrew met a similar fate with the same shoes he had admired when he walked in now on top of him. Adrian waved his own hand toward Gabriel, who countered with a simple wave of his, and Adrian was once again knocked to the ground. Before Andrew could act, Gabriel raised his arm and Andrew was slammed against the wall, pinned. It wasn't long before Adrian was right next to him. Neither one of them could move as Gabriel inched closer to them.

"It's admirable the way you both tried putting up a fight." He stopped five or six feet away from them. He looked up at them and discovered they were staring at him—this was the first time they had seen their father. "I need you both to do something for me."

"Go to hell!" Adrian screamed, trying desperately to move, his voice filled with anger.

Gabriel noticed how upset they were as they struggled to move.

Gabriel stepped even closer to them. "Ah, my boys. How long I have waited to see you both. I've thought about this moment for so long during my stay in the Tower, counting down the days until I would be able to meet you. Wondering how you turned out. Wondering if you guys would love me." He looked at both of them. "Is that what you want to hear? Does that make you feel better?" Gabriel added, his face expressionless. "The truth is, you're both reminders of my moment of weakness I had when I was younger. When I decided to lay with your ordinary s a p i e n of a mother."

Andrew and Adrian both felt the rage building up inside as they tensed up, trying to move.

Gabriel clapped his hands to get their full attention. "Now listen to me very carefully." He got closer to them. "If you want to see your cousin again—"

Adrian interrupted, "You son of a bitch!"

Gabriel rushed up to him and violently squeezed his face until the insides of Adrian's cheeks were touching each other. "I believe I was speaking" He let go of Adrian's face and took a step backwards. "If you want to get Chloe back alive, you will need to retrieve Darwin's cane and bring it to me. It's that simple."

Adrian's blood was boiling. "You're so powerful, why can't you get it yourself? Or does it make you feel big and strong, picking on teenagers?"

Gabriel started to get frustrated over Adrian's comments. He was not used to people talking to him like that—in fact, everyone around him feared him, and for a kid to talk to him like that frustrated him more than words could say. "I only need one of you for this task," Gabriel informed them. He began lifting his arm and Andrew started to float off the wall and was now suspended in the air in front of Gabriel.

Adrian looked at his brother, whose muscles were starting to stiffen. Andrew yelled out in agonizing pain as each muscle in his body cramped up. It was visible even through Andrew's clothes what spell Gabriel was casting, the same one that their own aunt experienced in this very mall. Adrian couldn't take the sight of his brother in pain. "STOP!" The store around him began to shake, things hanging on the walls around the store falling to the ground as racks in the small aisles collapsed. Gabriel looked around as cracks started to cover the walls and floor around him, one coming directly at him and causing him to back up a few feet. Gabriel looked impressed by Adrian's show of power. It didn't last long, though, as Gabriel violently pushed Andrew back against the wall next to Adrian, who lost focus on what he was doing. As the store stopped shaking, Adrian saw tears fill his brother's eyes from the pain he was in.

Gabriel looked at Adrian. "Impressive." He looked around the store at the damage his son did. "Really impressive." He glanced back at Adrian, who was now staring daggers his way. The hatred in Adrian's eyes said everything as he stared at Gabriel. Gabriel stared right back at him, the building tension causing Gabriel to get angrier, like Adrian was challenging him. Gabriel was insulted over the way Adrian looked at him and snapped his fingers, instantly snapping the necks of the two girls behind the counter and a customer, killing them. When their bodies hit the floor, Adrian blinked in disbelief.

Gabriel inched closer to his sons. "See how easy that was for me? Now, unless you want me to do the same to Chloe, I suggest you bring me Darwin's cane. You have until sundown in three days to meet me where I tell you," Gabriel instructed as he moved closer to the wall they were pinned against. He was now an arm's length away as he stared at Adrian. "*Three days*, or I will send Chloe's dead body back to her mother wrapped in a pretty bow."

He got one last look at his sons before he teleported away, sending Andrew and Adrian plummeting to the ground. Both Andrew and Adrian were on their hands and knees, breathing heavily. They both looked at each other without saying a word as their eyes begin to fill with tears—tears for Gabriel killing the three innocent people and for the realization that their own father did it.

Chapter Twenty-One

Adrian was the first to teleport home, Andrew close behind. Instead of going directly inside, they met in the backyard to discuss what they should do. Adrian could see that his brother was still in pain after what Gabriel did to him. He could only imagine how it felt for Andrew to have all his muscles cramp up the way they did. Adrian experienced some of that himself when, after a week's worth of weight training, he would wake up in the middle of the night with his calf cramping up. Just the thought of that feeling multiplied by a hundred made him empathize with Andrew. He hated seeing his brother in that much pain, and not being able to do anything about it made Adrian feel helpless. Now the image of Chloe being tortured like that filled Adrian's head. He couldn't do anything for Andrew, but they could save Chloe if they gave Gabriel what he wanted.

"We have to get Grandpa's cane, Drew. It's the only way to get Chloe back safe."

"I know…" Andrew replied while using a patio chair to keep his balance.

Adrian bowed his head. "We can't tell mom and Aunt Liz about this, either."

"I think we should, seeing how three people were just murdered in front of us. We are out of our depths here, Adrian." Andrew's chin lowered to his chest, slowly shaking his head while tears filled his eyes. *Why would he do that?* he thought.

Adrian dashed over to his brother, placing his hand on his shoulder. "I was thinking the same thing, but we can't tell them. They will just make us stay out of it and treat us like kids like they always do." Andrew's eyes widened. "We can't risk that asshole doing something to Chloe," Adrian added. He opened the patio door and led his brother inside. Andrew didn't say anything but agreed with Adrian, no matter how much he wanted to tell his mother. Andrew wiped his tears, hoping his mother wouldn't notice.

Sara heard her boys as the patio door slammed shut. She rushed to the kitchen and instantly hugged both of her sons. She didn't want to let go of them, but knew she had to tell them about Chloe. She asked them where they had been, to which they told her they were at their friend Dean's house. Sara didn't second-guess them; she just continued to hug them. They waited for her to tell them what was going on with Chloe and when she did, they acted surprised and shocked. They didn't need to act worried, though, because they already were. Every second they did nothing was a second wasted not getting Darwin's cane.

Sara backed away from her boys, pushing their hair behind their ears gently. "I've been trying to get ahold of you since it happened, but neither of you answered your phones."

Adrian felt comforted by her gesture. "We don't get good reception at Dean's."

Sara pulled them back toward her, worried over what could happen to them with Gabriel out there. She couldn't even imagine what Liz must be going through right now. In the background, a news report about three people dead at Horizon Mall caught Sara's attention. She turned, went back to the living room, and listened to the coverage of the incident. Sara couldn't help but feel overwhelmed with all the bad things happening around her.

Andrew had to get his mother's attention away from the TV. "We should go to Aunt Liz's."

"Yes." Sara turned away from the television. "Yes, we should."

As Adrian and Andrew went to pack an overnight bag, Sara turned off the TV, so she didn't have to hear what was going on in her town, a town that used to be safe before Gabriel was set free. She wondered if Chloe's kidnapping would get the attention of the wizard chancellor—if it would finally show him that Gabriel was still up to his old tricks. *Who knows if the chancellor even pays attention to what goes on in the normal world?* Sara thought to herself. Before long, Andrew and Adrian were running down the stairs ready to go.

"We will drive there," Sara said before they could even think of teleporting. As they went to the garage and got in the car, Andrew asked if Liz had heard from Bianca yet. Sara didn't think so but wasn't too sure.

"Bianca isn't picking up her phone. It keeps going to voicemail," Andrew added.

"Why don't you call Brad and see if he's heard from Bianca?" Adrian suggested. Andrew agreed and took out his phone to call him. After about two or three rings, Brad answered.

"Hello?"

"Hey." Andrew was relieved Brad answered. "Have you heard from Bianca?"

"Not since she told me she was leaving for a week or two," Brad calmly responded.

"Ok. Can you call me if you hear from her?"

"Yeah, of course. Everything alright?"

"Chloe is missing. Something happened at school today. We are going to Aunt Liz's now hoping to find out more."

"Oh my god! I'll try calling B as soon as we hang up."

"Hopefully, you can reach her because I have been trying and can't. Thanks, Brad."

When they pulled up to Liz's house, they noticed a police car parked in the driveway with an officer inside. They got out of the car and rushed toward the house and let themselves inside. Liz immediately came up and hugged each of them. She was overwhelmed with emotion and the twins could see it in her face. Andrew hugged his aunt again just to comfort her, which she greatly appreciated.

She told them she tried to see Darwin but for whatever reason, the Tower was on lockdown. She also told them that Adrasteia was going to get a message to Darwin somehow explaining what's going on. Liz sat down on the sofa and Sara quickly joined her. Sara comforted her by telling her everything was going to be ok, and Chloe would be ok. Liz appreciated her words; they were reassuring, not long-lasting, but reassuring, nonetheless. Liz couldn't help but think of the horrors Chloe must be going through. She knew how much her brother loved to torture people—especially normal people.

Rage now built up inside her; she couldn't wait to get her hands on Gabriel. She would make him pay if it was the last thing she did. When the doorbell suddenly rang, it caught everyone by surprise. Liz dashed over to open the door and Brad's voice could be heard. Liz welcomed him the same way she welcomed the twins and Sara. He went on to tell Liz that after what Andrew told him, he heard on the news that a teacher from Arcadia High was found dead in his home.

Hearing this, Sara turned on the news to hear it for herself. Once again, Sara was saddened at what was going on in her beloved town. No one said it, but they all felt the same way; this was all clearly Gabriel's doing. Liz offered Brad something to drink and he followed her to the kitchen. She served him a cup of coffee and asked if he heard from Bianca. He told her that after he talked to Andrew, he called and she answered, but the only thing they were able to say was "hello" because the call quickly dropped.

That didn't matter to Liz; she was relieved to hear someone talked to Bianca. She offered Brad something to eat but he was happy with just the cup of warm coffee in front of him. As he took a sip of his drink, he noticed that Adrian went to the backyard and sat down on an open lounge chair Liz had set up in the back. Brad then told Liz he didn't understand why Bianca had to go out of town in the first place and for a second, Liz forgot that Brad didn't know about the whole other world that existed parallel to theirs.

She told him some lie that this trip was planned months in advance and hoped that would put an end to his questioning. Thankfully, it did. Brad then went outside to join Adrian, who was staring up at the sky, admiring all the stars that were out. The breeze that blew through was nice and refreshing, and they could tell that spring was right around the corner.

Brad stopped a few feet away from Adrian. "Nice night." He looked up at the sky.

"Yeah," was all Adrian could say.

Looking back down at Adrian, he looked amused. "How you holding up?"

"Not good. I'm really worried about Chloe." He wanted nothing more than to leave so they could do what they needed to get her back.

"I know, but Chloe is a tough girl, so I'm sure she will be fine. She's probably on her way home now after kicking whosever ass that abducted her," Brad said, hoping to reassure Adrian of something he knew wasn't true.

"Probably," Adrian agreed. He knew Brad was trying to be supportive and nodded at him to let him know that it was appreciated. "Thanks."

Brad returned to admiring the sky. "It's weird with what happened at the mall and with Chloe. You'd think more police officers would be out there."

Adrian needed Brad to go. "I'm sure the police are doing everything possible to find whoever killed those people at the mall."

"I'm sure," Brad replied. Adrian didn't see it, but Brad was smirking, as if it brought him pleasure knowing about all the destruction going on around him.

Adrian was getting anxious because he still hadn't heard from Andrew, who was upstairs looking for Darwin's cane.

How's it going up there? Adrian's voice was loud in Andrew's head.

I'm still looking, Andrew continued to look around in Liz's room. Andrew remembered Adrasteia bringing Darwin's cane there for safe keeping after he was taken to the Tower by Adele, so he knew it had to be somewhere. He kept on searching, hoping not to get caught in the process. The more he searched, the more he realized that Darwin's cane wasn't there. He went downstairs and out the back to meet up with Adrian. Brad saw that Andrew needed to talk to Adrian and got up to leave. Before Brad left, he gave each of them a hug and told them that Chloe would be ok, which made the twins feel a little better after being reminded that Chloe was indeed a tough girl. Once Brad was back inside the house, Andrew told Adrian he couldn't find the cane anywhere.

Adrian anxiously tapped his foot on the floor. "It *has* to be here. I thought Adrasteia brought it here after what happened."

Andrew was perplexed. "I thought so, too, but couldn't find it."

"Hey, boys! Time to come inside—it's getting late," Sara yelled. She was standing by the back door, holding it open to let them know she was waiting for them to come in. "We are also going to be sleeping here so Liz won't have to be alone."

Adrian and Andrew didn't seem to mind sleeping over. They knew their mom was right and their aunt shouldn't be left alone. When they got inside, they saw Brad saying bye to Liz.

After they hugged goodbye, Brad gave Sara one, too, and headed toward the front door. Once Brad was outside, he looked around and saw the police officer stationed in front of Liz's house was on his phone, so he used that opportunity to teleport to where Isabel was keeping Chloe.

When Brad arrived in the dilapidated building, Isabel didn't acknowledge him; she just stared at the monitor in front of her, watching Chloe. They stood in what must have been an old, abandoned police station, as there were desks pushed to the side and old chairs on the floor. The walls had cracks on them, and the cell Chloe was being held in was rusted with a rancid smell to it.

"Has she been a problem?" Brad asked as he joined her side. Isabel ignored him and continued watching Chloe. "You know I was just doing my job." He knew Isabel was aggravated about the comment he made at Adele's.

Isabel glared at him. "I'm going to see if she knows anything." She brushed by Brad and bumped him as she passed.

It only took a few seconds for Isabel to reach Chloe. Brad watched the monitor to see what would happen.

"Do you know anything about the map?" Isabel asked, needing a distraction from Brad.

Chloe looked over at her. "Screw you."

Isabel's nose flared. "I'm only going to ask one more time: Do you know anything about the map?" She got closer to the cell Chloe was in.

Chloe tilted her head up to meet Isabel's eyes. "And I'm only going to say *this* one more time: *Screw you.*" She slowly got to her feet.

"You're pathetic. Protecting secrets for a family you're not really a part of? Must kill you that you don't have the power the rest of your family does," Isabel said as she inched as close to the bars as she could.

Chloe took a few steps forward. "Let me be clear: I don't know anything, but if I did, I wouldn't tell you." Isabel turned to leave. "Oh, but I will say this…" Chloe added, getting Isabel to turn around. As she did, Chloe reached for Isabel's jacket with two hands and slammed her face-first into the bars, sending Isabel stumbling backwards and falling to the ground instantly.

Isabel crashed onto the floor. "You stupid—!" She got up, summoning her wand.

ISABEL! Darby echoed in her head, causing her to stop. *Don't do anything stupid!*

Isabel stopped instantly. "Oh. Let me guess, you care for this one, too?" she said out loud so Chloe could hear, causing her to wonder who she was talking to.

Stop being stupid! Gabriel would kill you if something happened to her and he wasn't able to use her to get what he wanted.

Fine, Brad. I won't do anything stupid.

Don't call me that, Darby responded coldly.

Isabel straightened her jacket and leaned her head forward a bit toward her prisoner. "I will take great pleasure in killing you when the time is right." Chloe just stared back at her; if she was scared, she didn't show it. Neither one of them blinked before Isabel turned around and stormed off. Chloe put on a brave face, but inside she wanted desperately to go home.

* * *

THE next morning, Andrew woke up on the couch and went downstairs to find Adrian, who was sleeping on a sofa in the basement. The stairs squeaked as he stepped down them, waking Adrian in the process.

Adrian yawned and stretched so wide that his legs were hanging off the sofa. "I think we should go check Grandpa's house for his cane."

Andrew agreed. "I was thinking the same thing."

"Now we just have to figure out what we're going to tell Aunt Liz and Mom." Andrew glanced at Adrian to see what he thought.

Adrian met his brother's gaze. "Nothing. We have two days to find Grandpa's cane and get it to Gabriel. Mom and Aunt Liz will only tell us we can't go anywhere and treat us like kids, and we don't have time for that."

"Then what do we do?" Andrew ran his fingers through his hair.

Adrian was put off by that remark. "Well, Drew, it's called 'sneaking out.'"

Andrew began pacing back and forth. "We can't sneak out!" He threw his arms up in disbelief at the suggestion. "They will freak out thinking something happened to us, and we can't do that to them—not with what's going on now." Andrew stopped pacing and stared at Adrian.

"We'll leave a note, then?" Adrian innocently suggested. "We should get ready. Meet back down here in twenty minutes."

When Andrew came back down, he read the note, which was simple. It read "Mom: Staying cooped up worried about Chloe was really getting to us, so we decided to get some fresh air. Call one of us if you guys hear something. And don't worry, we will be fine." When Andrew was done reading it he gave it back to Adrian, who put it on the sofa where Sara would surely see it. "Ready." With that, they both teleported to Darwin's house.

When they got there, surprisingly no one was there, not even Nigel. Adrian decided that the first place they should look was their grandfather's room, so he led the way up there.

Darwin's bedroom was on the third floor of his massive house, which was understandable since his bedroom took up most of the floor. When they reached the top of the stairs, there was a little sitting area off to the side that went out to a patio overlooking the stables. A few more steps forward and they came to these huge, beautifully handcrafted wooden double doors with six-foot dragons carved into them. Adrian and Andrew both admired the beauty of the doors before trying to open them. When Adrian turned the doorknob, it didn't open but the dragons moved, which startled them into taking a few steps back.

A memory came to Andrew. "I know this…" Adrian looked over at him, confused. "Know what?"

"These are tocsin enchantments." Adrian had no idea what Andrew was talking about. "Like a security system," Andrew explained, realizing he would need to clarify. "Very dangerous to people, but luckily for us, they know we are Darwin's grandchildren," Andrew explained as he began stroking the spine of the dragon on the left door. The dragons soon went back to their original positions and the doors unlocked. When Adrian opened the double doors to go inside Darwin's room, they were immediately stunned by what they saw.

Picture windows circled the enormous room, giving them a 360 view of Darwin's estate. A balcony surrounded the room as well with at least four sets of double doors that led outside on each side of Darwin's room. Up above, a loft area caught Andrew's eye because of the library of books lining the wall up there. Andrew was tempted to go up the black circular metal stairs to the loft just so he could examine the multitude of books in Darwin's collection. Adrian saw how fascinated Andrew was by the books. "You're such a nerd!" he told him. Andrew chuckled and decided to go look for Darwin's cane up there.

Adrian went further in and saw a huge bed with what had to be a custom-made headboard sitting in the corner. It had to be the biggest bed he had ever seen—built for a king, no doubt. On the other side of the room, Adrian saw a sofa and oversized chair facing a large flat-screen TV, which probably never got used; Darwin never seemed like someone who watched TV. Before Adrian could even start looking for his grandfather's cane, Andrew called him from the loft.

"What's up, Drew?"

"I found it!" Andrew answered. Adrian quickly ran up the circular staircase, joining his brother who was staring at the cane encased in what seemed to be a force field.

"How do we get it out?" Adrian stepped beside his brother. He stared at the cane, not knowing what to make of it.

"I don't know a spell. Maybe one of these books can tell us how to retrieve something from a case. You start with those books, and I'll start with these." Andrew pointed at the books on each end of the bookcase.

"Or…" Adrian looked at his brother as he reached down to grab the cane and as he picked it up, the force field faded away.

"How did you do that?" Andrew's mouth dropped open a bit, in disbelief at how easy that was.

"I figured it was like the dragon doors and it knew we were Darwin's grandchildren."

"Oh," Andrew said. He glanced back at all the books lined up before them.

Adrian rolled his eyes. "Relax, geek. After all this, I'm sure Grandpa will let you read these books, too."

"Finding it was easier than I thought it would be," Andrew told him, completely ignoring his brother's comments.

"I'm glad it was."

"I think we should cast a tracker spell on it before we give it to Gabriel," Andrew suggested, knowing they couldn't just *give it* to Gabriel.

Adrian approached his brother. "That might be risky. What if he checks for spells or enchantments?"

Andrew focused on Adrian. "It's a small spell. It won't even activate until the next day, and even then, he wouldn't be able to tell. Besides, he wouldn't even think to look for anything like that because we are new to all this."

"True," Adrian agreed. "And how do you know so much about this, anyways? Also, we actually *are* new to this." Adrian knew that Andrew had gotten really invested in this new world of theirs, but even he thought Andrew was advancing too quickly.

"It's called reading and studying. Maybe if you opened a book occasionally, you would know this stuff too."

"Well, I'm the jock of the family, I guess."

"I'm in wrestling too. And I still study!" Andrew looked over to his brother. "But you're right. You are the jock of the family, and I'm the wizard of it."

Breaking eye contact, Adrian turned around, hoping Andrew wouldn't see that he got to him. Adrian didn't like coming in second to Andrew after years of coming in first. "Well, I'm into wrestling and working out more than you. And for the record, I do read the books Grandpa gave us and practice when I can!" He looked back at Andrew. "I just don't tell you when I practice because I don't want to hear any more lectures from you."

"Whatever. We need to get some ingredients from Adrasteia's, anyways," Andrew told him. This wasn't the time to bicker.

✳ ✳ ✳

ADRIAN and Andrew arrived in Polaris, the capital of Avalon, the same place they had teleported to with Darwin on their first trip there. They began their familiar walk to Adrasteia's shop, not taking the time to appreciate the sights like they did before. When they arrived at the shop, the familiar bell rang overhead. They made a beeline directly to the counter where they saw Tavish standing.

"Adrian! Nice tae see ye again. An' you must be Andrew." His endearing Scottish accent echoed in the quiet shop.

"Drew, this is Tavish, Adrasteia's grandson."

"Hey, what's up? Nice to meet you." Andrew extended his hand to greet him. "So, what can I do ye fer?" Tavish asked the two of them.

"I need rat tail," Andrew replied.

Tavish smirked. "Interesting choice. Rat tail is a tricky ingredient. If ye tell me what yer goin' tae use it fer, I could make sure tae get ye the perfect one you'll need."

"Just give me a variety, then," Andrew replied, not wanting to tell someone he had just met what they were up to. Especially not Adrasteia's grandson.

Tavish insisted, "But if ye use the wrong one, it might nae work—or worse, it might backfire."

"Drew, just tell him what you need it for." Adrian rolled his eyes. "Just give me a few different ones," Andrew repeated.

"We need it for a tracer spell," Adrian blurted out. Now wasn't the time for secrecy. No matter how advanced Andrew thought they were, they didn't

232

have time to mess up these spells given their time constraints. Tavish had grown up here, so he knew more than both of them.

"Ok, then. I'll be right back." Tavish glanced at Adrian, nodding to thank him.

"Really, Adrian?" Andrew made sure Tavish was out of earshot. "What if he tells Adrasteia?" he whispered.

"Relax. He won't." Adrian looked to make sure Tavish wasn't around. "He's a cool guy."

Andrew waved his hands up and down. "UGH! Oh, ok. Let's just tell everyone what we're doing, then. I have an idea! Let's go to the chancellor and tell him we're trading a key to unlocking a crystal for our human cousin. How about that?" Andrew mocked.

"Ye know these are nae soundproof walls," Tavish could be heard saying from the back room. Adrian and Andrew both stayed silent as he walked back up front. "So, yer trading fer yer cousin?"

"Yes." Andrew started grinding his teeth; they didn't need this right now.

"Well, then, I would like tae offer my assistance," Tavish offered, bowing his head in jest. He looked up and winked at Adrian.

"No. It's going to be dangerous, and if Gabriel sees you, he might think we're up to something," Adrian replied.

"Then we just have tae make sure he doesnae see me." Tavish wasn't giving them a choice.

Andrew was quiet. *It might not be a bad idea to have some help*, he thought to himself. Then a plan started forming in his mind—a plan that would make sure Gabriel didn't suspect a spell on Darwin's cane.

Andrew turned so he was facing Tavish. "If you don't mind helping us, I think we could use you." Adrian didn't want to risk Tavish's life but knew he was outnumbered here.

A few looks were exchanged between Tavish and Adrian before Tavish broke the silence. "What's the plan?" he inquired, excited to be doing something other than minding the shop.

✳ ✳ ✳

EARLY the next morning, the sun was rising, and the tress swayed in the wind. Adrian stood at the entrance of the woods where only the chirps of the birds could be heard. Suddenly, a flock of birds scattered out of the center of the woods. Adrian knew it was time. He began his walk into the woods, the fallen leaves and branches crackling beneath his feet with every step he took until he came to a stop. Adrian saw him then, his cold black eyes staring directly at him like he was trying to stare into his soul. He didn't blink or move; he just stared at Adrian. Adrian's heart began to race, and anxiety started to set in—he was scared.

"Where is it?!" Gabriel shouted from up ahead, his voice deep and full of hate.

"Drew won't come until I see that Chloe is ok!" Adrian shouted back. If he was still scared, he wasn't letting it show.

"So demanding." Gabriel took a few steps forward. "Very well. Adamaris!" he yelled.

Another wizard suddenly appeared next to Gabriel, tall and muscular with black eyes and black hair. He was taller than Gabriel and had a scar over his left eye, and he was dressed in a long black leather coat as he held Chloe in a chokehold. Before another word could be spoken, a strong blast sent Gabriel and Adamaris to the ground. Tavish teleported in, latched onto Chloe, and teleported out.

Andrew quickly pointed his wand at Gabriel, who was just getting up, and another blast sent him flying against a nearby tree. Adamaris soon joined him. Adrian saw his brother and they both teleported, but something went wrong—they ended up right back in the same spot they just left. Confused, Andrew ran over to his brother but was pulled by the collar on his jacket toward Gabriel. "Enough with the games!" Gabriel yelled as he tightened his grip on Andrew's shirt.

Adrian tried to teleport to his brother, but Gabriel closed his palm into a fist while turning it, and Adrian was right back in the same spot he left again. Both Adrian and Andrew were stunned; they didn't know it was possible for a wizard to stop another one from teleporting, but here it happened—twice.

"The cane, or I will snap his neck!" Gabriel yelled, his hand around Andrew's throat, squeezing it.

Adrian summoned the cane and quickly tossed it up as high as he could, hoping to distract Gabriel long enough for them to get away. It worked; Adrian and Andrew were finally able to teleport away unscathed—physically, at least. Adamaris looked angry as he finally got up. Gabriel saw where the cane landed, and he held out his hand as it floated to him. "Don't worry about them. We will kill them in time," Gabriel told Adamaris, who was extremely angry that they had been outsmarted by teenagers. After a few seconds, Gabriel and his lackey teleported out of the woods.

✳ ✳ ✳

ADRIAN and Andrew teleported back inside their house where Tavish was instructed to bring Chloe. When the twins saw Chloe and Tavish standing in the living room, they ran to her. Chloe had never been happier to see the boys and them, her. All three of them hugged each other, happy that Chloe was safe. Adrian was the first to break from the group hug.

"Thank you," he told Tavish, grateful for his help. "Don't mention it," Tavish replied.

"Nice accent," Chloe said. She and Andrew turned to look at Tavish.

"Yeah. Thank you for your help," Andrew added, regretting being cold to him before.

"Oh, Chloe! This is Tavish, Adrasteia's grandson," Adrian introduced them. He didn't want to be rude.

Without saying anything, Chloe ran up to him and hugged him, whispering "thank you" in his ear. Tavish hugged her back; glad he was able to help. Andrew remembered that he had to get something from upstairs and told them he would be right back. Tavish decided that he should be heading back to Avalon and said his goodbyes. Chloe thanked him once again and Adrian led him out to the patio in the back.

Chloe followed them into the kitchen. She was extremely thirsty and needed some water.

As Adrian closed the patio door behind them, Chloe watched her cousin and his new friend through the window by the sink as she gulped down her cup of cold, refreshing water. She couldn't hear what they were saying, but she saw a familiar look in Adrian's eyes that she knew very well—a look that she always got when Collin was around. She watched Adrian talk to Tavish and say their goodbyes. When Tavish teleported away, Adrian just stood there for a moment with a smile, looking very happy. A few moments later, Adrian opened the patio door and came back inside. Chloe turned around and looked her cousin in the eye.

"You should ask him out."

Before Adrian could respond, Andrew ran down the stairs and into the kitchen, causing Chloe and Adrian to laugh awkwardly. Chloe just embraced her cousins; she had missed them both so dearly.

"I just want to say thank you, both of you. It—" Chloe started but couldn't get the words out. The trauma from what she had been through finally caught up with her and she choked up, tears streaming down her face. "Just… thank you," was all she was able to add before she started crying, the tears of sadness soon turning to that of joy as she felt happy to be with the people she loved. Adrian and Andrew hugged her tighter. They didn't want to let her go; they knew they had to get back to Chloe's house, but for now they were taking in the moment. They finally had their cousin back safe.

Chapter Twenty-Two

L ester started to say something else but before he could complete his sentence, he was hit in the center of his chest by a bright red light and nothing, but pink mist was left in his place.

Lester Sterling, who hid successfully from every wizard in the world, was dead. Bianca quickly turned in the direction the blast came from, summoning her wand in the process, and was shocked to see Brad pointing his wand at her. As he shot the same spell her way, she deflected it just in time, but the force of their spells hitting each other sent her crashing through the window behind her.

When Bianca hit the dirt pavement, the impact left her unable to breathe for a second. Fortunately, she had always been a quick thinker and was able to cast a spell to make a copy of herself—a spell Darwin showed her when she was younger—that laid helplessly on the ground as she tumbled backward and crawled into some nearby bushes for cover. The spell she just cast worked so well that it could fool almost anybody, even a skilled wizard such as Darwin. As Bianca lay quietly, watching Brad climb out of the window, the shock started to set in.

Her boyfriend, the man she loved, killed Lester and tried to kill her. Bianca watched and heard everything Brad was telling her, and tears started to fill her eyes as she watched him pull out a shard of glass that was sticking out of her thigh. The spell, being an exact copy, of whoever cast it, made Bianca examine her own leg and to her surprise, a shard of glass was sticking out from the same spot. That must have been why she was feeling so weak.

Bianca didn't move one inch as she saw Brad lean over and kiss her copy's forehead. When he teleported, Bianca looked on as her perfectly made copy faded away. She quickly turned around to assess the damage to her leg. She felt the glass deep inside of her, so teleporting was out of the question; a wound like that could cause her leg to be torn off during the process. She couldn't risk the glass coming out en route to whatever hospital was close by.

Bianca summoned her wand and put the tip directly on her thigh, where the glass was protruding from, and applied pressure. It hurt, but she knew that was nothing compared to the pain she was about to feel. Bianca looked at her wand. *"Cauterizo!"* The tip of her wand started to glow a fiery red. Bianca held the wand on her thigh as she slowly pulled the piece of glass out. She lay there in anguish as her wound cauterized, barely able to hold on to her wand, but she had to.

She winced in pain but knew that if she removed her wand before the bleeding inside was stopped, she would bleed out for sure. The smell of burning flesh didn't help either. The shard of glass was finally out in time, and she tossed it to the side, examining her leg. No blood was coming out; she was relieved. Bianca laid her head down, exhausted and in excruciating pain, but knew she had more to do.

Forcing herself to get back up, she squeezed the open wound shut and once again pointed her wand directly at it. She mumbled, *"Glutino,"* and her wound was closed. She would undoubtedly have a scar, but she didn't care— the main injury she had sustained was taken care of. Bianca could still feel little pieces of glass on her skin and other cuts and bruises, but nothing more serious than the one she just took care of.

Bianca lay on the ground flat to gather her strength. Once she felt that she could, she started to get up. Even though her leg was fine, she could still feel the pain caused by the glass being inside. It felt like she just had surgery on it, which, in some way, she did. Bianca was finally able to stand, the dirt from the ground making a small cloud of dust around her feet, as she stood there and looked ahead at what, for her, was going to be a long walk to Lester's house.

The blast from Brad's spell and her defensive spell really took a lot out of her, both physically and mentally. Her body was still in pain, and she felt it more as she stood there. She began to limp inside, each step a major hurdle she had to overcome. The only thing on Bianca's mind was getting inside so she could sit down. Little pieces of glass began to fall off her back the more she struggled to walk. Finally, she reached the back door of Lester's home.

Bianca leaned on the door to rest, just for a second, then turned the doorknob, which opened without any issues. She limped inside and hobbled toward the kitchen for paper towels. When she reached the sink, she took as many paper towels she could until there was nothing left on the roll. Bianca opened the cabinet above her and found a large cup. She filled it with water and took a few sips, then turned around, limped to the kitchen table, and planted herself on the first chair pulled out in front of her.

Bianca tossed the crumpled paper towels on the table next to her big cup of water. She examined her right arm first and began pulling out the little pieces of glass embedded in it.

Bianca kept replaying what just happened repeatedly in her head, each piece of glass she pulled, a painful reminder of what Brad did. Tears once again began to fill her eyes, but she didn't let herself cry; she had to focus on getting the glass out of her. She took two pieces of paper towel and dipped the tip in the cup of water beside her.

She gently rubbed the wet paper towel over her arm where all the pieces of glass had been removed until it turned pink from the blood it absorbed. She repeated the same steps for her left arm and stomach until there was nothing left but a pile of wet, pinkish-red balls of paper towels in front of her. As she sat there staring at the mess, she replayed the look Brad had on his face when he shot his spell at her.

So much rage was in his eyes—she knew it was Brad, but in that moment, he looked different to her. Gone was that caring, warm-hearted man she knew. She had never seen that look from him, but the anger and hate came across loud and clear as she was hit with his blast and sent flying through the window. She snapped out of her thoughts and stood up from the table to go to the bathroom. Her leg still caused her to limp toward the front room that connected to the hall leading to the bathroom—well, at least she hoped there was a bathroom down that hall; she didn't know for sure.

Bianca opened the first door she passed, but it was a closet. She closed it and continued to the next door on her right, opening it to discover it was, in fact, a bathroom. A big bathroom with a double sink on her left, clearly decorated for someone who was elegant but at the same time humble. The colors around her were neutral, yet classy. The bathtub was huge and had water jets on each side of it. She closed the door and saw a nice fluffy white robe hanging on the single hook behind the door.

She picked a towel from a nearby rack and slowly stumbled over to the bathtub. She turned the first knob and water began to pour out, steam quickly following. She turned on the cold water after a moment and the hot water rapidly became warm.

Bianca started to take off her clothes and climbed into the tub. She noticed the button for the water jets next to the faucet and clicked them on. Her body appreciated the soothing feeling the jets provided, but her mind couldn't break away from the thoughts of Brad and that spell that turned Lester Sterling to pink mist.

She submerged her entire body underwater and stayed under for as long as she could.

She heard the pebbles that were embedded in her back hit the bottom of the tub. She came up and took a deep breath, turned off the water, and dove back under. Bianca heard nothing but the water jets she set on high as she lay underwater. For a moment, it was peaceful. The peace didn't last long, though, as the image of Brad's angry face blasting her with a spell returned.

Coming up fast for air, she started breathing heavily as she sat there. It took a minute for her to fully catch her breath, but she eventually did. After a few minutes in the tub, she decided to get out. She took the towel she had neatly placed on a small stand next to the bathtub after she turned off the jets. She got up and began to dry herself off. Her cuts and bruises still very visible, but clean. Bianca felt a little better—physically, not mentally.

She wrapped herself in the fluffy white robe she found behind the door and walked over to the mirror. She wiped her hand over the mirror to clean off the steam from the moisture in the bathroom. She stared in the mirror and a flush of good memories she had with Brad came to mind, and she finally began to cry uncontrollably. She punched the mirror with her fist and violently knocked everything off the sink and shelf right next to it. She rushed over to another shelf behind her and did the same thing.

Bianca was overwhelmed with sadness as she leaned against the bathroom door and slid to the floor. She couldn't believe how fake Brad had been over the past few years; it was all just an act for him. Bianca finally pulled herself to her feet and stormed out of the bathroom toward a bedroom she saw at the front of the house. It was now nighttime, and she curled up on the bed, tears streaming down her cheeks.

She started to remember those romantic nights she had with Brad, the most recent ones more vivid than the others. Bianca then started to remember sleeping while Brad whispered in her ear—something that she now remembered sent chills down her spine. She vaguely remembered Brad asking questions about things she didn't even know he knew about, questions she didn't remember until now. She knew she should go home but couldn't bring herself to leave yet. Within a few short moments, Bianca fell asleep, something her body needed more than she thought.

The next morning, the sunshine was trying to break into the cracks of the curtain, but Bianca didn't even notice. She lay in bed all day, only getting up a few times to use the bathroom. She tossed and turned for most of the day, falling asleep a few times in between, but mostly she just reflected on her relationship with Brad, analyzing every moment she had ever spent with him. Day quickly turned to night and Bianca once again fell asleep.

In the middle of the night, Bianca awoke from what seemed to be a nightmare. She realized that every night she spent over at Brad's house, he asked her very specific questions about things she purposely kept from him. It was now clearer than ever before that Brad got things out of her that she never even knew she told him. He was a clever liar and manipulator, and she could not believe how stupid she had been.

How could I not remember saying those things? she thought to herself. She had never felt more foolish than she did now. Things were becoming clearer to her as time went on, presumably from the spell wearing off since Brad had revealed his true self to her. This realization only brought more tears to her eyes, and she lay back down, defeated. During the rest of the night, Bianca went in and out of sleep, sometimes because of the sounds of the coyotes outside scrummaging for food, other times because she had bad dreams about what happened with Lester.

She knew she had gotten Lester killed, but she couldn't dwell on it; She thought of calling home but couldn't. How could she explain to her mother what was going on? She knew that she was still in shock and needed to put it out of her head before reaching out to her mother.

She finally fell back asleep for the rest of the night. It was soon morning again, and the sun was shining, birds were chirping, and the trees swaying in the wind made a soothing sound. Bianca heard something that woke her instantly—the sound of a car driving on the dirt road in the distance getting closer to the house.

She got up from the bed and peeked out of the window to see a car making its way toward Lester's house, and she watched it until it came to a stop. She saw the lady from the hardware store get out from the driver's side and she was not alone. Three men got out of the car too, one a bigger man—six-two, maybe, and weighed about three hundred pounds give or take— and the other two of a muscular build and average height. All three of the large men wore trucker hats. Bianca started to quiver, and her muscles began to twitch.

When Bianca saw them walking toward the house, she quickly backed away from the window. She put her jeans and an old shirt of Lester's and stood quietly by the bedroom door. She heard the doorbell ring followed by a few knocks. "Mr. Darling?" the girl said loudly. She heard one of the guys say something, but she couldn't make it out.

She saw the shadow of one guy walking up to the closed shades of the bedroom Bianca was in. In that moment, she didn't move, not even to breathe, as he tried to get a peek inside. She hoped the four of them would just leave, but they didn't. Another guy yelled he was going to check the back.

Before Bianca realized what was happening, she heard him climbing through the broken window and stepping on the broken glass as he made his way inside. She heard his footsteps rush to the front door to let the woman and the other two men inside. She heard them tramping throughout the house and the woman sounded genuinely concerned about Mr. Darling and what could have happened to him.

Lester must have been a good man to the people of this town, Bianca thought to herself.

She was once again reminded of the fact that she got Lester killed. She couldn't let that get to her right now, as she knew it was only a matter of time before they came into the bedroom.

Bianca knew she could easily teleport out of the house, but she didn't want to leave and face the reality of her situation just yet. The footsteps of one of the guys got closer to the bedroom door. Before he could, Bianca opened the door, startling him and the other three in the process. He backed up as she inched toward him, seeing that Bianca was recently roughed up.

"You shouldn't be here." Bianca looked directly at the woman she met in town a few days ago.

"I know you! You're that girl that came looking for Mr. Darling. Where is he?" she asked, her Southern accent raspier than Bianca remembered.

"You need to leave—*now*," Bianca ordered. The big guy looked at her like she was joking. No stranger, especially an outsider, would tell them what to do.

"Baby girl, I don't know who you are or what you think you're doing, but this here is Mr. Darling's house and we ain't leaving until we see that he's alright," the bigger guy threatened, inching toward Bianca.

"I wouldn't come any closer if I were you," Bianca warned.

He stopped and just laughed at her. All the anger Bianca had built up inside of her reached a boiling point. As he started to walk toward her again, she warned him to stop once more but he didn't. He reached his hand forward but before he could touch her, Bianca waved her arm and he was tossed hard against the wall as if he weighed nothing, slamming down on the floor in front of it. The impact knocked him unconscious. The other three backed up in fear but did not run out of the house.

The woman and other two guys stared at her, scared but also angry at what just happened. The two guys finally gathered the courage to run after Bianca, but they were easily pushed out of the front door one at a time with enough force to send them six feet from the front steps. The girl backed up toward the door, terrified now. The big guy started to get up, but he struggled to find his footing and fell over again.

"Grab your friend here and the two outside and leave. Get in your car and drive far away from this place, and don't look back," Bianca ordered. The girl knew that Bianca wasn't messing around anymore.

The woman helped the big guy up and they quickly ran out the door, grabbing the other two in the process. Bianca watched as they all got into the car and quickly drove off. It was a relief for Bianca to let out some of that anger she had built up inside, but she knew it was wrong to take it out on normal people—especially innocent people looking for their friend. She felt bad, but she wasn't thinking straight right now.

She had let her hatred for Brad consume her. She had been doing nothing but having a pity party for herself for the last few days, and it needed to stop. All that moping around wasn't helping anything. Every second wasted dwelling over Brad's betrayal wasn't going to help find the crystal. Bianca now knew that it was time to go home, time to move on and focus. It was going to be hard, but she couldn't let what Brad did control her actions again. She would deal with him eventually, but for now she needed to get home and help Liz locate the Alexandro's Crystal before Gabriel did. With Bianca's newfound realization, she teleported home at last.

Chapter Twenty-Three

Adrian and Andrew decided on escorting Chloe home instead of teleporting. That way, they could come up with a good story to tell the police officers that had been stationed in front of her house since she was reported missing. The closer they got to Chloe's house, the more her heart began to race. She was nervous about lying to the police, but Adrian was right, a lie to the police was better than the truth. Still didn't change the fact that she was nervous about being caught in a lie, which could get her and her family in trouble.

She rehearsed what she was going to say repeatedly as they walked. Adrian corrected her story a few times but other than that, Chloe seemed to have what she was going to say memorized. Andrew didn't think the police officers would hound her about this anyway, seeing how Chloe had just been through a traumatic event, but it was always better to be safe than sorry. He asked her to tell them what happened once more as they reached the corner of her subdivision. Chloe saw the squad car parked in front of her house down the street.

Adrian reached out and pulled her to him. "It's going to be ok."

Andrew also reassured her that she was going to be fine, and they continued the trek toward her house. When they got there, one of the officers was a little shocked at seeing her and got out of the car quickly, his partner following behind. Chloe explained to both of them that she and Mr. King were taken from the school by a masked man with a gun. But before she went on, she asked if she could go inside and see her mother. The officers completely understood her desire to see her mom and said that was fine, and they were going to call in the detectives who were handling her case.

"Thank you." Chloe rushed past them.

The twins took her inside. When Liz saw the door open and Chloe on the other side, she screamed out in joy and ran toward her daughter like she hadn't seen her in years, scaring Sara, who was reading a newspaper on the other sofa with her back toward the door.

"Oh my god, oh my god! How are you here? Oh my god, I'm so happy you're back!" Liz leaped to her, hugging and kissing Chloe over and over. Chloe and Liz hadn't really talked since Chloe found out she was adopted, but Chloe was overwhelmed with joy after seeing her mother. She knew they still had their issues to work out, but for that moment, Chloe couldn't have been happier to be in her mother's embrace.

Sara quickly followed and rushed over to them, beyond happy to see her niece back home unharmed. She looked over to her boys, smiling at them, she knew they were involved with getting her back. Sara didn't care in that moment; the only thing that mattered was having Chloe back home in one piece. *Such a huge relief for the family*, she thought.

Chloe went on to explain what exactly happened the day she was taken. Liz was horrified to hear that a morpher was able to get past Adrasteia's sensors; however, that was a smart idea on Gabriel's part to send nonmagical beings inside the school. Liz told Chloe that morphers were the only ones that could help Gabriel because the second a wizard stepped on school property, Adrasteia would know, as long as the charms were in place. Chloe felt the need to tell her mom that she was knocked unconscious by a wizard the morpher called "Isabel" and Liz knew that Isabel was somehow able to get on school grounds because of the morpher. Liz kept Chloe close to her as she explained everything to them.

Liz leaned back, her hands still on Chloe. "Why did Gabriel free you?"

"We made a trade. Darwin's cane for Chloe." Andrew looked down to the floor, not wanting to make eye contact with his aunt or mother.

"What?!" Sara yelled. Her entire focus was now on her two boys.

Adrian wanted the focus off Andrew. "Gabriel came to us at the mall the other day and told us what he wanted." He didn't mind looking directly at his mother; he would do it all over again if it meant Chloe would come home safe.

"Why didn't you tell us?" Sara asked, her voice a normal volume now, not wanting to argue with her boys.

"Because you would have stopped us," Adrian answered.

"I would have done anything to get Chloe back. But meeting that man alone was extremely dangerous." Sara said.

Liz finally loosened her grip on Chloe and went to Sara's side. "Your mom's right. Not coming to us and taking matters into your own hands was extremely dangerous… but thank you. What you guys did was brave." Liz couldn't be mad at them—they had done something she couldn't.

Sara agreed with Liz. "Yeah, it was. And I understand that you needed to get Chloe back, but you need to keep us in the loop. Do you understand?"

"Yes, Mom," Adrian answered. Andrew was still quietly staring at the floor.

Sara couldn't be that mad at her children either because they were able to get Chloe back safely. She didn't understand why Gabriel would go through all of that just for Darwin's cane, but she didn't know much about the wizard world. Liz speculated that Gabriel wanted the cane just in case Darwin was released from the Tower. Darwin was a powerful wizard but without it, he would be limited in what he could do.

Liz stopped thinking about the reasons why Gabriel would want Darwin's cane. The only thing that mattered was Chloe was home, and she once again hugged her daughter. Right after that last hug, the doorbell rang. When Liz opened the door, two detectives introduced themselves and asked to come in. One of the detectives was of average height and weight with blond hair and blue eyes; the other detective was a woman with long black hair, brown eyes, and a mole on her cheek. She was really beautiful and introduced herself as the lead detective.

"Hi. I'm Detective Clark, and this is Detective Matthews. Glad to see you made it home ok," she told Chloe.

"Thank you."

"I know it's hard to talk about, but do you mind answering a few questions?"

"Not at all."

"We can sit at the table," Liz said. Sara took the twins to the living room to let Chloe talk to the detectives without the added pressure of her cousins watching her.

As Chloe described to the detectives what had happened, Detective Matthews started taking notes. Chloe felt the nerves building up inside of her; she knew that she needed to remember every minute detail she told them. Liz watched Chloe as she told the detectives about how a masked gunman came into the classroom a little after Mr. King entered and demanded they both go with him. Chloe told the detectives how they were taken out of the northwest entrance and through the woods to a nearby van that was parked off the main road.

Chloe paused in some places for dramatic effect, like telling the story made it hard to relive. It was, but not for the reasons she was saying. She knew she had to sell it so it could be a closed case. Chloe started to choke up, unable to speak; her eyes filled with tears as she pretended to finally regain the strength to talk about her ordeal and continue. Detective Clark hung onto her every word as Matthews wrote fiercely in his notepad. When Chloe told them that the masked man took them to Mr. King's house, Detective Clark stopped Chloe to ask a question but before she asked, she paused. Her eyes squinted as if she was putting together everything Chloe just told them.

"Do you know why he took you both to Mr. King's house?" Chloe crossed her arms. "No. He just cuffed us in the back of the van and drove us there." "With his mask on?"

"No. He took it off once he started driving." Chloe clarified.

"So, you got a look at his face?" Detective Clark asked, wondering if she should get her to a sketch artist as soon as possible.

Chloe paused for a minute. Her heart began to beat faster, and she worried that the detectives would hear it pounding against her chest and know that she was lying. Chloe knew where this line of questioning was headed. She leaned forward and started to twirl her thumbs together and stared at her hands. "Yes."

"Do you think that you can describe him for us?" Detective Clark asked, hopeful that this could be the break she needed.

"He was tall, had dark hair and a scar above his left eye," Chloe said as she looked directly into the detective's eyes the way only a confident person could in her situation.

"Excellent. We should get you to the station and have you work with a sketch artist."

Liz went to stand directly by Chloe's side. "Hold on, she just escaped this ordeal. Do you think she can have a day to recover?" She placed her hand on her daughter. "She's been through enough for one day."

Detective Clark leaned back. "Ms. Gabarra, that is precisely why it would be best to go now, while it's still fresh in her mind."

Chloe interrupted, "It's fine, Mom. I want to get this over with."

Liz finally agreed but wanted to drive Chloe herself. The detectives were more than ok with that and told them they would see her at the station. As Liz led them out, Chloe sat at the table, relieved that they were gone. Liz closed the door behind them and went back to Chloe.

"Are you ok, sweetie?" She caressed Chloe's face. "Yeah, I'll be fine."

"Liz, get in here!" Sara yelled from the family room.

Liz and Chloe rushed to the other room in a hurry to see what happened. They saw Bianca standing by the TV, her face covered in bright pink cuts. The bruises on her body were fading lightly but still visible. Bianca wasn't the same girl she had been when she left. They knew something had happened.

"Sweetheart, are you ok?" Liz rushed to her daughter's side, ready to catch her as if she was about to collapse.

Bianca started to tell them all what happened, every detail from taking Brad with her until now. Silence fell over the room when she finally finished her story. Her family stared at her like they didn't believe what she was saying. They just saw Brad the other day, and he seemed to have genuinely cared about Chloe missing. Brad was even close with the twins—how could what Bianca was saying be true?

Andrew couldn't believe it. "Are you sure it was him? 'Cause a morpher took Chloe and he looked exactly like Mr. King."

"Yeah. A morpher doesn't have magical abilities… wait, Chloe was taken?" Bianca was startled by that news.

"Apparently, a lot has happened since you left," Sara added.

"Why? How? When? How are you here? Are you ok?" Bianca asked, panicked. Everyone was shocked by Brad's betrayal but didn't want to force Bianca to talk about it.

They knew how hard this had to be for her and each of them silently resolved to put their feelings aside—for now.

"Long story short, Gabriel wanted Darwin's cane, so we traded," Adrian told her, trying to catch her up on the things she missed.

"Oh my god…" Bianca paced to the other side of the room, mortified. "Darwin's cane is the key to unlocking the Alexandro's Crystal."

"Gabriel," Liz mumbled under her breath. The hatred she felt for her brother started to consume her.

"What?" Adrian asked, causing everyone to look over at Liz.

"This ends *now*. My daughter's lives aren't to be toyed with." Liz stomped over to the kitchen for a pen and a piece of paper and began to write. "Sara. Can you take Chloe to the police station?" She walked back into the family room and handed Chloe the piece of paper.

"Of course." Sara stood up. "What are you going to do?"

"It's time to end my brother." Liz looked at Bianca. "Be ready," she told her and teleported from the house.

Sara could already see that her boys wanted to help and didn't like it. "Don't even think about doing anything." She told them.

Adrian and Andrew didn't say anything; they knew it was pointless to tell their mom why they should help.

"Chloe, go pack a bag because after the police station, you are coming home with us," Sara said.

Chloe went upstairs and the twins followed her. They would have preferred to go with Liz, but they couldn't. Sara would kill them if they disobeyed her again. Bianca went upstairs, too, so she could shower and be ready to go when the time came. It was obvious that Liz was going to need her help with whatever she was planning.

Back in Chloe's room, Adrian threw himself on her bed and Andrew took the chair at her desk. "Are you sure you're, ok?" Andrew asked.

"Yes. A little shaken up over the whole thing, but glad I'm home."

"They didn't hurt you, did they?" Adrian chimed in. He was agonizing over the possibility that someone did something to her.

"No. The girl that took me was a bitch, though." Adrian and Andrew got a laugh out of that. Her cousins risked their lives for her, and she had never felt more like part of the family than right now. Chloe took a few shirts and jeans and put them in a duffel bag. "How long do you think I'm staying over?"

"Until this is all over, I guess." Adrian said. He rolled his eyes and looked out the window. "This is a bunch of crap. We proved over and over again that we can help, and we're still treated like kids."

"Relax, Adrian. Mom's been through enough and she's just worried about us." Andrew made his way over to Chloe and hugged her. "I'm glad you're back."

Chloe returned the hug and realized something they had all forgotten about. "Oh my god.

I have to call Collin!" As Chloe grabbed her phone and rushed out of the room, Adrian went back to bed. Andrew returned to the chair and sat down.

"Hey, guys." Bianca entered the room. Adrian and Andrew didn't know what to say to her. Everything she went through with Brad had to be hard. Bianca limped over and sat on the bed next to Adrian. "Can we talk?"

"Yeah. What's up?" Adrian replied.

"Things are about to get serious, and—"

"We know. Stay out of it because it's dangerous. We don't have to keep being reminded that we're useless children." Adrian let out a heavy sigh.

"Are you done?" Bianca looked at him, obviously frustrated by his interruption. "I was going to say the exact opposite, actually. Gabriel has an army of followers, and we are going to need the same. You guys proved that you could handle yourselves, so I want you both to be ready when the time comes."

Adrian and Andrew didn't know how to respond to that. They were on edge over Bianca's confidence in them. On the one hand, they wanted to be viewed as if they were responsible enough to help but on the other, they were scared. It was a lot of pressure for two sixteen-year- old's, but Bianca believing in them helped them overcome that pressure.

"I will let you know when we have a plan in place." Bianca stood up and looked at both of her cousins. "Be ready," she said. With one final look, she teleported away, leaving Adrian and Andrew sitting there in silence.

Chloe went back into the room. "Where did Bianca go?"

"Probably to meet your mom," Andrew said.

Adrian turned his focus to Andrew. "Drew. Is that tracer spell active yet?" He needed that spell to work.

"I don't know, I haven't checked," Andrew had completely forgotten about it with everything going on.

Adrian leaned forward. "How do you check if it's active?"

Andrew looked around the room and took off the posters Chloe had hanging on a wall, leaving it bare. He summoned his wand and chanted a few words beneath his breath. Adrian tried to make out what he was saying but he couldn't hear him. Suddenly, outlines of buildings and fields started to form on the wall, resembling blueprints that an architect would use. On one of the outlined buildings, words appeared: "Sterling estate." Between the outline of the buildings, Darwin's cane appeared.

Adrian sighed. He couldn't believe it. "Gabriel has it in Avalon." Andrew shook his head in disbelief over how arrogant Gabriel was.

"He really doesn't think anyone can stop him." Andrew felt his face start to warm up. His father's arrogance triggered a hate in him he didn't think he had. Andrew's heart started to pound, and his body tensed up as his pulse started racing. *He thinks he's unstoppable,* he thought to himself.

"We should let Aunt Liz know where he's at," Adrian added.

"Mom won't let us go to Avalon," Andrew said through gritted teeth.

"We could text Bianca," Chloe suggested. She may have been a mere human, but she wanted to help her family, no matter what.

"Ok, good idea," Adrian agreed.

Chloe took out her phone and texted Bianca. Adrian, Andrew, and Chloe went downstairs where Sara was waiting.

"Did you ever get ahold of Collin?" Andrew asked. He needed a distraction from the thoughts he was having.

"Yeah. He's meeting us at your place after the police station."

"Aww. How adorable of him," Adrian teased as Chloe started to blush.

"Oh, ok, Adrian. You want to start teasing people about who they like?" Chloe asked, smiling deviously at Adrian. Adrian quickly stopped laughing over his cousin's remarks. He knew exactly what she was referring to.

"God, Drew, let's move on," Adrian blurted out.

"Wait, what?" Andrew was confused because he didn't even say anything. Adrian pushed Andrew out the door and Chloe started laughing.

"That's what I thought." She was happy her threat had worked.

"Ok, let's get going." Even though all of this was going on, Sara felt a huge weightlift off her shoulders after seeing her boys and their cousin laughing together again.

✳ ✳ ✳

BIANCA and Liz were at Darwin's house sitting at the huge dining room table as wizard after wizard teleported in and greeted them. One by one, wizards took a seat around the table.

Hekabe poured them each something to drink. As more wizards piled into the dining room, the seats around the table all filled except for one. The last wizard to teleport in took the seat for himself. Before he could get too comfortable, one more wizard who nobody was expecting to see there teleported in. Silence fell over the crowded room.

"Caleb. How nice of you to join us," Liz said.

Caleb was a tall, handsome man with black hair combed to the side who looked to be about the same age as Liz. He was muscular in stature. Liz and Caleb had a romantic history, but they didn't talk about it, although it was obvious there was still something between them. He wore a dark suit with a cloak that hung over his right shoulder and covered his entire back. The witches and wizards that were seated rose to great him with a simple bow of their heads.

"Please, as you were," Caleb said. All the guests proceeded to take their seats again and looked over to Liz, who was still looking at Caleb. "Genevieve apologizes for not being able to make it. As you know Liz, she is preoccupied with matters of the country. But she sent me in her place after Adrasteia got ahold of her."

Liz nodded, relieved that her mother was alright. "Can you help with Darwin?"

"I will get word to him about what's going on."

Liz turned her attention to everyone else in the room. "Ok. Now, to discuss the matter at hand. As you all are aware, Gabriel is after the three crystals once again."

Gasps and comments break out between the unique group of individuals.

"We all knew this was always his intention!" someone blurted out. Silence once again started to fall over the room.

"I, for one, didn't think he would go after them. And who's to say he is?" said a witch sitting to Liz's right. She was a short, pudgy woman with thick, curly blonde hair and blue eyes. Liz didn't even want to tell her about the meeting, but she was someone Darwin trusted.

"*I* say. But more importantly, Dorothy, Darwin says." Liz didn't even try to hide her frustration with her.

"Darwin and you also think that Adele is working with Gabriel. Look, we can't go after this man based on speculation. We need proof," Dorothy snapped.

"Lester Sterling is dead. Killed by one of Gabriel's disciples," Bianca chimed in. Dorothy was quickly silenced. The frowns around the room were a reminder that Lester was at one point an important member of Avalon. *What a sad end to a remarkable man,* she thought.

"What do you need from us?" Caleb asked.

"We need to find Gabriel and stop him," Liz said, feeling she was stating the obvious. "I know where he is," Bianca added. She looked up to her mother and showed her the phone.

✳ ✳ ✳

ADRIAN was looking out the window in the front seat of his mom's car. He could hear Andrew and Chloe talking in the back but was too focused on his thoughts to make out what they were saying. When they pulled into their driveway, Adrian was the first to see Collin sitting on the front steps. "Look who's here!" He looked back to Chloe, who was grinning ear to ear at who she saw.

Collin couldn't contain his happiness, either; as soon as he saw Sara's car, he ran over to it. Chloe got out and before she could even close the door behind her, Collin was already kissing her. Chloe returned the kiss and then they separated to find a surprised Adrian and Andrew staring at them.

Andrew's eyes opened wide. "Well, this is awkward."

"Come on, boys. Let's give them some privacy." Sara led the twins inside.

Andrew and Adrian followed their mom, but not without looking back a few times at Chloe and Collin. They couldn't believe those two had just kissed. For Andrew, it was weird seeing his best friend kiss his cousin, but that still didn't change the fact that Andrew was happy for them. When the door closed behind them, Collin went back to kissing Chloe. When they stopped again, Collin gently stroked Chloe's hair, outlining her face.

Chloe opened her eyes, looking at Collin. "It's about time."

"I was so worried," Collin told her, stroking her hair behind her ear. "I'm fine. My cousins wouldn't have let anything happen to me."

"I missed you so much." Collin grasped Chloe's hand and started to walk inside.

Everything that had happened to Chloe didn't seem to matter anymore. She rested her head on Collin's shoulder as they made their way inside, never feeling happier than she was now.

Chapter Twenty-Four

dele teleported inside an old house that looked like it hadn't been lived in for a while. She looked around and saw mold building on the walls around her. Water must have leaked in over the years of this old, run-down house, causing the mold to build over time. She could tell that when this home was in use, it must have been gorgeous. The place had an elegant feel to it despite the cracks in the foundation and the rats running across her feet. She marched a little further to meet Gabriel, who was sitting on a chair with his legs crossed.

"This is an interesting place to lay low. Not the kind of place I would expect for you to be in, but I suppose that's the idea, isn't it?" She inched in a little further, examining the room as she entered. "Interesting, indeed."

"The old Sterling estate," Gabriel pointed out. He looked around the room. "Felt fitting coming here given how big of a help old Lester was. I figure he wouldn't mind me being here— you know, since he's dead and all."

Adele ignored what she just heard. "Any luck on the map?"

"Please sit down." Gabriel gestured for her to take a seat.

"I'm fine standing," Adele told him. She wouldn't dare risk dirtying her designer clothes sitting in the filthy chair being offered to her, even if it was being offered by a hot-tempered wizard.

Gabriel looked at her. "I brought in an expert on old spells. Huckabee was a fan of the old ways, and I'm guessing that's why the map is hard to read."

"And how long has this 'expert' been working on the map?"

"A few weeks. I'm confident that she will find out something soon. Shall I introduce the two of you?" Gabriel got up from his chair and led Adele toward the closed door, glancing back. "Well, come on."

Adele followed him into the room. It was obvious that magic was involved in fixing up this room. The walls were clean, and a working light fixture was illuminating the room. Adele noticed the painting hanging on the wall in front of her, which still looked the same as the last time she saw it. She saw books piled on the desk in the center.

Then from between the book aisles emerged an older lady with dark brown hair with graying roots. Adele knew her from the capital library and knew there was no way she worked for Gabriel. That could only mean one thing: He abducted her against her will. Not only that, but now Adele's cover was blown. It was obvious the lady was shocked to see Adele there, too. Of course, she had heard the rumors, but she didn't ever think there was any truth to them.

Adele gulped, taken aback by how Gabriel didn't care if her double life was exposed. "Hello, Agatha."

"Hello," Agatha replied, uneasy about the truth just revealed to her.

Adele looked over to Gabriel, who found the introduction amusing. He knew Agatha was close friends with the chancellor but didn't care; it was worth seeing Adele squirm where she stood. Gabriel found amusement in it. Her precious standing in the council's office might even be compromised. It didn't matter to Gabriel, though, because soon he wouldn't need her at the chancellor's side—he would need her at his. Adele knew that Gabriel hated it when her attention   was split, but she didn't care. She had worked too hard to rise through the ranks to let it be taken away by a librarian.

"Are you closer to reading the map?" Gabriel asked Agatha.

"I think I figured it out."

"Then why does it still look like a horrible painting?" Adele needed to get closer to examine it and looked over to Agatha for an answer.

"Before I do anything, I want to be a hundred percent sure. Is that ok, Adele?" Agatha asked. Adele turned her head quickly toward Agatha. She was stunned at the lack of respect being shown to her. After years of working in the capital, the library and capital staff always included a "lady" in front of Adele's name as a sign of respect—something Agatha didn't have for her anymore.

"This is exciting. When will you know for sure?" Gabriel loved every moment of their strained back and forth.

"Another day of research will suffice," Agatha informed him.

Gabriel sauntered over to Agatha and placed his hands on the sides of her face. "If your idea works, I will let you live."

Agatha felt uneasy at his feigned graciousness. "I would greatly appreciate that."

"You have your day, librarian. Come, Adele. Let's leave her to her work." Gabriel stormed out of the room, leaving Adele and Agatha staring at each other. Adele finally followed Gabriel and locked the door behind her.

She rushed to catch up to him. "You are going to kill her when she's done, right?"

"You heard what I said in there. I gave her my word, and I intend to keep it."

"You *have* to kill her. If you let her live, my cover will be blown, and I won't have access to the chancellor. Years of hard work would be wasted."

"Are you giving me orders now?" Gabriel stopped, turned to face her, his tone deepening.

"Of course not. I'm simply saying it will be in your best interest to keep me in my position."

"Once we get the first crystal, it's not going to matter what position you are in. We will be unstoppable, and I will need you with me. Unless you like the positions the chancellor always has you in." Gabriel half smirked.

It took a lot of strength for Adele to be quiet and drop her request. Ever since he had been released, Gabriel thought himself to be untouchable. His only concern was getting these crystals and that was it. Gabriel may have been a powerful wizard, but it was Adele who got him out of the Tower. If it wasn't for her, he would still be locked up not even able to levitate a feather, the mighty Gabriel left disabled by a brick building.

"You wanted to see me, sir?" Darby chimed in. He must have been standing there the entire time, because neither Gabriel nor Adele heard him come in.

"I'll leave you two to talk. I have to get back to work anyways."

"Be back here tomorrow," Gabriel told her. Adele bowed her head and teleported away.

Gabriel paused for a moment. He needed to eventually put Adele in her place, but that could be taken care of another day. "Darby, Brad—whatever your name is, I need you to do me a favor."

✳ ✳ ✳

ADELE teleported into her office. She pushed her desk chair to the side along with everything else off her desk and grunted. After a few seconds, she rolled her chair back over and took a seat. She reminded herself that she had to stay calm. Two council guards came into her office to make sure she was alright after hearing the commotion from down the hall. She told them she was fine and ordered them to leave. Once they closed the door, she took several deep breaths and closed her eyes. After a few minutes she started to clean up her floor by putting everything back on her desk. She noticed a white envelope that made its way in front of her. She opened it and took out a piece of parchment with the words "the bay" written inside. She gathered her things and rushed out of her office.

Her steps pounded the ground beneath her feet as she rapidly made her way out of the capitol building. Once Adele was outside, she teleported once more, going to the farthest point of Avalon. Seagulls flew high in the sky. The waves of the ocean slammed against the rocks across from her, the sun getting ready to set. Children could be heard playing not far from where she stood, but were out of sight, nonetheless. Nobody ever visited this side of the bay. As beautiful the sights were here, they were even better on the other side. She cautiously crossed a wooden dock that led up to a bench where Isabel was already sitting, waiting for her.

"It's so beautiful here." Adele sat right next to Isabel.

"Why couldn't we meet at your house?" Isabel wondered.

"Because Gabriel has spies everywhere." She kept her focus on the beautiful blue water in front of her. "He's starting to get careless."

"He's closer than ever to finding the first crystal. And if any of the stories I heard about its power are true… well, let's just say I wouldn't care either." Isabel looked over to Adele.

Adele took a deep breath. "There is still a smart way to go about it. He still needs to find the other two crystals for them to fully work the way they should, so he has a long way to go. He shouldn't be so careless and underestimate people. That will be his downfall." She looked at Isabel. "He didn't even care if my cover was blown in the capitol. Even if he does find the first crystal, he will still need me in my high position to clear the way for his search of the other two. Especially since we won't be able to hold Darwin in the Tower forever."

258

"What do you need from me?" Isabel asked, ready to serve her master.

"Find out who within our organization will be loyal to me if Gabriel fails, or if people just want a change in leadership." Adele knew this was a dangerous path for her to take, but she felt she had to.

Isabel was thrown by this request. "You are second in command; I'm sure everyone would be loyal to you if the need arose."

"I'm sure there are those who won't care about that," Adele stated, then sat there for a few seconds. "With whom does your loyalty lie?"

"With you, of course," Isabel answered. She stood up and took a few steps forward before looking back to Adele. "But I wouldn't count Gabriel out just yet."

"I'm not. But it's always smart to have a backup plan."

Isabel thought for a few seconds. "I'll find out what I can."

"Be discreet. We don't need anything to get back to him."

Isabel nodded in agreement and teleported off of the docks. Adele decided to stay on the bench for a little while longer. The breeze blew through her hair gently and she stared ahead, watching as the waves slammed against the rocks on the other side. She had needed this break for a while.

✳ ✳ ✳

THE next day, Gabriel was standing by the small lake located in the back of Lester's old house. Two of his guards stood a few feet away watching over him. They didn't like how he was exposed to the other residents in the area; granted, the nearest house was a mile away. Still, where Gabriel was standing, anybody could see him from the other houses that surrounded this local lake. Another guard's footsteps could be heard approaching in the distance.

Gabriel didn't react to the footsteps until the guard spoke those two words he had been waiting to hear: "Agatha's ready." Gabriel rushed toward the house as the guards quickly followed. When he got to the door, they stayed outside to keep watch. He raced into the house and opened the door to the room where Agatha had been working. When he saw her, his excitement quickly changed to confusion, as Agatha was standing by the painting with a small blowtorch.

"What are you doing?" He rushed to her side.

Agatha stopped and stared at Gabriel. "This is the only way to see the map."

"You have to set it on fire to read it? Does that make any sense when said out loud?" Gabriel took a few more steps toward her. "If you destroy the only clue to where the crystal is hidden, I will kill you."

Agatha's chin quivered, her hands shaking. "I know."

She ignited the blowtorch, and the painting quickly went up in flames, sending Gabriel into a panic. Agatha took a few steps back as Gabriel quickly dashed to her side. He watched in horror as the painting burned, and Agatha started to doubt herself when she saw the fire die down. Nothing was left but ashes spread across the canvas. Gabriel was speechless, surely thinking of ways to kill Agatha for what she did.

Agatha approached the painting and brushed off the ashes from the bottom. Once the ashes were cleared off, she saw blue paint. She backed up again, lifting her arm and pushing Gabriel back a few steps in the process with her. She waved the same hand, sending all the burnt ashes off of the now-blackened canvas, revealing a new painting underneath. Gabriel was amazed at what he saw.

There was a huge island that looked like it was in the clouds surrounded by water. The word Naraka ran diagonally across the surface of the island. Gabriel couldn't believe it; after all these years of being told that the crystals were a myth, he had finally found where one was hidden. He approached the canvas and rubbed his fingers over the island. Agatha took a step back to let him bask in the moment. She suddenly realized what this meant to the wizarding world: Not only was Gabriel after them, but others might do the same now. They would be very stupid to go up against Gabriel, but stupid people did exist.

"You have made me very happy, librarian," Gabriel said as he turned to look at Agatha. "I definitely won't be killing you."

"Good, because if there is any truth to what I have heard about this island, you still need my help." Agatha had always been guided by knowledge, and this was no different. Gabriel was opening her eyes to something most wizards thought was a myth.

"You've heard of this island?"

"Yes. I came across it in an old book that belonged to Chancellor Huckabee," Agatha told him, mesmerized by the painting.

"Has anyone ever been there?" Gabriel asked as he turned to face the painting. He was captivated by it, finally understanding why clouds surrounded the island.

"No. According to the text—" Before she could finish what she was going to say, the sounds of people yelling, and loud explosions could be heard coming from outside. A guard came bursting through the doors, out of breath.

"Sir! We are being attacked!"

"Who would dare attack me?" Gabriel took a few steps over to the window and peeked out. He recognized a few faces of those loyal to Darwin—then he saw his sister leading the charge. "I don't have time for this! Grab the painting and let's go. Librarian, you come with me." Gabriel forcefully took Agatha's hand as his guard snatched the painting up. They all teleported away from Lester's old house, leaving everyone else to battle it out. Luckily for Gabriel, his disciples weren't there and only some hired guards would be compromised. The guards were expensive, but ultimately expendable, nonetheless.

Outside, Liz easily dispatched four guards who were coming after her with their wands drawn. Their magic was no match for Liz, who only saw them as obstacles in the way of her opportunity for revenge as she headed into the house to find Gabriel. Bianca followed her mom but was distracted by two guards shooting spells at her. Bianca deflected the first three, but another one caught her in the stomach, and she was sent hurling against one of her teammates.

Caleb saw Bianca fall and quickly rushed to her defense, killing the wizard trying to capitalize on his first spell against her. Bianca looked over to him, grateful for his intervention. The moment faded fast as more of Gabriel's guards ran toward Caleb. Bianca fired attack spells against the two original guards who came after her. The first one she hit flew against a nearby tree, hitting it hard, and the other got caught by the blinding spell she sent his way.

While he was confused, Bianca waved her hand and sent him through the air into a nearby tree.

He hit every branch on the way down to the ground, both guards now knocked unconscious. With her path cleared, Bianca ran into the house to join her mom. Caleb defeated the guards attacking him and followed Bianca inside. Bianca and Caleb passed two dead guards that Liz surely killed. When they finally met up with Liz, she was in the empty room where Gabriel just teleported from. The only things that remained were books and a few sheets of paper spread out across the table and floor.

"We must have just missed them!" Liz slammed her hand on the table.

"Ma'am, the place is clear. Those that aren't dead took off," one of Liz's people said.

"Thanks, Gunther. Have these books collected and brought back to Darwin's estate." She pointed at the books on the table and aisles, hoping they would reveal where Gabriel was going. "You have him on the run. That says something." Caleb got a little closer to Liz.

Liz scanned the room. "Which means he probably knows where the Alexandro's Crystal is, and he doesn't want to risk getting caught?"

"That's my point. Gabriel thinks he's untouchable, yet he runs from you. I find it amusing," Caleb said. Judging from Liz's face, he did have a point.

"Bianca, make sure Gunther gets all this stuff back to Dad's!" Liz yelled.

"Ok, Mom."

"And Caleb, don't you have something else to do?"

"First thing in the morning," Caleb replied. Liz teleported from Lester's house and other wizards came into the room as Caleb teleported as well.

"Pack everything up and let's get out of here quickly, before anyone else shows up," Bianca said. The wizards worked fast and made sure they packed every single thing that was on the table that could lead to Gabriel's whereabouts.

"Gunther, can you come here?"

"What is it, Bianca?" Gunther said, moving to her side.

"Can you handle all of this? I have somewhere else I have to be," she requested, concern etching itself on her brow.

"Yes, of course. I'll make sure we get everything."

Bianca thanked him and teleported from Lester's house to her cousin's backyard. She could hear her aunt making dinner in the kitchen and decided that she didn't want Sara to see her. She looked up to Andrew's window and teleported directly into his room. "Hey, guys," she said, taking a seat on Andrew's bed.

"So, what's going on?" Andrew asked. Adrian could see Bianca was tired and had a little dirt on her clothes.

"Are you alright?"

"Yeah, I'm fine. Do you guys know where Gabriel is now?" "We could find out," Andrew offered.

"I need you to tell me. Because he wasn't at Lester's house when we showed up. He ran, like a coward," Bianca spat.

"Can we go with you now?" Adrian asked. Bianca didn't answer right away. She knew that she told her cousins they could help, but what just happened at Lester's had her second-guessing her original decision. She always knew that it would be dangerous, but Gabriel's people were out to kill anyone who got in their leader's way and that scared her. She didn't want to put her cousins in danger and didn't know how to tell them.

"Look, guys. I know I told you I would come back for you, but I don't think it's a good idea anymore."

Andrew inched closer. "You said you guys needed all the help you could get, and now you are going back on your word."

"I know, but I didn't realize how dangerous it was."

"Well, look at that, Drew. Another lie told to us by a wonderful family member of ours."

Andrew grew frustrated. "Whatever. We knew you would go back on your word. After all, we are just children, right?"

"Guys—"

Bianca wasn't able to finish her sentence as Sara asked from the doorway, "Can I have a moment with my boys, Bianca?" She must have been outside the door listening to what was going on since she just peeked her head in slightly when she spoke.

"Sure. I'll be downstairs."

Bianca limped out of the room and downstairs. She knew that Adrian and Andrew were disappointed about not being able to help, but if something happened to them, it would be Bianca's fault. She knew that it would be best if they just stayed home. Bianca's train of thought was interrupted by what she stumbled into in the front room. Collin had his head lying on Chloe's lap while she stroked his hair. Bianca couldn't believe what she was seeing. When Chloe noticed her sister staring at them, she just smiled at Bianca then went back to watching TV with Collin, who seemed to be falling asleep.

Back upstairs, Sara started, "I know this whole thing hasn't been easy for the both of you." She took a seat on the edge of Andrew's desk. "You were given this incredible gift and thrown into this world that you never knew existed. The way you both have handled that—well, I have no words to say other than I'm proud of you both."

"Thanks," Andrew said. Adrian just looked at his mom and wondered what she was getting at. After a few seconds of silence, Sara stood up to go sit between them.

"You guys can go with Bianca." Adrian and Andrew looked at each other, surprised at what they were hearing. Their mom had always been so protective of them, and they didn't think in a million years that she would be ok with them going anywhere near what was going on in Avalon.

Adrian wanted to be sure he heard her correctly. "Are you sure?"

"Of course not, but I trust you guys and I trust that you will be ok. You guys wouldn't have been given this power if you weren't able to handle what's going on. I'm not saying to get into magical fights or whatever; I'm just saying if you can help your aunt, then help her, but make sure you guys stay safe." Sara knew that it would be dangerous, but she also knew that Liz needed all the help she could get.

"Wow. Of course, we will be safe," Andrew reassured her. He hugged his mom and Adrian joined them. Sara stayed there with her arms wrapped around her boys. She loved moments like these. Of course, she was worried, but she knew that Bianca and Liz would keep them safe. It still didn't change the fact that she didn't *want* to let them go deep down, so she was going to hold on to them as long as she could.

"Um… Mom?"

"What is it, Andy?"

"For us to go, you are going to need to let go," Andrew joked, his head resting on his mom's shoulder.

"I know…" She held onto her boys a little longer before finally letting go. "Let's not keep Bianca waiting any longer."

Sara took her boys' hands and escorted them downstairs. It was such a long time ago when Sara last held their hands like that—Andrew and Adrian must have been ten or eleven years old and much shorter then. *My, how they have grown to be such remarkable young men,* she thought to herself. When they reached the bottom step, Bianca looked over at Sara and she knew. Sara was allowing Adrian and Andrew to go with her.

Bianca approached them. "I will keep a close eye on them. I promise."

"Where are you guys going?" Chloe wondered. She was starting to get up from the couch, waking Collin up in the process. Chloe ran over to Andrew and Adrian, who were standing close to Sara.

Andrew looked her way. "To Grandpa's."

"I'm going with."

"Chloe. It's better if you stay here." Bianca moved closer to Chloe and put her arm on her.

Collin got up from the couch and joined Chloe next to her family.

"I won't get in the way! I just want to be with you guys," she told them.

"Let's talk about this in the kitchen," Bianca proposed. Chloe shrugged Bianca's hand off her.

"Oh, please. Collin knows everything." Chloe turned and went back to the couch, throwing herself on it.

"Well, this is awkward…" Collin murmured.

"How long have you known?" Adrian asked.

"A while, I guess."

"And you didn't tell us?" Andrew looked over at Collin, upset that he had been keeping a secret from him.

"Really, Andy? You want to go there?" Collin looked at Andrew and silence fell over the room.

"Look. I'm going with and Collin is coming too. We will stay at Grandpa's no matter what."

"We don't have time to argue about this. Let's just get going." Bianca walked over to Sara and took her hand, escorting her to the kitchen. "Aunt Sara, are you sure about letting them go?"

"I'm sure. You need their help, so it's ok," Sara said.

"I will keep them safe."

"I know you will, Bianca." Sara rubbed Bianca's shoulder and gave her a reassuring smile. "Once this is all done, we will all sit down to dinner— together. I feel like it's been a while since we have done that."

"Sounds like a plan," Bianca agreed.

Sara led Bianca back into the front room where everyone was waiting, then grinned at her boys and wished them luck and to be safe. Adrian and Andrew were happy their mom finally saw them as young adults. Her trust in them was the best assurance they were, in fact, capable of helping. They had never felt prouder, and they couldn't let her down. They all held hands to get ready to leave.

"Bye, Mom," Andrew and Adrian both said before they disappeared.

Sara went back into the kitchen to clean up. She was doing the dishes and staring out the window, looking at her swing that she would be relaxing on in just a few minutes. When she looked at the frame of the window, she noticed one of the amulets that Darwin hung up was missing. She assumed maybe it fell in the dish rack or somewhere else, so she started looking around for it when the doorbell rang. She strode over to open it, but no one was there. *Must have been kids playing around*, she thought to herself. When she closed the door and turned around, she saw a familiar face staring back at her.

"Hello, Sara," Darby boasted menacingly. He lunged forward, pushing her against the door.

Chapter Twenty-Five

Gabriel and Agatha teleported to a secluded farmhouse far enough away from Avalon that he wouldn't be found. When they arrived, they startled the couple living inside. In a fit of rage, Gabriel killed the woman and man who lived there along with their teenage son and dog. Agatha and the guard were shocked at Gabriel's display of ruthlessness but neither said anything.   Agatha wondered why he was so angry, but she wouldn't dare ask. She wanted nothing more than to go home; this was the first time she had felt fear since Gabriel abducted her.

"That girl was with Liz," Gabriel growled.

"Sir?" the guard trembled.

"Darby said he killed her, but she was very much alive and attacking me with her bitch of a mother." He stared at them coldly and marched over to a chair. "I'll deal with that later." He started to refocus on the task at hand. "Tell me more about this island."

"It's a dangerous place to go. The whole purpose of that island is to protect the Alexandro's Crystal. I remember reading a passage…" Agatha took a few steps forward and put her finger over her mouth, tapping her lips. "Something along the lines of 'magic created it, but it won't help you there,' but I'm not sure. I would need to read the book this information is in."

"No more books!" Gabriel slammed his fist on the armrest of the chair. "No. Librarian, you are free to go, and you —" he pointed to the guard"— you come with me. We are going to this island in the sky, and we are getting what is mine." Gabriel and his guard teleported elsewhere, leaving Agatha to stare at the bodies before her as thick, heavy bracelets dangled from her wrists.

These people didn't deserve to feel Gabriel's wrath, but Agatha knew there wasn't anything she could do now. She got one last look at them to remember how dangerous Gabriel really was and teleported home as well.

✳ ✳ ✳

DARWIN'S house was becoming the unofficial headquarters for the quest against Gabriel, and Hekabe didn't mind at all since it gave her an excuse to be in the kitchen. Adrasteia and Tavish sat on the sofa listening to Liz go on over Gabriel being a step ahead of them when Bianca, Chloe, Collin, and the twins appeared.

"WHAT!" Liz stood up and rushed towards Bianca "What are these two doing here?"

"We wanted to come," Chloe answered, but her mom hadn't been expecting an answer from her.

Bianca brushed past her mother. "I didn't have time to argue with her, so I said she could come. They said they would stay here, and I figured that would be ok."

Liz looked over at Collin. "Why is he here?"

Bianca glanced back. "Oh. He knows everything." Liz gawked at Collin, who couldn't have felt more awkward.

"Hi, Aunt Liz," Collin said nervously. Everyone remained quiet.

Liz blew off his pleasantries. "And Sara is ok with the twins coming?"

"They know how to find Gabriel," Bianca informed her.

Liz peeked over to her nephews. "How?"

"We did a tracer spell on Grandpa's cane before we gave it to him," Andrew informed her. Andrew strode over to the nearest wall and took off some of Darwin's priceless paintings that were hanging on it. Andrew summoned his wand and chanted a few words under his breath. After a few seconds, the wall turned into a three-dimensional canvas with waves forming around an island that seemed to be in the clouds. The name Naraka appeared across the island with an image of Darwin's cane on the surface of it.

268

✳ ✳ ✳

GABRIEL and his guard landed on the island, and it was a beautiful place. They were on what appeared to be the beach, but the only water around was off in the distance behind them. Gabriel felt weaker, like his body was draining, but he chalked it up to how far they had teleported. Gabriel could see that this island was high up. He looked toward two bigger-than-normal palm trees that appeared to be an entrance to a tropical forest. Gabriel knew that was where he needed to go but before he could take a step forward, he and his guard collapsed to the ground, finding it difficult to breathe.

Gabriel started coughing up blood the more he tried to take deep breaths; he could feel his lungs filling up with what must have been blood. He looked over to his guard and saw him doing the same. He tried teleporting but couldn't; he tried summoning his wand, but it didn't come. His guard started to panic, but he couldn't stand up and more blood poured out of his mouth. Gabriel couldn't believe what he was seeing.

He looked back behind him out into the distance where he saw the water and began to crawl toward it, leaving his guard behind. Every move forward was a struggle for him; he was gasping for air at this point, exhausted, but he continued crawling. Finally, he reached the edge of the island and looked down. He saw a cloud a little way down and the ocean waves below that.

He looked back at his guard, who was convulsing on the white beach, and looked back out into the distance. With all his strength, he pulled himself over the edge and fell. As he fell through the air, passing through clouds at high speeds, he felt like a skydiver who had just jumped out of a plane, spinning out of control. Gabriel could feel his lungs emptying and could start to breathe again. That was when he knew he was far enough from the island and he tried teleporting again, only this time it worked.

Adele stumbled in on him, collapsed on the floor and rushed to his side. Gabriel took her arm and lifted himself up, then quickly pushed her off of him. Adele slammed against the wall hard but didn't say anything. Her jaw was clenched but she still said nothing, but for a split second she thought about how easy it would be for her to kill him at his moment of weakness.

"Find the librarian. *Now!*" Gabriel yelled. He had never felt more normal than he did in that moment. The thought of almost dying like that enraged him.

"Of course, sir." Adele complied. She pushed herself off the wall and her temples began pulsating. "I will get right on that." Adele teleported away,

269

leaving Gabriel to recover by himself. Gabriel stood up and tried to walk but he only stumbled a few steps forward. He got over to the couch and fell, barely making it.

* * *

AT Darwin's, the wall showed the staff fall off the island but before they could see what else happened, the locator spell faded away. Silence once again fell over the room. Andrew backed away from the wall and looked at his aunt to see if she knew where or what that was.

"Naraka Island. Does anybody know where that's at?" Liz asked, looking at the wall, puzzled by what she saw. No one answered her question, but Dorothy had a suggestion.

"Maybe the library at the capitol building might have some information on this floating island."

"Maybe. Take Bianca and the twins with you and see if those old books have any information on this island. If Gabriel went there, then that is where the crystal might be," Liz ordered.

"Tavish, go with 'em. The more people reading, the faster we can find oot somethin'," Adrasteia added. Tavish stood up and went over by Dorothy, and Adrian quickly followed.

Chloe exchanged a smile with Adrian as she passed him.

"Adrasteia and I will stay here and see if Dad's books have any information on this island."

"Ok. Everyone hold hands because you won't be able to teleport into the capital yourselves," Dorothy said. She took hold of Bianca's and Andrew's hands and moved so they would have enough room to be side by side. Tavish gently gripped Adrian's hand and lightly rubbed his thumb over his just before they all teleported from the house.

"Hey. Do you want to go see some cool horses?" Chloe said as she looked at Collin, taking his hand.

"I really do," Collin replied. When Chloe told him about these flying horses, he had wanted to meet one ever since. Hand in hand they went out of the door, which surprised Liz. She didn't have time to talk to Chloe about what she was seeing but felt happy her daughter was happy.

"Nigel!" she yelled. Nigel came into the room and looked over at Liz. "Can you keep an eye on them?"

"Of course, madam."

✳ ✳ ✳

ADELE was sitting in her home office going through some papers. She circled one location then stood up, putting on her long coat that casually fell over her. She took one last look around before teleporting to a mudded area surrounded by trees. The only sound was the owls in the trees above.

It must have been the middle of the night in this part of the world because only the stars above illuminated her way forward. With every step she took, she could feel her shoes becoming heavier with the wet dirt she had to walk through. Once Adele was out of a section of the woods, she came to a stop and looked ahead. She saw a little cabin with smoke coming out of the chimney with more trees behind it. Adele marched toward this modest cabin and when she was finally on dry dirt, her stiletto pumps magically started to clean themselves until she got to the front door. She let herself in, catching an unsuspecting Agatha off guard. She looked like she may have just woken up when she heard the clicks of Adele's heels approaching.

"How did you know where to find me?" Agatha said, terrified.

"It wasn't that hard. It's like you weren't even trying to hide. Must be the side effects of working as a librarian, I suppose," Adele said, her English accent making her comment sound even more insulting.

Agatha stepped back a little each time Adele approached her. "What do you want?"

"Right to the point. I like that." Adele slowly strolled over to a table that sat in the middle of the room, a divider for where the kitchen ended, and the living room started. She pulled back a chair and took a seat. "Gabriel needs your assistance again and asked me to find you and bring you back to him."

"Oh. Ok." Agatha took a deep breath and finally felt relaxed again—well, the most relaxed she had been since Adele got there. "Let me pack a few things and then we can leave." She turned toward her room, which wasn't far from Adele.

"I actually don't care what Gabriel wants!" Adele yelled. When Agatha turned around to look at her, she was hit in the center of her chest by a bright red light. Pink mist filled the air where Agatha once stood. Adele was still sitting down with her legs crossed, wand in hand. Before the pink mist reached her, Adele was gone.

THE capitol library was bigger than any library the twins had ever seen. There were six levels of books along with little flying creatures that soared between each level, pulling out books and putting them away and assisting whoever needed it. Dorothy told the twins that those creatures were called Argos. They ranged between three and four feet tall and had fairy wings on their backs. Their skin color was dark green, and their foreheads were bumpy to the touch.

Dorothy told them they were harmless and lived beneath Avalon. They helped out around the capital and served the wizards of Avalon any way they could. Andrew and Adrian thought they had seen it all, but even this surprised them.

After they were done taking in the amazing place that was the capitol library, they got to work looking for any information they could find about this mysterious island. Books were spread out on two tables, each of them reading through their share of volumes. Adrian got frustrated because after a few hours, they still weren't anywhere near finding out what or where that island was. Adrian got up to put one of the books away, telling an Argo who wanted to help him that he could do it himself. Seeing an opportunity to go talk to him, Tavish followed him into the stacks.

"This is a big waste o' time," he mumbled. Adrian turned around and saw that Tavish was close behind him.

"Seems like it," Adrian agreed. He turned back around and put the book in his hand back on the shelf.

Tavish marched to his side. "Maybe when all this is done, we can hang oot?"

"Hang?" Adrian stared intently into Tavish's eyes, who put his own book back and stood closer to him. "Not sure if this is the right time to make plans like this."

"True, but it gives us something tae look forward tae, I guess. Just us two. If ye want," Tavish said quietly. His Scottish accent sounded raspier when he whispered.

"That would be cool."

They looked at each other for a moment, but their time away from the group was over when they heard Andrew yell, "I found something!"

Tavish and Adrian rushed over to him, Dorothy and Bianca already there. Andrew told them where the island was and that no magic was allowed until "what was hidden was found." Dorothy seized the book from him to read it herself. After she was done, they all went back to Darwin's to speak to Liz and Adrasteia. After an hour of discussing what they knew and what options they had, Liz sat at the table with her arms crossed.

"She's the only nonmagical one that is connected to Darwin," Bianca reminded her mother.

"I still don't like it." Liz got up from the chair and paced over to the window of Darwin's study.

"I'll do it," Chloe muttered. Everyone looked over at the door, not knowing that Chloe and Collin were standing right there.

Liz quickly joined the others in looking at her daughter. "How long have you guys been standing there?"

"Long enough to know that I can help." Silence fell over the room and Liz went back to looking out the window.

Liz sighed. "We're going to need a lot of potions." With that tacit approval, everyone got to work on the plan they had created. Now that they knew where the island was, they didn't have much time.

✳ ✳ ✳

THE next day Adrian, Andrew, Bianca, Chloe, Tavish, and Collin were at the stables talking about what they were about to do. "Is anyone else nervous?" Andrew asked. Bianca and Chloe looked at him, a little confused. How could he even ask that? In fact, Bianca and Chloe were sure that Liz and Adrasteia were more than a little nervous over what the day might hold.

"Granny an' Liz are comin'," Tavish stated. They all looked over to see Liz and Adrasteia walking their way with six floating messenger bags behind them. "Must be the bag o' tricks," Tavish added.

Bianca whistled and out came four Pegasi from the stables. Andrew was the first one to get on his and Adrasteia got on after him.

"Ye an' I are travelin' companions now," Adrasteia joked. Andrew laughed it off. Adrian got on his Pegasus followed by Tavish, who was traveling with him. Collin tried to get on with Chloe but was instantly teleported behind Bianca.

"Nice try, Collin," Liz said. She climbed on behind Chloe. "Everyone ready?"

They all said yes and one by one, they teleported from Darwin's estate to an island not far from Naraka. "This is how far we go with magic," Adrasteia

273

told them. They all looked out into the ocean and could see Naraka Island floating in the air about twenty miles away from them.

Collin squinted, trying to get a better look at that floating island. "Why can't you all just teleport there?"

Adrasteia came up next to him. "I feel sorry for any poor soul who shows up there by teleportin'."

Collin just stared at her. *I feel sorry for asking*, he thought.

"OK. This is it. Everyone ready?" Liz asked. Nobody answered, but she knew they were and away she went. They all followed Chloe and Liz and soared high in the sky.

"Wow, this is really high!" Collin screamed, his voice a little muffled by the intense winds. His grip on Bianca tightened the higher they went.

"Hey, Collin?"

"Yeah!?"

Bianca wiggled a little. "You think you could loosen your grip just a bit?"

"No."

"Ok," Bianca sighed.

As they approached Naraka Island, each Pegasus flew as close to the surface as they could without landing and everyone jumped off of their steeds, tumbling to the white-sand beach below. Adrian and Tavish watched as all four Pegasi flew away. Liz was dusting herself off when she saw Chloe staring up ahead at two of the biggest palm trees she had ever seen.

"That must be where we go," Adrasteia pointed out, wiping away the dirt on her clothes from landing on the ground.

Liz glanced at the group. "Everyone, be ready for anything."

Liz led the way into the forest, making sure that everyone was right behind her and safe. Adrasteia was at the back of the group doing the same. They could see the entrance of the forest getting farther away as they made their way deeper into this unknown place. Liz stopped suddenly when she heard movement above her.

"Sounds like it's coming from the trees," Bianca pointed out, looking up frantically.

They were surrounded by trees with vines hanging down on almost everyone. Liz took a few steps forward when she was snatched up by someone who swung down from a tree, sending everyone into a panic. Soon enough, they were all surrounded by the natives of this island. They looked unlike anything the twins had ever seen.

Their bodies were charcoal black, and they had horns sticking out of their heads and had hooves for feet. Some were muscular, others looked like they were malnourished, but they all carried long spears in their hands, creatures of the island. Bianca was the first one to throw a potion at the natives in front of them, sending each of them flying into trees and bushes.

"RUN!" Bianca yelled. They all took off running, looking back to make sure that they had a good lead over the creatures. Liz was about to get stabbed when she fought off her attacker and managed to wrestle the sharp blade away from him and stabbed him in the gut, sending him plummeting to the ground thirty feet below. Liz watched as he fell and when he hit the ground, he turned to smoke. Liz was weirded out by that but didn't have time to focus on it; she had to figure out a way to get off the tree.

She looked over and saw a vine hanging across the way and used it to swing back down to the ground. She encountered some of the other creatures that didn't chase after her group and she threw potion vial after potion vial, sending them through the air. Liz couldn't have been happier that she had packed a lot of defensive potions for her journey here. Adrasteia looked back and saw that despite their progress, the creatures were catching up rather quickly.

She reached into her messenger bag and took out a vial of dark-purple liquid and threw it on the ground behind her. When the vial shattered, a thick cloud of purple smoke filled the air and the creatures that ran through it didn't make it out—instead, they ended up running off the side of the island. The other creatures seemed confused by what happened to their counterparts and didn't dare go through the thick purple smoke themselves. Adrasteia glanced behind her and saw Liz running at full speed toward them, but it wasn't long before she was behind the thick smoke and out of sight.

Adrasteia was worried that Liz suffered the same fate as the savages but was relieved to see that Liz took an alternative route around some trees. "Everyone stops!" Adrasteia yelled.

Everyone froze and turned to face her. Liz finally was close enough and Bianca threw a blue vial on the ground, causing a force field to surround all of them. The purple smoke cleared, and the savages were running up to them. Two of them ran directly into the field and turned to ash on impact, stopping the other ones in their tracks.

"This force field won't hold for long," Andrew noted. Based on his reading, potions were always temporary and not as strong as when they were cast with magic. He looked around and saw more of the native creatures surrounding them. "Guys, we need a plan here," he added, scared and regretful they hadn't made him stay behind.

The force field started to fade and that was when they all made a run for it. Liz was once again taken by two creatures, and they began playing tug-of-war with her arms. Adrasteia rushed over to try to help while Collin got hit on the head with a rock and fell to the ground at the same time. Chloe ran to his side and started to fight off two of these natives herself.

Chloe caught a spear thrown at her and used it to fight off the other two. She stabbed one, who turned to dust, and sliced another one, leaving more dust in her path. She saw one getting on top of Collin and she rushed it, kicking it off him. She then spun her spear and stabbed it through him once he was on the ground safely away from Collin. Adrian saw everyone around him in a fight for their lives and went for a vial that Adrasteia said to use only as a last resort, tossing it to the ground.

When it shattered, the vines and trees came alive, grabbing everything around them. The roots of the tree wrapped around the creatures' necks and pulled them away. One of the vines latched onto Tavish's waist, but he quickly was able to cut it off. Once they had a clear path away from the chaos, they all ran toward the next entrance that wasn't far from them. Once they passed two remarkably similar palm trees into the second entrance, they looked back and saw that the native creatures who managed to get free didn't dare follow them.

"That's interesting." Liz was trying to catch her breath, just like everyone else.

"Yeah. That can't be good," Collin added as he rested his hands over his knees, looking at the natives, who were starting to turn away. Tavish was looking around at their new surroundings. This part of the island had a lot of dead trees around them and not even the wind blowing through the air felt the same.

"What could possibly live here?" Andrew asked.

"Stay close to each other," Liz instructed. She got in front of them and once again Adrasteia followed in the back. They seemed to be getting through this part of the island a little faster than the first. "It can't be this easy…" Liz stopped, and everyone could see the third entrance up ahead.

"Maybe we got lucky? And come on, it can't be worse than those things back there chasing us," Collin teased as he looked back to make sure nothing was following them.

"Don't be a bampot," Adrasteia scolded. Everyone looked over at Collin for saying that. They all knew if there was *one* thing you didn't say during a dangerous adventure, it was that.

"Oh my god. What the hell is that?" Adrian couldn't believe what he was seeing. When they all looked ahead at the third entrance, they were greeted by the body of a snake that had to be a hundred feet long and as thick as a passenger plane slithering across the pathway they needed to take. Liz tossed down another vial and a force field surrounded them once more.

"What potions do we have left?" she asked, her heart racing. Tavish, Bianca, and Adrian were all out. Chloe, Adrasteia, and Andrew looked through their messenger bags hurriedly.

"Not enough," Adrian said. The snake was now circling them, hissing.

"Um, guys? The shield?" Collin started to panic. They all looked up to see the shield starting to die down.

Chloe tightened her grip on the spear she still had in her hands and the second the shield went away, Liz threw down one of her vials that created a ring of fire that circled the snake, causing it to hiss loudly. The snake began to circle outward, away from them, and brought its massive head within striking distance. Somehow through all of this, they managed to get a few yards closer to the next part of the island. Chloe then saw her chance and took it. She threw the spear directly into the snake's head, making it lift its head into the trees above. The snake rocked side to side before falling and blocking the third entrance.

"We won't be able to climb over that thing," Bianca told them.

"Aunt Liz. You and Chloe should go," Adrian suggested.

"Ok. Chloe are you ready?" she reached into her messenger bag for the two vials. She tossed one over the motionless snake and when it shattered, a small, portal-like square opened in the next part of the island. "Grab my hand," Liz told her. She threw the other one down in front of her and the same thing happened.

Liz and Chloe ran through the opening and came out through the other side. They looked back but couldn't see the others over the enormous snake that remained motionless on the ground. With no other choice, they approached cautiously through the next part of the island, not knowing what it might have in store for them.

Back by the twins, Adrasteia noticed that the snake was starting to breathe again. "Everyone. Give me whatever force field potion ye lot have left!"

Adrasteia ordered as she brought them all in close to her. She would be their shield if needed. They all handed her what little they had, and she threw each one to the ground. "This should hold a little longer than the last one."

The snake was once again up and slithering around them, striking the force field every few seconds trying to get to them. "Holy crap. This thing isn't getting tired!" Bianca shouted, her lips and chin trembling as her heart raced.

✳ ✳ ✳

LIZ and Chloe approached a tall wall with a circle in the middle of it.

"I would have never thought to bring potions." Gabriel voice could be heard but they didn't see him. Finally, he and some of his lackeys emerged from a dark shadowy corner that Liz hadn't seen. Adamaris lunged at Chloe while Gavin grabbed Liz. "I only brought *this*." He held up Darwin's cane. "You should have seen how scared those things back there were of this."

Chloe and Liz struggled to get free but couldn't.

"And you, my dear sister—you brought me the other thing I needed." Gabriel's face showed off a freakishly malicious grin. He came toward Chloe and rubbed her head. "Nice to see you again."

✳ ✳ ✳

AT the Tower of Avalon, Darwin sat down to eat dinner. Since Darwin was a different kind of prisoner at the Tower, his eating quarters were different than those of the other residents. He was able to eat in a nicer dining room and wear nicer robes, naturally in his color of choice, dark blue, and made of expensive, durable fabric. Another special resident came walking into the room, someone Darwin had seen many times during his stay on this side of the Tower. Only this time, that resident took a seat at Darwin's table and took his hands, startling Darwin.

"One of your grandsons will change the course of our world forever." He held onto Darwin's hands tightly.

"Let go of me," Darwin said calmly.

"He will be a new kind of evil," the resident told him as he looked Darwin straight in the eyes. Neither of them blinked but Darwin felt a sudden cold sensation expanding in his core.

"Can you get this guy away from Lord Darwin?" Caleb marched in and took a seat in the now empty chair in front of Darwin. "I hear that old man

278

thinks he's a seer." Darwin didn't say anything. "You know, a clairvoyant. I wouldn't listen to anything he had to say."

Darwin was quiet for a few seconds before speaking. "I'm surprised to see you here, Caleb." He didn't acknowledge what Caleb just told him.

"Leave us," Caleb instructed the guards. When they closed the door, Caleb looked over to Darwin. "Liz found out where the crystal is hidden."

"Where?"

"Naraka Island. That is where she's at, along with your grandchildren." Before he could say anything else, the guards that had just left came barging back in. "Didn't I say to give us some privacy?" Caleb repeated.

"Sorry, sir. We just received word that Lord Darwin is not to have any visitors, not even Avalon's defense secretary," one of the guards said. Caleb stood up and stared at them, each guard swallowing a knot that had formed in their throats.

It's ok, go. I can take it from here. Darwin's voice was a whisper in Caleb's head. He quickly turned and looked at Darwin. How was he able to communicate that way—in here, of all places? Darwin gave him a wink as the guards escorted Caleb out.

Caleb hadn't been able to give Darwin what he needed to escape but felt like maybe he didn't have to.

Two other guards came to escort Darwin out. "It's time to go back to your room."

"I'm afraid I have been locked up in here for too long," Darwin told them as he stood up. "Oh, have you?" the other guard asked sarcastically. Each guard took a position next to Darwin. "MOVE!"

"Not necessary. I'll be leaving now." Both guards couldn't help but laugh uncontrollably.

Darwin raised his hands like he was surrendering but flicked his wrist forward, sending both guards slamming against the wall behind them, knocking them unconscious. He took a step away from the table and teleported away from the Tower.

✳ ✳ ✳

GABRIEL was forcing Chloe to take Darwin's cane and place it into the opening in the middle of the circle on the wall. She had no choice but to comply, causing the ground to shake and the wall to crack. Gabriel pulled Chloe a few steps back and watched as the wall split open to reveal the crystal he had long sought. Gabriel couldn't believe his eyes and went to grab it. While his guard was down Chloe back kicked him in the stomach, sending him back a few steps.

Chloe turned around and punched him in the face a few times until he fell to the ground.

Liz dropped a potion that she had up her sleeve that sent three of Gabriel's disciples flying through the air. Chloe rushed toward the wall to get the crystal, then bolted toward her mom. In doing so, she gave every wizard on the island their powers back, and Gabriel started pulling Chloe back toward him.

He turned her around, snatching the crystal, and slapped her to the ground. Liz tried to stop him, but Gabriel shot a spell at her that threw her violently against the wall. More of Gabriel's disciples now teleported to the island to back up their leader. Adrian, Tavish, Bianca, Dorothy, and Adrasteia felt their magic flowing through them and they, along with Collin, soon rejoined Liz and saw that they were vastly outnumbered.

Everyone drew their wands and spells were sent flying through the air, some connecting to their targets and some missing, landing in the trees around them. Dorothy noticed one of Gabriel's men pointing his wand at an unknowing Andrew and ran out in front of him to block the spell, instantly turning into pink mist. Andrew was startled but managed to point his wand at the culprit and send him flying. He then pointed his wand at Collin and a force field was put up around him. Andrew glanced over to where Dorothy once stood, grateful for her sacrifice but feeling guilty that she died for him. Adrasteia shot a spell at Gabriel, who deflected it but was hit by Liz's and promptly sent to the ground. Adrasteia took Chloe's arm and led her to Collin so she could share his force field.

"Ye both stay absolutely still in here," she told them.

Collin and Chloe watched in fright at everything going on around them.

Gabriel was bored with all of this and tried to teleport from the island, but he couldn't—he kept trying but only got a few inches from where he originally stood.

Gabriel didn't understand what was happening until he saw Darwin emerging from the cloud of blue smoky light that always accompanied his teleportation spell. Six of Gabriel's disciples immediately went after him, but Darwin effortlessly defeated them and still managed to keep Gabriel from leaving.

Gabriel and Darwin were now face-to-face.

"How nice of you to join us!" Gabriel yelled as he summoned his wand.

He began shooting spells at his father, but Darwin deflected a few and caught the last one in his hands. Gabriel was stunned by what he was seeing. "How is that possible?"

"You still have much to learn," Darwin told him as he took that spell and flung it toward three more of Gabriel's guards who were ganging up on Andrew and Adrian. Gabriel managed to get off one more spell while he was distracted, and it pushed Darwin to the ground. Gabriel tried to teleport but still couldn't, his frustration mounting.

"STOP IT!"

"There is no escaping, Gabriel. Not this time." Darwin's eyes were focused on his son. Gabriel ran after his father with his wand drawn, but Darwin flung him to the side.

Darwin stood up and pushed every single one of Gabriel's people away while bringing all his allies beside him. Finally, he summoned his cane, and it flew out of the wall and into his hands. He caught it and spun it around, transforming it into a true wizard's staff before he banged it on the ground.

Within a few seconds, walls of water from below surrounded the island like a series of reversed waterfalls. Everyone looked up and was shocked at what they saw, not realizing what was about to happen. The water came crashing down onto the island, smashing down on Gabriel and all his people. Gabriel struggled to hold onto something as he gasped for air each time his head came up from underwater.

Darwin and the rest of his people weren't immune to what was going on around them, and soon the waves began racing toward them. Darwin turned his staff vertically across his chest, pushing outward, causing the water to part and go around him and his family while everyone else was washed away. Gabriel managed to hang onto a tree and was left on the floor, spitting out water and trying to catch his breath. Isabel teleported up on a cliff and looked down, seeing that Gabriel was exhausted.

She quickly lay down on the ground to keep from being seen. Only the water washing over the sides of the island could be heard. Gabriel got up to his feet but could barely stand. Darwin pointed his staff at him, and golden ropes shot out, wrapping around Gabriel's body, and binding his ability to use his power like a snake winding around its prey.

"Liz!" Darwin called out, looking back at her. "Get everyone out of here now!"

Liz didn't hesitate and called out for everyone to leave, and one by one they teleported off the floating island. As they fled, Gabriel was suspended in the air, his arms pressed tightly against his body. Darwin slowly paced toward the edge of the island, pushing Gabriel along with him with each step until Gabriel dangled above the clouds and ocean below. Darwin held out his hand and the crystal that Gabriel had wanted his entire life was ripped from his pocket, gently landing in Darwin's hand.

"Fine, Dad. You win. Just put me back in the Tower like you've wanted to ever since I was released."

"Not this time."

"You can't kill your only son!" He began to laugh at his father. "Oh, please! You couldn't kill me back then, and you can't now."

Gabriel's eyes glowed a golden hue like the rope that bound him, only a little darker. Darwin was caught off guard and looked on, horrified, as he witnessed the restraints, he had placed around his son start to burn off until Gabriel was left levitating by his own will. He smirked at his father, but before Darwin could react, Gabriel summoned one of the most powerful wind spells Darwin had ever seen. Everything that wasn't held down to the island was pushed backwards, including Darwin.

Darwin desperately buried his staff into the ground as he battled the wind to regain his footing, the ground parting at the weight of his staff as it sliced through the gravel below. Before Darwin could get his feet to the ground, Gabriel surrounded him in the hottest of flames, bringing them in tighter around his father. Darwin could feel his eyebrows getting singed and knew he had to act fast. With what little room he had, he raised his arms above his head, summoning the remaining water from all around him. It started to build as it spun equally as intense as the fire, growing greater and greater until it snuffed out Gabriel's flame. The cascading water caused Gabriel to lose his balance and he took a few steps back. When Gabriel regained his balance, he stared daggers at his father, who looked exhausted.

"You underestimate me, old man." Gabriel shot out a green orb from his hand that sent Darwin violently thrashing through the air until he crash-landed on the ground.

"You couldn't kill me then, and you can't kill me now. But I, on the other hand," Gabriel said as he investigated the palm of his hand as a circular flame started to form, "have no qualms about killing you!"

He flung the flames as fast as he could towards his father—only Darwin stopped it in midair, using its energy to change the flame to a reddish orb the size of a bowling ball and then he pushed it toward his son, who took the hit dead center in the chest. Gabriel lay on the floor in agony, wincing with every move as he tried to get up.

Darwin summoned his staff from where it landed, leaning on it for support, and approached his son. Gabriel looked up at him. "What are you going to do, Father? Kill me?" Gabriel took deep breaths as he got to his feet. "You don't have it in you."

Darwin once again shot golden ropes out of his staff. More ropes wrapped around Gabriel tighter and faster than before, covering nearly every part of him, leaving only his head exposed.

"Now, to the Tower I go."

"You're wrong, Gabriel. There is no hope for you. No redemption for you."

"You're still pathetic. Nothing has changed—" Gabriel said.

"You're wrong again." Darwin thought of his family, then looked Gabriel in the eyes. "I have other people to think about now. And I will do whatever it takes to keep them safe." The ropes started to loosen until Gabriel stood on his own.

"So, what now? You know the Tower can't hold me, so you might as well let me go! After all, you have the crystal now." Gabriel took a few steps back, still not able to teleport.

Darwin put his staff down and thought for a moment as he stared at his son before him.

Suddenly, Darwin's grip tightened around his staff, and he pointed it at Gabriel, shooting a streak of red light at him with so much force that his hand jolted back hard in the process, turning Gabriel into pink mist that slowly cascaded backwards in the wind.

Darwin took a minute to soak in what he just done before he grabbed his stomach and stared down at the ground, tears filling his eyes. Isabel, stunned at what she had just witnessed, teleported away, escaping notice. Darwin composed himself and left to rejoin his family.

When Darwin appeared, Adrian, Andrew, and Chloe ran over and hugged him. Darwin was overwhelmed with joy, hugging his grandchildren tight. Bianca couldn't resist and ran over to join in.

A few hours went by and the twins, along with Chloe, were in the stables checking up on their Pegasi before they headed home. "Tavish is a cool guy.

He and his grandmother helped a lot," Chloe noted. Adrian laughed off her comment and continued to pet his Pegasus.

"They're good people, indeed," Andrew added.

Darwin, Liz, and Bianca went over to meet them at the stables. "You guys should get home so your mom can stop worrying. She left me so many voicemails checking up on you," Liz informed them.

"Yeah. We should really get going, Drew."

"Yes, we should," Andrew agreed. But before they left, they both ran up to their grandfather and hugged him tightly. Adrian was the first to let go. "Thank you." He turned to his aunt and embraced her as well. Andrew followed. They were exhausted over everything they went through, but as they both looked at the people around them, they couldn't be more grateful.

Chapter Twenty-Six

Adrian and Andrew teleported to the back of their house like they normally did when they got back from their grandfather's, only they were a little more exhausted now. They opened the sliding door and saw that Ms. Haynes, their neighbor, was sitting at the table. When they entered, she stood up and stayed behind her chair.

"Hi, Ms. Haynes. Where's Mom?" Adrian threw his bag down.

"Boys, sit down for a minute," Ms. Haynes told them. Her voice was shaky, her chin quivering.

"Where's Mom?" Adrian repeated, his eyebrows drawing together. Not wanting to take a seat, he stood firmly in place.

"A few days ago, Sara came over to my house and asked if I could take her to the emergency room because she wasn't feeling too well."

Andrews's mouth was dry. "Ok. So is Mom upstairs resting?" He proceeded toward the stairs.

Ms. Haynes quickly stepped in front of him, causing Andrew to stop while Adrian went next to his brother. "When we got to the ER… your mom collapsed on the floor and the doctors had to rush her into the OR…" Ms. Haynes's eyes started to water and she couldn't keep her voice from cracking as she spoke. "The doctors did everything they could, but it wasn't enough."

She ambled over to them and put her hands on both of their faces, tears rolling down hers. "I'm so sorry. Your mom died, and—"

"Ok…" Adrian took two steps back. "That's impossible and not funny." Adrian's breathing getting deeper. He ran upstairs. "Mom, you can come out now! This isn't funny!" He frantically searched her room, panting.

Andrew couldn't bring himself to move. The noise around him started to fade, replaced with just his heartbeat pounding against his chest.

Adrian continued frantically searching for his mother. "Mom! This isn't funny, please come out! Please, PLEASE, PLEASE COME OUT!" Tears flowing down his face, he dropped to his knees as one last whisper left his mouth. "Mom… please…"

Ms. Haynes ran to the stairs, sobbing as she heard the pain in his voice.

Tears started to fill Andrew's eyes, but he still couldn't move. He wondered if this was real—he hoped it was all a bad dream, but it wasn't. Adrian's screams brought him back into reality; they were a reminder of how real this was. Ms. Haynes's hands were shaky as she struggled to find her breath. She couldn't bear the pain she caused. Liz came barging into the house then.

"Adrian!" Liz yelled when she saw him at the top landing of the stairs. She rushed by his side after she saw him fall to the floor and took him into her arms. Snots and tears filled Adrian's face when he saw his aunt.

"Aunt Liz…" He sniffed, trying to clear his nose. "This isn't real." He buried his face into her shoulder.

"Oh, sweetie. I'm so sorry…" Liz held him tighter. "Where's Andy?" Before Adrian could answer, she heard Andrew in the kitchen. He had fallen to his knees. "Oh, Andy…" She got up and brought Adrian with her as she went down to Andrew. Both of them fell to the floor, joining him. She hugged both of them, holding on to them tighter than she ever had before.

Andrew couldn't contain his emotions anymore and began to sob uncontrollably. Hearing his pain, Liz squeezed tighter. Ms. Haynes wiped away some of her tears and quietly left the house to let the family grieve.

✳ ✳ ✳

A FEW days later, everyone was at the cemetery to pay their last respects to Sara. It was cloudy out, but the sun was trying to break through, hopefully to brighten up this horrible day. No child should ever go through this so soon. Sara was young and had so much to look forward to.

She would never see her boys grow into the men she knew they would become.

Andrew and Adrian hadn't said much the past few days. They had many visitors but couldn't bring themselves to say anything more than "thank you" when they were offered condolences. When the service was over, Adrian was the first one to approach the casket as it was lowered. He reached down for a fistful of dirt and let it drop down below. The dull sound of the dirt hitting the surface that contained his mother's remains made him start crying.

Andrew followed and got the same results. Liz quickly comforted her nephews and took them back to the waiting cars. Darwin was the next person to go, followed by Bianca and Chloe. Lisa and Dean followed Collin and they walked back to the cars as well. They saw how hurt their friends were and couldn't imagine their pain. Lisa was the first to embrace Adrian. She told him everything was going to be ok. Dean hugged his friends as well and couldn't help crying himself.

Darwin was standing over by a tall oak tree watching his grieving grandchildren being comforted. The pain they were experiencing was unbearable to see.

"How are ye doin'?" Adrasteia put her hand on Darwin's back.

"These poor kids." Darwin stared at the boys "They don't deserve to suffer like this."

"They will heal in time. I'm sure o' it. I've also talked tae their teachers an' with only a month o' school left, we decided tae let 'em take that time aff."

"That's excellent. Thank you." Darwin was still watching his grandchildren and he felt numb, his eyes red and raw. He wished he could take their pain away.

"I was also asked tae tell ye the charges against ye were dropped, an' the chancellor wants tae meet with ye as soon as possible tae thank ye fer yer service."

Darwin cleared his throat. "There isn't a need to thank me. The only thing that I did was confirm the existence of the elder crystals." He couldn't take his eyes off his grandchildren.

"Aye, but ye protected it from getting into the wrong hands."

"And now I have to find the other two before anyone else does."

"An' then?"

Darwin stared directly into her eyes. "And then destroy them like someone should have done centuries ago." A singular tear slowly streamed down his face.

BACK at their house Andrew sat on his bed, staring at the last picture he took with his mother. His tears fell onto the photo as he focused on her face. He still couldn't believe it.

Suddenly, the door swung open, catching him off guard.

"Sorry, didn't mean to kick it that hard." Adrian was standing there with a pillow in one hand, a sleeping bag in the other. He tossed them onto the floor next to Andrew's bed and took a seat next to him. Without saying a word, Andrew leaned on his brother's shoulder and started to sob. Adrian couldn't do anything but lean his head onto Andrew's.

About the Author

Daniel Xavier Luna is from the west burbs of Illinois. He is a fan of all things nerdy and is a huge dungeons and dragons gamer. He doesn't consider himself an author but loves to write.

Learn more at: Danielxavierluna.com